"*Victim Six* is a bloody thriller with a nonstop, page-turning pace."
—**The Oregonian**

"Olsen is a master of writing about crime—both real and imagined."
—**Kitsap Sun**

"Thrilling suspense."
—**Peninsula Gateway**

"Well written and exciting from start to finish, with a slick final twist. . . . a super serial-killer thriller."
—**The Mystery Gazette**

"Gregg Olsen is as good as any writer of serial-killer thrillers writing now—this includes James Patterson's Alex Cross, Jeffery Deaver's Lincoln Rhymes and Thomas Harris's Hannibal Lecter. . . . *Victim Six* hooks the reader . . . finely written and edge-of-seat suspense from start to finish . . . fast-paced . . . a super serial-killer thriller."
—**The News Guard**

Heart of Ice

"Gregg Olsen will scare you—and you'll love every moment of it."
—**Lee Child**

"Olsen deftly juggles multiple plot lines."
—**Publishers Weekly**

Also by Gregg Olsen

THE BONE BOX

BETRAYAL

ENVY

CLOSER THAN BLOOD

VICTIM SIX

HEART OF ICE

A COLD DARK PLACE

A WICKED SNOW

A TWISTED FAITH

THE DEEP DARK

IF LOVING YOU IS WRONG

ABANDONED PRAYERS

BITTER ALMONDS

MOCKINGBIRD (CRUEL DECEPTION)

STARVATION HEIGHTS

CONFESSIONS OF AN AMERICAN BLACK WIDOW

FEAR
COLLECTOR

GREGG
OLSEN

PINNACLE BOOKS
Kensington Publishing Corp.

PINNACLE BOOKS are published by

Kensington Publishing Corp.
119 West 40th Street
New York, NY 10018

This book is a work of fiction. Names, characters, businesses, organizations, places, events, and incidents either are the product of the author's imagination or are used fictitiously. Any resemblance to actual persons, living or dead, events, or locales is entirely coincidental.

ISBN 978-1-62090-913-3

Printed in the United States of America

For Rebecca Morris,
who arrived at just the right time.

PART ONE
GIRLS GONE

*"You feel the last bit of breath
leaving their body.
You're looking into their eyes. A person in
that situation is God!"*
—TED BUNDY

CHAPTER 1

The teenagers had been waiting for the mother and her two children, a towheaded boy and girl, both of whom had found a million things to cry about all afternoon, to finally leave. It was after six and the sun was beginning to dip downward in the late summer sky. Across from Point Defiance, where Samantha Maxwell and Brant Logan were sitting in a tangle of driftwood, they watched the sun as it inched lower to the tops of the craggy Olympic Mountain range, the western-most reaches of the United States. They'd been drinking beer smuggled from Samantha's father's supposedly secret stash in the garage refrigerator. It was better beer than they were used to, and there was no denying they were feeling the effects of the alcohol.

"I thought they'd never go," Brant said, running his fingertips along Samantha's inner thigh. He grinned at her in that dopey way that he did when he'd been drinking.

Samantha pushed his hand away. "Hey," she said, "I'm not *that* drunk."

"But you look so unbelievably hot," said Brant, a lanky six-footer, said, rolling on his side on the blanket, throwing his leg over hers. "And I've been good all day."

"You're gonna have to do better than that," Samantha said, pulling away, and applying the last bit of coconut-smelling lotion to her lightly browned skin. She pulled her hair back into a loose ponytail and got up. "I'm going in," she announced, getting up and starting toward the cold blue water.

Brant rolled his eyes in a very dramatic manner. "You're crazy. Freaking cold out there," he said.

"Then you should come with me," Samantha said, turning back to look at him. The sun framed her head like a halo. "You need to cool off."

"Oh, I do, do I?" he said, his brow arched as he shielded his eyes from the sun. "You really want me to cool off?"

By then Samantha was already halfway to the water's edge.

"Last one in's a rotten egg," she said, laughing at the absurdity of the statement. *Why a rotten egg? Who but my mother comes up with these dorky sayings?*

Brant watched his girlfriend step into the clear, cold Puget Sound, but with the sun in his eyes, he turned away and put his head back on the blanket. He put his earbuds in and turned up the volume on his iPod. Soon his feet were twitching as he listened to Nickelback's newest music. *Not classic. But good enough*, he thought.

Good enough, he'd later think, *to lose track of the time.*

About an hour later, Brant sat up with a start. He'd drifted off to sleep. He looked at the spot on the blanket next him, but Samantha wasn't there.

He looked toward the water. "Sam?" he called out, getting up to see where she'd gone. "Where the hell are you, babe?"

He looked south, then north. The pebbled stretch of the beach was deserted. *Maybe she'd gone off to the restroom?* Brant slipped a T-shirt over his head and started walking up the beach toward the restrooms. He called out Sam's name several more times, but there was no answer. His eyes scanned the shore. There was no one to ask if he or she had seen Samantha. There was no reason to worry, really, but he did anyway. Later, he would say he'd just "had a feeling" that something was very wrong. He couldn't explain it; it just was something deep inside telling him over and over that Samantha was gone.

Where is she?

The restroom by the parking lot was smelly and empty. Adrenaline and beer made him feel anxious and woozy. He planted himself in front of the urinal, reading graffiti and wondering where Sam went. A second later, he was out the door and back where they'd spent the day. He told himself that she'd be back any minute. By the time the sun started to slide behind the Olympics, however, Brant's worry increased tenfold.

He picked up his phone. No messages. No calls. He dialed Sam's number, and her phone, still in her purse, rang next to him. He told himself he wouldn't mention that he'd left her purse unattended.

Sam wouldn't have gone off somewhere without her phone. Brant knew that. The phone was almost a part of her. Next, he pressed those three digits, in that sequence that sends a palpable wave of anxiety through the phone lines. It was the number no one ever wants to need to call.

"My girlfriend is missing," he said to the 911 operator, after giving his name.

"Okay," the operator said, "missing. What do you mean by that?"

"Samantha is gone. I can't find her."

"You two have a fight?"

"No," he said, suddenly feeling defensive. "I fell asleep. I'm kind of worried about her."

"Did she go off with someone?"

Why is she saying that? Sam would never. We're in love. Have been since we were sixteen.

Brant bristled a little. "She would not do that. That's not Sam."

The operator kept on questioning Brant. Her tone cool and clinical. Brant wondered if she would act that same way if a caller was inside a burning house. Didn't the operator grasp the urgency of the situation? Sam was gone!

"When was the last time you saw her, exactly?" she asked.

Brant continued to scan the beach. "I can't say for sure. Maybe an hour or two hours ago? She went swimming in the sound. Like I said, I fell asleep and when I woke up she was gone."

"Are you sure she just didn't leave, Brant?"

Again, why was the operator acting like that?

"Without her purse? Without her phone? Not Samantha. No way. What girl would?"

"All right. Sit tight. Police are on the way."

A half hour later, a team of first responders arrived at the beach to mount a search-and-rescue effort. It had turned to dusk by then and a helicopter hovered along the shoreline with a searchlight punching through the thickening air. Someone gave Brant a blanket and he wrapped it around his shoulders. As he watched everyone, he thought to himself that it was like some kind of scene out of a movie. Not real. Just pretend. No one used the words "possible drowning," but all of them figured that was likely what had happened. To their credit, the searchers showed no sign of fatigue. Even as the stars replaced the pink hue of sunset, they gamely continued doing what most all of them knew was futile.

If Brant's story was true, Samantha had been yanked from the shore by the swift water.

No one needed to point out the obvious. Ten feet from where the teens had put their blanket and pilfered beer was a sign: DANGER! NO SWIMMING! RIP CURRENTS!

Every day for the five years since her husband left her for their dog sitter, Abby, Colette Robinson had walked a stretch of beach along the southern end of Puget Sound. Low tide. High tide. When the shore was pelted with raindrops the size of dimes. Or, the best of all, when the sun lit up the edges of the water like a fuse. It didn't matter what time of year, there was always something to stick into her bag. Colette collected bits of beach glass that she'd used to fill four mason jars in the window of her bathroom. She'd recovered enough fishing floats to string a garland over the fireplace in the living room, too. Every time she ambled over the rocky shoreline near Tacoma, Colette found at least one thing that got her blood pumping with the excitement of discovery.

That day her eyes caught an out-of-place hue a few yards down the beach. It was a fragment of pink and white, absolutely not colors evocative of the Pacific Northwest, a brooding landscape fashioned of grays, blues, greens, and blacks. This was a spray of light against the dingy, dark backdrop of a cliff.

What was it?

She turned away from the water's foamy brink and started toward the base of the cliff. As she drew closer, she set down her Albertsons plastic grocery bag of sea glass and bone-white sand dollars. *This is special.* She'd read in the paper how the flotsam and jetsam of the tragic Japanese tsunami was headed for Washington's coast. Among the silver mass of driftwood that barricaded the cliff from the water, Colette saw the arm of what she was all but convinced was a doll. She ventured a bit closer. *Not a mannequin, smaller, maybe a doll.* It was white with amber-colored fingernails. Pretty, but creepy. Twenty feet away from what she was all but certain was the find of the day—find of the week even—Colette stopped and screamed. It wasn't just an arm. The arm was attached to a body. *A girl's body.* Nearly out of breath, she dug her phone from her pocket and called 911.

Colette Robinson had found Samantha Maxwell. That wasn't all she discovered. Colette didn't know it at the time, of course, but Samantha wasn't alone. She had company.

* * *

Tacoma Police Detective Grace Alexander braced herself against the suddenly very cold wind coming off Puget Sound. Summer was over. The weather had turned nasty in the afternoon in the way that it does in Washington whenever a rare sunny day managed to sneak in to bring sunburns and happy memories. The sky looked more silver than gray, but make no mistake about it, rain was coming. Rain had always been the price for the green surroundings and everyone who lived there knew that all too well. Grace was an attractive woman, small in stature, but with the kind of open face that invited people into her brown eyes. She had the eyes of someone who had seen a lot, more than most, but still invited people inside. Her ability to remain open was her greatest gift when interviewing witnesses.

She brought empathy. With empathy, came trust.

The petite brunette detective bent down, setting her right knee on the driftwood log that had caught the girl's other arm and kept her body from being pulled away by the outgoing tide.

The victim was wearing a bright yellow one-piece bathing suit that had somehow managed to stay in nearly pristine condition in the tides that had carried her away, then brought her back. Neither detective touched the body, but it was clear by its position tucked in among the logs that rigor had come and gone. She was not a floater, or bloater, a puffed-up figure, a kind of gas-filled balloon that a body becomes when left out in the elements. She looked like a young, albeit slightly blue and white, teenager. It was as if she'd been tossed there and then fallen asleep.

"Drowning vic," she said to her partner, Paul Bateman, a skyscraper of a man with pointed eyebrows that always made him look slightly perturbed, even when he wasn't. "Samantha Maxwell, nineteen. Missing for four days."

Paul studied the body, face down, the dead girl's dark hair melding with scraggly bits of seaweed. A crab crawled out from under her slackened curls. It was disgusting, but both detectives had seen far, far worse. Neither gave it a second thought.

"How can you be positive it's her?" Paul asked.

"The ink," Grace said, "here." She pointed to the small four-leaf clover on Samantha's right shoulder. "Don't you ever read the paperwork? It's in the report."

Paul turned up his jacket collar to ward off the breeze. "She wasn't all that lucky," he said.

"Understatement of the year."

Grace got up and looked around, scanning the lonely section of beach. She knew that the area wasn't a crime scene per se, only the sad site of the discovery of a dead girl.

"Accidental drowning?" Paul asked, as the coroner's techs made their way over the rocks and logs to collect the body. A seagull screamed overhead. A little more rain fell. The detectives took a few steps back to let the others do their work.

"Autopsy will determine what happened," Grace said. "Nothing to suggest anything other than an accident, at least nothing I've read in the missing persons report. Boyfriend said she was drinking a little and went toward the water to swim. Never saw her again."

"Not going to see her now," Paul said, pulling away from the putrid odor that rose up from Samantha's remains as the coroner's team cocooned the body in a bright blue neoprene bag. It zipped silently with the kind of closure found on a sandwich bag.

"Beachcomber over there found her," Grace said, indicating the woman who was sitting on a log clutching her plastic bag of shells and glass. "Officers are getting her information."

Paul walked a few yards down the beach toward the base of a cliff.

Grace called over to him. "You coming?" She repeated her question, but Detective Bateman didn't say anything.

She let out a sigh and followed him.

He was on one knee, looking at something.

"What is it?" she asked.

Paul looked up. "Not sure," he said, his eyes staying locked on hers. "Looks like a femur."

She shook her head. "Driftwood," she said. "Not a bone."

"Really," he said. "I think so."

"Human?" she asked, now joining him on her knees to get a closer view. Neither touched the bone. If it was human, it was evidence of a possible crime. It was likely that it had been dragged there by an animal, far from where it had been hidden. That is, if it had been hidden at all.

And if it was human.

"Not sure," Paul said. "But I think so. Been out here a while."

Grace got up and went a couple more yards west of the femur and, almost immediately, found another bone, a rib.

"It is human, isn't it?" she asked, feeling that mix of

excitement and horror that comes every time discoveries like bones on a beach were made.

"A woman? A child, maybe."

Grace stepped back and studied the outcropping above the breach. A cedar and a fir had sloughed off the top of the cliff and lodged themselves in a ledge about fifty feet above where Paul had seen the first bone. If the bones had once been concealed in a grave, it was a good bet they had literally come from above.

Samantha Maxwell had been the victim of a tragic accident. There was no doubt about that. She was a dead girl. A teenager. A daughter. But she was something else in that moment.

Samantha had been a messenger.

"It was like she led us here," Grace said.

Paul didn't care for that kind of woo-woo sentimentality, but he let Grace go on about her "feelings" and intuition. She'd been more right than wrong when it came to moving a possibility into something real, turning a "what-if" into a scenario that made sense—and helped solve crimes.

"I guess so," he said.

"We're going to need some techs over here," Grace said, calling across the windy rocky beach to the investigators who'd come to collect Samantha's remains. Samantha Maxwell wasn't going home alone.

She had company.

Grace wouldn't have told anyone—not her partner, her husband, even her mother—that *it* passed through her mind, as the bones were recovered amid the seaweed and silver-colored driftwood that had also cradled the remains of Samantha Maxwell. The *it* was like the grandfather clock in her parent's Tacoma home, always ticking, always there. The *it* was like a kind of leech that had planted itself on her skin and just never let go. She drew a deep breath as she tried to put it out of her mind. While Samantha Maxwell's case was never considered foul play, only a terrible accident, the scene had to be processed with the skill and decorum befitting the tragedy that had stolen the pretty young teenager's life.

The clouds had darkened and rain began to fall through a tear in the sky. The techs were dressed in dark blue rain gear as they methodically worked over an area that had been cordoned off with bright yellow tape. No telling how long the bones had been there. One young cop suggested they wait out the rain.

"Not like this is a fresh kill and there's any evidence to be had," he said.

"Are you an idiot or is your brain running low on fuel because you skipped a meal?" Grace asked. "We don't wait for the weather when we find a body."

The tech turned defensive. "You don't have to get all high and mighty with me. I'm just saying the obvious. Bones that old probably belong to an Indian or something."

Grace held her tongue. She could have reminded him that "Native American" was the preferred term, but there was no point in coming off as a bitch.

Or *high and mighty*, as the twerp put it.

By the end of the day, the bones recovered—nine of them—were tagged and bundled in a plastic lidded box of the same kind many home owners use to store their Christmas decorations. The femur had been the largest bone; ribs and fragments of a pelvis were also recovered from the beach. Techs moved up to the top of the cliff, at Grace's request.

"No telling what happened," she said, "but if those bones are from a homicide victim I'd say it was a good bet that the body was buried up there."

The cliff had sloughed off a van-sized chunk of earth.

Paul Bateman nodded.

"We don't even know if the remains are human, you know. And don't you go thinking that it's *her*."

Grace nodded. Her partner knew her so well.

"Hadn't even crossed my mind," she lied.

CHAPTER 2

The Salmon Beach neighborhood of Tacoma was all about the eclectic. The different drum. The doing your own thing. The charm of the neighborhood just north of Point Defiance had long been its hippie and hipness factor. Some of the houses had been brought in by barge, rejects that found new lives and the astounding view that came with being on the beach. Most, however, had been built there on stilts over the water as fishing cabins. It was a tiny village of some eighty homes with wind socks and birdfeeders, and people with strong hearts. They needed them. No cars could make their way down the sharp cliff to anyone's front door. It was a couple hundred steps down, and more important, when there was something to carry up, a couple hundred steps to get to the top.

Grace and Shane Alexander weren't at all like the couples on either side of their 1940s house perched on pilings. She was a Tacoma Police detective, he an FBI agent working out of the Seattle field office. Their lives were certainly law and order, but they were very much a live-and-let-live couple. If they smelled a little pot smoke from the older couple with the tie-dyed curtains a few doors down, they never said a word about it.

Their house, a cabin really, was only twelve hundred square feet. Cozy or cramped? That always depended on the mood of its occupants. When they disagreed—which was more than occasionally—no house, not even Aaron Spelling's former mansion in Hollywood, would be large enough for either to find solace in a quiet corner.

The discovery of Samantha Maxwell's body and the sad call she and her partner had made to the Maxwell home in nearby Spanaway had left Grace edgy. Telling a mother the worst possible news always did. And yet as bad as that was, Shane knew what was really percolating around his wife's mind.

"When will the lab have the results back on the bones?" he asked, finishing a beer and slipping past his wife for another in the refrigerator. He opened the freezer and retrieved a second ice-cold pilsner glass, a habit he'd had since college days at the University of Washington.

Grace, who had been mincing some chives snipped from a deck planter for Dungeness crab cakes she was making, looked up, but only for a second.

"A few days," she said. "They'll be in Olympia tomorrow."

The state crime lab was located in Olympia, a half hour's drive from Tacoma.

"Are you doing all right?" he asked, putting his hand on her shoulder and stopping her from her task.

"Fine," she said.

"Slim to none," he said.

Grace stopped a beat. "Excuse me?"

He took a drink and swallowed. "Chances are the bones aren't hers."

Grace scraped the chives from a wooden cutting board into the bowl of luscious pink and white crab-meat.

"I know," she said.

He looked at her with those eyes, the eyes that could tap in to her soul like no others.

"Do you really know that?" he asked, taking that first foamy sip from the second beer.

"Yeah," Grace said, looking up as the news came on. "Hang on." She reached for the remote and turned up the sound on the wall-mounted TV over a living room fireplace that was as fake as a reality show. Fireplaces were not a good idea in a place as hard to get to as Salmon Beach. Several beach homes had burned to the ground over the years because the fire department couldn't reach them in time.

"Tonight the coroner identified the body of Saman-tha Maxwell, missing from Point Defiance. While there has not been an official ruling, sources tell KING-5 News that the death will likely be ruled as a swimming accident."

Behind the reporter was a shot of Grace and the other police at the scene.

"Hey, you're on TV," Shane said.

Grace held her hand up. "Shh! I need to hear this."

"While investigators were at the beach," the reporter said in the kind of exaggerated earnestness that never seemed even remotely genuine, *"they made the discovery of human remains, unrelated to drowning victim Maxwell."*

Colette Robinson, the woman jilted by her husband for a dog sitter, appeared on the screen.

"I saw the dead girl first," she said, her eyes wandering from the camera lens to the interviewer. *"Poor thing. I've seen her picture on TV. Beautiful. So, so tragic. I never saw the bones, but I watched the police detectives collect them."*

The reporter finished the short segment by saying that *"the bones are of unknown age and origin. They might not even be human."*

Grace turned on the stove and poured some olive oil from a ceramic decanter.

"Have you talked to your mother about it?" he asked.

"Of course I did. She had a right to know before it came on TV, Shane."

Shane took another drink. "You shouldn't get her hopes up."

The skillet smoked. Grace reached for it and in doing so, knocked over the oil.

"Damn! Look what you made me do!" she said, going for the dishcloth that hung on the oven door's handle.

Shane took the skillet off the heat to let it cool a moment. "I'm sorry," he said, though he knew he really hadn't done anything wrong. "I just want to be a help to you and your mom. I'm on your side."

"What side is that?" she asked, immediately wishing that her tone had been absent of any impatience or sarcasm.

To his credit, Shane ignored it.

"The side of truth and peace," he said.

* * *

As she looked across the table at Shane that night, Grace couldn't help but remember that day she'd first laid eyes on him. It had been years ago, but not long enough to be a distant memory. Shane was on leave from the FBI at the time, promoting his book, *Birth of a Serial Killer*, a compendium of cases he'd worked on at the Behavioral Analysis Unit in Quantico, Virginia. Shane wasn't a "profiler," at least he didn't like to use the label. He felt that the status that came with that particular moniker was beyond the true grasp of those working in the field trying their best to catch a killer. He considered himself "more of a criminal genealogist" than a profiler.

To understand what makes a serial killer, he'd written in the introduction to his book, *law enforcement and other interested parties need to dig in to the killer's family tree. No one becomes the ultimate evil merely because they were born bad; they become evil because it is almost a part of their DNA.*

As he talked to a sizable group in the auditorium on the campus of Pacific Lutheran University the night he met his future wife, Special Agent Alexander showed slides of the crimes that he'd worked in his relatively young and exulted career at the FBI.

"Toni Caswell, nineteen, was the first victim of the Naperville Strangler, Ronald Chase Mitchell," he said, his voice projecting low and deep in the darkness of the auditorium. "The nineteen-year-old college student was not the first victim to be discovered, but actually the fourth." He paused, not for dramatic emphasis, as Grace would later learn, but because of the devastating guilt that came with his next words, an admission of sorts.

"Had her body been found earlier," Shane said, pausing to click to the next image, one of a young woman with a halo of blond hair and piercing green eyes, "I think that Cassandra Kincaid would likely not have been killed."

A hand shot up.

It belonged to a young Tacoma Police detective named Grace O'Hare. It was the first time she'd spoken to the man who she had considered an idol, then later, her husband.

"Yes, in the front row," Shane said, his blue eyes squinting a little in the dark.

Grace nodded, and a woman with a microphone came toward her.

"Yes, Special Agent, I still don't understand why— with all of the vast resources at the bureau—that you were unable to ascertain what became obvious years later, that Toni was Ronald Chase Mitchell's girlfriend and that all the victims after her were dead ringers for her?"

Shane Alexander nodded a little. He'd heard that question before.

"Look," he said, his tone even and not the least bit defensive, "we are really learning the truth of what's behind the mask. What is obvious after the fact is sometimes painfully so."

The comment was a none-too-subtle reference to the *New York Times* profile that had led to his book deal.

"I guess," Grace said, holding on to the microphone.

The young woman next to her, whose job it was to pass it to the next person, made an irritated face. "What you're saying is that as much as we know about sociopathic personality disorder, we really don't know enough to actually stop them from killing."

Shane stepped closer to get a better look at her. She wasn't going to back down. He knew he hadn't seen the last of her, and in that minute, that was just fine.

"No, I guess we don't," he said, as politely as possible. He turned around and indicated a young man in the second row. "Question?"

After the lights went up, Grace found her place at the end of the line for the book signing. She let several others go ahead of her, even putting up with the crime groupies and their over-the-top gushing about the agent's work at the Behavioral Analysis Unit.

One young woman, a reasonably attractive redhead who had a too-heavy hand with her eyeliner and slashes of blush that looked like they'd been applied with a stencil, served up the line of the night.

"That analysis would be above my pay grade," he said.

"I don't know which is sexier," she cooed, "serial killers or the hotties who catch them."

Grace watched the special agent deal with the crime groupie. He smiled and signed her book.

After she departed, clutching a book that she'd likely fall asleep while reading, he looked up at Grace.

"I don't know what is more repulsive, serial killers or the groupies they attract," he said.

"Your job puts you in danger a lot. I guess that's sexy to some," she said.

"We're well trained," he said.

"I didn't mean the FBI. I meant your job as an author and lecturer. That's the scary one."

He laughed. "I'm Shane Alexander," he said, stating the obvious, but doing so to break the ice and get her to say her name—without being too forward.

Grace nodded. "I know. I read your book."

"And you are?"

She looked at him with those eyes that could never tell a lie. "Grace O'Hare. My sister, Tricia, was one of Ted Bundy's victims. At least we think so."

"You want to talk?"

Grace, back in the moment, offered Shane the last crab cake. The sun was down and the water had turned from golden to black.

"You made 'em, you have the last one," he said, patting his slightly expanding midsection.

"You could burn off the calories by going up to my car. I left my book up there."

"You need to get an e-reader, Grace. We don't have the storage for any more books around here anyway."

He was right about that. The north wall of their small house was floor-to-ceiling books, most of them nonfiction crime, though there was the occasional serial-killer thriller—more for a diversion from the reality of the dark professions they'd both chosen.

Grace had always been interested in crime, murder especially.

"I think it's in my blood," she'd told Shane when they first met.

"Me too, but not because of personal connection.

Just a deep need to be close enough to the bad stuff to be able to stop the bad guys from doing whatever it is they're doing again."

"I understand," she'd said. "For me, for my family, murder has always been personal."

Some saw their strange alliance as a linkage between two individuals who were obsessed with crime. What those people missed was that they needed each other. He loved and understood her.

She loved him with all her heart, but she also knew that he could help her.

CHAPTER 3

It was dusk when Lisa Lancaster looked at the newspaper vending box. The headlines of the day's *News Tribune* touted a state legislator's brilliant/bogus idea to sell the naming rights of the Narrows Bridge to ease a disastrous state budget shortfall. She wondered why Tacoma was so provincial. Why Washington was so backwards. New Yorkers would never think to sell the naming rights to the Empire State Building. No one would ever give voice to such a ridiculous scheme.

While Lisa got most of her news from Internet sites like Gawker and TMZ, she did crouch down to read a little of a news story that caught her interest in that kind of ghoulish way that some stories do.

*HUMAN BONES FOUND: WHO IS JANE DOE
AND HOW DID SHE DIE?*

The article detailed the discovery of the bones and how the Tacoma Police Department was looking into a number of missing persons cases involving young women from as far back as the 1950s.

Lisa, a willowy brunette with shoulder-length hair

and forget-me-not blue eyes, stopped reading because the idea of an old body grossed her out. She turned her thoughts inward as she stood outside the student union building on the Pacific Lutheran University campus near Tacoma and tried to determine what she should do.

With her hair.

Her major.

Her life.

Lisa had been a history major, a communications major, a songwriter, a papier-mâché artist, and even a member of the university's physics club. She thought her indecision had to do with the wide breadth of her interests, but family members didn't agree. Lisa was twenty-four and had been in college for six years. She'd leveraged her future with more than a hundred and twenty thousand dollars in student loans.

And she still didn't know what she wanted to be.

Lisa roulette dialed until someone picked up. Her best friend of the moment, Naomi, took the call and promptly used up half of her "bonus" minutes talking about her boyfriend and how selfish he was.

"Like he acts like I'm supposed run right over to his parents' garage whenever he's horny," she said. "I told him if he's looking for a hookup then he should go on Craigslist like every other loser."

As she listened, Lisa watched a young man with a heavy backpack and crutches walking across the parking lot. It had rained earlier in the evening and the lot shimmered in the blackness of its emptiness. His backpack slipped from his shoulders and fell onto the sodden pavement.

Lisa turned away. "Some dork with a broken leg or

something just dropped his stuff into the mud," she said.

"That campus is full of dorks. Is he a cute dork?"

"That's an oxymoron," Lisa said.

"Oxy-what?" Naomi asked.

Lisa rolled her eyes, though no one could see them. There was no one around. Just her and the guy struggling in the parking lot.

"Never mind," she said. Naomi wasn't nearly as stupid as she often pretended to be. Neither was she all that smart. She was, as Lisa saw it, a perfect best friend. "I can't decide if I should skip dinner and go home. My parent's fridge never has anything good," she said.

"Mine, neither," Naomi said. "Even though I make a list, they ignore it. I practically had to kill myself in front of them to get them to buy soy milk for my coffee. I hate them."

"I know," Lisa said. "I hate my parents, too."

The young women continued to chat while Lisa kept a wary eye on the dork with the backpack.

"God," she said. "I don't know why the handicapped—"

"Handi-capable is the preferred term, Lisa."

Lisa shifted her weight from one foot to another. She was impatient and bored.

"Whatever," she said, "like I wasn't the president of that dumb club. I don't understand why they don't get a dog or a caregiver to help them get around. Or just stay home." Lisa stopped and let her arm relax a little, moving the phone from her ear. "He dropped his pack again."

"You know you want to help him," Naomi said. "Remember when we both wanted to be physical therapists?"

"Don't remind me. But I guess I'll help him. I'll call you back in a few."

Lisa turned off her phone and started across the lot.

The young man fell to the pavement. One of the crutches was just out of reach.

"Can I give you a hand?" Lisa asked.

He looked up with an embarrassed half-smile.

"No," he said, trying to get on his feet. "I can manage."

Lisa stood there, a hand on her hip. She was pretty. Prettier up close than she'd been when he first spotted her. She was smaller than he'd thought too. That, like her looks, was also a good surprise.

"Let me help you," Lisa said, bending down and hooking her hands under his arms. He stood wobbly on one leg, like a flamingo at the zoo. A good wind would knock him over. Lisa handed him his other crutch and picked up the backpack.

"You must be taking some heavy courses," she said, instantly feeling embarrassed about the unintended pun. She got a good look at his face. He actually was handsome with dark hair, large brown eyes, and stylish stubble above his upper lip and on the tip of his chin.

A goatee in the works?

Lisa grinned, not outwardly, but inside. The cute dork existed after all. She'll tell Naomi the minute she helped him to his car.

"Where are you parked?" she said.

"Over there," he said. "I'm Ted, by the way."

So sure he was about what he was about to do that he didn't think twice about using his father's name.

Lisa glanced over at the burnished orange Honda Element, a boxy mini-SUV that was destined to be the VW bus of the new millennium.

"Fun car," she said.

He shrugged, although with crutches under each arm, shrugging was not that easy an endeavor. "Good for outdoors stuff. If you go hiking and get mud in the car you can literally hose it out."

Lisa nodded. "I guess that's good. You like to hike?"

"I do. Sometimes I like to drive out to the middle of nowhere, pull off the road, and just find something cool to look at. A lake. A forest. Someplace where no one goes."

"I'm Lisa, by the way. What are you taking?" she asked, moving the heavy backpack to her other shoulder

"Biology. Pre-med," he said, though it was a lie. Inside his backpack were the A, B, and C volumes of old, outdated encyclopedias from his basement recreation room.

He was looking even more handsome.

When they arrived next to his car, he directed her to the passenger side.

"Can you put my books there?" he asked. "Easier to get to later."

She nodded.

He pushed the electronic door lock button on his key fob and Lisa popped open the door.

"Did some other good Samaritan take a nap in here?" she said, a little teasingly, as she set the backpack on a seat that had been completely reclined to form a bed.

He didn't answer and Lisa turned to look over her shoulder.

The young man was standing without crutches, framed by a lamp partially blocked by a dying cedar tree. Braided shadows crisscrossed his face like a spider web. He was holding one of the crutches like a Louisville Slugger.

"What the—" Lisa started to say, but her words were cut short.

He'd filled the aluminum tube of the crutch with his grandfather's lead fishing weights, thinking that a little more heft would be helpful when he swung it at his victim's head.

Which he did.

And it was.

Lisa's shoulder bag fell into the gutter and her cell phone cartwheeled on the pavement and broke into pieces. The college student offered no final scream. No real sound but the slumping of her body against the doorjamb of the Element.

In a moment marked by a blur of swift movements and a gasp of air from the victim's lungs, he had her inside.

He looked at her through the passenger window, satisfied and excited. He fixed the image in his memory like a photograph that he'd retrieve later. Moments like this were to be savored and relived over and over.

Lisa Lancaster was so beautiful. *Sleeping*. Like a doll with a swirl of lovely dark hair and perfect little features. He owned her right then, and a broad and unexpected smile came to his face. *Not fear*. Not a thumping heart sequestered behind a rib cage. None of that.

At that moment, the young man understood something about the power of the hunt that had eluded him as he'd planned and stalked his first kill. The rush. The excitement of doing something few dared to do.

And doing it better than the father he'd admired, though never known. He climbed behind the wheel and turned the key in the car's ignition. He let out a little laugh at the pun that came to him just then.

He really was in his element. In every way.

At ten minutes before midnight, the 911 communications center received an anguished call from the mother of a missing young woman. The operator, Mary-Jo Danforth, thirty-one, took down the information provided and created a file she'd pass along to law enforcement. It was close to break time and Mary-Jo was feeling bored and restless. After she hung up the call, she swiveled her chair to talk to her friend and co-worker, Kirk Aldean.

A video camera installed for training purposes captured their conversation.

MARY-JO: Some mother thinks her daughter's been abducted or something. Didn't come home from college today.
KIRK: Probably out whoring around.
MARY-JO: You said it. I didn't. I just told her that we usually don't get involved if someone's only been gone a few hours. I mean, Jesus, if my old man called every time I was late getting home from shopping . . .
KIRK: Shopping? So that's what you call whoring around?

MARY-JO: You're such a brat. Anyway, she was crying and saying it wasn't like her daughter to be so, you know, irresponsible.

KIRK: Such a ho.

MARY-JO: You want to have coffee?

KIRK: You hitting on me, MJ?

MARY-JO: I guess. Let me finish the report. We can take our break out back.

She returned to her keyboard and finished her record by typing in the name: LISA LANCASTER.

CHAPTER 4

One of the highlights of the lobby of the Tacoma Police Department was without question the Mug Shot Café. Forget the historic placards and the tributes to the fallen officers that filled part of a wall. The espresso shop served up decent lattes and cappuccinos to the men and women of the department that perpetually seemed understaffed—it was appreciated *and* needed, especially after late-night investigations that turned into early-morning case reviews. The officer who greeted visitors from behind a bulletproof glass enclosure had summoned Grace to come downstairs.

"Your mother's here," he said.

"Why does this feel like I'm in school again?" she said, trying to make light of it. Her mother had been a frequent visitor to the department. So frequent, in fact, that it had almost cost Grace the job when the department reviewed her application. Her mother wasn't "crazy," but she was a little on the annoying side. At least that's what they said to each other. Inwardly, each of them felt a little different. Grace's mother was a persistent advocate for her daughter.

The one who had gone missing before Grace was born.

"You said you'd call me," said Sissy O'Hare, a woman who never waited longer than a blink to get to the heart of any matter. She was referring to the bones.

"Mom, there wasn't any more to say." She looked over at a pair of black leather chairs in front of a turn-of-the-century paddy wagon that was part of the department's mini museum of Tacoma's law enforcement history. "Let's sit."

"You didn't tell me that the bones were a woman's or a girl's."

"I didn't know what they were. I told you that."

"The news says female."

"They've made a calculated guess. We don't know what the gender is," Grace said.

Sissy pressed her daughter. "Look, you're here. You know what's going on. The very least you could do is keep me informed."

Grace looked around. She didn't like the sentence that her mother had just uttered. Her job was to solve crimes, not be a tipster whose purpose was to slake her mother's insatiable need to know every detail of every case that could possibly help solve the mystery of what had happened to Tricia.

"Mom, the evidence collected at the beach is in the hands of a very capable lab unit in Olympia. They will let us know what, and if possible, who, those remains belong to. Besides, getting any DNA from those bones will be difficult."

Sissy put her hand on her daughter's knee. "Then you have to find the rest of her. Was—was there a skull?"

Grace shook her head. "No. Not that we could find. We're not sure how the bones got there, Mom. We don't know for sure if there was a grave above, up on the cliff. We're still looking."

"She had a retainer when she went missing," Sissy said. "You remember that I told you that."

"I remember everything, Mom. And yes, while the retainer could be a helpful clue, the confirmation would come from teeth. The blood and tissue inside the tooth is often well-preserved."

The conversation was both strange and strained. The two women in front of the vintage paddy wagon were talking about a daughter Sissy hadn't seen for decades, and the sister Grace had never known. They were detached from the idea that they needed a dead person's teeth. It was a conversation they'd had before.

Later, when they would separate and go about the rest of their day, they'd think about what had driven them to the point of obsession.

Back in her end cubicle on the second floor, Grace flipped through the stack of reports that had somehow managed to appear in the twenty minutes she'd been downstairs talking to her mother.

"You doing all right?" Paul Bateman said, setting down a morbidly stained white coffee mug—one that needed a trip home to someone's dishwasher. Anyone's.

She took it anyway. She needed more caffeine. "Yeah. I don't know what's worse, my mother or our caseload."

"Speaking of caseload—we're following up on the Lancaster case today."

"Of course we are," Grace said, already scanning the report.

When Lisa had gone missing just after Samantha Maxwell's body was found, one of the local radio stations had tried to make something of the coincidence. The on-air hosts ignored the department's public information officer when he reported that Samantha's drowning was nothing but a tragic accident and had nothing whatsoever to do with the Lancaster girl.

"Short-staffed," Grace said, getting her coat. "Remind me to remind our wonderful sergeant that we can't do it all. No one could."

Across town, a man wallowed in the same beleaguered state. So much to do. So, so little time.

That afternoon Catherine Lancaster's haunted brown eyes stared at the lens of a Seattle TV news camera. A pediatric nurse at Tacoma General, Catherine was a tall, lanky woman with angular features and a wide, almost slotted mouth. With dark eyes and light brown bob, she had never been a beauty queen, but those who knew Catherine would only describe her with one word: *beautiful*. She'd devoted her life to serving others and the irony of what had happened to her wasn't lost on anyone. Among her friends, Catherine was the first to offer help—and the last to leave when someone needed her. There was no time of day too late to call. No question that could not be asked.

She was a woman who didn't deserve the lens of the camera on her. Not then. Not ever.

"Please," she said somewhat stiffly, her voice surprisingly strong given her obviously fragile state. Her thin lips trembled as she strung together the words that no mother would ever want to utter: "Help me find my daughter."

Catherine was on the news that evening doing what she'd been doing from the first moment Lisa vanished from a parking lot at the Pacific Lutheran University campus. A single mother, she had only one purpose in life at that moment. She wanted to find Lisa. No one but another mother could understand the true torment that comes when a child is missing. That was not to say that fathers didn't feel true anguish. But while in the world of political correctness no one dared to say so, it was true: It was a million times harder on a mother than a father. It just was. It just *is*.

"Look," she said, tears welling and threatening to roll down the crisp planes of her face, "I know that everyone says their kids are perfect, but Lisa was. She really, really was."

The reporter went on to cite Lisa's achievements, and there were many: basketball letter as a freshman, honor roll every year through high school, leader of a group of students who sought greater understanding for those with handicaps. Lisa was a dream child.

"She wanted to be a social worker or maybe a counselor for troubled kids. She wasn't sure exactly what she was going to be because there were so many things that interested her."

The tears finally fell.

The camera cut away to a wide shot of the campus parking lot, then the reporter, who stood shaking her head slightly.

"Such a sad story unfolding here in Tacoma. If any-one has any information—saw, heard anything, please contact the Tacoma Police Department."

The last image on the screen was a photo of Lisa and a phone number.

Down in Olympia a few miles south of Tacoma, a man named Dennis Caldwell was watching the Seattle TV news when the image of Lisa Lancaster made him do a double take and reach for the phone. He was almost shaking when the detective handling the case of his daughter's disappearance answered.

"Hey, Dennis," Detective Jonathan Stevens said. "I know you're calling for an update, but, sorry, nothing new."

"No update. I mean, I think I might have an update for you," Dennis said, his voice quavering.

"How's that? Remember something, did you?"

"No. I just saw something I think you should check out. I saw on KING-5 just now. There's a missing girl's case in Tacoma. The girl was abducted from one of those colleges up there. Taken, just like my Kelsey."

"I'm sure it might seem that way to you, Dennis," Detective Stevens said. He was not trying to shut down the anguished father. Although it sounded like he'd been drinking, he wasn't going to hold that against him. His daughter had been abducted. No one ever gets over that. Never. "We're still on top of the case."

"Like hell you are. You don't know who took her now any more than you did the day she went missing. You don't know a thing."

"We're on it," he said.

"The girl up in Tacoma looks just like my Kelsey. The same hair. Same features. A beautiful girl. Maybe the guy who took her is the same one who took my little girl. Will you promise to check it out?"

Jonathan Stevens never failed to check out any lead, no matter how tangential.

"You hang in there, Dennis," he said.

"You catch who abducted her."

After the call, Jonathan did a quick computer check and found information about Lisa Lancaster's disappearance. Lisa did look a lot like Kelsey, that was true. But she was much older. Kelsey Caldwell was seventeen and had been abducted after drama practice—she had been cast as Fiona in *Brigadoon*. Lisa Lancaster was twenty-four, a college student. He did have to hand it to Dennis Caldwell, drunk or not. He was right. The two girls looked like sisters.

Jonathan Stevens made a call up to Tacoma. It was more due diligence than anything. The chances of the two cases being connected in any way were slim to none. He just didn't want to be the cop who didn't act on a desperate father's request for justice. He couldn't live with that at all.

CHAPTER 5

Like the others before him, and undoubtedly the many more to follow, he was watching the TV news with a keen interest. His kind liked to be informed. They needed to get the update, the 411. Men like him always needed to know what their work had wrought. It was a thrill to see how someone reacted when his or her little girl was snatched. Most cried. Some like Lisa's mother, Catherine Lancaster, let tears fall slowly, as they fought for control in front of the camera. Those *boohoo-ers*, as he called them, were interesting, though kind of predictable.

Of course you are miserable, you idiot. You should have taught your daughter to be careful. Ever heard of stranger danger? Cry me a goddamn river, you idiot mother!

He sucked in everything Lisa Lancaster's mother had been saying, like he would suck the marrow from Lisa's bones. Hard. Quick. She was a classic boo-hoo-er. And a bit of a bore if you asked him. Which no one ever would, because no one would ever know it was he who'd taken her.

The ones who got his adrenaline pumping were

those who showed more anger than fear. They were the ones who jabbed at the camera and threatened to come right out of the TV to throttle the perpetrator.

"Bring her back or I'll make you so damn sorry!"

He smiled. They seemed so angry, so determined. It was almost a joke to him. They'd be the first ones to run from him if they knew he was nearby. All talk. All bravado. He imagined going to a candlelight vigil or a missing persons office to rub shoulders next to the finger-jabber. He'd lean over and whisper.

"She begged for her life, you know."

And when the person spun around, he'd pretend he'd said something else.

"She's a survivor, you know."

The only thing better than the finger-jab threat of some pissed-off dad was the truly inconsolable mother. The ones who could hardly get a word out of their trembling lips.

He liked those kinds of mothers. Their words and palpable fear were like a drug. They sparked. They sent a charge of adrenaline, spasms of excitement, through his body. It was as if their pain, their deepest hurt, brought him the greatest joy that he could imagine. Better than sex.

Almost.

Sometimes he was so drawn to the mother's pain that he'd drive by their house. It was a risk, a big one. Risks, however, were part of the game. The one he admired over all the other men who were just like him, had taken more risks than anyone. He'd escaped jail twice. He'd killed more girls than any other—though others were pretenders to the crown. He was the best at what he'd sought to do. A legend.

At times, he knew that following in the footsteps of a legend was like walking a tightrope in the dark. Yet he had no choice. He never really had.

Police detective Grace Alexander stood on the front doorstep and let her eyes pierce through the opening in the curtain between the small window and the door frame. The fabric moved and a woman with dark, penciled-on brows and eyes that had obviously cried a thousand tears stood there waiting. The women's eyes met, and in a flash both knew that what they were about to share was nothing either would have wanted.

Not ever.

"Let me do the talking," she said to Paul Bateman, who was standing a step behind her.

"You always do the talking," he said. "But I guess that's one of the things you're good at."

If it was a dig, it was a subtle one. At least for Paul, who'd been anything but subtle. He'd been angry over custody issues concerning his daughter, Elizabeth, a twelve-year-old girl who did what a lot of kids of police officers did—whatever she could think of when it came to torturing her father.

And her mother, too. Paul's ex, Lynnette Bateman, was the sergeant in the same detectives' unit—the one who'd insisted her unit "man up" and get the work done with less. For the past few months, Grace and other members of the department had half-enjoyed the drama of two of their own tussling over a kid who it seemed was going to end up on the wrong side of the law.

At that moment, none of that mattered, of course.

The woman on the other side of the door twisted the knob and spoke with the kind of anxiousness that was the hallmark of a mother in her position. She couldn't fathom that the world had conspired to drag her down lower than she'd ever dreamed possible in the beautifully restored turn-of-the-century home in Tacoma's Proctor district.

"You found her," she said, stepping backwards as the door widened to let the detectives inside the foyer, a large space of gleaming mahogany trim.

"Ms. Lancaster?" Grace asked.

Catherine Lancaster gave a quick nod. "You found her," she repeated.

"I'm Detective Alexander," Grace said. Without allowing her eyes to move from Ms. Lancaster's, she twisted a little toward her partner. "This is Detective Bateman."

Paul Bateman nodded but, sticking to his word for a change, said nothing.

"You've found Lisa, haven't you? She's dead, isn't she? My baby's dead!"

"No. No, Ms. Lancaster, we haven't found her."

A brief look of relief came over Catherine Lancaster's face, and she steadied herself. She led the detectives inside and motioned to a pair of chairs across from a sofa draped with an afghan. It was a large room, deceptively so. Most homes of that vintage were warrens, small spaces. This one was spacious.

The detective who had originally had the case had been injured in a car accident the previous evening— the night of the news telecast. Grace and Paul had taken the case—and the urgency that came with it—

that morning. They explained the accident and how they'd be taking over.

"I hope you're better at finding my daughter than he was," Catherine said. "It has been four days, you know."

Grace let the cutting remark slide. Detective Roger Goodman was an excellent investigator. His notes indicated that he had been following up the possibility that Lisa had left with a boyfriend.

Catherine offered coffee, but no one wanted any. They sat around the kitchen table, a refrigerator plastered with magnets and postcards was a chronicle of the family's life—Disney, Grand Canyon, Hawaii. On the counter were shopping bags from Macy's and Nordstrom and a shoebox. A chalkboard above the wall phone carried a message.

Lisa, let me know about Friday!

"We want to follow up on Marty Keillor, your daughter's boyfriend. He left town the same day as Lisa."

Catherine shook her head, an irritated look on her face.

"Look," she said, "I told Detective Goodman that Marty was a good kid. They weren't seeing each other anymore. They dated on and off for years, and when they finally broke up it was amicable. He came over here the day before yesterday."

Grace had read the name in the report. "We've been looking for him. Why didn't you let us know?"

"I did. I called it in to Detective Goodman," Catherine said. "Left a message on the machine. I guess he was in the hospital already. Probably my hospital, too, but no one told me."

"Where was Marty?" Paul asked.

"He and some buddies went over to Sun Lakes on the other side of the mountains, where there's still some summer weather. They had no cell, no Internet. Marty had no idea Lisa was missing. He's as devastated as I am."

The sound of a car door slammed and footsteps made their way to the door.

As if on cue, it was Marty.

"He's here right now. Talk to him."

Catherine got up and opened the door. A handsome young man with dark hair and biceps that indicated daily curls embraced her. Lisa's mother and former boyfriend hugged.

"Police," Catherine said.

"Good," the young man said, finally loosening his embrace as they walked across the living room to the kitchen.

Grace looked at Paul. The hug was a little strange— not the embrace of the heartbroken, but something else.

Marty Keillor slid into a seat. He was taller than Paul. His legs barely fit under the table. He wore a tight black V-neck T-shirt and dark washed Wranglers. On his snowshoe-sized feet were brand-new Carhartt boots.

The detectives introduced themselves to the former boyfriend.

The young man leaned across the table, his face full of concern.

"Where is she?" Marty asked.

"That's what we want to know," Paul said. "We thought maybe you could tell us something. Did you know we were looking for you?"

He shook his head. "How could I? There's no cell service. I got the other cop's messages, when we came over the pass. I came right over here. Didn't I, Catherine?"

Catherine? Whatever happened to Ms. Lancaster? Grace thought.

"Can anyone verify where you were when she went missing?" she asked.

"Yeah, like about fifty people. Huge party at Sun Lakes," he said.

"Can you provide us with names, numbers, for any of the fifty, specifically?"

Catherine spoke up. "I don't like where this is going," she said. "I can see that you're trying to blame Marty for something here. That's ludicrous."

"Maybe. But it is routine, Ms. Lancaster," Grace said.

Marty glanced over at Catherine, then back at the detectives. "No problem. I get it. Missing girl—boyfriend, ex-boyfriend, gets dibs on being a person of interest."

"If you have to investigate Marty, do it fast," Catherine said, patting him on the arm. "He's got nothing to do with this. He's my support system and he's a good one. I want you to find out who took Lisa. *Please.* Find out who took her and bring her home."

Grace could feel the mother's pain. Despite the odd vibes she was getting of something going on between the mother and former boyfriend, there could be no denying that Catherine Lancaster was in tremendous pain.

"We're going to do our best," Grace said.

"But to be fair, there isn't much to go on," Paul said.

"I'm sorry your detective got injured, but you better

hope that his misfortune didn't put my Lisa in greater
danger. You better hope that big-time."

The detectives handed over their business cards,
promised open lines of communication, and took a list
of names and cell numbers from Marty.

Detective Goodman had interviewed campus police
at PLU—which yielded nothing. He made a note of a
meeting with Naomi Carlyle, the girl who had likely
been the last person to talk to Lisa before she'd disappeared.

"Let's go see Naomi," Grace said.

"Yeah," Paul answered, as they got into the car.
"Was it just me or did you get a weird feeling? Maybe
something going on between those two?"

Grace started the car and looked at Paul.

"Oh yeah," she said. "Did you notice the shoebox on
the kitchen counter? Carhartt boots size thirteen."

"No, so?"

"Marty was wearing brand-new Carhartts," she said,
backing into the street.

"Didn't catch that," he said. "Methinks they've been
knocking those boots."

Grace nodded. "Methinks that, too."

Roger Goodman's initial report indicated that Naomi
worked at the Melting Pot. Since she wasn't picking up
the cell number they had for her, Grace and Paul drove
down the hill toward the restaurant in Tacoma's best
stab at urban renewal—a slew of restaurants along Pacific Avenue not far from the Washington State History
Museum and the Dale Chihuly–stuffed Museum of

Glass. Grace and Shane had been to The Melting Pot a couple times before. It was an expensive fondue restaurant whose price point kept it in the "special occasion" category. On the drive down, Paul complained about Lynnette, his ex-wife, and Grace pretended to agree with everything he said. To disagree just meant more mind-numbing examples of why Lynnette Bateman was a complete bitch and control freak. Since she truly was, there was no point in getting that litany from her pissed-off former husband.

"You know," Grace said, "Lynnette is my sergeant."

"I know," he said. "I feel sorry for you."

"I appreciate that, Paul. But what I'm trying to say is I just can't go there conversation-wise. I get what you're saying. I trust your opinion. Can we just leave it like that?"

"Okay," he said, his face a little red. "I just need someone to talk to. You know, she's really messing up the custody deal."

"You're a good father," Grace said. "It will work out."

He looked out the window. "Hope so. I need my kid."

Grace nodded. She pulled into a parking space behind The Melting Pot.

"Naomi drives a light blue VW," she said, pulling into park.

"Yeah. That's the one. Guess she's working."

Inside the restaurant they found Naomi Carlyle, front and center. She was an attractive young woman with long waves of blond hair and green eyes that flickered in the light of her workstation, the hostess podium.

After the detectives introduced themselves, the trio went to a quiet space in the back of the restaurant.

"I told the detective on the phone that I couldn't think of anyplace Lisa would have gone. I mean, I can think of places she would like to go—Maui, for example. But I doubt that's where she went. She would never have left that car of hers. She loved it. Plus, when you get right down to it that little bitch would have never gone anywhere good without me."

"Little bitch? That's kind of harsh," Paul said.

Naomi laughed. "No. That's just nickname we had at Stadium High. We were the little bitches—LBs. We ran that school."

"I see. High school was a while ago," Grace said. "You and Lisa have been close for a long time."

"Yeah. Like sisters," Naomi said. A waitress offered them water, but all three indicated no.

"Then you probably were around when she was dating Marty Keillor," Paul said.

"Party Marty," Naomi said. "Yeah, I was. The dude was fun but so wrong for her. He kept cheating on her. She'd break up. Go back to him. Break up again. You needed a tally sheet to figure out what their relationship was. Glad that's over."

"Was it a hard breakup?" Grace asked.

"No. Not really. I mean, look they had a yo-yo relationship. Each breakup and makeup was easy. By the end they were only a booty call anyway. What's all this about Marty? He's a dope, but he'd never hurt her. You should follow up on that capper she was talking to before she disappeared."

"Capper?"

Naomi shrugged. "He had a broken leg or something. She was talking to me when she was going to her car and said she'd call me later, but I fell asleep. I never even looked to see if she called until the next day."

"What did she say about the guy with the broken leg?"

"Just that he was a dork and she was going to help him. She used to be in a club that helped those people."

"The 'cappers,' " Paul said with obvious disdain for the young woman's choice of words for handicapped individuals.

"Don't be a judger," she said, her eyes now icy. "Just do your job and find her."

Grace cut the tension with a question. "What did she say about the guy?"

"Not much. She went to help him because he dropped his books. I guess some of our diversity training actually took root. I would have just let him struggle. I don't believe in helping people who you don't know."

Naomi was a jerk, but she'd been the last one to talk to the vanished girl.

"Marty and Lisa's mother seem very close," Paul said.

Naomi shrugged. "I guess so. I'm sort of creeped out by the two of them."

"Creeped out?"

"Yeah. There were a few times when I was over there in high school that I thought they were a little too close. I told Lisa and she didn't care. She was just using Marty for his car anyway."

* * *

Grace checked her messages when she and Paul returned to the car. None from the state crime lab. And
thankfully, none from her mother. While the possibility
was always out there that her sister's remains would be
discovered sometime, somewhere, Grace also knew
that for many family members of the missing and presumed dead, there was never a final answer.

"Let's go back to the office," she said.

CHAPTER 6

Dismembering a human body was much harder than it appeared. It was messy, took considerable strength, and no matter how tough one thought he or she was, it took a very, very strong stomach to get the job done.

And yet, when the endeavor was part of the family business, there was no getting around it. It must be done.

The man looked down at his tool kit—knives, a handsaw, kitchen shears—and the oozing red that flowed like a sluggish river toward a rusted, hair-clogged basement drain.

He let out a sigh.

The *Saw* slasher films, the charming but bloody cable TV show *Dexter*, and assorted episodes of *Criminal Minds* had done him wrong. They'd not prepared him for the smell of torn human flesh. They'd done a poor job putting him in the picture to see what it felt like doing the necessary but nasty. He winced slightly as he moved the blade deeper into the widening crimson canyon of the dead woman's abdomen. The vibra-

tion that came from a serrated blade against the impasse
of a bone rankled him whenever the steel of the blade
met one. Femurs were particularly resilient. He hated
femurs because they called for the swinging of an axe.

Hoisting an axe overhead and driving it into his victim meant breaking a sweat.

He hated to sweat.

The young man had read everything he could on the
subject, at least subjects that were parallel to what he
was undertaking. He'd watched videos of hunters dismembering deer on YouTube. He'd even practiced on
the turkey that his mother had served that Thanksgiving.
It was a twenty-five-pound tom, fresh, not frozen.

A very uncooperative turkey at that.

"Poultry can be tricky. Aim for the joints," his mother
said, pulling all the air in the room through her cigarette.
"The leg will come right off."

He'd glared at her back then. Never a beauty, any
looks she'd had were long gone. She was dour, with lifeless eyes. She had the kind of smoker's mouth that
looked more like a shrunken gash than a smile.

"Hmm," she said, as the juices ran in the platter.
"Might not be done," she said, snuffing out her cigarette into raw giblets in the sink. "Looks red, not clear."

He ignored her.

He liked red.

Everything was red.

That evening Grace and Shane Alexander shared a bottle of Riesling and a wedge of creamy Brie that she had
somehow found the time to bake with pecans and brown
sugar. It was gooey, salty, sweet, and completely deca-

dent. Something wonderful that she thought would help take their minds off the long day. Shane had finished a weeklong special project for the bureau and wanted just to forget about all the politics that came with the job that he'd once thought was about catching the bad guys and making the world a better, safer place. Grace had office politics to contend with, too, and the crumbled marriage of Paul and Lynnette Bateman had been dissected over and over. There was nothing more to say about it. Besides, she had the concerns of the missing girl on her mind.

"So you think there might be some liability with the Lancaster girl's investigation stalling because of Goodman's accident?" Shane asked as they sat on the deck of their Salmon Beach home and watched the seagulls and boaters pass by.

"That's what the mother thinks," Grace said. "If Lisa's been abducted and some scuzzball has her and kills her you can bet she'll file a wrongful death on the department."

Shane offered her more wine and she held out her glass.

"Any leads?" he asked. "That is, any you can tell me about?"

She smiled and shook her head. It was kind of a game they played. Their lives were about crime, murder, violence, and the cases that consumed them, but they pretended that the information they held couldn't really be shared—not if it hadn't already been on the news or disclosed by someone else. Bureau policy carried more weight than the edicts issued by Lynnette Bateman.

"No," Grace said. "One minute she was on the phone and the next minute she was gone."

He put his hand in hers.

"I'm sure this, even more than the bones at the beach, dredges up bad memories," he said.

She nodded. "Not my memories, but yeah. Bad ones."

"You'll catch the guy," he said.

"I hope so. I wouldn't want Ms. Lancaster to live through all the stuff we have had to endure in our family."

He nodded. "No one should have to," he said.

Grace took a big sip of her wine. "No one should have to live with a ghost." She stopped as a kayaker came close enough to hear. She waited until the coast was clear, until it was safe to speak. "The funny thing about ghosts is that they can seem so real. Always there. Hanging over you. Almost taunting you."

"You'll solve this, Grace. And you'll solve the other one, too."

She nodded. Her mind racing back to the memories that were such a part of her. So deep. So entrenched. And yet like a ghost, not really there.

Her phone vibrated and she looked down.

"Mom calling. Did I tell you she came to see me today?"

Shane shook his head. "Take the call. She needs you."

Grace wanted to say something about how she needed *him* right then, but she didn't. She picked up the phone.

"Hi, Mom, just talking about you . . ."

* * *

After hanging up the phone, Sissy O'Hare looked out her kitchen window at the same view she'd seen in the O'Hares' backyard since she and her husband, Conner, bought the house shortly after Tricia was born. The pregnancy had been a difficult one and doctors told her she should not have any more children. The house was for Tricia, a place to spoil an only child. A swing. A kiddie pool. A patio for riding her tricycle. Sissy held those memories and turned on the water. Steam rose and she squirted dish soap into the water. The pear tree on the far side of the yard was no longer producing decent fruit, but it was too pretty during its spring bloom to cut down. She closed her eyes for a moment, remembering. Tricia had begged to be pushed skyward there, higher and higher. Grace, too. The branch where Conner had strung a swing had broken off in a storm and a massive burl had formed, a gnarled hump of healed wood. As she looked out that window, she wondered about the bones that were being pored over by the scientists in the lab in Olympia. She wondered if her little girl had been found. As the tap water filled the sink and a billowy cloud of suds heaped over the water's surface, Sissy knew her firstborn was dead. She'd known so for decades. Yet in that moment, she half prayed that the bones were not Tricia's. If they were, it would really be over. *Final.* There would be no little drop of hope that Tricia had run away and started a new life somewhere. Tears came to her eyes. She turned off the water.

Mother and daughter had argued that last day. It was a silly argument, one that Sissy was all but certain had not been the cause of whatever it was that had happened to her. It was so silly, yet so painful; she'd never told Conner or the police about it.

"That top, honey," she had said, "makes you look like a streetwalker."

"Everyone is wearing them," Tricia answered.

The top in question showed a four-inch band of skin on her midriff.

"March yourself into the bedroom and get yourself something decent. I don't want your father to see you looking like that."

"I hate you, Mom. You're always telling me what to do."

"I love you, Tricia, that's why. Now, go."

She expected Tricia to come back into the kitchen wearing a more sensible top and give her a hug before she left. She didn't. She slipped out the front door.

Sissy never saw her again.

CHAPTER 7

For most of Grace's life, Tricia's room had been off-limits. She was able to go inside only when her mother and father allowed her to do so. That was once a year, when the family would gather to observe the anniversary of Tricia's birthday. When she looked back on it later in life, she could envision that the entire bedroom was but a shadowbox of her phantom sister's life. Her high school diploma was framed above a desk. On top of the desk were miscellaneous papers—a letter, a drawing of a cat, and other things that were so mundane that even though Grace had never known Tricia, she was sure that those things would have been thrown in the trash. They were not keepsakes at all. There were some items that truly were—her Bible, a desiccated corsage from her senior prom. The rose was no longer red, but black and brown, with petals that clung to the stem with fragility.

Her sister's room was the larger of the two secondary bedrooms. When she was younger, Grace had resented how even in death, Tricia would always trump her for everything—a larger bedroom, a closer relationship with her parents, even a dog. When Grace was five, the family poodle, Mirabelle, succumbed to cancer at sixteen. Mirabelle had always been known as Tricia's dog, a trusted companion, a possible witness to whatever had happened the night of her disappearance. Grace cried a fountain after the dog died, and begged for another puppy. Her parents said no. It had been too hard to say good-bye to Mirabelle.

Tricia's beloved dog would be the only pet the family would have.

A photo of Tricia taken when she was fifteen, her mouth a train track of braces, Mirabelle at her side, hung above the desk.

Grace's teeth were crooked, too. Yet her parents didn't get her the benefit of orthodontics. Tricia, she had everything.

And yet whenever she snuck into the bedroom and sat on the bed, Grace wondered how it was that for all the reasons she could conjure about why she could hate her sister, she didn't. Instead, she felt the kind of aching loss that her parents did. *Why,* she asked herself over and over, *did Tricia have to die?* She couldn't compete with a dead sister and she didn't really want to. She simply wanted to know the same things that her parents agonized over.

Who had taken her? Why hadn't she been found? Was she still alive?

It didn't take a radio shrink to figure out the genesis of Grace's interest in a career in law enforcement. She'd grown up inside a family subsisting on tragedy and anger. She'd seen her mother stuff envelopes for a crime victims' group, her father drink until he could no longer walk. She'd heard the arguments that ran from the darkness of night to the first splinter of morning light.

"If you'd loved her more, she wouldn't have left us."

It was her mother's voice, accusing and cuttingly cruel.

"Sissy, you're out of line and you know it."

Her dad, sober for once, had a point. Grace knew it, even as a teenager. Her sister's disappearance was the fault of no one—other than the perpetrator—and her mother's anger was completely unfair. Her sister's vanishing had been random. She'd been a type of girl—pretty, slender, fine-featured, dark haired—that had been favored by a potential serial killer, one who'd never had the kind of name recognition that Tacoma's most infamous son, Ted Bundy, enjoyed once he was finally arrested for a string of murders. Investigators had tried to link Tricia's case and the disappearance of another Tacoma girl, Susie Sherman, to Bundy, but there was no real connection—at least none that anyone could find. After Bundy was arrested in Florida and the spotlight once more shined on potential crimes he might have committed, investigators took another run at trying to make a case that he'd been the perpetrator.

The Tacoma News Tribune ran a story about the possibility with the headline: DID TED KILL TWO TACOMA GIRLS?

The article indicated the similarities among Ted's murders in Washington, Oregon, Idaho, Colorado, and Utah and how the Sherman and O'Hare cases might have fit into the time line. Ted had been in the area off and on, but a gas receipt in Ellensburg on the other side of the Cascades at the time of Susie's disappearance put her case in doubt. Ted, had, in fact, been in Tacoma visiting family when Tricia disappeared. That didn't mean anyone had a shred of evidence, but a shred wasn't needed when it came to what many saw as the country's most prolific serial killer. Ted was always good for speculation. He was kind of the spaghetti serial killer—attribute a case to his name, throw it on the wall, and see if it sticks.

"Look, we're not saying he killed every girl who ever died in the Pacific Northwest," a Tacoma PD detective said in the news article, "but only a fool would ignore the distinct possibility that he could have been a particular killer. After all, the guy really got around."

The statement was made in 1974, what cops and crime writers later called the "Summer of Ted." That was before Theodore Robert Bundy was *Ted Bundy*, of course. He was simply an almost mythological man with a bright white smile, a gimpy arm in a sling, and a metallic VW bug. After the hysteria swung into full gear when two young women vanished on the same day, there wasn't a sorority girl with long, dark hair, parted in the middle who wasn't halfway certain that she had encountered Ted somewhere during that time. And, if a girl didn't actually have a Ted sighting of her own, there was always a friend who'd escaped being his victim.

Whoever Ted was. *Wherever* he was. He was like a handsome boogey man. Everywhere and nowhere at the same time. He was, many thought even at the time, a legend in the making.

Not long after Grace met Shane they went for a long walk along Ruston Way, a stretch of restaurants and beachfront park along Tacoma's Commencement Bay. It hadn't really been love at first sight when they'd met at the University of Washington. He was dark, handsome, and had the kind of disarming smile that put everyone at ease. He was tall, too. In fact, more than a foot taller than she, which was a huge relief. Although she'd always planned a career in law enforcement, she still wanted a life that included heels. During that walk after dinner, Grace truly opened up the first time about her sister's death and its impact on her life.

"She died before you were born, but you still mourn her," he said, as they took a place on a bench. A group of teenagers roughhoused nearby and a continual parade of couples, just like them, strolled by.

"It is hard to explain, but it really isn't mourning. Sure, sometimes I'm sad about Tricia, but most times she just casts a big shadow," Grace said. "Remember that case where a couple had a baby because their older daughter had leukemia and there was no donor?"

"Kind of," he said. "They needed a match for her bone marrow and they decided to take a chance and have another child." He put his arm around her and said, "Just in case." It wasn't supposed to be a sexy move, just a kind of reassuring gesture from someone who cared about her. Grace could feel it.

"Right," she said. "Just in case. And, you know that it worked. The little girl was a match."

"I'm not sure what you're getting at, Grace," he said, after a pause.

"I'm not saying it is exactly the same thing, but I grew up knowing that I was a kind of replacement for Tricia. Don't get me wrong, I know my parents loved me. But they just missed her so much, loved her so much, that I was there to fill the void. You know, like a family sometimes rushes out and gets a new cat the day after their cat is run over."

Shane looked off at the water, thinking.

"That's a little severe, Grace."

"Maybe, but that's how I felt. It was always Tricia this, Tricia that. Do you know that Tricia and I wore the same outfit to our first day of school? It was a pink sweater with a poodle appliqué. I thought it was cool because it matched Mirabelle. I didn't even know it was the same sweater until years later when I was going through an album tucked away in the basement."

"Okay, I'll grant you that is a little creepy," he said.

"That's not all. I mean, I could tell you stories all night about what it was like being the sister of a dead girl. Even though she was gone and had been gone before I was even born, there was never a time when her name didn't bring my dad to tears. There never was a time when I didn't feel that they wanted her so much that if there was a knock on the door from someone with a potion or promise that could bring her back and the only caveat would be that I was to be traded for her, they would have done so without so much as a thought."

Grace held Shane's gaze for a while. She could see trust, understanding in his eyes. Yet she was unsure how much she could really say. She had never been abused or anything like that; she understood that a parent's loss was undoubtedly greater than whatever anyone could imagine unless they'd been there themselves. As she grew older she could see a haunted look in the eyes of those who had suffered great loss. When she was a small girl, her parents hosted a support group for mothers and fathers of murdered children. Her mom had her serve cookies at many of the meetings and she could feel the longing stares coming from the club members as they watched her move from the kitchen to the living room, where a semicircle of chairs had been set up.

"How old is your little girl?"

"Nine," her father said.

"My Tracy would be about her age now."

"My Danny would be driving a car."

"Paula would be married by now."

It was always that way. The parents talking about their loss in terms of what their children would be doing at that very moment had they survived their killers. Yet, like Tricia, the reality was that they were frozen in time. Forever stuck. Just like the pictures that hung in all the sad little bedrooms of those kids who never came home—always there, as if waiting for the inevitable and relentless tears of those who mourned them.

CHAPTER 8

Emma Rose set out a pair of black pants, a white cotton blouse, a SAVE THE SOUND T-shirt, a black sweater, and a pair of black heels. She was short and no matter what the occasion, heels were always in order. Even for work at the Starbucks adjacent to the Lakewood Towne Center, just outside Tacoma. Starbucks dress code was much more relaxed than her clothes indicated, but Emma was the kind of girl who liked buying her work attire at Target in batches of threes. It just made everything easier not to worry about what she was going to wear when working. There was no disputing that she was a creature of habit. Never late. Always ate at the same place—on a bench in the parking lot in front of the coffee place. Emma always wore her long, dark hair the same way too—parted in the middle and held in the back with a loose clip.

She worked with Oliver Angstrom until just after nine.

"Do you hate this place as much as I do?" she asked as they wiped down the counter space and loaded the dishwasher for the last cycle of the night.

Oliver, a twenty-five-year-old in search of a publisher for a graphic novel about the end of the world, looked up. "I don't even like coffee," he said.

"I used to. Now the smell of it makes me sick," she said. "I don't know which I hate more—the people who come in here or the coffee."

"Tell me about it. I think that fat guy that sat over there," Oliver said, pointing across the room to a leather lounge chair under the plasma screen that touted the supposedly hip music that provided atmosphere all day long, "was actually watching porn with his hand in his pants."

"You're kidding me," Emma said, clearly disgusted.

Oliver nodded. "No lie. No one complained, though. Everyone who comes in here is too self-absorbed to pay attention to what anyone else is doing."

"Coffee-drinking Facebookers!" Emma said, with mock outrage. "Why don't they just go home to do their social networking?"

Oliver nodded in agreement. Emma was right. Over the past couple of years Starbucks had changed from a place where people breezed in, got a latte, and left for work. Oliver theorized that the declining economy was an invitation for whole groups of patrons who didn't have anywhere to go. No rush to get anywhere. Now people planted themselves at a table and Facebooked. Sometimes they didn't even buy a drink, which totally sucked in a business plan built on making people think they could sit and visit, when really turnover was needed.

"What did you think of the woman who bitched that her quadruple-pumped caramel macchiato didn't have enough syrup in it?"

"Gag me, is what I thought," Emma said.

Oliver laughed. "Or the dude who spilled his mocha and told us it was all our fault."

"Like we were going to argue with him, even though I saw the whole thing, too." Emma stood across the counter and surveyed the scene. She liked Oliver, but she could feel what was coming next. Some girls have a kind of sixth sense about when a guy is going to hit on them. Emma did.

"You want to hang out some time?" Oliver asked. It was a question that he'd wanted to ask for weeks, but until that moment he just hadn't had the nerve. He'd even asked his manager what he ought to do and she'd told him to go for it. He stopped what he was doing and looked over at her.

She lifted a shoulder and shrugged. Oliver wasn't bad looking. He had a lean build, nice features, dark, expressive eyes magnified through horn-rimmed lenses. So the physical side wasn't bad. Neither was his personality. One thing bugged her, however, and she couldn't get past it. He was a video game developer and graphic novel geek who lived at home with his mom and splurged once a year for a trip to Comic-Con. She lived in the real world—and she wanted to fix it. The T-shirt she wore under her work blouse said it all.

She wasn't really interested, but she didn't want to hurt his feelings, either. Emma Rose simply didn't want to live in the world of geekdom. She didn't even want to visit it. Oliver was too, too into it. He'd once brought everyone out one at a time to look at his latest purchase in the trunk of his car.

"What is it?" Emma had asked. "Looks like a lamp."

"Are you shitting me?" Oliver had looked at her like she didn't know what day it was.

"Er, no," she'd said. "Not shitting you at all."

"This is a lamp used on the set of the *Green Lantern* movie."

"Oh," she'd said, looking at the ordinary desk lamp with some feigned interest. "I heard that movie got terrible reviews."

"It wasn't a masterpiece, but this is genuine movie history. Got it online. Paid a lot for it."

As she played that memory over in her head, she tried to find the right words to let him down easy. A lie seemed to be the best course of action.

"I'm seeing someone," she said.

Oliver nodded, his face turning pink with embarrassment. Right then he wanted to kill the manager who had told him to go for it. Some great advice.

"Oh," he said, looking down. "I didn't know."

Emma didn't like to hurt anyone's feelings. "It's kind of new," she said quickly. "He lives in Seattle. Goes to the U."

"Cool," he said, lying through his teeth. He watched Emma as she went to fetch her coat.

"Yeah, don't know where it's going. I mean, I know it isn't serious, but it is kind of new and I want to focus on hanging out with him."

Oliver finished what he was doing and he gave the restaurant one last once-over. It was clean, ordered, and, he thought, perfectly bland. Just right for the customers who started the next day's shift. He dimmed the lights and the pair exited. Emma went toward the bus stop and Oliver left on foot to wherever it was that he'd parked his mom's car.

He stood still a moment and watched her, wondering why it was that no one had told him about her boyfriend.

Before turning in for the night, Dan Walton and Diana Rose checked all the locks on the windows and doors in their two-story Craftsman on Proctor in North Tacoma. It was a lovely neighborhood of fine old homes, a couple nice restaurants, and antique shops, but there had been a series of break-ins in the neighborhood over the past few months and caution had segued into routine. It wasn't that the Roses were the kind of family to leave the front door unlocked at night, but neither were they the paranoid type who insisted on doing a perimeter sweep every time the sun dipped down behind the Olympics to the west.

Lately everyone was feeling a little uneasy. Tacoma neighborhoods had been experiencing a rash of violent crime—including the murder of a man who'd simply posted an ad for his late wife's diamond tennis bracelet. He'd been robbed and bludgeoned five blocks away from the Roses' house. Another case that had made headlines in the *News Tribune* was the story about a missing Pacific Lutheran University student, Lisa Lancaster. The last time anyone had seen the slender brunette had been in a campus parking lot.

Dan was an engineer with the city and Diana taught music at Annie Wright, an ivy-clad private girls' school not far from their home. Diana had been depressed the past few weeks as her fiftieth birthday was approaching. She'd had breast cancer three years prior and had more cause to celebrate her half-century milestone than most, but Diana Rose was vain enough to try to thwart any semblance of advancing age. She readily admitted to friends that she'd had Botox treatments a time or two, but lately she'd been contemplating something a little more extreme than having toxins injected into her face. She wanted something more permanent. At least as permanent as could be, given the fact that no matter what anyone did, time did not stand still.

"You are as beautiful as the day I met you," Dan said to his wife when she ruminated on getting older, losing their daughter to college in the fall, being empty nesters. Dan was a heavyset fellow, with stout arms, grey eyes, and hair that he combed over with such meticulousness each morning that many people who noticed it wondered just how it was that he'd managed to stretch so little so very far.

Diana, who was rail thin with angular features and wiry black hair, looked at the clock with a fixed gaze. Much longer than needed to determine it was ten-thirty.

"Emma must be out with friends," she said. She'd always been a worrier, which, of course, accounted for the lines she wanted erased from her face.

"She's fine," Dan said, touching her shoulder gently. "She's nineteen and you can't control every minute of her life." The words were said with more love than harshness and Diana quickly nodded. He was right. Emma was very, very responsible.

"Usually she texts me," she said, "when she's going to be late."

Dan turned off the dining room light. "Ten-thirty isn't late and she is—hate it or not—a grown woman."

"Yes, but . . ."

"Let's go to bed," he said. "You've got an early day tomorrow."

Diana knew Dan was right. She *did* have an early day. She was helping their church get things in order for a big fund-raiser, an auction. She had no one to blame but herself for the fact that she'd worked countless hours on the project. When no one wanted to take the lead on getting everything organized, Diana Rose raised her hand. Nearly from the minute she did, she remembered why it was she hated to lead anything at church or school. Leading meant doing all the work and getting all the blame when things went the slightest bit off course.

Diana picked up her phone and started to text a message.

"You need to give her some space," Dan said.

"Just a minute." She pushed the buttons on her phone and sent a message.

Be gone early for the auction setup. See you tomorrow night. Love you.

Diana followed Dan upstairs, passing by Emma's shut bedroom door. Emma had become allergic to cats and Mocha, a brown and white Persian mix, had been banished from her bedroom—something neither Mocha nor Emma really liked. She loved their cat.

Diana set her phone on her bedside table just in case Emma texted back.

The next morning, Dan and Diana left the house in tiptoe-like fashion. Emma's door was still shut. She had probably gotten in very, very late. Mocha was curled up in the downstairs bathroom sink. The house was quiet and very peaceful.

Diana made a mental note to remind Emma that while she was a grown woman, she still needed to be a courteous one. Throughout the day, Diana texted her daughter four times. Each time the note was a short missive about what to put out for dinner, to remember to feed the fish in the tank in the sunroom, and finally, a simple I love you.

When Emma didn't respond, Diana figured that she'd probably forgotten to charge her phone.

She'd talk to her about that later, too.

At 7:40 AM, that same morning, a parking lot maintenance crew cleaning that section of the Lakewood Towne Center recovered a small black purse. Inside were a set of house keys, a tampon, a pack of Life Savers, and a wallet containing twenty-one dollars. The wallet also held a Target credit card imprinted with the name DIANA L. ROSE. The crew collected the purse and put it in a locked box along with a pair of glasses and a dog collar they'd found on their rounds. By the end of the day the purse would be buried under an avalanche of things discovered in the acres and acres of parking—a family album, a baby rattle, a glow-in-the-dark Frisbee, four jackets, a baseball mitt, and a six-pack of beer.

The beer was the only thing that didn't get earmarked for the Lost and Found department at the mall's headquarters. No one was going to ID a six-pack and since it was pretty good beer, the two guys working that day figured it was something they'd split later when they kicked back to talk about how much they hated their jobs.

The purse and the other things sat in the back of the crew's maintenance vehicle until the end of their shift, about 2:30 PM.

CHAPTER 9

Tavio Navarro knew he'd had too much to drink and was never going to make it home from a landscaping job in Puyallup, just east of Tacoma. He'd been crewless that afternoon as he worked on a small rock wall that he'd been hired to build. The rocks he'd been moving into position were known as "two man" rocks and he could surely understand that they were aptly named. His shoulders ached and his forearms, unprotected by long sleeves, were beat up. All afternoon, he'd been guzzling sweet tea from McDonald's. Not because he loved it so much, but because it only cost a buck. Tavio wanted to save every penny possible for his family— both in Spanaway and back home in small village south of Guadalajara, Mexico. He'd been in the United States for more years than he had spent growing up in Mexico. And yet, even though he'd earned a green card, married, and started a family, he still kept his distance from some things American.

The law was one of them. It wasn't about him or his papers, of course, but about the extended family that lived in and around the mobile home he rented at the end of a dusty lane in Spanaway.

Tavio's legs started twitching as he drove and he winced. He'd missed his last chance to take a leak at the McDonald's he'd passed ten minutes ago as he drove the long stretch of flat roadway along the Puyallup River. It was dusk, the end of the day, and he knew when he pulled off the roadway to relieve himself, he'd be able to do so in complete privacy. It was a familiar place to him. He and his brother Michael had often stopped there on their way to and from the Indian smoke shop where they bought discount cigarettes.

Tavio parked his battered Ford pickup and looked up and down the riverbank. He could see a couple of white guys hooting it up as they fished about fifty yards away. Other than that, the coast was clear. The truck still running, mariachi music playing, he widened his stance and assumed the position and unzipped. *Ah, relief!*

As the stream of urine weakened and he shook off the last drops and zipped up, something in the grass caught his eye. For a second he thought it was a child's toy, or maybe even a photograph from a magazine.

It looked a little like a hand.

Tavio, curious more than anything, swung the truck's door closed so he could walk past without stepping off the narrow pathway through the bramble of blackberry vines and the scourge of the Northwest, Scotch broom. He wanted to see just what he was looking at. The hand. The photograph. The doll.

Whatever it was.

As he inched forward, a smell, a hideous odor, wafted into Tavio's nostrils and he pinched them shut with his grimy fingertips.

Three steps closer and he knew what he was looking

at something very, very wrong. His heart rate quickened and he knelt down a little, his eyes following the hand up a slender arm attached to a girl's body. She was lying facedown and he noticed that it appeared that an arm, maybe a leg, was missing. Her dark hair was tangled around her neck. He captured what he needed. Nothing more. Tavio knew she was dead. He knew that because of the smell, but also because of the peculiarity that comes when a living thing is no longer so. It was strange, scary, and he wanted to get out of there as quickly as he could.

By his feet he saw a crushed cigarette pack. Its brand was familiar. *Too familiar*. He bent down and picked it up, his heart rate accelerating by the nanosecond. Tavio spun around and ran for his truck. As he backed out, he told himself to do so slowly. He didn't want those white guys fishing and drinking beer to notice him. He knew that the girl had been murdered and hidden there, but he didn't want to be the one to tell the police. It wasn't that he didn't feel frightened and sick for the girl and her family, because he certainly did. He remembered how his young brother, Juan, had been killed coming across the border between Nogales and Tucson when they were boys. No one in his family could say a word because no one wanted to be face-to-face with the authorities. Tavio knew that sometimes silence was an awkward protector.

His right to be there, to be a responsible young man in world of possibilities—all of it would come into question. Back then, there was no doubt that he'd have been deported to Mexico. That couldn't happen now, but even so there was always the risk. They'd question him. *Why were you there?* They'd want to see his ID.

They'd ask his wife all sorts of questions he didn't want asked. He didn't want to leave. He didn't want Mimi to know that his papers were forgeries.

Instead, Tavio drove home as carefully as he could. He didn't want to be stopped. He didn't want to talk to anyone. He rolled his window down low and hoped that the stink that had coated the inside of his nostrils hadn't found refuge on his clothes.

Tavio hadn't seen the girl's face, but he had an idea who she might be.

The night before, he'd seen her mother on the news. She was a nice-looking older white woman with the saddest eyes he'd ever seen. She looked like she was middle class or better, the kind of person who would hire him to work in her yard. She looked kind. But more than anything, the mother of the girl he'd seen on TV was very frightened.

"If anyone knows where she is," she had said, tears rolling down her smooth cheeks, "please help the police. Please help bring our daughter home."

Tavio remembered thinking as he watched that the mother did not seem very hopeful that her daughter would be coming home anytime soon. *Or at all.*

As he pulled into the driveway in front of the trailer he and his wife rented in Spanaway, Mimi emerged from the open door. As always, she was a vision. Her black hair tied back, her brown eyes accented by a pale cocoa eye shadow, and her full lips, red. The instant he saw her, he knew that she was, as he always called her, his "angel."

"Dinner's ready," Mimi said, calling from the front steps as her husband emerged from his truck.

"Hungry," he said, unconvincingly.

Mimi picked up on that. "You all right?" she asked

Tavio shrugged a little and rubbed the back of his neck. "Hard day," he said.

"I'll make it better," she said, putting her arms around him and planting a kiss on his lips.

"I probably smell like manure," he said, though he hadn't touched the stuff all day. It was that *other* smell and though he doubted that it clung to him, he felt he needed to lie. Make an excuse. It felt funny that he didn't want to be close to his wife. Tavio didn't like holding back, but he knew that Mimi would tell him to go to the police. He knew she'd be right, too. He didn't want to tell the police because they'd question him, but something more was weighing on him, heavier than an anvil laid across his throat.

It was Michael, his brother.

"Michael home?" Tavio asked as they walked up the narrow concrete pathway to the front door.

"Nah. He's out again. Seems like he's always out now."

"I thought he was sick."

"Must be better now. He left just before you got here."

"I haven't talked to him for three days."

They went inside; the wonderful smells of his wife's cooking—a roast chicken and vegetables—would have brought a river of salivation from his mouth down his throat on any other day. Tavio had no appetite. None at all.

"I'm going to shower before we eat," he said. "Need to get the stink off me."

Mimi patted her abdomen.

"Baby kicking today?" he asked.

She smiled and nodded. "Your son is a future soccer player."

"Baseball," Tavio said.

He turned and went toward the bathroom, his heart pounding and the look on his face far from the joy of the moment. He pulled the cigarette package from his jeans pocket and proceeded to tear it up into little pieces. He lifted the lid to the toilet and the confetti of paper and cellophane fluttered into the bowl.

He flushed and the bits of paper swirled downward. Tavio was shaking then, hoping and praying that what he was thinking would not be true.

Could Michael have done this?

That night Tavio Navarro couldn't sleep. With Mimi curled up next to him, he tried to stay still and not wake her. She was a light sleeper and needed her rest. Every day she woke up at 4:30 to make her husband's lunch before she left for the school cafeteria where she worked preparing breakfast and lunch, then off to classes at Tacoma Community College. Mimi Navarro worked hard. They all did. As Tavio stared at the ceiling, he reminded himself that there was nothing but worry to be gained by making assumptions about someone. Although he'd never had the kind of brush with the law that his brother Michael had experienced, he'd been looked at with suspicious eyes in the past. He figured it was always the other guy's problem, not his. If they wanted to think poorly of him because of his light brown skin, black hair, the accent in his speech, so be it. He could not stop them. He couldn't explain what they could never understand: He was just like them.

And yet he was thinking the worst of his brother. He was thinking, just maybe, he had had made a terrible mistake, a mistake like he'd made once before . . . times one million. A mistake that would send them out of the country

That summer there had been several high-profile cases in nearby Seattle in which illegals had committed some crime only for the authorities to discover that they'd already been deported once. One man ran over a girl pushing a grocery cart across a busy roadway. Another man had raped a woman. Both cases had drawn considerable fire and ire from anti-immigration proponents because the offenders had used the legal system for nothing short of a ride back to their homeland after committing a serious crime. They barely even waited for the dust to settle before they'd returned to the U.S.

Tavio wanted only to raise his family in a place of opportunity. He followed all the laws, he paid his taxes, and he even employed other workers. He was living the American dream.

Michael, he feared, was another matter. Michael was six years younger, had a slighter build, and was different from his brother in every other way. Tavio thought hard work was the answer to every problem. Michael wanted to party and live a life of no responsibility. He liked hip-hop, not mariachi. He liked tequila, not beer. He liked girls who were younger than him—girls who were lithe and pretty.

Like the one Tavio had seen on TV.

"I'd like to get me some of that, bro," he said when

they were watching a news report about a missing Tacoma girl.

"She's too young," Tavio said.

"Young feels good to me, Tav."

"You said you were going to date someone your own age."

"Those girls are all used up."

Mimi came in the room just then.

"You are a pig," she said, giving her brother-in-law a cold look. She put down the laundry basket and started folding hand towels. "Pig," she repeated.

"I don't get many complaints," Michael said, almost at once knowing that he'd said the wrong thing.

"What about Catalina?" Tavio asked.

Michael jumped up from the sofa. His jawline had tightened and his eyes flashed anger.

"Are you always going to bring that up? When am I going to be able to put that behind me?"

It was a fair question, but Mimi didn't bail him out by saying so. She continued to fold the laundry, barely glancing at her husband.

"You want to talk about it, do you?" Tavio asked Michael.

"I want you to forgive me. It wasn't my fault. You know that. I am your brother. You are supposed to be on my side."

Tavio reached for the remote control and turned off the TV.

"I will always be on your side," he said. "Even when you are wrong. You are my blood, Michael. But that doesn't mean I won't worry about you and worry about the things you have done."

Mimi looked up. "Yes, Catalina will always be a worry."

Michael put his hands up in the air and stomped out of the room.

Tavio nodded at his wife.

"You said what needed to be," he said, turning the TV back on. "Catalina was a good girl."

There were dozens of photos pasted on a board in the Tacoma Police Department's cold case room. Grace Alexander wasn't officially part of the cold case unit. But she found herself in that space whenever a conference was called on a major case.

Her eyes always landed on the board, first on her sister's high school portrait, and then up two rows to the picture of the little girl who was the first of the many unsolved cases that would forever hold the attention of the department.

Ann Marie Burr was her name. Ann was just nine. She vanished in the night from her Tacoma home a half century ago and was never seen again. *Just gone*. It was as if the little girl had gone to answer the door and just followed her abductor into oblivion willingly.

Grace didn't want to be the sister of a Bundy Girl— the cop with something to prove. Though that's just what she was. She never said a word and she never allowed her eyes to linger on that scoreboard of unsolved homicide. She refused to remark upon the juxtaposition of Tricia's photo and little Ann's.

CHAPTER 10

Catalina Sanchez was a lovely teenager with a cascade of black hair that she let wave down her back, never constricted by a ponytail. She was only nineteen when her body was found alongside a riverbank near Selah, an eastern Washington farming community known for apple, pear, and cherry orchards. The police did a poor job investigating the case. Not so much because she was an illegal migrant worker, but because they were so short staffed. Catalina had the misfortune to die when budgets were so tight that if cases weren't solved within say a week, they were shuttled off to a file room and into oblivion.

What police detectives did know was that Catalina had been raped before she was bludgeoned with a river rock and left for dead. They swabbed her vagina for semen and took scrapings of the skin caught under her red-painted fingernails. All was tagged as evidence. The detectives also noted how she had defensive wounds on her wrists from being pinned down. Her skull was fractured. Blunt-force trauma was the cause of death. Homicide was the manner of death.

The Navarros knew Catalina. She was a girl from

their village who had come to the United States with her family about a year after they did. She was just a kid then, of course, but even so, it was plain to see that Catalina Maria Sanchez was a true beauty in the making. Michael Navarro fixated on her. He pestered her over and over for a date, and finally, she said yes. He was giddy with excitement over the prospect of going out with her. He'd planned to take her to a nice place for dinner in Yakima and on a moonlight walk along the river. For the occasion, he bought a bottle of tequila and a brand-new shirt—pale blue fabric with mother-of-pearl buttons. It was western style, something that Michael knew Catalina had admired whenever she saw a ranch hand wearing that kind of garment.

"Handsome cowboy," she'd say. "Not a pretender, but a real one. That's what I like."

It had rained hard the night of Catalina's disappearance. Precipitation was scarce on the Eastern side of the Cascades in Washington state. Later, when he thought of what happened that night, Tavio Navarro would remember two things more than anything else. The sound of the rain hammering the tin roof of the migrant workers' bunkhouse was almost like a lullaby, soothing him to sleep. It had never rained that hard in his life. So sudden. So much water. The other memory was the sound of Michael as he lay whimpering in the bed next to him.

It was after 3 AM when Tavio went over to his younger brother to stop him from making that awful, annoying noise. When he stood next to Michael's bed, Tavio noticed a series of muddy footprints from the door ending at the foot of the bed next to a heap of sopping clothes.

"Shhh!" he said, tapping Michael on the shoulder.

"Mistake," the younger brother said, his voice falling into whimpered shards. "I made a mistake. I didn't mean to."

Tavio leaned closer, as if the proximity would keep his brother from being so embarrassingly loud. "What mistake, Michael?" His eyes landed on a pair of parallel scratches across his brother's cheek. "What happened? Did you get into an accident? You are hurt."

Michael, who up to that point seemed coiled into a ball, sat up. He did not want the others on the other side of the bunkhouse to hear. He motioned for Tavio to follow him to the small porch by the door.

"Something bad happened, Tavio. It was an accident."

"Was it my car?" he asked referring to the old Chevy that he'd been driving for the past year.

Michael shook his head, violently so. "No. No. Your car is fine."

"What then?"

"Mi Catalina."

Tavio lowered his eyes and touched his mouth, signaling to his brother to be very, very quiet. "What about Catalina?" he asked in a whisper.

"She . . ." Michael stood in the dank light of a soggy early morning and started to cry. It was not a soft cry, but a guttural sound that Tavio thought would wake up everyone in Yakima.

"Stop!" he said, his voice growing louder than he'd wanted. "Do not cry! It cannot be so bad."

Michael started shaking. He no longer looked up at his brother. It seemed he didn't want to face him at all. The words, like the rain, like muddy footprints, would never be forgotten.

"You have to help me, Tavio. Catalina is dead. I killed her. I didn't mean to. I am sorry. I thought she wanted me to make love to her."

Tavio's eyes widened to such a degree that it seemed it was very possible that they would pop out and fall to the floor. "What are you saying, Michael?"

"I'm saying the truth. I'm sorry. Do you want me to show you?"

Tavio was stunned. "This has to be a mistake!"

"No mistake. They will kill me. They will hang me. Cut off my head. Do something terrible. I did not mean to kill her. I loved her. You know that, right?"

Tavio nodded. He would have thought so, but killing someone was too hard to forgive.

"They will cut off my head," Michael repeated.

Tavio shook his head. "No. No they will not."

"There is no forgiveness in this country," Michael said as he pulled on a dry pair of pants and a clean T-shirt.

"Bring those clothes," Tavio said, not even sure why. "Let's go. Show me."

They drove mostly in silence. Tavio tried to get his brother to tell him exactly what had happened, but Michael was inconsolable by then. He managed to sputter out a few words as he directed Tavio to the turnoff by the river where he'd last seen Catalina. The ground was muddy and the sun had started to light the weeds with the morning light that would forever seem hideous instead of lovely.

Catalina Sanchez was sprawled out next to the riverbank. Her beautiful dark hair swirled in the mud and her brown eyes gazed upward into nothingness.

Tavio dropped to his knees and frantically began

shaking her. It was a futile effort and he knew it. Her eyes confirmed what his brother had told him. She was dead.

"Who saw you tonight?" Tavio asked.

"Here?"

"Anywhere. Yes, here. Yes, the restaurant."

Michael shook his head. "No one. We were alone."

"The restaurant! Who saw you there?"

"We did not go to the restaurant. She brought tamales. She made. I think, I thought she liked me and wanted to be with me here."

"Tell me, are you sure no one saw you?"

"No one. I know of no one."

"Good." Tavio got up from the body and looked around. "We have to hide her."

"I don't know. I don't know if we should."

"Do you want your head cut off?"

He shook his head. "No. But shouldn't I just tell the police what happened?"

Tavio looked down at the body. Catalina's blouse was torn and her pretty blue and white skirt was pushed up in front. It was obvious what happened. The scratches on his brother's face had made it so very clear. And yet, he had to ask one more time.

"No. Tell me. Tell me what happened."

Michael slumped on the hood of the car.

"She let me kiss her. She did. She let me put my hand on her. She liked it. She did. She told me to keep going, to make love to her."

He stopped for a moment as a car, out of view, passed by on the main road.

"What happened?"

Michael looked away. "I don't know. She didn't seem to want me anymore. I told her it wasn't good for me to get all excited and not make love to her, but she laughed at me. She said that she didn't want me. She wanted some other guy. I tried to kiss her some more and she slapped me . . . laughing at me. I told her, 'No, don't laugh. I love you.' But she kept laughing so I grabbed her and well . . ."

"Did you rape her? Did you do that to her?" Tavio could scarcely believe that his brother could do such a thing to a woman, a girl. It was disgusting. Vile. Against everything that their parents had taught them.

Michael locked eyes with his brother. "I didn't rape her. I made love to her. She just got so mad at me. So embarrassed."

Tavio looked directly at the scratch marks on his brother's face, but said nothing about them.

"How did she die, Michael? What did you do to her to kill her?"

"It was an accident. It was. I was making love to her and her head hit a rock and I didn't know it. I thought she was just finally, you know, relaxing."

There was something insane about what Michael was saying, but Tavio saw no way out of it. He did not want his brother's head cut off . . . or whatever they did in Washington.

"Let's hide her now."

Catalina weighed no more than ninety-five pounds, but her dead body felt like a ton. The Navarro brothers dragged her to the edge of the riverbank where there was a shallow pool—a place marked by candy wrappers and pop cans—where young kids liked to swim. The morning light had brightened considerably and anyone close by could easily see that they were not a couple of kids swimming, but two grown men and a dead girl. Tavio held her feet; Michael had hooked his hands under her armpits. Her head, at once bloody and pale, hung limply from her slender neck. With each step, it swung, like a bell counting off the moment of her final good-bye.

"I'm sorry, *mi corazón*," Michael said.

Tavio just looked at his brother with disbelieving eyes. The words meant nothing. He meant nothing just then. It was hollow. Empty. Just words to soothe his own guilty heart.

Straddling the rocks, they waded out and gave the body a decisive shove, sending it down the lazy waters of the river to a place where someone would find it. Not soon, they hoped. But they didn't want her to never be found. She was a girl from their village. She'd given up everything to start over in the United States.

She'd given her life.

Neither brother knew a thing about DNA right then. Later, they would wonder if the police who found her body would have thought to have taken a sample. If they did, would they somehow find Michael Navarro?

And if they did find him, would they cut off his head?

CHAPTER 11

It was early the next afternoon, that time of day when nothing happens, the so-called dead shift. Snickers bar in hand from her trip to the employee vending machines, 911 dispatcher Luna Demetrio was barely in her chair when she picked the next call from the console that fed calls from all over Tacoma and Pierce County, one desperate caller at a time.

LUNA: What's your emergency?
CALLER: I need to tell somebody something bad happened.
LUNA: All right, sir. Can you tell me your name?
CALLER: (muffled noise, no answer)
LUNA: You there? I hear you breathing, are you all right?
CALLER: I'm not going to give my name. I'm calling from a pay phone. I'm going to leave the second I'm done with you so don't send someone.
LUNA: I can barely hear you. Please speak louder. What's your emergency?
CALLER: I think, I mean, I'm pretty sure there's a dead body by the river. I saw it.

LUNA: What river?

CALLER: I didn't know we had more than one. The Puyallup. Off River Road. Over by the bridge there's a gravel lot.

LUNA: Sir, please tell me your name.

CALLER: No. Good-bye.

The call ended one minute and twenty seconds after it started. Luna typed up a message that was transmitted to the first responders for calls of an urgent nature. Luna was a very thorough operator, one who'd been honored for her attention to detail with two Starbucks cards and a potted hibiscus from her manager.

She typed the details of the call into the report and added: *Caller was almost inaudible. Not sure if male or female. When I asked for an ID, which he/she refused, there was a long pause. During that pause I heard the sound of someone else talking. Maybe the radio. Not sure. That's all.*

The tip from the informant or witness had yielded a grisly discovery as a team of CSIs, Pierce County Sheriff's Department officers, and two homicide detectives from Tacoma gathered around the edge of the lazy Puyallup River, just east of Tacoma's gritty downtown. Three-foot-tall grass and a noxious weed called tansy ragwort had drawn a partial curtain around where the body had been put to rest. As a cacophony of crows hurled their calls through the air, the group of men and women went about their tasks. Some took photos. Some ran the length of a tape measure. Others merely secured the scene. There was no question when Grace

Alexander laid eyes on the figure that they were looking at the remains of Lisa Lancaster.

Or rather, most of Lisa.

While the sum of her body parts had been laid out in a hellish repose, they were in pieces. Lisa was all there, but she'd been butchered with the kind of hideous brutality that could only be the work of a madman.

And not a very skillful one at that.

Grace kneeled down next the victim. Her eyes carefully tracing the tentative cuts that had severed her right arm.

"Look," she said, "he hesitated a little."

"Yeah, I see that." It was Paul Bateman, who had joined her while the medical examiner pushed everyone else away from the scene.

"Found some cigarette butts. Bagged and tagged."

"Saw it," she said. "Did you get the fishing bait bag?"

"Yeah, but I doubt anyone would kill someone here and go on fishing."

Grace's eyes stayed on the body. "Probably not. But maybe this is a favorite place. A good place he thought to hide her. I mean, it is a good place in a way. It isn't that far off River Road. Anyone could just go by and miss her."

It was true. More than a thousand cars passed that spot per hour, as people commuted to jobs in Tacoma or the Puyallup Valley. The only thing that brought any solace to the tragic scene was the fact that, however long Lisa had lain there, she had not been alive. She had not been one of those victims who were stashed alongside the road trying to summon the strength to call for help. Grace thought of the case of the California woman who'd crawled to the roadside after being left for dead—her arms severed from her body, but her will indomitable. Lisa Lancaster hadn't had that chance.

Lisa had never said a word. Her final words, her final screams, had likely been given in a place where no one could see her, hear her. There was very little blood around the body. It was obvious that she'd bled out somewhere else.

Grace could feel the bile in her stomach rise. A sick person like the one who'd done this had probably savored her last breath as though it was something to enjoy. To revel in. What lay in pieces in the tangle of weeds just above the muddy riverbank had been brought there and reassembled.

"Hey!" a Pierce County deputy called from a tangle of brambles. "Got something over here."

Grace stayed with the body, while Paul went in the direction of the deputy. He was a young officer, a total newbie. It was easy to spot those. They still allowed the excitement of finding a piece of evidence come to their faces.

"Plastic garbage bag," the kid said. "Looks like blood on it."

Paul nodded. "Good work. Now, please step back."

It was a black Hefty bag, the heavy-duty kind that Paul had used when his ex, Lynnette, threw him out and told him to get his stuff out of the house. He shook his head. He hated how thoughts of Lynnette infiltrated his mind all the time. Having to see her every day at work was bad enough, but having even the most common objects recall some incident with her was beyond cruel.

The black bag had been carried out into the water and tossed into the brambles about twenty-five yards from where the killer had deposited Lisa, bit by bit. It was hard to tell in the flat light among the Himalayan blackberries if there was blood on the bag, but from where Paul Bateman stood it appeared that there could be. If so, the bag was a monumental discovery and a major mistake by the perpetrator. Plastic bags held latent prints. Trace evidence from the killer's vehicle could easily adhere to the sticky, bloody plastic. If this was the bag he'd brought ninety-five-pound Lisa Lancaster in to reassemble on the riverbank then it also had topped its manufacture's promise of holding "up to seventy-five pounds without tearing."

Grace joined Paul by the thorny vines.

"They're transporting her now," she said.

Paul pointed to the bag. "Techs will process this and the cigarette butts. Are you sure it's Lisa?" he asked, his eyes unblinking.

"Sure enough that we better get over to Ms. Lancaster's before the press does."

CHAPTER 12

It was almost dark when the detectives arrived at the Lancaster house. Grace scanned the street for any of the usual suspects—the press, that is. Thankfully, there weren't any. One vehicle did catch her eye. Marty Keillor's souped-up Honda Accord was parked behind Ms. Lancaster's car.

"Marty's here," Paul said. "Hope we don't wake 'em up."

"Enough of that," Grace said, though she'd thought the same thing.

"Just saying," he said.

Catherine Lancaster opened the door. She was wearing a white cotton blouse and jeans. It didn't escape Grace's eyes that the second button from the bottom was unfastened.

"Is it true?" she asked, her voice trying to find a breath. Her eyes were ablaze with a curious mix of anger and fear.

While both detectives knew to what she was referring, they didn't give any indication. A rookie would blurt out that they'd found a body when the mother might only have asked if it was true that they'd eaten at the local Sonic. Never, ever give up any information first. Always, both knew, wait and see what the subject is really talking about.

"What?" Paul asked.

"I heard that someone found a body," she said.

Marty Keillor appeared behind her.

"Is it Lisa?" he asked.

"May we come inside?" Grace asked, and Lisa's mother opened the door wide to allow them entrance into the living room. She stopped them with a cry.

"I knew she was dead!" she said. "I knew it in my bones. My girl's gone. My only baby! Gone!"

"Ms. Lancaster," Paul said, trying to calm her.

"Are you going to tell me everything is going to be okay? Maybe you'd know how I feel if this had ever happened to you. Lisa is gone." She glanced at Marty. "Except for Marty, I'm alone."

The remark was strange. *Why acknowledge Marty as her boyfriend now?* If that was, in fact, what she was doing?

"We aren't sure it is her," Grace said. "The medical examiner will be analyzing"—she stopped herself short of saying the body or body parts, which sounded as horrific as it really indeed was—"analyzing the, uh, evidence."

By then Ms. Lancaster was inconsolable. Marty Keillor slumped silently into the sofa where Lisa's mother had sunk in a sobbing heap. On the coffee table adjacent to the sofa were an ashtray and a stack of laser prints with images of beaches and tropical flowers, printouts from a travel website.

As the detectives left the house, Paul leaned close to Grace's ear.

"Looks like Ms. Lancaster and Marty were planning a vacation."

"Saw that," she said, walking down the driveway a few yards before stopping. She started for the pair of galvanized garbage cans that sat next to the curb.

"What are you doing? Dumpster diving at a time like this?"

"Hardly," she said, prying off one of the lids and peering inside. "Look here," she said, hoisting up a half-full black plastic bag. "Look familiar?"

Paul shrugged a little. "Like who doesn't use those bags?"

"I admit Shane and I use them, too, but let's bring this in to the lab to see if they are the same manufacturing lot as the one recovered from the scene."

"You really don't think that Ms. Lancaster and that creepola Marty offed Lisa," he said.

"Maybe. You saw the printouts on the table."

"Maui does sound nice," he said.

She nodded. "Yeah, a great place to run away to."

"Okay, so the daughter's ex-boyfriend is shagging her mother," Paul said. "Disgusting on all grounds, but why kill her? If anyone should have been hacked up it would have been Party Marty."

Grace smiled grimly at the mention of the nickname Naomi had given Lisa's ex.

"Agreed. There something more going on here," she said. "Maybe there's a conspiracy here? Maybe Mom was mad at Lisa."

"She said she was a saint on that TV news report."

Grace glanced back at the house. "She oversold that, didn't she? The guilty often overdo it when it comes to lauding the victim."

"Right. But why kill the girl?"

Grace opened the trunk and put the plastic bag and its smelly contents inside. "Maybe there was a money reason."

A money reason. Aside from jealousy and rage, money was the most frequent flash point for crimes that led to murder. People killed because they had too little money. Because they were afraid someone would take some of their money. Sometimes they killed for profit. Although children were rarely murdered by their parents for insurance proceeds, there had been cases in which that had occurred. Indeed, more than one wary insurance salesperson had begrudgingly sold a policy in the tens of thousands on a child whose earning power— the measure of a person's worth—was nil. How they slept at night was beyond Grace Alexander's comprehension. In one notorious Northwest case, a couple purchased nearly a million dollars on the life of a child who later died in a terrible and suspicious house fire.

The kicker there was the little girl had been adopted only seven months before the fire swept through the couple's house in Yelm, southeast of Tacoma. Law enforcement speculated that they had adopted the girl only to kill her for the insurance money. The case could never be proved and National Life had to make good on its policy. The couple took the proceeds and disappeared, leaving observers to wonder if they'd do it again somewhere else.

Could Lisa's mother be one of those coldhearted

people? By all accounts she was a devoted nurse, a caring soul whose compassion for others knew no limits. Why was she sleeping with her daughter's ex? Why was she going to take a trip to Maui? And if she wasn't the worst kind of a mother in the world, was Party Marty the ultimate evil?

CHAPTER 13

It was after 7 PM when Diana Rose returned home from work. The day had been brutal; as of late, that was more a common occurrence than a rarity. She'd spent two hours at the church before going to her class at Annie Wright. Mocha was waiting for her by the back door and she bent down to give the cat a little attention before setting her purse on the counter. She made a face when she noticed that Emma hadn't put out the frozen chicken to thaw. She'd have to microwave it and that was always risky. More often than not, she'd learned over the years, defrosting meat semi-cooked it.

"Emma?" she called up the stairs. She noticed the cat's bowl was empty, so she filled it with water.

No answer.

She went upstairs and opened the bedroom door. The room was such a mess. Like always. The bed was unmade, a tangle of clothes were heaped on the floor, and dishes were stacked on the nightstand.

Diana speed-dialed her daughter, but it went right to voice mail, a surefire sign that Emma had let the battery run down again.

She punched in the speed dial number for Starbucks.

"Hi," she said, "this is Diana Rose. Can I speak to Emma?"

"Hi, Ms. Rose. This is Devon, her manger. She's not here. We tried calling her phone, but no answer."

Diana was confused. "What do you mean, not here?"

"She's two hours late. She didn't even call to let us know. Really had us in a bind."

"Are you sure she was supposed to be in today?" Diana asked, trying to stave off the uneasiness that had started to sweep over her. She found herself sinking onto her daughter's crumpled linens on the edge of the bed.

"Must have missed the bus," Devon said, picking up on the mother's anxiety.

"Maybe," Diana said. "Maybe one, but there are buses every half hour. She'd have to have missed at least three or four. That's not possible. I'm really worried, Devon."

The sound of coffee grinder churned in the background.

"I'll let you know," Devon said. "We're super short-staffed today. Besides Emma, I have another no-show today. Gotta go."

"Wait!" Diana said, nearly yelling into the phone.

"What? I'm, like, super busy."

"Call me as soon as she gets in."

"Okay. Will do. Thank you for calling Starbucks."

It was early evening when Diana phoned her husband, Emma's stepfather. Dan Walton answered on the first ring. From the background sound, it was obvious he was in his car heading home.

"Need something from the store?" he asked.

"Honey, Emma didn't show up for work today. I don't think she came home last night, either."

"What do you mean, didn't come home?"

She looked around the room. "I really can't tell for sure, but I called Starbucks and they said she didn't make it to work today. We have to call the police. We have to find out where she is. This isn't like her. Something bad happened to her. I know it."

"Calm down," Dan said. "I'll be home in five minutes. I'm sure she's okay."

"Hurry," she said. "Please, Dan. Get here as fast as you can. Something is very, very wrong. I'm her mother. I feel it."

Dan promised he would. He dialed 911 and explained the possible emergency to the dispatcher. He gave his address and said he was headed home.

"My wife is there now," he said, running a hard yellow light—something Cautious Dan would never have done. "I'll be there in three minutes."

"We'll send a car out," the dispatcher said.

Dan Walton had an uneasy feeling, too.

At 6:45 a Tacoma police officer named Antonio Lorenzo knocked on the Roses' front door. He was a young officer, barely thirty. He had warm eyes and an instantly soothing countenance that no doubt served him well responding to calls such as the one made by Dan Walton.

"Let's back up a little," he said. "Tell me what's going on with your daughter."

"Emma didn't show up for work today," Diana said, her words coming out in quick gulps. She hadn't cried yet, but Officer Lorenzo could easily see she was on the verge.

"May I come inside?" he asked.

"Yes, please," Dan said. "I'm Dan Walton. This is my wife, Diana. Our daughter is Emma Rose. We didn't see her last night after work and they said she didn't show up today."

Officer Lorenzo had a kind, calm face, which in that moment and in the hundreds of others that preceded it, was put to good use.

"Is this unusual for Emma?"

Diana's face tightened. Not facelift smoothed out, but stretched with worry. "*Very*. Of course it is. We wouldn't have called the police if it was commonplace, now would we?"

Dan, now sitting next to his wife on the sofa facing the officer, who'd taken a seat on the brown leather recliner in the living room, put his hand on her knee. He patted her a few times to remind her to stay calm. Thinking the worst was ludicrous. Their daughter was a good girl. An environmentalist. A great student. If she'd gone off somewhere they were going to hear from her.

"Are you sure she didn't come home last night?" the officer asked.

"I didn't hear her come in. I'm a very, very light sleeper," Diana said.

Officer Lorenzo made some notes.

"Are all of you getting along?" he asked, his voice soft and nonjudgmental.

"What is that supposed to mean?" Dan asked.

"Just asking. Just need to know if there were any problems here at home. Were all of you getting along with Emma?"

Dan leaned closer. His brow narrowed. He didn't want to be angry just then, but the implication of the police officer's words seemed directed at him.

"Do you mean to suggest she's run away, left home?"

"Did she, Dan?"

"There would be no reason I could think she would do that. She is our only child and we're a very close family," Dan said, still stiff with resentment.

"My husband is right. We are extremely close. Sometimes too close, I think. Emma didn't go to college this year because of my illness."

"Sorry?"

"I'm cancer free now," she said. "But the past couple of years have been rough and Em didn't want me to go through it all on my own. Even though the surgery was a year ago and I'm fine, she just decided to postpone college for a year. Does that sound like a girl who would run away?"

"No, I don't think so," the officer said. "Is it possible that all the responsibility became too much for her and she needed a break?"

"But I am fine now! Look at me! My daughter even got me Mocha when she's so allergic because she knows how much I love cats," Diana said, looking over at Mocha as the furry feline wandered across the living room floor, her dust mop tail pointing upright like a skunk's.

Officer Lorenzo took a few more notes about Emma's height and weight, and asked for a picture. Diana got up to get one off the bulletin board in the kitchen.

"We can't report her as missing until she's been gone for twenty-four hours," he said.

Dan looked at his watch, an old Seiko that had belonged to his father. "Well, as far as we know, that's in two hours. She closed up the Lakewood Mall Starbucks last night. She gets off between nine and ten, depending on how much cleaning is needed after a day of coffee drinkers."

Diana returned and handed over a five-by-seven.

"Her senior photo," she said.

Officer Lorenzo looked at the photo and then looked up quickly. He didn't want to say what he was thinking, so he said something else.

"She looks like a very nice girl," he said.

"She is. Very nice," Dan answered.

"She's everything to us. She would never not come home. She would never not call us. Never," Diana said.

The officer got up, still looking at the photo.

He didn't know Emma Rose, of course. But he'd seen her face before. The nineteen-year-old was a ringer for Lisa Lancaster and Kelsey Caldwell. All three wore their dark hair long, parted in the middle. Kelsey's was slightly wavy, but her mom said she'd taken a flatiron to it over the past year to give her the long, straight look that she'd sought. It was very, very seventies, which in turn, was very, very cool.

"I'm going to make a run over to Starbucks to see what I can find out," he said. "It will be close to nine when I get back to the department. When I do, I'll make the report. One of our detectives will get with you for a more detailed follow-up."

Diana, so wrapped up in her deepening worry, didn't get the change in mood just then, but Dan did. There had been a seismic shift. If the officer with the kind manner had been calm and professional when he first arrived, he no longer seemed quite so composed. There was something about the photograph that seemed to change everything.

Smaller bones likely meant—though he was inexperienced and unsure—an easier go of it in the basement when he went about the business of butchering her. Butchering her, by the way, was as far as he would ever go.

The idea of sex with a corpse sickened him. The idea of visiting human remains in the woods of the Pacific Northwest was wholly unappealing. This wasn't about some psycho sexual conquest, but about control and technique.

He wanted to take what had been done before and improve it. As if he was revising code on a slow-moving, jagged-looking computer game. That was cool. It was about the cool factor and the fame that came with being the best, being better than his father, a man he had never even met, but one he'd admired and fantasized about from the time his mother told him the truth. He'd been cheated a little and he knew it. Other serial killers had unwittingly or purposefully involved their family members. When he read about Green River Killer Gary Ridgway's proclivity for bringing his little boy while hunting prostitutes along the SeaTac strip, he felt a pang of jealousy. He'd never had that time with his dad.

That had been taken from him when he was but a child and his father was strapped into Florida's Old Sparky. The flip was switched. Human flesh burned and his dad was electrocuted to death. That moment, as much as anything, set things in motion. Not right away, of course. He was a sleeper cell and it was that night on the Pacific Lutheran University campus, he was awakened.

The dark-haired girl with the pretty eyes had done that. She was a shot of adrenaline. She was just like the others.

The day after Kelsey Caldwell's father called the Thurston County detective with the suspicion that his daughter's case might have a connection to Lisa Lancaster's disappearance, detectives from the Tacoma Police Department and the Pierce and Thurston County Sheriff's Offices conferenced by phone. Grace and Paul were among those on the call, a brief one to make sure that all were aware of the purported similarities in the two cases. After a number of serial cases had gone undetected in the Northwest for a number of years, no law enforcement professionals wanted the blood of future victims on their hands. Most of the connecting of dots among the counties along Puget Sound yielded nothing more than increased awareness. The chances that a true serial was at work were slim to none.

Serial killers, or rather the proliferation of them, was a kind of Hollywood invention. There just weren't that many. And yet, in reality, the gloomy Pacific Northwest had had more than its share of famous cases. To many crime aficionados, the Northwest was serial-killer central. Seemingly mild-mannered Spokane resident and military man Robert Lee Yates had killed sixteen women, all prostitutes, in a two-year string that started in 1996. Gary Leon Ridgway was granddaddy of them all, at least in terms of confirmed victim count. The dull-witted truck painter, like Yates, also hunted and murdered prostitutes—a common prey among those who kill for sport. While the Seattle man was eventually convicted of killing forty-nine, he confessed to almost a hundred victims in total. There was no real diabolical brilliance displayed by Yates or Ridgway, yet they managed to elude capture for a number of years because of the victims they selected, girls and women on the fringes trying to survive by selling the only thing they felt they could offer—their bodies.

Of course, the most infamous of all serial killers in the Pacific Northwest, and possibly in the entire world, was Tacoma's own dark son, Theodore Robert Bundy. While most serial killers were stuck with the perpetual and requisite use of their entire formal names, Tacoma's killer was simply known as Ted.

Grace's connection to Ted was deep and personal, and until her sister's case was resolved, she knew it always would be.

The Tacoma detective shut out the world around her and put her laser-like focus on the electronic case files of the two missing girls on her computer screen. Lisa's had been a missing persons case, initiated by Detective Goodman. It also included updates from the interviews she and Paul conducted with her mother and best friend. Next, she turned her attention to Kelsey's file, a more detailed accounting of the seventeen-year-old's sudden absence from the planet. While Grace could see similarities in their physical descriptions—serial killers fre-

quently stalk a specific type—there was something else
that jumped out at her. Something she was sure was
merely a coincidence.

The circumstances of the girls' abductions were
more than familiar. They mirrored what Ted Bundy had
done when he took a Washington girl and a girl from
Colorado.

Grace put it out of her mind.

Or rather she tried to.

Grace felt that saying much more about it would
only serve to bolster her reputation for being obsessed
with Ted Bundy. One time when she was in the bathroom, she'd heard a couple of other women, a records
clerk and a lab assistant, talking about her.

"I think she's kind of weird," the records clerk said.

"I don't know," the lab assistant said. "I guess she
seems nice enough."

"I read her file. You want to know what's in it?"

"You aren't supposed to disclose that stuff."

"We work here. It's all right for us to share. We're
not supposed to tell anyone outside. It's okay to talk
about stuff here because we're all, you know, working
together."

"I don't want to know."

"Really kind of interesting."

"Okay. I guess you can tell me," the lab assistant
said, lowering her voice.

"Now you're making me feel bad."

A long, seemingly, exasperated pause followed before the lab assistant gave up. "Just tell me."

"Fine," said the records clerk. "Says that she had to
be evaluated by the shrink twice because of her sister's

disappearance. They've cleared her. No reprimands. But they told her to stay out of the Ted Bundy files. I read her files. Interesting and disgusting stuff. Anyway, there is a lot of crap in there about how her mom, Sissy O'Hare, kept pestering our guys here back then. She was sure that her daughter was a Ted victim. Never proved it. Maybe she was. Grace was digging around trying to see if they missed any clues."

"I guess I could understand why she'd do that. You know, why she'd want to know."

"Don't you think it's creepy?" the records clerk said.

"Probably. But really, you shouldn't look in her personnel files."

"I have clearance. I'm very responsible. I've never told anyone what I've seen. I would never, ever breach my duty to be confidential."

Grace waited for the women to leave. She didn't report them. To do so, she'd felt, would only make matters worse. She believed her background was an asset, one that made her a more effective investigator and victim interviewer. She could connect with anyone who'd felt his brand of incompressible and evil influence in the trajectory of their lives.

After reading the Lancaster and Caldwell files, she needed a moment.

"Paul," she said standing behind him as he finished a phone call in his cubicle adjacent to hers.

"What's up?"

"I'm heading out early. Hold down the fort, will you?"

Paul nodded. He'd seen that look before.

"Anything new on the bones?" he asked.

Grace pulled her coat from the hook next to her chair and shook her head.

"Not yet," she said, heading out the door. "Might take a while. If anything, I'm patient."

PART TWO
PEACE, TED

*"We serial killers are your sons, we are
your husbands, we are everywhere.
And there will be more of your
children dead tomorrow."*
—TED BUNDY

CHAPTER 14

Grace Alexander had read every book written on Ted Bundy. In fact, true-crime author Ann Rule's famous account of her friendship with Ted, *The Stranger Beside Me*, had been required reading when she was growing up in the family's white and gray Craftsman home in North Tacoma. It sat on the shelf alongside first editions of *Of Mice and Men*, *For Whom the Bell Tolls*, and *To Kill a Mockingbird*. The novels were genuine and undisputed classics, of course. Grace's mother, Sissy, insisted that Rule's book was on par with those famous tomes.

"A story like Bundy's deserved the ring of truth," she'd said one night when Grace was eleven and reading the book for the first time. "*Stranger* is a choir bell."

Later, Grace wondered about a mother who would have her not only read such a book, but discuss it as if they were having a chardonnay and Brie book club meeting.

What do you think motivated Ted to lie about things that weren't even important?

Do you think Ted has any feelings whatsoever?

What kind of a mother was Louise Bundy?

Grace had immersed herself in Ted's life. Given the circumstances of her birth, had there ever been another path to follow? It had all been ordained by heartbroken parents, who had lost their oldest daughter, their first-born, to a phantom.

Grace knew how Ted had been born at the Elizabeth Lund Home for Unwed Mothers in Burlington, Vermont, in November of 1946. His mother's Christian name was Eleanor Louise Cowell—though later she was known only as Louise. Grace imagined what it might have been like for a young woman finding herself pregnant. Louise more than likely lied on the birth certificate that Theodore Robert was the son of an air-man named Lloyd Marshall. While no one from her family ever gave voice to the rumors, some suspected that the pregnancy was darker than a mere casual relationship between a young woman and a serviceman.

Grace's feelings regarding Louise were like wipers, moving back and forth over an oily windshield. Louise hadn't set out to give birth to a monster. No mother does. Sometimes Grace felt sorry for her; other times, mostly because of her mother's stories, she hated Louise. She had a vivid recollection of the time her mother actually confronted Louise when they were out shopping. Grace was eleven at the time. Louise, dressed in a plain cotton shirtdress and shoes that were so sensible they could easily have been worn to work on a factory floor, was shopping in the linens department of the Bon Marché at the Tacoma Mall. Sissy, looking for a wedding gift and dragging Grace along, spotted Ted's mother from a table of marked-down china.

"Stay close," she said. She set down the oh-so-slightly chipped platter, and walked over.

Louise's eyes fluttered a little, but she offered no indication that she knew Sissy.

"I know who you are," Sissy said.

"Excuse me?" Louise answered without really even looking up. Ted's mother ran her fingertips over a piece of the fabric exposed through a small slit in its plastic wrapping.

Grace's mother reached over and touched Louise's hand.

She was trembling a little.

When their eyes finally met, Sissy saw something that she hadn't expected to see.

Fear and recognition.

"I know who you are, too," Louise said, finally and softly. "I know what you believe and I know in my heart that nothing I can say would make a bit of difference to you."

Sissy O'Hare's heart rate had accelerated by then. She had seen the picture of Louise on the night of Ted's execution, the phone pressed to her ear, around her the simple furnishings of a hardworking couple's life.

"Do you know anything about my daughter?" she said.

Louise tightened her grip on her purse and stepped back a little. She kept her eyes fastened on Sissy.

"I know what it's like to lose a child," Louise said, her voice a slight croak. "If I could ease any mother's pain, I would."

Sissy, who had imagined all sorts of scenarios had she ever had a moment alone with Ted's mother, hadn't expected that she would feel pity. She told Grace that's just what happened. While it spun through her mind to shoot back a cold remark about how Louise couldn't possibly understand what it was like to have her child missing or murdered by a monster, Louise had experienced a profound loss, too.

"I imagine that you and your family have suffered a great deal, too," Sissy said, finally, and not without compassion in her heart.

A salesclerk interrupted the conversation.

"Can I help you two find anything?" she asked.

Both women shook their heads. Louise loosened her grip on the sheet set and put it back on the shelf. There was an irony to the younger woman's question, of course. Both women had needed help in finding answers—Sissy, for the identity of the killer; Louise, for the reason her beautiful boy had turned into the worst kind of evil.

And yet, as her mother replayed that encounter with Grace when she was a little older, it was clear that she didn't hold Louise responsible. Grace was in the middle of a social studies course at school that introduced the nature versus nurture debate.

"We don't know everything about what makes a person evil," Sissy said.

"That's only partially true, Mom," she said.

"If you're thinking that Ted's mother is a factor in what he ended up doing later in life, I think you're overstating things."

"She abandoned him when he was a baby, Mom."

Sissy nodded. "Yes, but she went back for him. She didn't leave him at the home. She loved him enough to bring him home."

Grace pressed her mother. "She led him to believe that he was her brother."

"Those were the times, Grace."

"He never knew who his father was. His family had wrapped up his entire young life in lie after lie."

Sissy knew where her daughter was going, and she knew that she was probably right. And yet, she debated her right then. Grace was smart, tenacious, and well equipped to do what Sissy wanted her to do above everything else. She didn't say it out loud. She couldn't. She didn't want Grace to think that her own environment, her own upbringing in the shadow of Tricia's murder, was artificial. The love between them was genuine.

Louise Bundy may have given birth to a monster, and she'd certainly played a role in the miserable trajectory of his life, but not all of it was her doing. Grace and her mother parted company on that. Sissy felt that there was such a thing as "a bad seed" and that Ted had been evil from the outset.

One time when Grace was a teen, a story about a young woman who grew into adulthood not knowing that her grandfather was in fact her father appeared on a TV talk show. The young woman had lived a life of crime, unable to resolve just why it was that everything she touched turned ugly.

"She was born evil," Sissy said as mother and daughter pulled weeds from a garden bed under a beloved pear tree.

"Maybe she was bad because her mother hated her?"

Sissy stopped what she was doing.

"You mean, her mother's hidden feelings were not so hidden? Is that what you are saying?"

Grace dropped a dandelion into an old galvanized bucket. "Think about it, Mom. If she was treated like she was garbage, like she was vile, maybe she would grow up to be that way."

"A self-fulfilling prophecy, maybe?"

"I guess it might be. Maybe we can never understand what makes people do the ugly things they do. We try, though. Don't we?"

It wasn't the greatest mystery in the annals of crime, but it was one that Grace pondered over and over as she tried to understand the man who would have such an influence on her life. Ted was an obsession, one that had been passed on through her own personal history and the desires of her own mother. They kept coming back to this: Who was Theodore Robert Cowell, Ted Bundy? Really? Was he the son of an Air Force veteran named Lloyd Marshall? A sailor named Jack Worthington? Both were names that Ted's mother had ascribed to the man who'd made her pregnant. Over the years, the Cowells suggested that Ted was the result of incest between Louise and her father, Sam.

"He hated his mother for doing that to him," Grace had said once, revisiting a familiar conversation with Shane when they took a drive to the peninsula to visit friends. It was summer, hot, dry. It was the kind of day that would bring out young women in bathing suits and predators on the hunt for them. Somewhere. Anywhere. There was always someone on the hunt. Those days often evoked Ted.

"I never talked to Ted," Shane said, his eye on the road. "So I wouldn't know for sure."

"You've profiled him. You know."

"When he found out that he was a bastard—his

words, not mine—I expect it was an epic betrayal. He probably knew he wasn't one of Johnnie Bundy's kids—he didn't look like them. He probably entered the room more than once when things fell silent. He knew that there was a secret about him."

"If he hated his mother so much," Grace said, "maybe it was her that he was killing. Maybe everyone had it all wrong. Maybe it was his way to get Louise to pay for her lies."

"We'll need to stop for gas," Shane said, flipping on the turn indicator.

"I'd like a pop, too," she said.

Shane took the next exit. "Back to what you were saying, babe. I get it. I can see his rage directed toward Louise, but I think it was toward all women. All the women in his life. He was selecting a kind of everywoman, to stand in for Louise, maybe his grandmother, his girlfriends. Remember, as much as we know about him we really can't say for sure any of it is absolute."

"He was all contradictions," she said. She was thinking about how Ted had professed a deep love for his grandfather—a man who some family members were all but certain was his actual father. In some ways, that kind of misplaced devotion fit the profile. But there was more to it. If there had been a genetic component to Ted's aberrant behavior, it came from his grandfather. Family members talked about how Sam Cowell abused his wife, children, and even family pets.

"Brain studies indicate a fundamental difference between sociopaths and normal brains," Shane said.

"I've done the same reading," Grace said, her tone a little defensive. She regretted it the second the words passed her lips.

Shane didn't take the bait.

"Sociopaths like Ted sometimes learn the behavior from a family member," he said.

"Sam literally pushed one of his daughters down a flight of stairs because she dared to oversleep," Grace said. "Another said he swung a cat by its tail like a lariat."

Being a young woman in Tacoma had gotten decidedly more terrifying. Lisa Lancaster had been found butchered along the river. An unknown female's remains had been uncovered along the beach. Emma Rose was missing. Farther south of the county, Olympia teenager Kelsey Caldwell's name had been aligned with the missing girls cases, but that was more by the press than the genuine belief of law enforcement. She wasn't a part of the Tacoma cases.

That all changed one morning.

"How did we miss this?" Grace said, studying the highlighted section of the autopsy report that Paul Bateman had planted in her hand the minute she'd sat at her desk.

"A mistake," he said, almost more of a question than an answer.

"That Lisa had two left hands?"

Paul didn't say anything more. It was all there. The medical examiner's report noted that there had been body parts from more than one victim recovered from the dump site along the Puyallup River. An assistant taking autopsy photos had been the first to discover what should have been patently obvious—that the hands that had been severed and recovered from the site were both lefties.

"This is a colossal screwup," Paul said, facial muscles tightening.

Tissue samples had been analyzed and hand number one was a match for Lisa. The other, hand number two, was not a tissue or DNA match at all.

"The hand's size, overall condition, and traces of pale pink nail polish, indicate a female in her teens or early twenties. . . ."

Grace's blood was boiling too. "We're going back," she said.

Paul nodded.

"To the river," she said.

A half hour later, the two parked on the same dusty shoulder alongside River Road. The crime scene tape had been removed and rainfall had washed away the evidence of hundreds of footprints of the crime scene techs, coroner's staff, and police detectives who'd been there when Lisa's remains had been tagged and bagged.

Grace walked over to the river's edge. Paul finished up a call and followed.

The river had swollen and sloshed over the thin shelf that served as its bank. A fisherman, unaware of the fact that they were police detectives or the grisly reason that had brought them there, paused and waved from the other side.

"Thurston County is sending a sample of Dennis Caldwell's DNA right now," Paul said, getting off the phone. "No one is telling him, though. The detective there, Jonathan Stevens, knows how to keep his mouth shut. We don't want this out."

"If it's a match," she said, "it'll get out anyway. Probably sometime today."

She studied the bank and looked over humps of grass

and Himalayan blackberry vines that rambled around the perimeter of the river.

"The rest of Kelsey's got to be around here," she said, her eyes tracing the scene, inch by inch.

"Maybe just that one part was ditched here," Paul offered.

Grace didn't think so. She shook her head and started walking. "Ridgway and Bundy both dumped bodies in clusters. They went to places they knew would be undetected, places where they could go back."

"And defile the bodies," he said.

Grace nodded. "That, too. But I wasn't thinking that. I was thinking about how they liked to relive the conquests, from the hunt to the kill. At the after-party."

"They really got off on it," Paul said.

It made her sick to her stomach, thinking of Ridgway and Bundy's victims, their final moments. How even in death they'd been made to suffer the worst indignities that anyone could imagine. In fact, no normal person could even conjure up the activities that Ted had enjoyed with the dead girls.

"Sick pieces of crap, those two," she finally said, stopping and bending at her knees to get a closer look at a piece of paper that had attached itself to the damp earth. It was narrow and white, probably a receipt.

"Let's collect that," she said, pointing to it with the tip of her shoe.

Paul shrugged a little. "Wasn't there when we processed the scene."

She looked at it and gave her head a slight shake. "Exactly. Maybe it's nothing. Or maybe he's come back."

"I hate that you always call the unknown subject a *he*."

Grace shot Paul an irritated look. "Jesus. You're

going PC on me now? Fact is ninety-nine percent of these twisted pukes are male, Paul. No offense meant."

"Just kidding you," he said, the smile falling from his face. "Don't you laugh anymore?"

She shook her head. "Haven't heard anything funny for a long time."

With that, she walked ahead, and Paul returned to the car to get the requisite supplies for collecting the receipt or anything else they might find. With each step on the nutrient-rich river soil, Grace Alexander thought about the kind of person who would come back to re-live his murders. She knew that both Bundy and Ridgway had had sex with their victims post-homicide. Yates had emphatically denied that he had, as if that was some kind of an accolade he could give himself. There were differences detected in the clusters, too. Ridgway had posed his dead women. Bundy had admitted to moving his victims' bodies, but never in a ritualistic manner.

Again, as if there was a distinction between being merely a serial killer and being sick enough to pose a body in a provocative and shocking way.

Kelsey Caldwell was out there. She just had to be.

Unsurprisingly, Lifetime was not Grace Alexander's go-to cable channel. She was more of an Investigation Discovery viewer. Yet when scrolling through the TV channel guide while she waited for Shane to get home, she noticed the umpteenth rerun of *The Deliberate Stranger*, the TV miniseries about Ted Bundy. She had watched the two-part series once with her mother, who hadn't thought the facts were at odds with the truth. Or at least some TV writer's version of the truth. One thing that had rankled Grace however, had been Sissy's insistence that Mark Harmon was too handsome to play Tacoma's evilest native son.

"Bundy was not that good looking," Sissy had said when they'd watched the marathon of serial-killer TV movies one day, the pinnacle of which had been *The Deliberate Stranger*. "He wasn't some ogre, I'll give him that. They always tried to glamorize the bastard."

Grace cringed whenever her mother swore. It just didn't seem to fit her personality. Her mother was tough, but gentle. She lived her life like she was from the South or England—tea in the afternoon, sandwiches with the crusts removed, pinochle games, and ladies' auxiliary meetings. Not women's, but *ladies'*. Grace knew the source of the bitterness that came from her mouth was because of the hurt of losing Tricia.

The one she loved more than me.

"Just a movie, Mom," she said.

"More than a movie," Sissy said, snuggling next to Grace on the sofa that commanded most of the living room in their cozy house. "It is a reminder."

Grace thought about it. She was just a girl then, but she knew that she probably shouldn't push too much even when she wanted to know more.

"A reminder of what?" she asked anyway.

Sissy looked at her, in that unblinking way that she did when she needed to prove a point. "That sometimes the bad guy gets away."

"But they caught him," Grace said.

Sissy didn't blink. "They didn't catch him for all that he's done."

Grace was aware that her mom was writing to Ted at

that time. She knew that she was trying to get the death row inmate to confess to his crimes—all of them, including the murder of her sister. It wasn't that Grace wasn't interested in what her mom was doing, but she really didn't talk to her about the letters. At the time, talking to either of her parents about anything related to Tricia just made her feel so second place.

"Mom," she finally said, "maybe you'll never, ever know."

Sissy O'Hare glanced away from the TV and held her daughter's gaze.

"That's not acceptable," she said, her eyes dampening a little. "I will never rest until I know. I need you to understand this. I need you to stand with me on this. *We* can't ever rest until Ted Bundy has admitted to everything that he did to us. To your sister. To all of the people who were so unfortunate to have met him, talked to him, got into his car."

Grace just sat there. Her mom was obsessed. There was no doubt about it. What could she say to calm her?

She swallowed. "I love you, Mom." She put her hand on her mother's and gripped it. "Stop. You're scaring me."

"I love you, baby. And you should be scared. When the monster comes into your house he doesn't ever leave. I need you to help me. I need you to take up the cause—if anything ever happens to me. *You* need to find out what happened to your sister."

Handsome Mark Harmon grinned on the TV screen. Mother and daughter sat in silence as the actor in tennis whites charmed a young woman. The woman was a brunette, slender, and very, very pretty.

"Don't go with him," Sissy said to the screen. She

squeezed Grace's hand, pulsing it a little so as not to put a full-on hand lock.

"She can't help it," Grace said. "She doesn't know what kind of person he is."

"That's right," Sissy said, now turning back to her daughter. "Remember that. Remember that no one who knew him could believe he was so heinous. He looks like he couldn't hurt a fly, but he's worse than a spider. Spinning, spinning, spinning."

Her mother's statement was a warning, but it also carried a challenge. Was stopping Ted Bundy something that she could do? Or if not Ted, could she stop another killer?

Whenever she looked back on watching *The Deliberate Stranger* with her mom, Grace could see why she became a detective. It wasn't so much for her sister, it was for her mother. It was for all the mothers out there curled up and crying at some stupid movie that reminded them of the baby someone had taken.

In the days before Trivial Pursuit, Sissy O'Hare had created homemade flash cards to teach her daughter both the mundane and shocking facts about the man she was sure had murdered her beloved Tricia. Later, when Grace thought of it, she wondered if her mother's obsession was almost a form of child abuse—even though her mother's intentions had never been evil. She only wanted her daughter to understand as much as she could.

The devil is always in the details, she could say.

Yes, the details.

Grace had found the index cards tucked away in a

plastic sandwich container years ago when she was sorting things for the Goodwill after her father died. She was in the garage, where she had placed a piece of plywood atop two sawhorses. On one end were the boxes of clothing that were to be given away. She pondered over a few of the items as the memories associated with a particular garment came back to her. A dress she'd worn to a job interview at Nordstrom when she was in high school. She'd gotten the job, and immediately found that liked it—but not for the reasons that many her age assumed, the generous discount on new clothing. The girls she worked with were studying fashion merchandising and were giddy when the newest arrivals came in from New York. She mirrored their own enthusiasm, in the way that people do so as not to ruin a moment of joy for another. Yet their ambitions and desires seemed so inconsequential. A pair of white pants made her grimace. White pants were never a good idea.

Never.

Carefully, as if she didn't want to spill its contents, Grace opened the sandwich container and took out the first three-by-five card, its edges no longer crisp, but soft and fuzzy from wear.

She had held those cards so many times.

Written in her mother's handwriting:

What is Ted Bundy's favorite novel?

She didn't have to flip it over to see the answer. It was emblazoned on her brain.

"*Treasure Island*," she said softly, as though she didn't want anyone to hear.

She remembered how she'd despised that book, not because it was a boy's book—the reason her friends hadn't liked it—but because it was Ted's book. She hated everything about him; everything that brought him joy, or sadness, brought her the opposite emotions.

Grace set it down and looked at the next card. She recalled sitting at the big kitchen table, her mother facing her with her sweet but steely eyes, urging her to get it right.

What was the make of Ted's family's car in Tacoma (the car he was embarrassed to be seen in)?

That one was easy. Her father always pointed them out on the rare occasion when one was on the roadway, once when he'd been scavenging for parts at a junkyard and she'd accompanied him there. The answer was a Nash Rambler.

So many of Grace's own memories were blended with Ted's life that sometimes it was hard to separate her own from what she'd been taught about the serial killer by her parents. She turned the cards over one by one and flipped through the answers.

By age ten he was dragging girls to the woods to urinate on them.

He was a Cub Scout.

He stole ski equipment in high school.

None of his teenage friends ever visited his bedroom in the basement of his childhood home.

He hated the way Tacoma smelled.

Grace smiled at that one. Who, but the owners of the smelter that gave Tacoma a nose-plugging reputation, didn't hate the stink, the so-called aroma of Tacoma? She looked back down at the cards.

He picked through garbage cans in search of porn.

He was jealous of his cousins because they had a piano in their home.

He never bonded with his stepfather—refusing to call him Dad.

Grace knew all of those things and more. She probably knew Ted better than he knew himself. She knew every tragic, disgusting, disturbing detail of his life. She knew how he'd come into the world as an imposter, something less than a human being. She knew how cunning he could be when it came to winning over the sympathy of a pretty young girl. She knew that he understood that as a perceived weakness, like an arm in a sling, was a far better approach than the thuggish behavior of wrestling a woman down in broad daylight. Later, that lesson would be forgotten as his rage escalated into a frenzied rampage at the Chi Omega sorority house in Tallahassee, Florida.

The next index card was about Chi Omega, the location of the second to the last gasp of Ted Bundy's toxic life.

Grace ran her fingertip over the image of an owl, the mascot for the sorority on the card. She'd researched the sorority at the Tacoma Public Library. She decided that if she were ever going to pledge, it would be to Chi-O. She'd drawn the owl on the card, not to cheat or remind her with an obvious clue. She was only a girl then. She drew the owl because she liked the bird. Nothing deeper. Nothing that drilled down into anything more than just that. She thought about how her mother had let her paint a big mural behind her bed, the gnarly branches of a maple tree with four owls against a daisy yellow moon. A brief smile came to her lips, but it passed the instant she flipped over the card. The answer printed, again in Sissy's controlled penmanship:

Fifteen minutes.

Just fifteen minutes. Grace knew that was the length of time it had taken for Ted Bundy to slip into the sorority house in the early morning hours of January 15, 1978 and molest and rape and murder. He used a wooden club, something that he'd found en route. It wasn't planned and it was beyond risky. Four sorority sisters had been beaten, two of them had died. Survivors said that Bundy had worn panty hose over his face to disguise his appearance.

Only nine hundred seconds. That's all he'd needed.

Grace drew a short breath. It was the last card that always got to her.

Who killed your sister?

The answer to that one was all incumbent upon her. It always had been. It was the reason she'd been born and it was the driving force behind everything she did. It was a curse, and yet it was also empowering. She needed to succeed where others had failed. At times she felt that her parents had created her for the purpose of hunting their prey, but that didn't always bother her. She felt sorry for people born into the world without any kind of purpose whatsoever. What was the point of being on the planet, if not to do something right and good for someone else? All other options seemed hedonistic, selfish.

She flipped the little white card over.

Theodore Robert Bundy.

Grace was thirteen when it should have ended. She and her mother were watching TV nonstop, waiting for Ted to die. It was January 24, 1989. She remembered seeing on TV a man from Florida who was standing next to a hand-lettered sign that said FRY DAY IS TUESDAY and wearing a BURN, TED, BURN T-shirt, which he was selling (twenty dollars for two). He unflinchingly told a reporter that he didn't think there was anything wrong with selling the shirts. After all, Bundy was a killer, and that certainly was far worse than making money off one.

Sissy O'Hare didn't agree with the man and told Grace so. She didn't agree with all the profiteering that came with Ted. The authors who insisted their books were about "educating" rather than making money, the movie people who wanted their films to "tell the true story" and ghoulish women who followed Ted like he was some kind of Pied Piper to hell. All of them sickened her. All of them. There was something so very wrong about those people who were making their livelihoods off someone who made a sport of killing young women.

"See that man selling T-shirts?" she asked Grace as they watched the pending execution unfold on TV.

Grace nodded her head, her eyes glued to her mother's.

"He's doing something evil and he doesn't even know it. He doesn't know about the pain behind what Bundy did. He doesn't understand that turning Bundy's execution into a carnival only celebrates what he did."

Grace nodded.

"There is only one type of person with any honor in this, that's the man—or woman—who carries a badge."

Grace looked a little unsure.

"Police, honey. They are the only ones I want to see happy in a mess like this one. They are the ones I want to see smile because they put the bad guy right where he belongs."

CHAPTER 15

In the second-floor offices at the Tacoma Police Department, Grace Alexander and Paul Bateman looked at the photographs of the three faces who'd commanded the attention of the homicide unit for the past few weeks. The first, though this had been unknown to Tacoma police, had been Kelsey Caldwell, seventeen. The second to go missing had been twenty-four-year-old Lisa Lancaster. The newest face put up on the wall, adjacent to the pictures of every member of the police department, belonged to Emma Rose. They were in the war room, the detective's conference room. It was the place where cases were discussed, evidence was weighed, and theories were shared. Until the possibility of a third missing girl made its way to that room, there had not been a pattern. Two does not make a pattern. Two can be a coincidence. Random. Just one bad bit of bad luck after the other.

But three? Everyone knew that like in the old game tic-tac-toe, three in a row was significant. All three girls were similar in age, size, build. Their facial features were blandly pretty, their hair long and dark. On their own they might not have been noticed, but in a group of three everything that was common about them became remarkable.

"They guy's obviously hung up on a type," Detective Bateman said. Coming from him, the comment was almost funny. After his wife ditched him, he'd hooked up with a woman who looked so much like her a few people thought they'd gotten back together.

No one had used the "S" word yet. Calling something a serial killer case was the epitome of TV-style police chatter. But there they were. Three young women, girls really. Pretty maids all in a row.

"The newest girl has been missing for a little more than a day. Parents called it in after they found out that she didn't get to work," Grace said.

Paul nodded. "Yeah. Last seen at her job," he said.

"Where does she work?" she asked.

"Starbucks. Lakewood Town Center."

Grace went for her coat. "Good. I could use a cup of coffee."

Just before they left, Paul picked up the phone. The call was brief. He locked his eyes on Grace's.

"ME's office. Tissue's a match. It was Kelsey's hand."

Grace didn't say anything. In her bones, she'd already known that.

Where were the rest of Kelsey's remains? And, more important, who would have done that to her?

The Lakewood Towne Center Starbucks was like a lot of such places—loud with people talking, blenders buzzing, and a thick layer of the aroma of coffee permeating everything and everyone. The only thing of note

was that one of its workers was missing and the staff
that was behind the counter was jittery when the police
detectives arrived. Not jittery in the overcaffeinated
way that its patrons often were, but the kind of jittery
that came from deep concern.

Emma Rose was dependable. If she wasn't at work
and she wasn't at home, no one thought there could be
a good outcome.

"When she was fifteen minutes late, I texted her,"
Sylvia Devonshire told the detectives.

"Did she text back?" Grace said.

Paul added three packets of Splenda to his drink and
stirred. Grace looked over at him and shook her head,
but said nothing.

"Is it that unusual? I mean, fifteen minutes. That's a
tight leash you've got on your people."

Sylvia shrugged. "It is what it is. You try making
twenty drinks for some schmo's office suck-up and you
need everyone you can." She looked up and smiled at
one of the schmos in line. "Just a second. Aphrodite is
making your drinks now."

The man nodded impatiently, obviously indifferent
to anyone's needs but his own.

"See?" she said, this time in a low voice.

Paul stopped stirring. "Okay, so Emma is dependable and you were worried. Anything you can tell us
about her last shift?"

Sylvia pretended to be busy and looked away.

"Sylvia, you're thinking about something," Grace
said.

The young woman looked up. "I don't know," she
said.

Grace leaned a little closer. "That means you know something."

Sylvia wrapped her arms around her chest, trying in a very real way, though unconsciously so, to hold it all inside.

"Tell me," Grace said.

"I don't want to get anyone in trouble."

"No one is in trouble but Emma Rose," Paul said.

Grace looked over at her partner. "Look, he's right. But Emma's parents are very, very worried."

"Is there something going on with Emma and her parents?" Paul asked.

Sylvia shook her head. "Oh no. Her parents were cool. They used to come in and sit over there." She pointed to a pair of leather easy chairs. "You know, hang out before she got off and then they took her out for Thai."

"That's nice. But something is bothering you," Grace said. "What are you thinking? We've got to find her."

"I hate to bring it up."

"What? Sylvia, what are you thinking?"

"I don't know. I don't want to cause trouble. He's a nice kid."

"Who? Who's a nice kid?"

"Oliver. Oliver Angstrom. He was always talking about how hot Emma is and, you know, how he wanted to ask her out."

"She's a pretty girl," Grace said. "I'm sure she got a lot of attention."

"Right. Customers liked her, too."

"We need you to focus now, okay? What about Oliver?"

Sylvia looked down at the counter. "He was going to ask her out. Finally. I knew she wouldn't say yes, because, well, she's so pretty and he's so geeky. Sweet, but geeky. But not geeky and scary."

Grace knew the difference. She'd once dated a geeky guy in high school. Smart, brainy, was sexy. Loving *Star Wars* too much, not so.

"I don't know if Oliver asked her out or not, but I do know that they were together. They cleaned and closed."

"Did you see Oliver today?"

An uneasy look came over Sylvia's face. She shook her head. "No, I didn't. No one did. He called in and used one of his floating holidays."

"Was that unexpected?"

"Totally. If I'd gotten the call directly I would have told him no, but he called in the store's voice mail and left a message before opening."

Grace knew that approach. She'd done it a time or two herself. So had Paul. Always call in to the sergeant when you know he's not at his desk.

Just then, another Starbucks worker made his way through from the back room. He was a thin, gawky teenager, with a faint black moustache struggling to survive on his upper lip. The goatee he'd tried cultivating was even less successful. He was carrying a small black purse.

"Talking about Emma?" he asked.

"Yes," Grace said, looking at the teen with the purse.

"Lost and Found brought this over earlier today," he said. "Emma's purse. Said the maintenance crew turned it in and the guy at Lost and Found knew her name and picture ID so he brought it over here."

"Why didn't you tell me?" Sylvia asked the young man, whose tag identified him as Tony G.

Grace took the purse. "Did they say where they found it?"

"Yeah. She must have dropped it by the bus stop. Found it over there," he said, indicating a place outside the front of the coffee shop. "Want me to show you where it is?" He looked at Sylvia for permission and she reluctantly nodded.

Sylvia let out a quivering sigh. She was, apparently, all business. "We're very, very short-staffed, Tony."

"It's all right. We'll only keep him a minute. Then he can get back to his important work here." Paul's tone was condescending, more than it really needed to be. Sylvia had pretty thick skin, but she got the gist of what he was saying without words.

"Fine," she said. She turned her attention to Grace. "Emma's a sweet girl. I hope you find her soon."

There was a slight chill in the air as the trio walked over to a section of the parking lot, in front of which sat a Plexiglas-enclosed bus shelter. With the exception of an elderly woman laden with shopping bags from several mall stores, the enclosure was empty.

"Here's where she caught the bus," Tony said.

"Thanks," Paul said.

Grace nodded as she scanned the area. The Starbucks was in full view, not more than thirty yards away.

"You need anything else?" Tony asked. "Gotta get back."

Grace smiled and nodded, and the young man backed

away, his green apron disappearing around a swarm of parked cars.

"What are you so happy about?" Paul asked.

"Not happy," Grace said. "Just glad."

"Glad about what? And what's the difference, by the way?"

Grace's eyes traveled up a parking lot light standard. "We might have a witness."

"Huh?" Paul squinted, but he needed his glasses to really see anything at any distance. "Some birds?"

Grace resisted the desire to roll her eyes. He would notice that for sure. "The video camera," she said, extending her index finger in the direction of a small surveillance camera pivoted toward the bus stop. "Let's see who monitors the feed."

Where am I? Emma Rose looked around. She could barely move. Every inch of her body ached. She remembered that she'd been kidnapped, by some pervert no doubt. She tried to lift her head, but it was heavy like a bowling ball. Her eyes moved around the darkened room. In the corner she saw the shadowy figure of a man. He was just out of the beam of the reading lamp.

"What are you going to do?" she asked, almost editing her words to ask, *What have you done to me?*

Emma waited for an answer. Instead, she saw him flip the switch that powered the gooseneck reading lamp. The room was now completely black. She felt the air move around her and the door open and shut. Next, the sound of the dead bolt as it fell into place.

She reached down and touched herself. Her clothes

were on. She wasn't a virgin and she knew what it felt like after sex. She hadn't been violated when she was unconscious.

A moment later, she fell asleep.

When she woke up, it was to the sound of the hatch and tray being opened. She went over to the tray. Lying on it were a brush and mirror. She went back to the light and looked at herself. Her hair had been washed and detangled. The bruising of her eyes had faded from a dark purple to an almost imperceptible yellow hue.

Her long hair. Shiny. Clean.

Her thoughts raced in a circle.

What was he doing to her? Why was he holding her? Why didn't he speak to her? Who was he? Was it a stranger or one of those Starbucks customer creeps? The ones who always winked at her when she handed over their drinks?

CHAPTER 16

Grace drove past the First Methodist Church every week on her way to visit her cousin, Vonnie Joanna, or Vo-Jo as the family called her, in that part of Tacoma. The church was a little out of her way, not enough to make her think that her obsession was out of control, but enough to make her dismiss the route if she was in a hurry to VJ's little house. Nine times out of ten on those drive-bys, it would enter Grace's mind that the church had likely been the starting point of all the hurt that was to come. It was the axis of the evil. It was there that Johnnie Bundy had met Ted's mother, Louise, at a church gathering for singles, mostly older ones, some with kids.

There were a lot of what-if games that Grace played when it came to her sister's murder. This was one of the weaker ones. She wondered, if not for that meeting between Louise and Johnnie that day in 1951 would Louise have maybe left town? Ted would have gone with her. To California or Nevada. Somewhere far, far away. If Louise had not stayed in Tacoma, would things have been different enough in Ted's life to stop him from doing all that he did? Or had any of the places or people that had made up the trajectory of his life mattered at all? Maybe he'd been evil at birth. Maybe there'd been no stopping him.

Grace looked over at the pretty, but plain, church as it filled the frame of her rearview mirror. She wondered almost out loud, *If not for Louise meeting Johnnie Bundy, would I have ever been born at all?*

With his parents upstairs rearranging the furniture for what had to be the fiftieth time that year, Oliver Angstrom set aside his latest video game and channel surfed in the basement rec room of the family's home just south of Lakewood. His interest perked up a little when he landed on *The Texas Chainsaw Massacre*. It wasn't a comic or graphic novel come to life—those had been pretty lame lately anyway—but there were elements of the horror classic that stoked his imagination.

Oliver had cracked open the little basement window and smoked a little pot. He was feeling something right then, but he wasn't sure if it was anger or anxiety. He'd asked Emma out the evening before. *Finally*. He hadn't asked a girl out for more than two years, though he'd nearly stalked a few as he tried to find a way to overcome his nerdy nervousness. He'd read self-help books. He role-played in front of a mirror. He worked out. He shaved his chest. He did whatever he thought he could do to make himself more attractive. The one thing he couldn't fix, however, was his essential geekiness. Being a comic fanboy, a computer nerd, or anything along those lines was fine if a guy wanted to attract the female equivalent. But that's not what Oliver was after. He'd wanted to date Emma Rose from the first day she walked into Starbucks looking for a job. She had only wanted part-time work because her mother had been sick and she didn't want to be away from her very long. He'd overheard Emma tell Devon that her mom loved Starbucks and that she wanted her to work there as a way to get out of the house a few hours a day.

"Don't get me wrong," Emma said, "I love coffee, too. But I'd rather be home with her. She's pretty strong about me needing to get out and be with people my own age. So here I am."

She's so pretty, he'd thought. *So sweet*. She was also sexy in the way that some girls are when they don't even know it. Oliver was hooked. He just didn't know what to do about it.

And then that night he'd finally asked her. Finally. After all the practice. After telling almost everyone who worked there that he was interested in Emma, he did it. And it was a big, fat flop.

He balled up a fist and punched it into the cushion of the old sofa.

Dammit. Damn her! Why hadn't she seen that he was special, so very special? Why hadn't she said yes? He was Spiderman! She was his Mary Jane! He was Superman! She was his Lois Lane. He couldn't remember the Green Lantern's love interest. Emma was right. It had been a terrible movie.

She was always so right. Why hadn't she seen that he was perfect for her?

He looked down to the coffee table, where he'd set the photo he'd taken from the employee bulletin board when Emma was recognized as barista of the month.

She was so beautiful in her crisp white blouse and perfectly pressed green apron. *So sweet.* She was always nice to him, listening with keen interest to whatever it was that he'd finally summoned the courage to tell her about.

Boyfriend or not, Oliver Angstrom was utterly determined to make her fall in love with him. He'd do whatever it took. He would not, he told himself over and over, be denied. Batman needed his Catwoman. Oliver needed his Emma. He turned up the volume on the TV as his favorite part of the *Texas Chainsaw* reunion came onto the screen. The roar of the saw. The scream of the girl cowering in the basement of the abandoned house.

Oliver stayed glued to the screen. Leatherface was in love. He was willing, ready and able to do whatever he needed to do go get the girl. Oliver wasn't violent like that at all. Not really. Even so he admired the character central to the *Texas Chainsaw Massacre* as a tormented figure who was willing to do anything to get the girl.

He wanted to think of himself just like that. Without the power saw, of course. Oliver Angstrom wanted nothing more than to possess Emma Rose. He wanted nothing more than to take her out on a date. Kiss her. Tell her that she understood him like no other. The only problem with all that he'd planned was that she'd said no. She'd said she already had a boyfriend.

He doubted that and that hurt him as much as her answer. She didn't even think that he'd be able to find out that there was no boyfriend. It was like he was nothing to her. Not even worthy of the truth. He'd never rejected anyone before, but if he did, he'd never lie. The only good thing about the fact that she'd lied was that there was no boyfriend. There was no one else in the way.

The only thing about him that didn't interest her seemed to be . . . him. But he could change. He could make her love him if only he knew just what in the world that was. He took another draw on the joint he was smoking, held it, and then blew the smoke out the open window. He took a seat on the sofa and plotted just how he'd make her fall in love with him.

"What are you doing down there?" his mother called from the upstairs doorway.

"Nothing! Leave me alone, Mom."

"There's someone here who wants to talk to you."

"Who's that?"

"The police. That's who!"

Oliver jumped up from the ratty old sofa and prayed to God that he didn't smell like a grow operation just then. *The police? That can't be good.*

CHAPTER 17

Grace Alexander and Paul Bateman were standing in the Angstroms' living room when Oliver emerged from his basement lair, rubbing his eyes a little and hoping against hope that the police didn't think they were too red.

Shana Angstrom, a large woman with room-filling hair and a rope of gold around her neck, introduced her son, while Clark Angstrom, a stump of a man with twitchy eyes, just stood mute.

"Ollie," she said, in her nails-on-chalkboard voice, "there might be some trouble and you can help out."

Oliver blinked hard. "I don't know anything about Emma."

Grace nodded, a little surprised that the young man standing in front of her in a T-shirt and jeans and smelling of bong water had immediately invoked the missing girl's name.

"What do you know about her?" Paul asked.

Clark Angstrom seemed to fade into the background while his wife directed the group to the living room, where they could talk "more comfortably."

"Clark," she said, "be helpful, will you? Offer them a drink."

"No," Paul said. "We're fine. Thank you."

"Ollie," Shanna Angstrom said, "sit up and answer their questions. These are busy people and they wouldn't be here if it wasn't of some importance. Right, Detectives?"

Oliver Angstrom, it seemed, didn't have it easy.

"Work called and told me Emma's missing. That's all I know."

"Really? You don't know where she is?" Paul asked.

He shook his head and slumped low in to the sofa next to his father. "I don't know her that well," he said. "I mean, don't get me wrong, I asked her out, but we just didn't click that way."

"What way is that, Oliver?" Grace asked.

Oliver glanced at his parents, his mother, now seated on his other side. "Hook up," he said, sheepishly. "We didn't hook up. She was cool and all, but we just didn't, you know, hook up like . . ."

"Like what?" Paul asked. "Like how you wanted to?"

Oliver didn't say anything.

Shana got up and started for the kitchen. "Would you like a beer?"

"No," Paul said. "No thanks. We're working."

"I'll take a water," Grace said, more to be polite than anything. "Let me help you."

She followed her into the kitchen and Shanna fished a couple of glasses from the cupboard.

"Your son seems like a nice boy," Grace said.

Oliver's mother smiled nervously. "Oh, he is. I mean,

I wish he'd get a real job. Trying to make video games all day and night."

"Really? That's cool," Grace said, almost choking on the word "cool." She considered video games the scourge of a generation of young people. Sure, they had stellar reflexes from working the controls with faster than lightning speed, but many were almost handicapped— incapable of dealing with humans. Oliver, she noted, almost never made direct eye contact.

"Is he working on a new game now?"

"I think so. He's always hanging around in the basement. Maybe he'll show you around. Probably a pigsty, but that's the way kids are. No respect for what their parents do for them day in and day out."

Grace took the water and returned to the living room.

"Oliver, your mom was telling me about the video games you're producing. I'd love to see what you're working on. I've always loved video games. I think of them as the art form of a generation."

Oliver brightened slightly. At least he seemed to.

"Me, too."

Grace set down her glass. "Do you mind showing me where you work on your latest? I have a nephew who wants to be a game developer. He's just a kid, but I think I'd earn some cred if I said I saw what someone with his same dreams was actually doing."

"Sure. Messy down there, but I'll show you."

Grace followed Oliver down the stairs, while Paul remained with his parents.

The basement was dark and smelly. The couch in front of the TV was a thrift market reject.

"This is a great space. Really private," she said.

"Thanks." Oliver looked over at the door to his grow room. Grace followed his gaze.

"Mom's doll collection's in there. Off limits to all," he said.

Grace nodded and backed off. "When did you last see Emma?"

"At work," he said.

"Right. Did you leave together? See where she went?"

Oliver shook his head and fiddled with the controls next to his TV.

"Not really. I had to clean up."

The TV went on and he started to demo his game, *Babe Hunter*.

Grace watched for a moment, but something else caught her eye. On the coffee table in front of the TV was a picture of Emma.

Oliver stopped what he was doing. "Oh, that? I found it. Just kept it. She could get another."

"Get another?"

"Yeah, it was her mall photo ID. No biggie. Just kind of wanted to keep it. You don't think that's weird, do you?"

Grace did, but she shook her head no.

"No," she said. "Not at all."

After a few more moments watching Oliver Angstrom play the world's worst video game, she thanked him for his time.

"We'll be in touch," she said.

"Do you want me to burn a disk of my game for your nephew?"

"That would be great, but no thanks. He's too young for your game. Looks kind of adult for his age."

Oliver nodded and went back to the screen.

The detectives waited until they got back into the car before saying anything. It had been one of those kinds of interviews.

"What did you find out downstairs in the creepy kid's crash pad?"

"He had a picture of Emma. Said he found it. Seems like he might be a stalker or something. Maybe obsessed with her. Wouldn't let me go in one of the rooms. He said his mom had a doll collection that was off limits. You? Anything with the parents?"

"Mr. Angstrom said about two words, maybe three. Mrs. Angstrom went on and on about what a disappointment her boy was and how she wants to kick him out. She actually said she wished he was a suspect in Emma's disappearance because that would mean he'd made a move on a girl. Think about it. Domineering mother, creepy basement, if there was a dead dog and wet bed we'd have the address of a serial killer."

Grace smiled, but it was a grim smile. "Oliver's no serial killer. He's a dope. I'm kind of with his mother," she said. "Even with all that, I'm kind of curious about what's behind that basement door. Doll collection? That really would be the topper."

"Agreed," Paul said as he turned the ignition.

"You mind dropping me off at my mom's?" Grace said.

"Wednesday night, is it?"

"Yeah. Love my mom, you know I do. But since Dad died I made a promise. Every Wednesday is our night."

"At least you'll have lots to talk about," he said.

She nodded. "That we will."

CHAPTER 18

Sissy O'Hare was an exceedingly attractive woman, the kind who didn't think old age was an excuse to fall apart and give in to the inevitable ravages of time. She didn't chase after youth with facelifts, exotic oils, or clothing that wasn't appropriate for her age. Sissy changed her hairstyle with the times—refusing to be one of those women who looked like a sorry depiction of their high school yearbook photo. She ate right and exercised. In a nod to her favorite fashion icon, Jacqueline Kennedy Onassis, Sissy O'Hare wore a strand of favorite pearls when she was gardening.

She let friends call her Sissy O.

Grace adored her mother, even when she resented the circumstances of her birth. There had certainly been hard times between them, bouts where they hadn't spoken for days on end. Most of that dissipated when Grace left home for college. It was around that time that she'd really gotten to know her mother and what made her do all that she did. Grace didn't have children of her own, but through Sissy, she imagined she understood just how powerful the love for a child really could be.

Since her father's death, Grace and her mother talked almost daily. At least once a week she and Shane would have her over to dinner or take her out. Wednesdays were a mother/daughter day, a date carved in stone. The conversations were no longer about when Grace and Shane were going to have a baby, though that sometimes slipped through in veiled ways.

"I saw the cutest baby clothes yesterday at Nordstrom," Sissy said one time, knowing full well what she was doing.

"I'm sure you did, Mom," Grace said, refusing to take the bait.

"Can you believe that Octomom woman? All those children! Wouldn't you be happy with just one?"

"Yes, Mom. One day, one would be nice."

"I didn't mean *now*," she said, not too gracefully, trying to step back a little.

"I know."

That all was then. Water under the bridge. Done and gone. Their relationship was on solid ground, and though neither woman said so out loud, both were grateful for that.

Sissy liked to eat at 6:30 on the dot, a holdover from her days when Conner would come home dog tired, belt down a Manhattan, and slide himself into a chair at the dinner table. *The table.* As Grace picked at her mother's eggplant parmesan casserole—a specialty that had always been her "company's coming" dish when she was a girl—Grace couldn't help but be transported back to that time and place. Her mother in the kitchen, wearing a strand of pearls, stirring the marinara as it simmered over the blue flame of the stove and soaking the eggplant in a light, acidulated brine. On the refrig-

erator was the usual cavalcade of children's artwork—
a tracing of a hand made to look like a turkey, a self-
portrait of a little girl with pigtails, a cat lumbering
along the top of a fence.

All were drawings that had been made by Tricia, the
sister she'd never known.

Grace couldn't remember, all those years later, if
she'd ever asked her mother or father about why they
insisted on keeping those relics front and center. It
wasn't that she didn't command some display space,
because she did. While Tricia's artwork was on the front
of the refrigerator door, hers was relegated to the side of
the appliance.

One time when her mother must have noticed the
disappointment on Grace's face, she'd remarked on it.

"Honey, your drawings would only get faded. There's
less light where I put up your lovely work."

Grace hadn't bought the excuse. Yet by then it had
been clear that there was no competing with the memory of a dead, murdered girl. Never could be.

Her mom served Grace a plate and watched for her
approval.

"Delicious, as always."

"Glad you like it, honey."

"Company's coming, Mom," she said.

Sissy grinned, her teeth as white as they had been
when she was young. Teeth, she liked to boast, that
were all her own. "You remember!"

"I remember everything, Mom," Grace said, leaving
the "everything" to mean whatever her mother wanted
it to be. It didn't have to be anything about Tricia.

And yet that was why she was there. As the investigation of the Tacoma girls went on, the subject at hand

was driven by Grace's need to talk about the cases. Not specifics, really. And not really about the cases at all.

"Mom, I know I'm supposed to understand what motivates these killers, but it is beyond me."

Sissy wiped her mouth with the corner of a chambray blue cloth napkin. "It is beyond everyone, honey." She placed the napkin back in her lap and smoothed out the wrinkles. "It riles me that there are complete morons on TV every single day talking about the evil that men do to young, unsuspecting girls."

One helmet-headed blonde was particularly irksome.

"Oh that ninny!" she went on. "She always talks with complete authority. Who but Jonathan Edwards can get into the heads of others, let alone a sociopath's? Sure, these idiots have their degrees—" She stopped, realizing that her daughter held such a degree. "No offense," she added quickly.

"None taken," Grace said. Her mother was venting and that was a good thing. Her mother had always been the kind to hold things deep inside, and then, when she could no longer do so, explode. "Who do you think knows the motivation, then?" she asked, knowing full well what her mother was going to say.

"Only another monster knows. Only they can understand their own kind."

"I thought so. That's why I'm here, Mom. There's a monster out there and we have to stop him."

"Understood," Sissy said, offering some extra cheese that she'd grated before dinner.

Grace shook her head. "What did Ted tell you?"

"I knew that was coming," Sissy said, setting down her fork and searching her daughter's eyes. "I knew you were going to ask me."

"I'm sorry, Mom, but maybe you can help. You faced him."

Sissy nodded. "Yes, I did. A lot of good it did, but yes, I did."

After dinner, Grace and her mother went downstairs to the basement where the O'Hares had kept a war room for the sole purpose of finding out who had taken Tricia. In more than three decades, it had barely changed. On one wall was a whiteboard, the kind that uses erasable markers. It had long since been wiped clean, though in the light coming in from the window wells, the faint tracings of letters emerged. Wiped off, but not removed.

Suspects. . . . Location . . . Detective in charge . . .

Standing there against the whiteboard and the collection of Rubbermaid tubs labeled with a Sharpie pen. Some indicated newspaper clippings, some held photos, still more had the clunky video technology that had long since disappeared—VHS tapes. As her mother moved toward a stack of the plastic boxes, Grace was clear on at least two things. There was no way she could have grown up in that house and become anything other than a police officer. Trying to catch Tricia's killer was a family obsession. The other certainty was that her parents had never ever been able to move on from their search for justice.

Conner O'Hare's last words on his deathbed were incontrovertible proof of that.

"When I'm in heaven, I will finally be able to ask Tricia who killed her," he'd said.

Grace watched her mother pick up a medium-sized

box and slide it on top of the pool table that Conner had covered with a sheet of wood so they could use it as a meeting table for the victims' families meetings.

No one played pool in the house after Tricia vanished, anyway. She and her father had loved the game. Grace had learned never to acknowledge that the table had once had a function other than being a place for the grieving and angry to meet once a week.

On the top and sides of the plastic box, Sissy had written, in block lettering, TED.

In the family they'd always been known as the Ted Letters. They were a collection of missives written by Ted Bundy while he was on death row in Florida. Grace had been led to believe that it was some kind of cat-and-mouse game that her mother employed to get Ted to tell her if he, in fact, had killed her daughter. There were other potential Bundy Girls and she would have liked to have closed the case on any of them. She wrote to Ted more than fifty times over a two-year period. He never failed to answer. And while she loathed Theodore Robert Bundy over any other human being in the world, she never told him so. Ted might have thought they were friends. On the morning after Ted's execution, a prison chaplain called her with a message from Ted.

"He wanted me to tell you thank you for the correspondence over the years. He also said that he wished he could have helped you find out who killed your daughter."

"He didn't say anything about Tricia? The other girls?"

The chaplain sucked in more air. He wasn't being impatient, just resigned to the fact that the monster that he had tried to lead toward salvation had done nothing to ease the minds of those who needed it the most. "No. Just that he wanted to wish you well. To wish you peace."

"Nothing?" she asked, pressing the question to the chaplain one more time.

"No, sorry. Ted said nothing specific."

"I have something specific for him. In case you pray for his soul," she said.

"I do and I will."

"Tell him I hope he rots in hell. Good-bye."

Sissy had hung up the phone feeling angry and numb at the same time. If Ted had the truth somewhere in his evil and diseased brain, it was possible that he was making one final attempt to show up the world that he was gentle and misunderstood. A feeble attempt, for sure. Deep down, Sissy was sure that the nation's most notorious serial killer had been responsible for Tricia's death.

It wasn't just wishful thinking, either. Her daughter fit the profile of Ted's so-called type—not only in her physical appearance, but her personality, too. Most of the girls whom he'd killed were the kind who could be called upon to be helpful. Tricia was without question the kind of girl to give a stranger directions, help an injured student with his books, provide money for an emergency phone call.

There was one more bit that played into the possibility that Ted had been Tricia's captor and murderer. After Bundy was apprehended, a detailed accounting had been made of every traceable moment of his life. Every receipt with his name on it, every phone call that he'd made or answered, was logged into a master file by

the King County Sheriff's Department, which had as-
sembled a major task force to catch the man who'd been
murdering pretty young women in Washington state.

On the day that Tricia disappeared, a credit card receipt from a gas station in Shelton was logged into evidence. Shelton was less than an hour away from the
Pacific Lutheran University campus. While it didn't
carry as much weight as a charge slip from Tacoma, it
was very, very close.

A clerk who'd sold Ted seven dollars of gas and a
Mars candy bar said that he hadn't been traveling alone.
It provided the third leg of the stool on which the possibility that Tricia O'Hare had been a Bundy victim
rested. The transcription between King County Detective Gerry Montrose and Super Seven Gas station attendant Lee Wong was the go-to piece of evidence for
Sissy and Conner O'Hare, and later, Grace. The choic-
est bit of the transcript appeared on the twentieth page
of the twenty-page document.

DETECTIVE MONTROSE: Did you actually talk to
    Mr. Bundy?
LEE WONG: Weird that you call him *mister*. Guy's a
    real dick. Yeah, I did talk to him. I remember how
    he waved me away when I approached his car. I
    went over to him, you know, to see if he wanted oil.
MONTROSE: Waved you away?
WONG: Yeah. Like I said earlier, he jumped out of his
    car to pump his own gas even though he was at the
    full-serve pump. The dick said, "I'll do it myself.
    No oil needed." Then he actually pushed me back
    from the car like he thought I was going to fight
    him for the dipstick or something.

MONTROSE: Was he aggressive with you?

WONG: No, and it doesn't matter if he was. I pack a thirty-eight. You practically have to, working at a gas station or mini-mart these days. Customers will kill you if they don't like the way you screw on their gas tank lid. And yes, in case you're going to ask it, I have a CW permit.

MONTROSE: Good. Did you get a look inside the car?

WONG: Not really. I mean, I sort of think he had someone sleeping in the backseat. I can't be sure because I didn't get a real look. You know, out of the corner of my eye when he was hassling me about the oil fill-up.

MONTROSE: So you didn't see anyone, really? Just more like an *impression*?

WONG: Yeah, an impression. That's a good way of looking at it. I got the impression of a girl sleeping in the back. Now . . .

MONTROSE: Now, what?

WONG: Now, I guess I wonder a little if it might have been a girl. Maybe a dead one. If she was dead, then I'm sorry for her family. If she was alive, well, I don't even want to think about how bad I feel. You know, how I could have maybe done something.

MONTROSE: You would have no way of knowing, either way. Don't beat yourself up.

WONG: Okay. Thanks.

[End of transcript.]

And then there were the letters. The Ted Letters.

"Can I take these, Mom?"

Sissy scrunched up her brow and thought a moment.

"Oh, I don't know. I loaned them to *The National En-quirer* and it took more than a year to get them back. Goodness, I was stupid. I should have photocopied them."

"I'm not the *Enquirer*. I'm your daughter. Besides, the *Enquirer* paid you. I seem to recall that you got ten thousand dollars for your group."

"I'm a tough negotiator," Sissy said, a slight smile on her face. "Yes, you can borrow them. Not sure what you're looking for, but yes, if you think it will help, take them."

Grace looked down at the letters. Her mother had tied them with a periwinkle blue ribbon, like some young girl might have done to a batch of love letters. These, however, were far from love letters. These were letters from the devil.

"I'll bring them back in a few days, Mom," Grace said as they walked back up the stairs, away from the pool table that wasn't really a pool table, from a war room that had never ceased to be the central location for a group of men and women bonded by the murders of their children.

"Don't forget to turn out the light," Sissy said.

"Lights out, Mom. Lights out." Grace turned down the switch and the room behind them went completely black.

CHAPTER 19

Sissy O'Hare wore a platinum locket around her neck. A gift from Conner the year after everything happened, the locket was heart-shaped and when opened revealed a photograph of the child she would mourn forever. Grace had never known a time when her mother hadn't worn the locket. She'd also seen her open it, look at it, and with tears streaming down her cheeks, snap it shut and close her eyes. Grace, though jealous of her murdered sister, always hoped that Sissy was remembering something beautiful about Tricia. As jealous as she could be—and as foolish as it was—she loved her mother. Some solace was needed. The locket was a symbol of loss, love, and the awareness that everything precious could be taken away by anyone, at any time. There was never any doubt that when her mother passed on, she would be buried with the locket around her neck. It was such a part of her.

Although Sissy's memories of her eldest daughter varied, as those of most mothers do, there were two etched in her brain so deeply that for the longest time others struggled to surface. The first was the day Tricia had gone missing.

It was the first of October. Vine and big leaf maples had started to turn the previous week, and the snap of autumn made all Pacific Northwesterners think of New England and what truly splendid fall colors might look like if the region had more deciduous trees. Pumpkins for carving and apple cider served in big, red mugs fueled the fantasy. Conner had gone to work, and Sissy and Tricia were alone at the breakfast table. Sissy had made her daughter's favorite—a toad-in-the-hole fried in so much butter that if the cholesterol police had been invented back then they surely would have handcuffed Sissy and taken her away to serve time for overindulging her daughter.

Tricia didn't have classes until noon, so mother and daughter used the extra time to talk about everything that interested them—Tricia had just switched her major to art history, the same degree that Sissy had earned at Western Washington State College in Bellingham. They talked about the merits of Cézanne over Van Gogh.

"Van enough already," Sissy had teased.

"I know you don't like his work, but you have to admit he had an ear for good painting," Tricia joked lamely.

Her mother laughed anyway. Tricia kissed her mother on the cheek, picked up her backpack, and went to wait along the curb for her friend, Carrie, to take her to work.

As she went out the door, Sissy made a comment about Tricia's attire, and that was it.

It wasn't until after 7 PM that day that Sissy began to worry about Tricia. She was usually home from class by five—and if she was going to be late, there was never a time that she didn't phone her or Conner to let them know.

"Carrie and I are going to hang out on campus for a while. There's a cute guy that she wants to accidentally meet," she'd said one time, quickly adding, "Again."

"How's that accidentally meeting someone actually working for her?" Sissy asked.

"You know Carrie, Mom. She's no quitter."

"That she's not," Sissy said.

Sissy and Conner ate dinner without her that night. Though later others would insist their observations were tainted by the eventual tragic outcome, the O'Hares were quite nervous. Scared even. They made the first of three calls to the Tacoma Police Department at 9 PM. Two others followed at ten, and then, finally at three minutes to midnight.

With each call the fear had been ratcheted up. With each connection, the cool voice of a desk officer answered in the same way.

"Girls these days do stuff like that. She probably ran off with a boy to a party or something."

"My daughter isn't like that," Conner said.

The officer sighed. "She's a girl, isn't she?"

"Yes," Conner said, bile rising in his throat over the insinuation that he didn't know Tricia very well. They were close. Extremely so.

"Trust me, she's like that. These are different times than when we grew up. Kids take more risks. They don't want to be like us."

"My daughter is a good girl."

"Wasn't implying that she's not. Besides, she's not missing until she hasn't been seen for twenty-four hours. That's the statute."

"All right," Conner said, knowing that anger over what he was hearing wouldn't advance his cause. Anger never did. It wasn't a pissing match over who was right, either. It was simply a plea from a father trying to get some help.

The third call was made by Sissy, who had been coached by her husband.

"My daughter Tricia O'Hare has been missing since Tuesday morning. I have no idea where she is."

That worked. The dispatcher sent a cop out to make a missing persons report.

And yet, resourcefulness and a little white lie aside, there was very little to be gained by getting the police to respond right away in the first place. The reason for that, Sissy would later tell her victims' families support group, was that "girls abducted by a madman have about a 10 percent chance of recovery."

"Ten percent?" asked Sheila Vinton, whose daughter, Shelley Ann, had been murdered by a stranger who'd held the fourteen-year-old hostage for seventeen days in a cabin in the foothills of Mount Rainier. "Not very good odds."

"No," Sissy said, folding her arms across her chest, a little unhappy with Sheila's response. She knew that Sheila had been accused of being a bad mother because she hadn't reported her daughter's disappearance for two days. The reason, she insisted, was that her ex-husband had visitation. He committed suicide, which Sheila only admitted to herself, gave her a sense of relief—a way to put all the blame where she could.

Not on herself.

All of that would come back to Sissy whenever she thought of her daughter and that terrible night she went

missing. *Ten percent! Ten percent! How could that be?*
What kind of police force do we have here in Tacoma?

She would later learn that the Tacoma Police Department was one of the best in the country, but law enforcement is seldom a match for someone who seeks to
do evil. Catching an abductor is a million times easier
than finding a killer *before* he kills.

Sissy, bleary-eyed but wired like Grand Coulee
Dam, stayed by the phone in the kitchen all night praying and hoping. A couple of neighbor ladies sat with
her for part of the evening, though they left when she
lay down on the sofa to pretend to get some rest. She
didn't eat, either. She couldn't. Something inside told
her that there would be no good outcome.

No 10 percent.

Conner got into his silver Mazda 626—the one in
which he'd taught Tricia to drive—and drove all over
the PLU campus, the streets of Tacoma, and even as far
as Lakewood, south of the city. He was armed with an
anguished look on his suddenly haggard face and Tricia's Stadium High School senior portrait, pulled from
the hallway in its honey oak frame. In time, most
Tacoma residents could identify the image of the girl,
either by name or just with a sad shake of recognition.

"Is that the girl who . . . ?"

Grace returned to her sister's case file, the one her
mother had made. Sissy had once told her that the collection had been made over time—whenever a detective on the case retired she'd make a play for more
access. Open investigation files were never shared with
victims' families or the press. Not anyone. There was

good reason for that, too, but Sissy had a way about her. She could be the freshly-baked-cookies-in-hand type with teary eyes and a need to know, or she could turn those eyes to glacial ice and criticize the cops for not doing their jobs. Whatever worked. It was always about that.

Grace supplemented the file, page by page, over time, with trips into the records room. She didn't care if the nosy records clerk turned her in. There were worse violations that could be written up about any number of the people who worked at the Tacoma Police Department—all the way to a famous case in which the chief of police sexually harassed and abused his staff and murdered his wife when he could no longer control her. That was huge, of course, and had been covered widely by the media. The other transgressions were smaller. One police officer routinely viewed porn on his laptop. One stole from a fallen officers' fund. Grace only took what she felt was rightly hers— her family's history.

She studied the witness statements. Her mother's was twice as long as her father's.

She was supposed to be here Saturday
morning, 10 am sharp. Like always. We were
going to get my hair done and go out to lunch. . . .

Grace could never remember a time when she and her mother had done that sort of mother/daughter activity. Their relationship, while close, was a bond formed because of tragedy, not because of her mother's loving nature. Certainly, her mother loved her; there was no doubt about that. The difference was they didn't do things like get their nails done or go to the salon for a color and style.

A student at the university, Melissa Reardon, twenty-two, had told detectives how she'd found Tricia's purse and keys—the first concrete proof that Tricia was not a runaway, but a victim of something terrible. Melissa's statement had been taken in her dorm room on Sunday, a full day after Tricia hadn't shown up for the appointment with her mom.

> My work study job requires me to pick up trash
> in the parking lot on Saturday mornings. The
> school doesn't want any parents to see any
> evidence of drinking and whatnot. I found
> Tricia's purse. I know it was Tricia's purse
> because when I opened it, it still had her wallet
> and ID. I took it to campus security for lost
> and found. . . .

Close friend Peggy Howell's interview was more innocuous, not really adding much to the investigation—though Peggy would tell her story over and over to the media. A female detective, who died in a tragic accident on Interstate 5 a year later, had interviewed Peggy at her mother's place on Ruby Street in Ruston.

> Tricia and I had talked about going to a party
> off campus that night, but when I saw her around
> 6 pm, she'd changed her mind. Said she had a
> stomachache. I think she was going off to see a
> boy or something. We were best friends, but I
> don't know who it was.

It was Phillip Marciano, a world literature professor at the university, whose statement put him in the hot seat during the early part of the investigation. His voice was recorded during three interviews at his office on campus and one, a very short one at his home near Browns Point, north Tacoma.

> She was one of my best students. We had
> coffee—nothing more—two or three times a
> week. I last saw her Friday afternoon after class.
> She'd been over at her parents' house, was upset
> with her mother or father about something. I
> don't know what. I think she wanted to talk a
> little, but I didn't think that boundary should be
> crossed.

As Grace well knew, Dr. Marciano had become the subject of considerable scrutiny for a couple of reasons. First, his wife, Jackie Marciano, had, only four weeks before Tricia disappeared, made a complaint to the university that he'd been involved with a student. Second, the class for which Tricia had been enrolled convened on Thursdays. *Not Friday*. Investigators put the screws to the professor, but he never faltered, never changed his story. Detectives were all but certain they'd caught him in a lie, but they were wrong. The reporting officer had made an error when transcribing his handwritten notes to the typed report. The professor had, in fact, said he'd last seen the missing young woman on Thursday. Further digging turned up another error in his favor—his wife had lied. She had been the one having an affair with a neighbor and thought by casting aspersions on her husband, she'd be in a better position to retain a larger chunk of his state pension.

The file was thick, at least two hundred pages by Grace's estimation. Page after page of false hope, innuendo, and empty promises of resolution stared up at her—and all the others who read the documents trying to tie Tricia's disappearance to a crime—Ted Bundy? Another killer? Kidnapping? It could have been any of those things.

Or none of them.

It was possible that she'd just vanished because she'd wanted to. Maybe she'd been sleeping with the professor? Maybe he'd told her that it was over? Maybe she'd been so hurt she'd just decided to go away and never be found. People did that. Not often. But they did. Parking attendants at airports all over the world find cars whose drivers never, ever return to claim them. They just get on a plane and leave.

Did Tricia do that?

Though her sister's case file had been started before she was born, Grace could see how some of her own files might turn into the kind of documents that she'd scattered about to study and read, long after the fact.

She knew she'd be judged by those who still loved their missing and who still ached for a resolution.

The families want an answer. Even the worst possible answer.

CHAPTER 20

Grace sat up in bed reading. Shane was doing the same thing. Neither gave a single thought to the idea that they might have sex or even talk about what had transpired throughout the day. They'd kept in touch with text messages already. Grace had come from dinner at her mother's and Shane from a long day dealing with bureau politics at the Seattle field office. Their bedroom window faced the water, and when an enormous freighter bound for Asia passed—an occurrence that usually stopped them from doing whatever they were doing to watch—it was barely noticed. Both were deeply immersed in what they were reading. Shane was editing an afterword that he'd written for a book by a forensic pathologist, a friend from his days before Grace. Grace, maybe rightly so, was normally skeptical about the pretty and accomplished author/friend, but that night she made no mention of her. No slightly sarcastic quip along the lines of "You're not bringing her into our bed, are you?"

Her tired eyes were glued to the letters her mother had loaned her. She'd seen some of them before when she was a teenager, but this time urgency drove her, not curiosity.

"Didn't realize that serial killers had such great penmanship," he said. "Thought they were more erratic in their letterforms. At least that's been my experience."

Grace looked over, a sly smile on her face.

"My mother wrote this," she said, barely looking in his direction.

"Your mother? You said these were Bundy Letters."

She nodded and started to fold the thin white paper with the florid cursive writing. "My mother is one smart woman. She actually copied the letters before she sent them so that she'd know exactly what Ted was responding to."

"That doesn't look like a photocopy," he said.

Grace nodded. "I know. Get this, my mom handcopied them. They didn't have access to a home copy machine back then and dad didn't want to spend ten cents a copy. Less money for the cause. Plus, I don't think he thought this writing to Ted Bundy would get them anywhere."

"It didn't," Shane said.

"It did," she argued.

"How? In what way? He never admitted anything."

"Not Tricia's murder. There were some other tidbits that he spread throughout the letters that actually did help close cases in Utah and Oregon."

"I didn't know that," he said, a little surprised by her disclosure. What else didn't he know? They'd talked about Tricia's disappearance hundreds of times.

Grace didn't say so out loud. She didn't need to. Somewhere in the letters of a crafty lunatic were the answers to what had happened to her sister . . . and just maybe what had happened to Kelsey, Lisa, and Emma.

A line her mother had written was both poignant and devastatingly true.

Sometimes, Ted, I think all of us are products of the good and bad done to us as children. Maybe that's your story, too.

The other side of murder, the side from which the darkness was born, is not the need for some measure of sympathy. While most people blamed the mother, the father, the environment from which the murder emerged, Grace always considered homicidal tendencies to be generational. The road that Ted Bundy had been on when he killed his first victim had been one that was paved with the messy combination of evil and mental illness that his parents and *their* parents likely had unwittingly laid down before Ted was a sorry glare in his father's eyes. Ted's own grandmother had reportedly been treated for depression with electroshock therapy. She was also an agoraphobic, refusing to leave the safe confines of the family home. And while the confusion of his paternity would certainly traumatize any young person, Ted had exhibited a pathology and propensity for violence long before that issue emerged.

A relative, a teenage aunt, told the story of how she'd stirred from an afternoon nap to find Ted, only three, smiling at her in that way that really isn't a smile, but an acknowledgment of something he'd done—or intended to do.

All around her were kitchen knives.

No one knows for sure why Louise left Philadelphia

with five-year-old Teddy in 1951, although it is easy to guess. Shame and abuse had likely reached a level she could no longer endure. Louise needed a new life. She didn't need to be the woman with the little boy who never knew his father. She could not have gone a greater distance than Tacoma, and that probably figured into her thinking, too. When she met Johnnie Bundy, a cook for a local hospital, he was everything she'd ever wanted. A Steady Eddie. A man who kept his promises. Decent with a capital D.

"Ted was grandiose even as a kid. He must have hated having a dad who was a hospital cook, not an airline pilot," Grace said while Shane shifted his weight on the mattress and doubled up the pillow under his head.

"Or a lawyer," Shane said.

"Right, one of those glamour jobs that he could brag about with the other boys. His dad worked in a hospital cafeteria. Even in working-class Tacoma that had to have been at the lower end of things," she said.

"In a way, he always thought he was better than the Bundys," Shane said. "He thought his stepfather was boring, didn't make enough money, and wasn't too smart."

"Ted wanted to be better than them. Johnnie Bundy wasn't sophisticated. He was just the quintessential average Joe, but his averageness was his goodness. He married Louise and adopted her son and raised him as his own."

Shane shook his head. "He didn't know what he was getting into."

"No one could have seen what was coming." Grace reached over and turned off the bedside light.

* * *

Tacoma is called Grit City, and it's a nickname that fit like a grimy garden glove. And while there are stately mansions in the north end—places that were the homes of the lumber barons like the Weyerhaeusers—Ted's world as a boy and a teen was decidedly more prosaic. Johnnie Bundy's living was modest and their home, clothing, and cars reflected that. Ted's true young adulthood is bit of a mystery. He'd tell people that he was addicted to magazines of murder and bondage, pornography with the most disgusting and vile images of evil done to women for the gratification of a small segment of the male audience. He immersed himself in true-crime documentaries, reveling in the depictions of lifeless, bloodied, female bodies.

And then, like a switch, he'd put on the mask and deny it all.

Ted was a teenager of the night, a junior night stalker. He'd steal beer, guzzle it down, and then start the walk. He'd follow the sliver of light from parted curtains and press up close to get a glimpse of a girl or woman in a state of undress. A voyeur, a peeper, whatever it was that Ted Bundy was before he became a killer, he perfected it.

A hunter. That was Ted.

Among Grace's mother's files was a photocopy of a letter that Ted had written to a television producer who had promised "to set the record straight" and tell the true story of Theodore Robert Bundy. In this missive, Ted reflected on his teenage years at Woodrow Wilson High.

*You will put up any kind of piece of garbage that
you want to and then try to justify it with some
quick cutaways to people who really didn't know
me at all. That's mostly everyone. I just wasn't a
joiner. I didn't want to be part of the in crowd. I
didn't think that there really was an in crowd at
that second-rate high school anyway. I had more
going for me. So, yeah, I understand that you
will do what you do. I did the minimum to just
get through high school. Probably, Dan* [the
producer], *you were a lot like me. Most people
are. I know you are asking me to be introspective
and I guess there is one thing that I could give
you in that regards. I honestly didn't see the
point in having any of those people as friends.
Or why I'd even want to?*

peace, Ted

It was after two in the morning, when Grace's phone
rang on the bedside table of the Alexanders' Salmon
Beach house. Shane stirred, but didn't awaken completely. Among the many things they had in common,
were nighttime calls from dispatchers, special agents
in charge, partners, anyone who carried a badge and
worked a case. At least a few times a month either's
phone would ring at this hour. This time it was her turn.
Grace dropped her feet into her perfectly positioned
slippers and grabbed the pink terry robe she left slung
over a chair and started for the hallway.

It was Paul.

"What is it?" she asked, in a whisper.

"We found Emma or Kelsey, or maybe someone else."

Grace had expected to hear this, but even as she did, it sickened her.

"Where?" she asked.

Some dogs barked; wherever he was calling from, the canine unit was there.

"The other side of the river," Paul said. "Where that guy was fishing."

"What?"

"Right. I'm there now. You want to come down."

"Wouldn't miss it for the world. Be there in twenty."

"Make it twenty-five. Stop for coffee. Could use some out here. Colder than crap."

The river's surface was striated and black, like wide-wale corduroy stretched between the banks on either side. Nine police and sheriffs' units, dogs, and personnel were congregated there. Paul's ex-wife, Lynnette Bateman, was there, too. Watching the two interact was usually fun, but it wasn't going to be just then. Not with a dead teenager on the edges of the Puyallup.

"Over there," Sergeant Lynnette Bateman said. "Detective Bateman is with the medical examiner."

Grace nodded and went toward the lights that pierced the starry sky like a supermarket's grand opening.

Paul thanked her for the coffee and took a swallow before he spoke. "Pretty sure it's Kelsey," he said. "Tech says left hand is missing."

"Just the left hand?"

He nodded and drank some more.

"She wasn't completely dismembered like Lisa?"

"Guess not."

"What else?"

"They think she might have been frozen. She's in pretty good condition. You know, considering how long she's been dead. No decomp. The bastard."

"So you think it's a man who did this?" Grace said.

Paul pulled off the top of his Styrofoam cup so he could guzzle the coffee more quickly. He was a man in dire need. "You got me," he said. "No more PC. Only a seriously messed-up maniac of a dude would do this to a little girl."

Grace nodded. "Who found her?"

"Transient over there," he said, raising a shoulder to indicate a figure with short dark hair sitting on the bumper of a cruiser.

"Talk to him?" she asked.

Paul allowed a smile to come to his face. "It's a *she*."

"Right."

"She said she was looking for cans for recycling along the river and, well, found something I doubt she'll ever forget. I know I won't."

"Techs process her?"

"Yeah. She had this on her." He held up a T-shirt inside a plastic bag.

Grace pressed her fingertips to the plastic to read what was printed on it.

Save the Sound

"She said she found it near the body, but not *on* it. She said she actually found it first, before the body."

"Where?"

"Almost on the road." Paul suddenly turned his attention to the coroner's assistant, who was preparing a gurney and a body bag to transport Kelsey's remains to the Pierce County Medical Examiner's Office for autopsy. "Hold on! My partner needs to see the vic."

The men backed off and Grace followed Paul over to where the body was lying.

It was Kelsey Caldwell, all right. No need for forensics to verify it, though the techs would do just that during the autopsy. Her eyes were open staring up at the stars; her long dark hair shimmered as if she'd been placed there after a salon blow dry. And while she was nude, her most intimate parts had been covered by bunches of grass.

"The transient did that," Paul said, looking back over at the woman sitting on the cruiser's bumper. "She said she didn't think it was right to leave that girl naked like that."

The scene had been compromised, which was frustrating, but Grace understood the sentiments, too. Nothing about what had happened to the seventeen-year-old was right at all.

"Somebody's going to have to call the father," she said. "This will be in the papers faster than you guzzled that coffee."

CHAPTER 21

Emma Rose was no longer consumed by fear. She was beyond that. She hadn't been raped. And as far as she knew she hadn't been murdered. It was possible that she had been murdered, of course, and that she'd done something so terrible that she'd been assigned to a space in purgatory. She dismissed that after the first two hours of her captivity. She was not exactly sure how long she'd been held in that dark place, a mattress on the floor, a bucket to use for her toilet. Her captor had provided copies of *People* magazine, a reading light, and a green, unbearably scratchy army blanket. She'd been fed a cheese sandwich—American cheese, which she thought was completely disgusting—and Sam's Club diet cola.

It surprised her that she even thought that the American cheese was terrible, considering that it really was the least of her most pressing concerns. She was also surprised that she'd gotten used to the bucket so soon. Since there was no window, she had no idea what day it was, how many days had passed.

And then there was the matter of her captor. He came to her with only a single whispered utterance—

"Stay back or I'll fill your apartment with poisonous gas and you'll be dead in five seconds."

Apartment? That hole? An apartment?

Calling it that scared Emma a little. If that was his idea of an apartment, he was even more whacked than she might have thought. Besides being a girl snatcher. And if he was calling it an apartment, did that mean she was going to be held there forever?

"Did you contact my mom?"

No answer.

"Hey, I want to go home," she said, trying not to cry.

Silence.

"I know you are listening. I want to know what you're going to do to me. I mean, I want you to let me go home. I haven't seen you. I don't even know what it is that you want from me. Please. Call my mom!"

Like all of the times she tried to start a conversation with him, whoever he was, he ignored her. She could hear his breathing, or at least she thought it was his breathing. A small fan had been installed in the "apartment" presumably to provide fresh air intake. It was on all the time, whirring and spinning.

Emma waited, thinking it all out. She considered that maybe a more submissive approach might be more to the creeper's liking.

"Why won't you talk to me?" she asked, sitting on the edge of the mattress. "I wish you would say something. I'm a very good listener. My teachers always said that I had excellent listening skills."

Nothing.

Emma pushed on. She was not a quitter.

"I wonder if you're as lonely as I am. I know you're

smart and talented. You made this really nice apartment," she said, nearly choking on the phrase. "Please, sir, talk to me."

Sir, she thought, was a nice touch.

And still nothing.

Emma got up and walked to the entrance to the apartment. Her captor had fashioned some kind of a narrow horizontal hatch on the door. It was only wide enough for a soda can turned on its side.

"Please," she said, trying to remain as calm as she could. Freaking out, Emma believed, might make whoever it was breathing on the other side of the wall see that she wasn't a threat.

For a second, when she heard the twisting of the lock on the other side of the hatch, she thought she was finally getting somewhere.

The hatch opened and the tray pushed forth.

Emma looked down at a *People* magazine with Selena Gomez on the cover. It was an article about some troubles the young actress had overcome recently. Emma took the magazine and went to her mattress. She twisted the gooseneck of the reading lamp and slumped against the army blanket.

God, Emma thought as she fanned open the magazine, *this girl thinks she has problems. I'm probably going to be raped and murdered.*

As she read, her mind wandered all over the place. She tried as hard as she could to remember exactly what she'd been doing before she blacked out. She remembered being at Starbucks and getting ready to close for the night. She remembered how she and Oliver had raged about the customers who had the nerve to bring their own food in to the coffee place that they now used as home offices. One guy had even had the gall to bring a thermos of coffee from home.

"It's Starbucks coffee," the young man said. "What's the big deal if I buy it here or at Safeway? You're still getting the profits."

She remembered leaving Starbucks and walking toward the bus stop. After that, *nothing*. Her memory was a complete void. She felt the back of her head. The bump where she surmised she'd been struck had shrunk by then. The touch of her hand made her wince. Her long dark hair was getting tangled, the back strands turning into a white girl's bad idea of dreads. When she adjusted the lamp, Emma noticed the shade's interior was lined with reflective silver.

It was hard to see her face with the bulb glowing right in her eyes. But in a fleeting instance she saw what she looked like just then.

Around her eyes were dark circles. Emma gasped. She'd seen that kind of bruising around a woman's eyes before when a neighbor had been battered by her husband.

"What did you do to me?" she asked softly, sure that the creeper couldn't hear her above the omnipresent din of the running air intake fan. A tear fell down onto Selena Gomez's pretty face. Emma refused to cry out. If she'd had thought for one moment that she had a chance to get out of there, she knew it was wishful thinking.

No one who captures a girl, beats her, and traps her in a so-called apartment ever lets her go.

CHAPTER 22

The next day, Olympic Security, the company with the contract to monitor the parking lot—and to tow cars that had stayed too long—gave up the video without so much as a whisper that they needed a subpoena in order to do so.

"Quality is the shits," said the office manager, a big fat guy whose butt seemed permanently affixed to an office chair on wheels.

"That's all right," Grace said, as she took a small box of tapes. "We're used to that."

She'd arrived alone. Paul was back in the office "working," whatever that meant. She wasn't so sure.

"You want to watch it here? I have a TV in the back room," the manager said, pushing off in his chair like a hermit crab toward the doorway.

"No. No thanks. We'll watch it back at the office."

Grace got in her car and started to drive, the box of small videotapes on the seat next to her. It really was a long shot, of course, but she hoped that the feed would show whatever had happened to the young woman. What had caused her to leave her purse behind? Had there been a struggle? Had she fought for her life only to succumb to someone stronger, more powerful than she was?

Oliver Angstrom was a complete weirdo, but the world was full of those types. Being weird was often an affectation. Like nipple rings on some accountant. That might only show when he took off his jacket, just a hint. Just something to get one noticed. More often than not, weirdoes simply ended up living benign, unremarkable, lives. Few were abductors or criminals, though they might have looked the part. Grace knew that it was the average guy or gal who was the biggest threat. They lived among everyone, their averageness a mask.

Weirdos like Oliver were too, too obvious in their quest for perpetual attention. They were on everyone's radar.

Oliver was just some lame kid with a crush. He could not have butchered two girls and dumped them by the river.

Or could he? Ted killed his first victim as a teenager.

Grace and Paul sequestered themselves in a conference room and fed the videotape into the player. It was not lost on either one of them that video, like other technology, was changing. Most of the video feeds collected for evidence now had been handed over on thumb drives and disks. This was old school, like a lot of Tacoma was. The black-and-white images were not HD quality. They looked nearly as bad as the video that one of the blues had brought to show her sonogram.

"Right there!" she'd said. "See that? It's a boy!"

Paul had turned to Grace and lowered his head. "You see anything?" he asked.

She shook her head and whispered back. "Looks like a girl to me."

Paul grinned. "Hope she doesn't name the baby Rocky or something."

Grace smiled back. There were times when she and Paul really got each other. Not often, but enough to ensure that they had each other's backs. When he and his wife split up, it was easy for Grace to choose whose side to be on. Paul could be a doofus, but he was real at least part of the time. His wife? Not so much. She was all about getting ahead.

Thankfully the parking lot videotape had a counter that actually had been reset to reflect the correct time of day when the images were recorded.

"This almost never happens," Grace said. "Remember that time when we watched eighteen hours of tape because they'd failed to reset the counter?"

"Don't remind me," Paul said. "I about busted a nut when that idiot admitted that he was too lazy to change the time stamp and didn't tell us because he didn't want to ruin his chances for the employee of the month prize."

"Oh yeah," Grace said. "I remember that. That was the worst." Grace fast-forwarded the video to 9 PM.

"Closing time," Paul said. "Let's settle in for some more exciting police work."

Grace pushed a bottle of water toward her partner and he sucked it down like it was oxygen.

"Thanks. Must have eaten a pound of salt today."

"Stay away from the chips," she said. "You'll live longer."

"You my mother now?"

"No," she said. "Not your wife, either. You need to pull yourself together. You shouldn't be letting yourself go." She looked over at his gut, which hung over his belt buckle like a sagging car bumper.

Paul ignored her gaze.

"Sylvia said that they close at nine," she said, "but it takes the crew about forty minutes or so to clean up."

"Right," Paul said, getting up to dim the lights, his eyes on the photos of the missing Tacoma girls. "Movie time."

The first few minutes were run-of-the-mill parking lot scenes. Busier than either detective might have guessed, but considering that the mall closed around that same time it should not have been much of a mystery.

"God, how many people take the bus these days?" Paul asked, his glasses on and his eyes scrutinizing the plasma screen set up for PowerPoint presentations and the projection of evidence photos. "I've never seen so many people in uniform."

He was indicating all of the food service workers, dressed like they'd come from behind the Epcot attraction showcasing the world's cuisines.

They sat in silence for a few minutes as the cars left, the bus pulled away, and there was no sign of Emma Rose.

"Did we miss her?" Paul asked.

Grace noted the time. 9:45.

"Maybe. Let's give it another minute."

Just as she was about to press the rewind button, Emma Rose came into view. Even in the grainy eye of the camera, one could see that she was a pretty girl. Long dark hair, balanced facial features, a lithe figure.

"She's making a beeline for the bus stop," Paul said.

"Wait a sec," Grace said, now moving closer to the screen.

Emma Rose stopped and turned. She was saying something to someone out of view of the camera.

"She doesn't look agitated."

"Someone she knows?" Paul asked.

"Oliver?"

He nodded.

A second later Emma walked out of the reach of the camera's unblinking eye.

CHAPTER 23

No one who lived in the Northwest during 1974's summer of terror could ever forget the parade of missing girls whose photographs appeared on the front pages of all the newspapers in Washington. Before that summer, the people of Washington had assumed that killers did their evil for a purpose. *To get money? To cover up another crime?* Before that time, people had thought that victims carried some of the blame for their demise. They'd used drugs. They were prostitutes. The idea that a white college or high school girl could be stalked and murdered was beyond the comprehension of really anyone outside a psychology classroom or a police detective's office.

The first of the murdered girls had disappeared from her apartment in Seattle. She was young, pretty. She had long hair parted in the middle. While she was the first of the known victims, at least seven more followed.

Daughters and sisters, just like Tricia, disappeared. Their screams were never heard. One by one. Girl by girl. Gone.

* * *

It was a long drive, better than an hour from Tacoma to Lake Sammamish State Park near Issaquah. Long after Ted Bundy was named as the suspect for the string of murders throughout the western United States, Sissy drove Grace out there. It was a field trip of sorts—the kind of excursion that they embarked on more often than those more typical of mother and daughters. Sure, they'd gone to movies together. They went ice skating at Sprinker in Spanaway. They even went to a mother/daughter fashion show at the PLU campus. Many of their trips together, however, held a more specific purpose.

Sissy had to know what happened to Tricia. Wondering and waiting would never suffice.

They parked in the lot, their car facing the blue waters of the lake that had been the site of Ted's most notorious and brazen kills. He'd abducted two young women, one after another, from the park in the middle of a hot July day in 1974.

Sissy led her daughter to a picnic table near the restrooms. A couple of kids played horseshoes a few yards away. A teenage boy yelled at his mother for telling him what to do. A radio played an old Beatles song. The weather wasn't particularly great that day, but it didn't matter to Sissy. She hadn't brought Grace there for that kind of an outing.

"I came here with your father after we heard the news about Ted being arrested. I didn't know where your sister was," she said, looking up at the Cascade foothills behind them, "but I felt like we should honor the girls who came from here."

Grace didn't say anything. Her mother didn't need

her to respond. It was more about Sissy getting out the words and just letting them kick around in the wind until she was finished. It wasn't that she didn't value Grace's input; it was that the endless loop of her obsession had no place for another person. There was no pause. Just a stream.

"He told the girls that he needed help. And they helped him. They had been raised by loving and kind parents. It was their kindness that attracted him to them. I know that. I know that as much as I've ever known anything. Kindness can be a weakness, Grace. Please listen to me. Don't get me wrong. I don't want you to be harsh, uncaring. Not at all. I don't want you to be indifferent to the needs of others. I just don't want you to put anyone else above yourself."

Grace nodded.

"Okay, I guess I understand," she said.

When the words slipped from her lips they felt hollow. Deep down she knew that her mom did want her to put someone else above herself. *Tricia*. Her whole life was about her sister.

Sissy had brought a bag of stale bread and they walked to the shore where a small flock of mallards and one big white duck congregated. Sissy handed Grace a piece of bread.

"Break off small bits. You don't want to choke them." She stopped a moment and looked out at a water-skier zipping by a couple hundred yards away.

Grace met her mother's gaze and she did what she'd been doing too much of lately—she read into it what her mom might really be thinking.

Did Ted choke Tricia?

Were the girls who disappeared from the park in

1974 aware of their fate or were they knocked uncon-
scious?

Did they enjoy the summer sun on their faces like
the water-skier that day?

Did they know their families had never, would never,
forget them?

When Grace O'Hare was fourteen, her parents took
her on a car trip to Utah. Coming from Washington
State, where the landscape was dipped in green and
splattered in blue, Utah's vast vistas of orange, red, and
salmon seemed completely otherworldly. The landscape itself suggested Mars. They'd played road games
along the way—all but Slug Bug, because of the VW's
connection to Bundy. The stayed in motels with swimming pools, and one in Sandy that had a Jacuzzi—
Grace's first time in a tub of hot oscillating water.

"We need to get one of these," she told her mother.

"If we don't get to Granger tomorrow, we'll all be in
hot water," her father said, with a laugh at his own pun.

Grace climbed out of the water and took one, then
two of the thin white towels supplied by the Best Western. "What's in Granger?"

"Meeting an old friend," Sissy said.

"What old friend? Someone I know, too?"

Grace's dad got up and went toward the gate around
the pool and Jacuzzi.

"Someone who feels as we do about Ted, honey,"
Sissy said.

Grace didn't ask anything more. In fact, she felt de-
flated. The tone in her mother's voice was familiar. It
was if her vocal cords tightened and airflow was

restricted. She spoke through lips held tautly over her teeth. Grace knew then that there would be no time in their lives in which her parents' obsession would take a backseat to anything else. They were in a pinball game and every bumper they touched was the serial killer from Tacoma.

There was no getting away from Ted.

In August of 1975, after he'd murdered in the Pacific Northwest and moved on to kill in Colorado and Utah, Ted was arrested for the first time. It was the first instance that anyone back home in Seattle and Tacoma knew that the handsome stranger who called himself Ted was, in fact, named Ted. He drove a VW bug, too. That also fit what witnesses had told investigators that summer day at Lake Sammamish when two had disappeared. "Ted" had had his arm in a sling and asked several young women to help him retrieve his small sailboat from his car. One girl had refused because she'd seen that there was no boat and she didn't feel comfortable getting in his car to "drive up to his parents' house" to retrieve it. Two girls, whose only crime was the compassion they showed a man who asked for help, had agreed.

Their bodies were found on a mountain slope only four miles from the last place they'd been seen alive.

The detective who caught Ted in Granger had only done so after Ted refused to stop for a traffic violation.

Sissy started corresponding with Caswell Moriarty in 1977. She didn't like to spend money on long-distance calls, but she never failed in having a book of stamps at the ready. She'd written to others over the years, too, but this man was a true believer in her cause. She needed that. She needed her husband and daughter to see it, too.

"See, I'm not the only one who knows that Ted killed Tricia," she said more than one time when she needed to rally the flagging troops.

Caswell, or Cass, as his friends called him, was a pint-sized man with a walrus moustache and a swirl of molasses-colored hair. He'd taken medical retirement from the Utah Highway Patrol after blowing out his kneecap in pursuit of a jail escapee.

"The double irony here," he said when letting the O'Hares inside his tidy house on the edge of Granger, "was that scumbag's name was Ed Dundee. Welcome to my life."

While her parents sat in the living room, Grace played with Cass's dog, a small shivery creature named Taco.

"I took the file from the office. Made you a copy," Cass said. "Figured you'd get more use out of it now than the authorities here. Florida's got dibs on him. The SOB couldn't have picked a better state to kill in, if you want the ultimate justice, that is."

Sissy nodded, her eyes riveted to the eight-by-ten glossy black-and-white photograph of the objects Cass had found in the car.

"What did he say that ski mask was all about?" Sissy asked.

Cass shrugged and rolled his eyes upward. "He was a big-time skier, that's what. Funny thing, no skis or poles in the car."

They all looked down at the list, and the photograph that depicted each item in Ted's arsenal.

"Handcuffs? What about those?" Grace's father asked. Conner usually let Sissy do the talking, like she was the lead investigator and he was merely there to keep the ball rolling in the event that there was a slack moment.

"Dumpster diving. Yeah, that was his brilliant answer on that one. You know everyone talks about how smart he is, I'm not so convinced. I mean, think about it, who tosses handcuffs into the trash? Those things cost beaucoup bucks."

And of course the next items, those were the ones that would send anyone with a scintilla of compassion into a panic at the thought of how they'd been used—a crowbar and an icepick.

"His depravity knew no bounds," Sissy said. "I used to pray that he just strangled Tricia and killed her that way. I hoped that she could stare into his eyes and let him know that she was good, and he was a soulless piece of garbage. He didn't do that, did he, Cass?"

Cass didn't answer right away. He was one of the world's foremost experts on Bundy and his crimes. Others proclaimed that designation, even kind of fought for it, as if there were some kind of honor in knowing evil better than anyone else. But he knew. He knew beyond a shadow of a doubt that Ted's violence was never measured slowly. It was always a deluge.

"Sissy," he said, "you've always known the answer. Don't think about that. Don't let what he did to your little girl live on like that. She's at peace. It doesn't matter how she got there."

"It does to me," Grace said, putting Taco down and stepping toward her mother and father. "I would like him to suffer more than my sister did. In order to do that, we have to find out what it was that he did to her."

Cass nodded. "I understand, Grace. I really do. But there is no way someone without a conscience can be made to suffer. You have to be among the human race to feel, and Ted Bundy was one of those aberrations that come along every hundred thousand births. Maybe a million. He looked human, I'll give him that. I'll give him that some of the ladies thought he was easy on the eyes. He acted like he was. But really, it was an act. He was mimicking what others do."

"Honey," Sissy said, looking at her daughter, "I love you. I know that you understand."

Sissy squeezed Grace's hand and looked over at her husband.

It was a proud, proud moment.

CHAPTER 24

"**Y**ou've found Emma, haven't you? She's dead, isn't she? My baby's dead!"

Grace Alexander took a step toward the door that had swung open before she could even knock. She put her hand up and shook her head.

"No. No, Ms. Rose, we haven't found her."

"I saw the paper today," she said, holding up a copy of the *News Tribune*, its headline running across the top of the page:

SECOND GIRL FOUND BY PUYALLUP RIVER

"It isn't Emma," Grace said. "I promise."

A look of relief came over Diana Rose. She opened the door wider, and let the detectives inside. She indicated a pair of chairs across from a black sofa draped with an orange afghan—a look that gave the North End Craftsman home a distinct Halloween vibe. On the table next to the sofa was a photograph of Emma and her sister, Tracy. The two of them posed beaming in a mountain meadow—probably Mount Rainier, Grace guessed noticing the ocean wave of purple lupine behind them. It was a cruel reminder of what had already been stolen from that particular family.

And what might have been taken when Emma Rose vanished from the Starbucks at the Lakewood Towne Center.

Tracy and her father had been killed in a car accident coming off the Nalley Valley viaduct four summers before.

Grace never could rationalize why some families were a lightning rod for tragedy. It wasn't that people were cursed with bad luck. She didn't think that, no, not at all. And yet, there was something about the way cosmic forces conspired to pile on tragedy. It was more than someone being on the track to disaster; it was like the skids were greased and it was harder and harder to avoid calamity. It had nothing to do with socioeconomic status. The Roses were upper middle class. Arthur Rose had had a good-paying job. Tracy had been a straight-A student at Stadium High School. Father and daughter had been coming home from Spanaway. Tracy had been attending orientation at Pacific Lutheran University, where she'd intended to enroll the next fall.

They were T-boned by a drunk driver and the downward spiral, a hurricane of bad luck and disaster, sucked the life and the joy from what had once seemed the perfect life. Perfect girls. Perfect husband. Perfect house. Everything anyone would have wanted. And now, all that was left of it was the perfect house.

"Ms. Rose," Grace said, close enough to the trembling mother to touch her, but feeling reluctant to do so. "We haven't found Emma, but we found this and we need you to identify it."

Grace looked over at Paul and he handed her a

plastic bag. It was plain its contents were familiar to the missing girl's mother. It was a powder-blue T-shirt with faded graphics depicting a circle of seven dolphins swirling around SAVE THE SOUND logo.

"That's Tracy's," Diana said, reaching for it, feeling the crinkling plastic as she massaged the garment through its protective covering.

"You mean Emma's?" Paul asked.

Grace shot him a look, one that she hoped conveyed that he'd promised that she could run the investigation insofar as victims' families were concerned.

"It was Tracy's. She bought it the year before she and my husband were killed in the accident. Emma wore it. Often. It was kind of her way of staying close to her sister," she said, moving her gaze from the detectives to the photograph of the sisters on Mount Rainier. "They both loved the mountains and water. They were close."

Grace didn't say so right then, probably because Paul was incapable of understanding just what that might feel like. She easily could.

My sister is gone, too.

Grace gently pulled the bagged and tagged garment from the fingers of the grieving and anxious mother. "You said she was wearing a white blouse when she went to work. Was she wearing this, too?"

Diana snapped her attention back to the detectives, and shook her head. She buried her face in her hands and rubbed her temples.

"I can't be sure," she said, her words now coated in the distinct aguish of a mother who doesn't know where her child is. "I mean, I'm sure that the T-shirt was hers, was Tracy's. Where did you find it?"

Grace set the bag on her lap. "Some blues found it a quarter mile from the latte stand," she said.

Diana looked confused. "Blues?"

"Sorry," Grace said. "Patrol officers."

Diana didn't ask the question that both detectives were sure she was thinking. If her daughter was wearing a blouse with the blue T-shirt as an extra layer underneath, how was it that the T-shirt was no longer on her body? Had she taken it off? Or had someone else?

"May we see her room?"

"You think someone took her, don't you?"

"We don't know what happened, Ms. Rose," Grace said.

"She's dead, isn't she?"

It was obvious it was hard for Ms. Rose to let that phrase pass her lips, but she managed. It was almost like she was practicing. *Preparing*. Not wanting it to be true, but given the way her life had been going for the past two years, it was so sadly possible.

"Can we see her room?" Paul asked.

Diana got up and the detectives followed.

Emma's bedroom was at the top of the stairs. It was painted a peachy pink, a color that was somewhere between a little girl's dream hue and a more sophisticated young woman's idea of what was pretty. The room had a large bay window that overlooked the garden with just a hint of a view of Commencement Bay. The bed was an antique, painted white iron with small shabby-chic flecks of the metal showing. On the right side of the headboard someone had tied streamers of blue and white ribbons. Grace wondered if Emma had been a bridesmaid earlier that spring.

"Do you want me to leave?" Diana asked.

"Whatever makes you the most comfortable," Paul said.

"You speak," the mother said.

"When she lets me," he said, looking over at Grace, who had moved to the desk across from the bed. She was either engrossed in something or pretending not to hear. Diana left the room.

"What are you looking for, exactly?" he asked.

Grace turned over some cards and papers on the desk, but didn't look up.

"If we're going to find her, we need to *know* her. And if . . ." She hesitated and looked over at her partner, making sure that the mother was gone. ". . . and if she's the victim of an abduction of some kind we will need to know why she was picked up."

"If she was."

"Right. *If*." She held out a card. On the front was a photograph of a kitten sniffing a white rose.

"Cute," Paul said, though he really didn't think so.

"Ms. Rose?" she called out. A beat later, Diana Rose stood in the doorway. Her red eyes gave her away. She'd been crying quietly in the hallway.

"Did you find something?"

"Who is Alex?"

"Her boyfriend. They only dated a few months. She broke it off with him."

"Why was that?"

"I don't know. I think she was tired of being tied down. She wanted to go out with other guys. Have fun.

You know, you remember when you were a teenager, don't you?"

Grace nodded. "Barely. But yes, I do. Why did she keep this card if she was so over him?"

Diana took the card and looked at it. She shook her head. "I've never seen this before. Where did you get it?"

"Just here." Grace pointed to the desk.

"May I see it?" Diana said, not really waiting. She took the card and her eyes met the detective's. "You don't think he had anything to do with her disappearance, do you?"

"I don't know. We'll check it out. What is Alex's last name? And do you know where he lives?"

"Morton. He lives a few blocks over."

"Palmer Morton's son?" Paul asked.

She nodded. "Yeah, that's the one."

"*The* Palmer Morton?" Grace asked, though she knew by the way the mother and her partner were acting that it had to be the very same. Everyone in Tacoma knew Palmer Morton. He owned about a third of the downtown retail core, including a steak house named Morton's. He'd sued the famous Morton's chain and won a provision that there would be no Morton's steak house in Tacoma that wasn't his. Chicago. New York. L.A. But not in Tacoma.

Palmer Morton was that kind of a guy. Both detectives knew his son's reputation, too. He'd been picked up for shoplifting at the Tacoma Mall, a case that had been conveniently dropped. Something about a file being lost, though no one in the department thought it was anything other than a favor called in by a fellow who knew something about favors.

Before they got to the car, Grace turned to Paul.

"You know what it means?" she asked.

"That Morton kid is a creep?"

"Maybe. But not that. The T-shirt was Emma's. That means whoever killed Kelsey has Emma. Whoever killed Lisa killed Kelsey. The girls are linked. There's no doubt."

And there was no doubt that they didn't have much time.

Tricia O'Hare's yearbook photograph from her senior year at Stadium High stared up from atop the papers Grace had spread out on the kitchen table overlooking the water off the front of the house on Salmon Beach. Her sister's photograph. She could so very easily draw that exact image from memory. From the way her sister's long hair rested just past her right shoulder, the left side pushed back. The leotard top Tricia wore offered a classic and elegant neckline. The dove necklace, the only real adornment. Her ears had been pierced after the photo was taken. Conner O'Hare wouldn't let his daughter get them done until her eighteenth birthday. Grace could see herself in her sister's eyes, her mother's eyes, looking up at her in a serene gaze that could never have hinted what was to come. The image was in color, but over time the photograph had taken on a kind of pinky and orange cast, which only served to make Tricia seem even further away.

She was familiar, but there was no doubt she was from another time, another era.

If Tricia hadn't vanished, Grace knew without an iota of doubt that she would not be sitting there. She wouldn't exist at all. She loved her life. Her mother. Her husband. Yet gratitude for her very existence wasn't in the offing. Anger was. She'd lived in the shadow of a phantom. Two of them, in fact. Her sister and the deliberate stranger.

She flipped over the photograph to vanquish it from her thoughts just then, to put Tricia out of her mind.

As if.

The coffeepot beeped and she poured herself another cup. The day hadn't even started, but it already felt so heavy. She looked at the photo of Ted Bundy that her mother had taped to the outside of one of the folders. Sissy had used a thick red pen to write the words: *HE TOOK HER.*

If he did, the answers were there somewhere in the twisted story of the killer from down the street. She knew his story, but still she reread the pages her mother had written.

After a period of rootless travel, Ted returned to the University of Washington and focused his studies on psychology in 1970. He'd found his niche, and his grades reflected it. It was as if there was something in those classes that pushed him to dig in deep and actually do the work. He didn't skate on his handsome face, facile tongue. Later, in a moment of introspection, Ted would tell a confidant that he didn't know exactly what drew him to that area of study—or what it was that sucked him into it so deeply.

"It wasn't as if I wanted to be a shrink or anything. I guess I just wanted to know what it was that motivated people to do whatever it was they did."

The friend didn't answer back with the obvious. It was too inflammatory.

Ted, do you think you were looking for what made you into a monster? Ted, did you ever find out what it was?

In 1971, Ted Bundy took a job that always carried the ultimate in irony. At the time, Seattle was one of a few major U.S. cities with a suicide prevention crisis line. The Suicide Hotline, as it was known, was that number the brokenhearted and desperate called when they could think of no other way out of their misery.

One call, two months into his tenure there, was like so many of them. It came from a young woman at her wit's end, deep into the drama and depression that had enveloped her since a breakup with a boyfriend.

GIRL: I think I might hurt myself. I really do.
TED: Talk to me. I'm Ted. I care.
GIRL: I have a bottle of sleeping pills and I just want to take them and, you know, never, ever wake up.
TED: I've felt that way, too. Everyone has. What's your name?
GIRL: You have? But you're working at the crisis hotline.
TED: Everyone has their moments of despair. But this call isn't about me. I didn't catch your name.
GIRL: Annette, my name is Annette.

TED: Annette, what happened? I want to know how to help you. I don't want you to take those pills. I want you to live through this, all right?"

GIRL: I don't know if I can. I don't know if I want to live.

TED: Are you alone?

GIRL: My mom and dad are asleep.

TED: Where are the pills? Can you put them some-place away from where you are?

GIRL: I don't want to.

TED: What happened to make you so sad, Annette?

GIRL: My boyfriend, Brian, dropped me. Said I was "too much work" and that he didn't want me anymore.

TED: You don't sound like too much work to me, Annette.

GIRL: You're nice.

TED: Thank you, but this call's about you, Annette. I think you are nice. Tell me, are you really going to hurt yourself?

GIRL: (long pause) No, I guess not. I was just mad. I just wanted someone to talk to.

TED: Call me anytime you are sad.

GIRL: I'm sad a lot. I don't know what time you work.

TED: I'll give you my home number.

After the conversation was over, Ted set down the phone and swiveled his chair to face one of the other operators on the line, a pretty young woman with blond hair and light eyes.

"Ted Bundy, I should report you for giving out your

phone number to that girl," Iris O'Neal said, nearly wagging her finger in Ted's direction.

Ted grinned sheepishly. "Sorry, Iris. It just came out."

"Well, I won't turn you in," she said, looking over at another of the counselors, a Goody Two-shoes who walked around with a clipboard marking down everything that happened on the lines.

"Thanks. Why not?" he asked.

Iris smiled. "Because I know you. I know that you can't help but empathizing with these callers. You just can't help but do good, Ted. You'll be a legend around here, long after you're gone."

She'd thought about her way out of wherever she was from the moment she'd regained consciousness. Every conceivable scenario ran through Emma's first groggy and confused, then sharper and more determined, mind. She considered a myriad of remedies she could pursue to subdue her captor, that is, if she could only get close enough to strike. Emma didn't have many weapons at her disposal in the so-called apartment. There was the gooseneck lamp, of course. It was the most likely candidate. The teenager imagined how the fixture could do double duty. She could pick it up, hide it behind her back, and when the moment was right strike him over the head with it. In her mind's eye in that scenario, her captor would fall to the floor after a single blow. She was a better hitter than Alex Rodriguez. She'd been infatuated with the ballplayer before he became a Yankee. She was sure, like A-Rod, she could swing, swing hard, over the fence. He's out! *Dead.* Home run! Then, Emma believed with complete certainty, she would be able to take the cord and wrap it around her abductor's veiny neck, cutting off his air supply until he was absolutely, positively, for sure, dead. When he was dead she felt pretty sure no one would blame her. Although he hadn't raped her, she would say that he did—as if being held hostage God-knows-where wasn't enough of a reason to kill him.

She looked around the dimly lit space. The only other weapon was the bucket that she'd used as a toilet. She'd like to drown the pig in the stinking bucket, but as disgusting and fitting as that was, it wasn't practical. Her captor emptied it every other day. He filled it with fresh bleach-water and made her lay on the mattress while he took it and brought it back. She remembered how she'd been so embarrassed that someone had seen her feces in a bucket, but that kind of modesty was over by the first or second day. When Emma Rose came to grips with the fact that she had but one chance to get out of there she vowed not to blow it.

She just wasn't sure when that chance would present itself.

Emma lay still on the mattress listening. For a second she thought she heard the voice of Ellen DeGeneres. *Yes, it* is *Ellen!* She loved Ellen's show and the comedienne's voice calmed her. She listened more carefully. She was pretty sure that the man who held her captive had gone out. If he was out, then maybe there was someone else in the house. Someone, somewhere, watching *Ellen.* Maybe whoever it was would save her.

She screamed as loudly as she could. "Help me! Get me out of here! I'm being held prisoner by some creeper! Help me."

She stopped and listened. Ellen was no longer talking. The house was quiet.

Had she misheard? Was she hallucinating?

The space above her was soundless.

Emma started to tear up a little, but she fought the emotion. She didn't want to be weak. She didn't want to succumb to her worst fears. He would rape her, probably. He would kill her, too. And whoever was watching Ellen DeGeneres didn't give a rat's ass about her.

"It isn't right," she said, crying as softly as possible into the smelly mattress while pulling the scratchy blanket over her. "Ellen would never have let me suffer."

CHAPTER 25

Sometimes memories are manufactured. Sometimes it isn't intentional. Grace knew that from cases she worked for the Tacoma Police Department. Manufactured memories were different from so-called repressed memories. Grace's own life history had one. She had been only a small child when it happened, but it had been told to her so many times, it seemed real. Vivid. True. On June 8, 1977. Sissy O'Hare had braided her daughter's damp hair the night before so she could have "wavy hair." She dressed in her prettiest pink top with brand-new cropped blue jeans. It was a special day, the beginning of summer vacation. Sunlight poured through the open curtains and a robin pecked at its reflection on the glass, an occurrence that had brought more interest than annoyance to the O'Hares.

When the phone rang, Sissy set down the hairbrush and went to answer. Instantly, her cheerful demeanor fell like a stone tossed into a very still pond.

"He what?" She looked over at Grace, then turned away toward the window and the robin. The rest of the words came from her amid gasps, in a rapid-fire fashion that pelted the glass windowpane.

"No," she said.

And then: "What time?"

"Did he hurt anyone?"

"Where did he go?"

"Why is this happening?"

"Why does God hate all of us?"

By then her mother was crying. Sissy let the phone fall into the cradle of the receiver. Her tears were twin streams, just moving down her cheeks and dropping onto the floor.

"Mommy," Grace said, rushing to comfort her. "Daddy?"

Conner was away on a business trip.

"No. Worse than that, baby. Something terrible has happened."

"Mommy?"

Sissy steadied herself, her hands finding the back of a dining chair. She bent close to her daughter and held her, and then pressed her lips to her ear.

"Do not be afraid," she whispered. "Ted escaped."

Later the "memory" would become more complete as the bits and pieces of Ted Bundy's story emerged and filled her memory bank. Ted's incarceration had been short-lived. He was transferred from Garfield County Jail in Glenwood Springs, an hour away to the Pitkin County Courthouse in Aspen, Colorado, for a preliminary hearing. Ted was full-on Ted then—the Ted he wanted the world to see. He was acting as his own lawyer and in doing so was granted special—and, ultimately, foolish—privileges. He was able to shed the shackles and handcuffs that prisoners wore—items he said that were not only prejudicial, but made it impossible for him to maneuver around the second-floor law library. Moments later, the Pacific Northwest's lcast favorite son jumped from the window, landing on the ground and disappearing into the mundane spring day.

Later when she played the exchange between her and her mother, Grace escalated her vocabulary to concepts beyond her age.

"They'll catch him, right?" she asked when her mother told her what happened.

Sissy had pulled herself together and looked into her daughter's brown eyes and nodded.

"Yes. I think so. The police know that they can't let him be free. No one is safe. They told me they have already set up roadblocks all around Aspen. He can't go far."

The next morning the *Tacoma News Tribune* ran a story on the front page:

IS TED BUNDY THE REINCARNATION OF HARRY HOUDINI?

That brought a memory, too. Sissy immediatcly called the newspaper and screamed at the nice girl who answered the phone, telling her that in no uncertain terms the paper was glorifying a monster and in doing so diminishing the unspeakable evil that he'd done to an untold number of women and girls.

"If he killed your daughter," Sissy said, almost screaming into the phone after being transferred to the city editor's desk, "I doubt you'd be writing headlines like that!"

The first week of summer had not been as Grace had dreamed it would be. There were no trips to Titlow Beach and the massive saltwater swimming pool there.

Her mother didn't take her to Point Defiance for the picnic that she'd promised for that first Saturday. Instead, they sat around the house staring at the phone and playing Chinese checkers for six days—six days in which her mother ratcheted up her obsession with the man she was sure had been her daughter's killer.

Still later, when it came on the news that Ted Bundy had been apprehended again, it had not been because of fantastic police work. It had once again been a routine traffic stop that had been the suspected serial killer's undoing. He'd been picked up in Aspen driving a stolen car erratically with a sprained ankle. He had stolen a rifle and taken maps, food, and whatever else he could get his hands on. If he'd had a grand plan, it was a failed and ill-conceived one.

No one knew it at the time, of course, but it wouldn't be his last escape.

In Seattle and Tacoma, indeed all over the Pacific Northwest, pockets of people—law enforcement and civilians—were caught up in everything Ted. Sissy had her group of parents and siblings of murdered children and they were busy plastering photographs of Tricia and Ted on bulletin boards in supermarkets and telephone poles throughout Tacoma.

Under the black-and-white photos were six one-syllable words:

DID YOU SEE HIM WITH HER?

When news came that Ted's 1968 VW bug had been recovered from the teen in Midvale, Utah, to whom he'd sold it, the O'Hares all brightened and braced themselves. Sissy considered the VW a "kind of mobile crime scene" and she was convinced that if Tricia had gone with Ted, it had been in that evil car. She was equally sure that if Tricia had gone with him, she had not gone on her own accord. She knew better than to get into a stranger's car. When FBI lab technicians examined the car—literally every inch of it under a microscope—they managed to recover some vital evidence. Among the dust and debris of a car that had been all over the west, the lab collected a number of hairs matching two dead girls from Utah and Colorado; in addition to those samples, they found one that was certainly a match with Mandy Deirdre, the girl who got away.

The living witness, as she became known.

Mandy didn't speak of what had happened often— that was one of the distinguishing markers of a real Ted victim. The wannabes, those who needed the attention, were always there in front of a reporter's open notebook, or the camera of TV news crew. Mandy didn't clamber to be in front of anyone. She had come through the darkness of what-if, and didn't want to revel in it. Because of that genuine reticence, Sissy never phoned her to find out just what was going through her mind or if Ted had mentioned her daughter's name. It seemed like too much of an intrusion. Mandy was lucky to be alive and that kind of luck didn't need to be sullied by the curious, or even those desperate to know something. Anything.

In early October of 1975, potential Teds were placed in a row under the harsh glare of a jailhouse lineup. Mandy, all ninety-five pounds of her, did what no one had been able to do before. She fingered him as her assailant. There was no hesitation, like there often is when reality is thrown in a victim's face. Instead, just the confidence of a young woman with the burden of stopping evil.

"That's the police officer who stopped me," she said.

Witnesses in Colorado made additional positive IDs of Ted as the stranger who'd been lurking around the high school where Candy Detrick was last seen alive.

Ted, it seemed, was charged with kidnapping Mandy and attempted criminal assault and, as they would always do throughout his life, his parents stood by him. Johnnie and Louise came up with the fifteen thousand dollars sought by the court and he was released to await trial in Washington.

Grace was a girl then, but she could never forget how her mother had reacted to the news that Ted had been freed on bond. That was the day they needed a new TV.

Sissy stood up from the sofa and yelled at the TV.

"Can you believe it?" she asked, her voice nearly a scream.

She picked up her husband's trophy and slammed it down on top of the walnut console. She was so angry. So hurt. She didn't shatter the glass, but the tube flickered and the picture faded to that measly pattern that came on the channels for which there was no reception.

It was the first time Grace had seen her mother be aggressive like that.

"Mommy, are you okay?"

"How could I be okay? How could any of us be

okay? He's out. He's going to kill another girl. Mark my words."

Grace unplugged the TV. Just in case.

Sissy went for her coat and an umbrella. The weather had been nasty for two weeks, sending a cold rain over the faded fall foliage.

"Mommy, where are you going?"

"Come with me. We're going over to the Bundys'. I'm going to put them on notice. I don't care what they say. I don't even care if they call the police. In fact, I hope they do."

Grace followed her mother to the car and climbed into the passenger seat. Sissy didn't even wait for her to buckle up; instead she just put the car in gear and drove.

"I'm sorry about the TV," she said.

"I don't care, Mommy. Daddy might not be happy about it."

"I'm sure you're right. But you know what? He gets to go to work every day, away from the news, away from Tricia's empty room. He doesn't have to face the reminders twenty-four hours a day."

Fifteen minutes later, they were at the Skyline Drive address where Ted had lived in his last year of high school. Police cars and a TV crew from KVOS were outside the Bundy home, a nice wood-clad house with small, almost eyehole, windows in front.

Sissy parked behind the news van.

"Looks like I'm not the only one with the need to talk to the Bundys," she said.

Grace followed her mom.

A police officer stopped them.

"Are you friends of the family?" he asked.

Sissy shook her head. "No, I wouldn't say friends."
"What's your business here?"
"I want to talk to Louise and Johnnie," she said.
"So you do know them?"
"No. I think Ted murdered my daughter—*her* older
sister." She pointed to Grace, who just stood there say-
ing nothing, taking in all the drama around her.
"I understand, ma'am," he said, "But you don't need
to be here."
"Is it against the law?"
"No," he said. "It's just that there's no point in it.
Ted's not here. The Bundys aren't coming out. We just
want everyone to go away, leave them alone."
"Leave them alone?" Sissy asked, he eyes popping.
"They helped to make him into whatever it is that you
want to call him. I think they should come out. They
should face everyone and tell us why it is they want to
support a murderer."
"He's their son. It just is the way it is. Please go
home."
Sissy stood there, her pant legs wicking up water
from a mud puddle.
"How is it that I have to go home to an empty house,
a room without my baby anymore because of him?"
The officer looked over at Grace, who stood next to
her mother, shivering in the cold October air.
"Because you have her to think about," he said, indi-
cating Grace standing quietly next to her mom.
Sissy looked down at Grace, and their eyes locked.
She noticed for the first time that Grace was freezing.
She didn't have a jacket or a sweater. She was shaking
and her face was streaked with rain.
"Tell Louise I hope her son rots in hell, but before

he does that, I want you—any of you—to make him tell me what he did with my Tricia! Do you understand? Do you copy?"

The officer seemed to.

"We're together on this," he said. "I promise." He looked around the Skyline Drive house, the cars, the people, the media. The buzzing of people all there for a reason, but none greater than the woman and her daughter. If anyone deserved answers, he was all but certain, it was that mother.

CHAPTER 26

A memory that could never ever be erased from Sissy O'Hare's brain, no matter how much she would have preferred, came ten days after the ordeal began. It started with a phone call.

It was Harold Masters from the Tacoma Police Department on the line. Detective Masters had been handling Tricia's case since the first real full day of her vanishing.

"Mrs. O'Hare?" the detective asked. It was immediately apparent that his voice was devoid of any hopefulness.

"Yes, it's me," she said.

The detective cleared his throat. "Mrs. O'Hare, can you and Conner meet me at the station?"

"This doesn't sound good," Sissy said, sliding backward into a chair, the air emptying from her lungs.

"We don't know for sure," he said, again as flatly as possible, without hope.

Sissy looked over at her husband, who had set down the *News Tribune* and was watching her face fall. "We can be there in twenty minutes," she said.

* * *

Detective Masters's sympathetic eyes were no longer as penetrating as they had been in all of his encounters with Conner and Sissy O'Hare. Indeed, when he met them by the front desk at the police department they barely landed on either of the missing girl's parents. It was obvious before a single word was uttered that the detective was about to say something that he didn't want to say and that the O'Hares most certainly didn't want to hear.

From the outset, Conner was shaking. He put his arm around Sissy, more for his benefit than hers. She was oddly quiet, stoic.

"You found her?" he asked.

Sissy stood there mute.

"Let's go in here," Det. Masters said, gesturing for them to follow into the open doorway of an interview room they had visited two days after Tricia's vanishing from campus. Tricia's best friend, Carrie, had joined them in that interview, one that yielded very little new information and plenty more tears. Carrie kept saying over and over that it was her fault for wanting to have some alone time with the guy she had set her sights on.

"Tricia went to get something to eat or something. . . . I never saw her again," she said. "It was my fault. All my fault."

Outwardly, the O'Hares didn't argue the merits of her guilty conscience. They patted the teenager on the shoulder and tried to calm her to see if their daughter's decidedly selfish best friend had a clue about what really happened to Tricia. Inside Sissy's head, a refrain ran on an endless loop.

It is your fault! You stupid girl!

That had been more than a week ago. And with each day, as Xerox-copied flyers with Sissy's smiling senior portrait went up all over Pierce County, hope faded. By the end of that eighth day, there wasn't a bus stop or telephone pole that hadn't been stapled, tacked, or even duct-taped with Tricia O'Hare's photograph and the loud proclamation: REWARD. Search parties organized by Boy Scouts and search-and-rescue groups from as far away as Spokane methodically inched their way across a large empty field near PLU, turning up a dead cat and another woman's purse, but nothing more. The police led by Detective Masters had worked around the clock, of course, but it was as if Tricia just walked off the face of the earth.

Now you see her, now you don't.

The detective folded his dark tan hands and set them on the table.

"A body has been found," he said, his eyes now gliding over both of the parents.

"Is it our Tricia?" Conner asked, his eyes already flooding.

"We're not sure. We need to make an identification."

Sissy spoke up. "So you don't know." She stopped herself before adding, *if it is her?*

"But you know enough to bring us here," Conner said, fighting back tears.

Detective Masters nodded. "Yes," he said, his voice so soft it might not have been heard in a normal conversation. This was far from normal. "I'm very sorry," he said, "but we do think we've found your daughter."

"Where? Where?" Conner asked, putting his arm around Sissy and holding her close as he finally let completely go and convulsed into tears. "Not our little girl."

"A fisherman and his son found the body just up from the bank of the Puyallup."

Sissy later told her victims' families support group that she looked at the detective's mouth as he spoke, trying to decipher what he was saying. It seemed like his words were coming at her in some strange foreign language. Nothing he said seemed to compute whatsoever.

She stared at Conner.

Why is he crying? What happened?

Later, Sissy learned, her experience was not so uncommon. She had shut down, a defense mechanism to stop her from experiencing the deepest pain a mother might feel. Nothing any mother could face could be worse than the realization that her baby was really gone.

"I'll need a family member to identify the body," he said.

"Where is she?" Sissy asked, now retrieving some of what was being said. Conner was a mess; she could see that she had to be the one. "I'll go."

"Are you sure, Mrs. O'Hare?" the detective asked, knowing that her husband was in no condition to do what needed to be done.

And that was the second memory, the trek in to the morgue, seeing her daughter while Conner waited in the hallway, his face in his hands. Tricia was laying on some kind of a table with wheels as she was pushed in front of a window, a light on, and an attendant in scrubs peeling back a pale green sheet. A light went on and the image of her daughter not as she'd been in life, but slightly bloated, a whitish gray pallor over her skin, came into view.

Sissy O'Hare looked over at the detective and motioned that she was going to be sick. She spun around and reached for the door, but there wasn't enough time. Though it felt as if she hadn't eaten for days, she began to vomit. At first it was simply that horrendous noise that accompanies dry heaves. It is the kind of noise that sometimes induces others to follow suit. A second later, a foul fountain came up out of her throat and splattered against the floor. In any other another time, Sissy would have been mortified beyond words by what had transpired. She was a woman in complete control. She was tidy. Her manners were impeccable. She was the strand-of-pearls-wearing gardener, for goodness sake.

"This isn't my Tricia," she said.

"Are you sure?"

"A mother knows her baby. Yes, I'm sure," she said, standing there crying, hunched over a coagulating pool of vomit, wishing that God would take her right then, too. The love of her life was gone. The baby she'd rocked since birth. Gone. Everything good. Gone.

Who could have done this?

It was a question that she'd later convince herself that she had to answer on her own.

Those two moments—learning her daughter was missing and the viewing of the lifeless remains of someone else's little girl —could only be supplanted by the memory she wished for more than anything. She wanted to live long enough to savor the death of the man or men who were responsible for the cruelest deed. Before going to sleep each night, Sissy O'Hare found a private moment away from Conner, then later, from Grace, and said a silent prayer.

Dear God, it is wrong for me to wish harm to anyone, but please answer me and spare my broken heart by making the Tricia's murderer pay for his crimes with his own blood. Forgive me for wishing another human being to suffer, but I cannot be a stronger, better person here. I want him to die a slow, painful death. I want him to feel whatever she felt times a million. God, please hear my prayers. Please show some mercy on my broken heart and release me from the torment of a killer walking free to cause more harm.

Sissy O'Hare knew it was distasteful and probably even wicked to ask God for harm to another human being, no matter how vile the individual. She thought somehow that it was possible that God, in his infinite compassion for her suffering, would understand and do what he could to help ease her shattered heart. She didn't tell Conner what she was praying for, because vengeance was not something he could truly comprehend. His devastation was his alone. He told Sissy over and over that he wanted whoever had taken and probably killed Tricia to be punished when he met his maker.

"Justice," he said, "will be done. It may not occur in our lifetime, but one way or another whoever took our girl will pay for it."

The year after Tricia's vanishing was the blackest time of the O'Hares' lives. It was a pendulum, however, that lurched back and forth from hope to despair. Any crumb of hope was devoured; each setback brought tears, drinking, arguments. They joined a victims' families support group the spring after their daughter died. Neither would say that it was something that didn't provide some solace, yet Sissy in particular found it a little too emotional.

"It's like a church potluck, but with tears instead of fruit punch," she told her husband after a few months of going to meetings in the basement of the Lutheran church on Pacific. The fifteen other members seemed focused on the tragedy of their circumstances, something none would have denied. Sissy saw a different purpose. She wanted to two things—justice for her daughter and another baby.

She was forty, not ancient, but hardly a young mother. When she told Conner she wanted to get pregnant, he was overjoyed by the prospect. No child could take their Tricia's place, of course, but Conner felt that they still had a lot of love to give. When she became pregnant just before the Fourth of July the year after Tricia was murdered, Sissy made her next move. She quit the support group at the church and formed her own. Hers would focus on the catching of the killer responsible for Tricia's murder.

CHAPTER 27

A crew from a Seattle TV station made its way to Tacoma to cover a story that would likely lead the 11 PM broadcast. A missing girl was a ratings grabber—and despite the second-city reputation of T-Town, it had been a good locale for such stories. Ratings had been boosted by images of crying moms, empty parking lots, and the morose intonations of Kelli Corelli, a reporter with big hair and big teeth and the kind of sad, savvy delivery that always ensured at least a few viewers would tear up.

". . . in a moment you'll see the last images of the missing teenager as she left her job at the Lakewood Towne Center. . . ."

The video, all grainy and practically useless, played for a second, and then another voice came on.

"If anyone has seen my daughter, please let us know." It was Diana Rose, her voice cracking under the emotions that came with the discovery that Emma wasn't where she was supposed to be.

The next shot showed Emma's mother standing on her front porch.

"She's all that we have."

The cameraman panned to the mother's hands. Inside one of her balled-up fists was a crumpled tissue.

"If anyone knows anything . . . I'm begging you . . . please, please help us find our daughter."

The reporter got back on camera and somberly reminded viewers that the case was a top concern "not only of this family, but of the Tacoma Police Department, which has been investigating a series of missing girls' cases."

People connected to the case were watching that channel that night—Paul, Grace, the Roses. All were hopeful that someone would come forward with information. Emma didn't just vanish like the fog off Commencement Bay. Someone out there had to know something about her whereabouts.

Someone watching did. A phone number was flashed on the screen.

Sienna Winters shut her phone and waited for a call back. She curled up on the sofa of her South Tacoma apartment. The neighbors were loud, as always, and it was hard to think, hard to figure out if she'd done the right thing. She was sick to her stomach about making the call, but there was nothing she could do. She felt that the Roses should have all the information they needed. They were nice people. An hour later, there was a knock at the door.

It was a pair of detectives from the Tacoma Police Department.

Grace spoke first. "Are you Sienna?"

"Yeah. You the police?"

"Yes, we are. I'm Detective Alexander and this is my partner, Detective Bateman. We got your message."

"I thought you'd just call me. Kind of weird that you're here."

"Sorry, but your message was so . . ." Grace stumbled, uncharacteristically, for the words. "So disturbing."

Sienna, a cranberry-headed girl with pale, pale skin, green eyes and twitchy nerves, didn't blink. "Yeah. I guess it was."

"Can we come in?"

"Yeah. Just don't let the dog out," she said, indicating a terrier mix behind her legs.

"No worries."

Sienna and the dog led the detectives to the living room portion of the studio apartment. It was a dark space with a wall draped in icicle Christmas lights, a TV on mute, and a pile of dishes on the floor next to the sofa.

"Obviously, I wasn't expecting company," Sienna said.

"That's all right."

"Am I supposed to offer you something? All I got is sweet tea."

"No, we're not here to visit. We're here about your message."

"Yeah that. I kind of regretted it after I left it," she said, settling into a molded plastic chair across from the detectives, who were now seated with the dog on the sofa.

"Sienna," Paul said, "let's go over what you told us."

"You mean about her telling me she was going to

run away? Hated her mom. I know that sounds ugly, but I just had to say it. I saw Diana crying on TV and it made me puke. Those two hated each other."

"Really. And you know this how?"

"We used to work together. Before she went big-time and got the Starbucks job."

"Where was that?"

"Food court. I was, still am, at Hot Dog on Stick. She was over at Mandarin Wok," she said. Grace's eyes landed on the ridiculous hat that was placed on top of the rest of Sienna's work clothes.

"Don't say how dumb the uniform is. I already know."

Grace smiled. "No, I won't. So you were friends with her?"

"Not BFFs, but pretty tight."

"And she told her that she hated her mom?"

"Yeah. It was no big deal. I hate my mom, too."

Grace nodded. She pretended to understand, when of course, she didn't. She always loved her mother.

"Anyway, she started telling me about her mom being sick and demanding. How she didn't get go to college because her mom was such a bitch about everything. A total control freak. One time she told me that she thought her mom was crazy enough to have faked her cancer just to keep her around."

"That's a pretty ugly thing to say," Paul said.

Sienna shrugged it off. "So, ever heard of the ugly truth?"

"You said on the message that you thought she was a runaway. Why do you think that?"

"Because she told me she was going to."

Grace narrowed her brows. "Told you, specifically?"

Sienna nodded. "Yeah. She said she was going to just walk away and disappear. She was going to start over somewhere. New name. New everything. She said she'd never be found because if she ever did her bitch of a mom would be right there telling her what to do."

The dog, whose name they learned was Toby, started to scratch and Grace was sure that she was going to end up with fleabites on her ankles. Bugs of all kinds loved her blood. She was a veritable smorgasbord for mosquitos, too.

"When did she say this to you?" Paul asked

"When didn't she? She was always complaining about her mother. She thought her stepdad was nice, but stupid to be stuck with that witch of a wife."

"Did she share this with anyone else?"

"How would I know? I told you that we weren't that close." ·

Grace made a few notes, asked a few follow-up questions, and the interview was over.

When they got out to the car, she stopped before getting inside.

"She's such a liar," she said. "If she's not, then I can't read people at all. Diana Rose is no bitch mommie dearest. She just isn't."

Paul got inside and turned the key.

"Get in, let's go."

"Are you listening to me?"

"Yeah. I am. But honestly, you know that no one has a clue about what goes on behind closed doors. Remember Candee?"

Grace slid into the seat. How could she forget?

* * *

Candee Getz was a seven-year-old girl who had been held captive by her father and stepmother for four years in a back bedroom of her Browns Point home. Patty Getz simply hated any reminder of the first Mrs. Getz, a woman who had died in a traffic accident and had never even been a rival of Mrs. Getz number two. When she and Don Getz married, she sold everything that was even remotely connected to Geneva Getz. Literally everything. Every. Little. Thing. Geneva's family would have loved to have had the old silver, the china, the family antiques, but Patty couldn't be bothered with returning any of the treasures. She wanted it all gone and she wanted it done fast. She ran an advertisement on Craigslist and let complete strangers pick the bones of her husband's first wife's memory. All gone but Candee, of course.

And yet, the small blond toddler simply disappeared. As far as the neighbors knew, Candee had gone off to live with relatives in Idaho. The Idaho family had given up on trying to stay connected to their sister's little girl.

Don Getz had been adamant that it was better for Candee to start over.

"She's been through enough. She needs to be part of a new family."

The family, heartbroken beyond words, didn't know what else to do. Don had always been a decent guy. If he'd wanted to start over, then they'd let him.

All of that changed when one sunny July afternoon a young man hired to clean the pool next door heard cries coming from the Getz house. At first it sounded like a wounded animal.

A coyote? Maybe?

Jorge Martinez knocked on the door, but no answer. He noticed a stack of *Tacoma News Tribune* newspapers heaped up on the steps, indicating that whoever lived there hadn't been home. The cries were so loud that he let himself in the side gate and wound his way around the house. At the back of the house was a bedroom with its windows covered with aluminum foil from the outside.

The sound was unrelenting.

"Hello?" he said.

The noise stopped. It was sudden. Just off.

"Hello?"

Jorge heard the sound of something moving beyond the aluminum-covered window. He rapped on the glass, a dull thud rather than the clear sound of a fist against glass.

Then he heard a sound that caused the hairs on the back of his neck to rise.

"Help," the voice cried.

It was no coyote, but the sound of a very scared child.

It didn't take Jorge much time at all to do the right thing.

"Move back," he said. "Move away from the window. Do you hear me?"

"Yes," the voice said.

Jorge pulled the concrete top off a bird bath and pushed it hard into the window.

From the opening he could see her. She was small. Pale. Frightened. Candee had been found.

The neighbors did what they always did. They told the police, the reporters, even Oprah Winfrey, that they'd had no idea she was held captive. No idea that the ideal family unit next door was nothing as it had seemed.

Grace ran the story through her mind. She knew that people like Don and Patty Getz existed. They had jobs. They put up Christmas lights. They attended the annual block watch meeting. And yet inside their beautiful home, with its stunning gardens and views of Commencement Bay, was a dark secret. No one could have seen it coming. No one would have ever guessed in a million years.

Grace looked over at Paul as he started to drive. They'd both worked the Candee Getz case. It was one of those cases that stayed with everyone a long, long time. Probably forever. That wasn't true of most cases. Most came and went. A good detective knew that when his work was done, it was done. To dwell on something terrible, as most such cases were, was to invite nightmares and regret.

"I heard from Geneva's sister. Candee's doing great," she said.

"Great or as great as could be expected?"

Grace looked out the window. "No, great. Really. She's going to be okay."

"Let's go see if Palmer Morton's kid is home," Paul said.

"Sounds good."

Emma Rose woke with a jolt. The clicking sound and the sense that someone was watching her had become familiar. She looked up, then over at the door. The hatch opened and a sandwich, American cheese on white bread with the crust trimmed, was presented on a paper plate. Alongside it was a can of cola. Emma took the items from the tray and watched it pull away, disappearing on the other side of the door. The hatch snapped shut. She turned away and started for the mattress when the hatch opened again.

That was unusual. The creeper normally waited about an hour or longer before the tray was submitted for the paper plate and the cola can.

Emma went back to the door and looked down at the tray. It was empty except for a single Hershey's Kiss candy, its shiny silver foil wrapping caught the light from the reading lamp by the mattress. There was a long list of things that she missed by then—her mother, her friends, her sense of feeling safe. Free. On the list, somewhere past everything else, was chocolate.

Had she said something about it to the creeper? She wasn't sure. In those first days of captivity, Emma had sputtered out a flurry of things amid her protestations that she didn't deserve this. She'd said over and over that she would do whatever he wanted if he only let her go. She'd screamed into her thin pillow how much she wanted to go home and how she never wanted to see an American cheese sandwich again. She might have mentioned she wanted some coffee or candy or something along those lines.

Had he given her the Kiss for any reason other than to be kind? Had he given it to her so that she would do something for him? To him?

In that moment, she didn't care. She unwrapped the foil and put the candy into her mouth. The first bite was silky, creamy, so wonderfully sweet. Then it tasted slightly chalky. She disregarded the texture of the candy. She wanted something that gave her a little bit of pleasure. Something that tasted good.

As she walked toward the mattress she felt a strange sensation. Her knees began to weaken.

CHAPTER 28

The Morton mansion sat defiantly on the edge of the bluff overlooking Tacoma's sparkling, but decidedly working-class, Commencement Bay. It was, arguably, the most magnificent setting for any home in the City of Destiny, as Tacoma boosters had nicknamed Seattle's stepsister to the south. It wasn't just a large home, but a true mansion with seventeen rooms, including a ballroom. The house had come with a bit of history, too. It had been the site of a famous kidnapping of a doctor's son in the 1930s—a crime that had never been solved. The home was painted an eggshell white with black shutters and was set off by a circular drive that wound around a fountain that was a replica of some Italianate antiquity that the original owners had sculpted on the spot. Before Palmer Morton bought the place, the home had been a regular on the historic homes tour. The incontrovertible diamond of the tour, patrons of the annual event agreed.

Grace suppressed the urge to roll her eyes when a servant dressed in a uniform of black and white answered the heavy, ten-foot door. Who but a jerk like Palmer

Morton would make the help look like they came with the historic home?

"May I help you?" asked the dour man with a shiny pate and razor-thin moustache.

"Yes, I guess you could," Grace said. "We're looking for Alex Morton. Is he home?"

The servant studied the detectives, first Grace, then Paul. "I'm Richard Mathias, the butler. What is your business with Alex?"

Grace spoke up. "We're investigating the disappearance of a friend of his."

"Ms. Rose?" the man said.

"That would be right. Yes, Emma Rose. Did you know her?"

"I'd seen her a few times. Plus I saw her picture on KING's news this morning. A lovely girl."

"May we come in?" Paul asked, asserting himself into the conversation.

"No," he said, backing off a little. "Floors were just waxed. Besides, no one is home. Just me and the housekeeper."

Housekeeper, too. Morton has it pretty good, Grace thought. She was lucky to get Shane to spring for a Merry Maid before Thanksgiving the previous year.

"How come you didn't tell us right away that Alex and Mr. Morton weren't here?"

"Sorry," Mathias said. "I made an assumption."

The remark interested Grace. "What kind of an assumption?"

Mathias rolled his shoulder a little; it was somewhat sheepish gesture done more for the effect of it than for any real feelings he had about offending anyone. "I thought you were collecting for the library or something," he said.

Grace was annoyed, but didn't show it.

The butler must be taking asshole lessons from his boss, she thought.

"Thanks," she said. "I guess. When will either Mr. Morton or his son be home?"

He started to close the door. "Next week, I think."

As the door clicked shut, a voice could be heard. It was clear and unmistakable.

"What did those jokers want?"

It was the voice of a young man. Grace looked at her partner.

"Guess Alex was home after all."

Paul nodded and Grace rang the bell again.

Mathias answered. "Did you forget something?"

"No, but evidently you did. You forgot that impeding a criminal investigation by lying is a punishable offense."

The servant looked flustered. "I don't know what you are talking about."

"Cut the Mr. Belvedere crap," Paul said. "We heard the kid. Get him. We want to talk to him."

"I don't know. . . . He's a boy. He'll need his father's permission."

"He's over eighteen. Get him for us now. We're trying to find a missing girl. Maybe he can help," Grace said.

As Mathias appeared to weigh his options, a voice from behind called out.

"I'll talk to 'em," a young man's voice said.

It was Alex Morton, a nineteen-year-old, wearing his

slacker uniform—a rumpled T-shirt and khaki shorts that hung so low Grace Alexander almost stared to make sure they weren't about to fall off in mid stride. He had bushy brows and the kind of fawn eyes that girls couldn't resist. That he was rich, had a restored Porche Targa, and had the attitude that the world owed him ("It isn't easy having an old man like mine to live up to.") probably didn't hurt him one bit in the dating department.

"Your father will nccd to be notified," Mathias said.

"Then, Jesus, Mathias, do your job. That's why you get paid the big bucks." There was no trace of irony in his voice.

Grace wondered how it was that a seemingly nice girl like Emma could fall for a boy like Alex. Date him, yes, but anything more? Out of the question. What Richie Rich didn't know was that he was a conquest as much as any girl.

Alex stepped outside, saving Mathias the quandary of whether or not he should invite the police into the house. Alex lit up a cigarette and offered the light to Paul—not to Grace. While neither detective smoked, it was clear just what Alex Morton thought of women in general. He looked only in Paul's direction when he spoke.

"Fire away. This is, like, cool to be talking to the police. Lame that you think I know something, but I'm guessing you don't have anything much to go on."

"Why is that?" Paul asked.

The teenager shrugged. "Because I don't know anything and you're wasting your time here. Girl's dead, isn't she?"

Grace bristled at the remark. "Why would you say she's dead?"

"Is she the good cop or the bad cop?" he asked, ignoring her question.

"She's a little of both," Paul said. When the teenager looked over at a small gathering of neighbors, Paul rolled his eyes and mouthed the words *Piece of work* to Grace.

She mouthed back, *Piece of shit.*

Paul grinned and looked back over at the oblivious teenager, whose glare at Grace became a full-on glower.

"I barely knew her. We messed around a few times. No biggie," he said, drawing on his cigarette like it was going to get him high. Really high.

"Her mother said that you were serious until a few weeks ago. Said Emma dumped you and you kind of took it bad," Grace said, refusing to be ignored by the twerp standing in front of the venerable mansion that would, indeed, be his one day.

"No one is serious at nineteen, lady," Alex said.

"Detective Alexander, if you don't mind."

"Whatever. I dumped her. Big deal. I was tired of her. Too clingy. Wanting too much of my time."

"That's interesting," Grace said. "Let me write that down." But she didn't. She just stood there letting her remark soak in along with the fact that she was mocking him with her proclamation that anything he said was worth believing. "Her mother said you Facebook stalked her, called her a hundred times in two days, and sent over ten dozen red roses."

"That's bullshit. I did not. I'm done talking with you. That bitch was crazy and so are you."

"Hey," Paul said, "that's enough of that. You mom and dad ever teach you manners?"

"My mom ran off with my dad's partner and my dad's an asshole. So I guess not."

"Where were you last night, say from six p.m. to midnight?"

"Home. *Here.* With my dad watching the tube. You can ask him. Ask Mathias, too. Don't treat me like some punk criminal. I'm innocent. I haven't seen her in weeks. No lie."

Alex Morton's words were strange. While it wasn't a huge leap from the idea that he was a person of interest in the case to punk criminal, it was a sudden one. No one was saying that they wanted him to "come down to the station" to make a statement. Yet Alex Morton was sure posturing like he'd been directly accused. *A guilty conscience, maybe?* That, naturally, presumed that he had a conscience at all.

"You didn't send her all those roses?" Grace asked.

"Never," he said.

She pulled out her cell phone and scrolled through some images she'd taken while at the Rose's. She turned the phone with the screenshot of Emma's Facebook page before Diana pulled the plug that afternoon. It was photo of bloodred roses, so many it could have been culled from a florist's website. But it wasn't. It had clearly been taken in Emma's bedroom.

She wrote: *Creep sent these. Some people have too much money.*

"Never saw that. Bitch unfriended me."

Paul brightened. "Unfriended you? That's interesting. Wonder why she did that?"

"I'm done talking to you. I've got stuff to do."

Grace didn't let him leave without a parting shot. She waited for that fleeting bit of eye contact that he afforded her. "Whoever bought that many roses had a lot of money . . . or his father's credit card."

Alex gave her a look, said nothing, and went back inside. It would be hard to say if the gargantuan door slammed or if it always sounded that way.

"He's a liar," she said as they walked toward the car. The onlookers, except for one, had quickly dispersed.

"Yeah," Paul said. "Through and through."

"We need to track him," Grace said as a woman started toward them. "Every minute of his day. Did he drive somewhere? Get gas? Was he on a video cam at a Target or something?"

"Dollars to donuts, he wasn't home," Paul said in one of his nonsensical retorts.

The woman who rushed over was middle aged. She wore a skirt, boots, and a jacket trimmed in leather. She was a little more Annie Oakley than the neighborhood, but she said she lived across the street.

"I'm Marla Hoffman. I rent the place over there. Are you here about our cats?" Her voice was breathless. "Minnie has been gone for two weeks, Sasha for seven. All of our cats are disappearing around here. I think that Alex boy is doing something to them."

Grace was caught off guard. "Cats? No, not here about cats. We're here about a missing girl." She pulled out Emma's photo and the woman nodded enthusiastically.

"Yes, I know her. Nice girl. Too nice for that kid. I saw him kick a dog and my other neighbor thinks that he's been taking our cats. God knows why. He's scary. If I didn't have a lease on this place I'd get out of here tomorrow."

It crossed Grace's mind that she ought to ask how the woman could afford the neighborhood. It wasn't the kind of address just anyone went to for a rental, that was for sure.

"Do you know when you saw her last?" Paul asked.

Marla thought a moment.

"That's easy. The day before yesterday." She glanced at the mansion towering behind the detectives. "In the afternoon. I came home from Pilates and she was standing outside stewing over something. We talked for a minute."

"What did she say?"

"Typical teen stuff. Mad at someone, I guess, mad at that asshole Morton kid. Excuse my French. She said that she wished people were nicer."

"Nicer?" Grace asked, her brow slightly raised.

Marla shrugged. "Yeah, nicer. I told her that people start out nice enough, but they shake that off soon enough."

Paul nodded. He, apparently, agreed.

"We might need to take a statement later," Grace said. "We'll need your contact info."

Marla reached into her purse and pulled out a silver-plated business card case. She worked in IT at Weyerhaeuser in nearby Federal Way. Despite the economy there was still money in IT. Marla probably made more than six figures, judging by her expensive clothes, Pilates class, silver card case. Maybe even platinum. That's how she could afford the neighborhood.

When the Tacoma detectives got back in the car, Grace spoke first.

"Two lies on the tally sheet for Mr. Morton."

Paul put the car in gear.

"Yeah, the fact that he hadn't seen her in a long time," he said. "The day before yesterday doesn't qualify as a long time in my book."

Grace checked her messages, her thoughts still wondering if Alex had any idea how things were shaping up against him. "Not hardly," she said. "Plus we've got him dead to rights on the roses, too."

They drove down the hill toward the bay, the waters smooth and dark as obsidian.

In the Morton mansion things were decidedly less tranquil. After the two detectives left, Alex Morton flopped on his bed and screamed into his pillow. Next he dialed his father's cell phone number. No answer.

He's never there when I need him!

Next, Alex dialed the office number. ("That one's for losers," his dad had said. "The people I want to reach me call direct.") Calla, his father's secretary for the past six years, answered. She was an attractive brunette with enough smarts to be an officer in the company, but for some reason, she never advanced out of the support function role she'd been hired into. A few speculated as to why, but no one dared to say anything. Her husband was Palmer Morton's real estate business partner, Byron Jennings.

"I need to talk to my dad," Alex said, barely hiding his frazzled nerves.

"Alex, he's in a meeting," Calla said. "Sorry. I can take a message."

"I don't care," Alex said, his voice rising in anger loud enough that Calla pulled the phone away from her ear a little. "I need to talk to him."

"He can't be disturbed," Calla said, looking through the plate-glass partition into the conference room, where Palmer Morton presided over an enormous architectural model of the mega condo and retail development The Pointe at Ruston Way, in Ruston. It was a crucial development that had the unfortunate distinction of being in the planning stages when the real estate market went kaput. New investors from Korea were in the conference room and Palmer was in the midst of his dog-and-pony show.

"You don't get it," Alex said, this time with a tone that was more than a little threatening. "Do you want HR, or better yet your husband, to know that you've been boning my dad?"

Calla looked around, swiveled her chair, and faced the window with the view to the choppy waters of the bay. Her back slightly hunched. She lowered her voice to a whisper. "Alex, I don't know what you're talking about."

"Calla, you do," Alex said. "Now go get him. I'm in trouble here and he needs to do some fixing. Get him now or you'll not only be out of a job, you'll be looking for a new man. But in your case, you better make that two."

The call went through to Palmer Morton's cell phone to a number even Alex didn't know. Phone records would later show that father and son talked for forty-five seconds before ending the call.

* * *

For the first time, Emma Rose noticed a small red light in the corner of the room. It was a pinprick of red, like a taillight of a little airplane far, far away. She slid her body to the edge of the mattress and got up. It was up on the ceiling over the toilet bucket.

What was that red light? What was the creeper up to now? She wondered if maybe it was a smoke detector to keep the so-called apartment safe in the event of a fire. She remembered how those lights were tiny green ones and, to be fair, if the smoke alarm went off there was no place she could run to anyway.

What is it?

She stood on her tiptoes and strained to get a closer look. She tried to swipe at it with her hands, but it was just out of reach. She looked over at the bucket, still full of urine and feces. She knew that the contents of the bucket reeked. She was used to the smell, in the way she thought that a mother must get used to the stink of a baby's vomit or diaper. Unpleasant, to be sure, but not something so terrible as to kill you.

Not like the creeper.

She looked over and the small red, white tip matchstick caught her eye. She went over, bending down to pick it up. She wished that it was a razor blade or something really useful. Something told her that she should hide it. She tucked the wooden match under the army blanket.

For later.

Next, Emma dumped the contents of the bucket onto the floor and turned it upside down. She climbed atop and strained to get at the little red light. She stood there on the bucket teetering as she finally made out four small letters on a small black box from which the light emerged.

S-O-N-Y.

Sony! She knew what kind of products the Japanese manufacturer of electronics made. Her mom had an old Sony Walkman that she'd finally ditched for an iPod a couple of years ago. Her uncle had a Sony video camera. Emma knew which of those items that had to be . . . a camera. The creeper had been watching her every move from the minute he held her in the prison cell he referred to as the apartment.

CHAPTER 29

Near the bottom of one of her mother's TED boxes was a letter to her mother from a minister, a man from Pennsylvania who had taken a train and a Greyhound bus to be one of the last people to see Bundy before his execution. The letter was dated two weeks after the high-voltage stream turned the serial killer's brain into some kind of evil casserole. Even though she'd been only a girl at the time, Grace held a vague memory of the day the letter arrived at their Tacoma home. Seeing the condition of the letter, not its contents, for the first time in so many years later only confirmed that recollection.

The letter had been shredded to pieces, and then carefully put back together with strips of cellophane tape, yellowed with age.

Grace had remembered how her mother had opened that particular envelope to read with the rest of the mail while she was making dinner. Pork chops, Grace recalled. Funny how she could pull that little, dumb, not-needed-to-be-remembered detail. Sitting at the kitchen table, Grace's eyes widened as her mother transformed;

her mom's face went from interest in what she was reading to complete and utter rage.

From calm to red as quickly as could be.

"Liar!" Sissy O'Hare had called out as she tore up the letter. Her father, who had been in the living room, hurried toward the kitchen to see what had provoked his wife to scream.

"Sis! You all right?" Conner called out, rounding the corner into the room.

"I will never be all right," Sissy said.

In a way, in that moment, it was clear that, even with Ted Bundy dead, she was right.

A snow of bits of paper littered the black-and-white checkerboard floor—the floor that appeared in a couple of eerie photographs later—photos in which Grace later concluded she had been purposely posed to resemble images of her dead sister. Those photos were disturbing to Grace and she was sure they were the source of a lot of her belief that she was a replacement daughter.

While the light of her desk lamp drenched the yellowed cellophane tape Frankensteining the paper shards together, Grace read the letter.

Dear Mrs. O'Hare,

First of all, let me offer my condolences for the loss of your daughter. While I have comforted many in my congregation over the years for the loss of a loved one, I have never had to share the grief of the mother or father of a murdered child. My only offer of solace to you is that I know that someday you and your

precious Tricia will be united in heaven and will
be together for all time, for all eternity.

Now, the other purpose of my letter. I guess,
the real reason. As you might have read in the
paper or viewed on the television, a number of
clergymen met with Theodore Robert Bundy just
before his execution two weeks ago. I was among
that collection of Godly men, which included
two protestants, two Baptists (like myself) a
Catholic, and even some kind of denomination
that considers crystals as magnifiers of spirit
power. I have not chosen take to the airwaves as
some of those have, as I find this kind of tragedy
personal and I find it beyond immoral to pro-
mote a connection with the notorious for the
mere sake of building name recognition or
expanding one's flock. And, to be frank, I don't
think that the New Age minister really has a
flock, as flocks tend to be made of people, not
magical thinking.

Grace recognized that as a none-too-subtle dig at
another minister who'd interviewed Bundy and announced during a press conference that, among other
things, Bundy's murder spree had been fueled by pornography and later, by demonic possession. In a taped interview, Bundy had said: "It was like coming out of some
kind of a horrible trance or dream. I can only liken it to
having been possessed by something so awful and so
alien, and then the next morning wake up from it, remember what happened."

Through that pastor, Ted had told the world that

pornography was the root of all serial homicide and that he was convinced that TV and movies shouldered the majority of the blame. Pornography was rampant, literally and figuratively shoved in a viewer's face. Conner O'Hare considered that reasoning "utter hogwash" and decades later, Grace agreed that there was no better phrase to describe it. It *was* hogwash.

She sipped her tepid coffee and read on as the minister who wrote to her mother went on and on about what he hoped to accomplish, and how everyone—even Ted—deserved forgiveness.

> *Mrs. O'Hare, consider this truth: By not forgiving someone you are not right with the Lord. You are letting your hate and anger fuel all of the wrong feelings. If you could find forgiveness somewhere in your heart, I assure you that you will find peace.*

Grace flashed on how Ted had signed his letters to her mother: *Peace, Ted.*

Fleetingly, because giving a Bundy apologist any semblance of genuine consideration went against everything she knew to be true, Grace wondered how it was that her mother was supposed to forgive the man that she was certain in her bones was her daughter's killer when he wouldn't admit to it.

> *I talked to Ted about his roster of victims and while everything he said to me sickened me to my soul, I did my best to remember every single word of it. He spoke to me with tears streaming*

down his face. This was a man in deep pain, a man with a desire to repent for his sins. Despite his chains and shackles, he got down on his knees and we prayed together. I'm no fool, Mrs. O'Hare. I know the truth when I see it. My congregants know that about me, and if you knew me personally, you'd undoubtedly agree. He told me the names of the girls whom he'd killed, the girls he was driven by demons to kill. But one of the names not on that very sad list was your daughter's. Ted said he did not kill Tricia. He said, "Tell Mrs. O'Hare when I'm gone that she should rejoice and revel in her freedom." He said—and he wanted me to carry this message to you as accurately as possible— "Be as free as a dove, to be anything else is to have an albatross around your neck."

Grace had never seen it, but the words in the stitched-together letter sparked another memory. When Tricia went missing, she'd been wearing a simple necklace with the charm pendant of a dove.

Free as a dove. Albatross around your neck. Peace, Ted.

Grace folded the letter, the adhesive on the cello-phane tape coming undone, and inserted it back into the envelope. Her coffee cup was empty and her stomach was in need of food. She touched her abdomen to stop it from growling, a noise that seemed louder than it really was. She couldn't shake the contents of the letter.

Had Ted challenged her mother in some strange way?

Had he taunted her with the mention of a dove, the albatross, and her neck?

Grace had the distinct feeling that was just what the serial killer had had in mind.

Grace couldn't sleep, a condition that had become entirely too common in the days since the first of the Puget Sound girls started to vanish—and when the bones were found. Part of it was her job, of course. She played the scenarios of what the girls' last moments might have been like, if indeed all three had had last moments. Until there was a body—or body parts— found there was hope for Emma Rose, but that hope only made it harder to sleep. Something else kept her up, too. It was the face of the sister she didn't know, the one who had been part of her life since before she was conceived. Grace crawled out from under the bedcovers, trying hard not to wake Shane. Her restlessness should not become his problem, too. She felt wired, as if she'd consumed ten cups of sugared coffee, but she hadn't. She just couldn't shut off her brain. No matter how much she needed rest. Peace eluded her.

She crept down the hall to the office that would someday, she still vaguely hoped, be converted to a nursery. She'd had plans for that space since they bought the house on Salmon Beach. She painted it in her head, blue, then pink, then yellow, then back to blue. Time was running out on that. Women were having children later and later, but she didn't want to be a mother like her own—the one other kids in the class thought was a grandma. Sissy had been over forty when she had her.

Grace hoped that if she and Shane ever became parents they'd start with a boy, a boy who would be just like Shane—responsible, caring, yet with just enough of a mischievous streak to keep things interesting.

Her nightgown provided only the thinnest layer of warmth and she nearly turned back to get her robe. But she didn't. The pull to the scrapbook that her mother and father had created about Tricia's disappearance and murder was impossible to avoid.

She opened it to the first page of the white and pink book. It was a strange color scheme, she thought. She wondered if it was a baby book that had been turned completely around and converted to a death book of sorts.

The eyes of her sister in the missing poster stared at her. The dot pattern was large, probably from the pages of the *News Tribune*, but it still didn't obliterate the lovely and haunted look in Tricia's eyes.

"Can't sleep?"

Grace swiveled around and looked up at Shane, standing behind her in his underwear. "No. I guess not," she said.

Shane stepped closer and put his hand on her shoulder, his eyes tracing the pages of the book. "I'd be an idiot to ask what's on your mind, because I already know. Want to talk about it?"

Grace nodded. She felt the strange flush of emotion coming to her, but she fought it. It was like the boy who'd rescued a girl from a stabbing and held it together like a champ until he spoke to his mother. Love and a safe place always invited a person to let go.

"Ted had something to do with my sister's death,"

she said, a single tear rolling. "I think my mom's been right all along."

He turned her chair to face him. "You know that's not true, Grace. You know Bundy and his crimes are among the most investigated cases in history. More FBI, more local PDs, historians, all of them have had a crack at trying to identify all his vics."

She nodded. "Yeah, I think I do know that," she said. "Thanks for the support, Shane."

"I'm just saying what you already know."

She looked up at him. No more tears had fallen, nor would she allow them. She loved Shane more than anything, but he didn't understand what her life, a life in the shadow of a dead sibling, had been like. Nor did he really understand her need to figure out once and for all what it was that drew her to law enforcement, to homicide.

"Look," she said, her fingertip tapping the poster image in the scrapbook.

He patted her shoulder, but not in a condescending way. "I've seen it," he said, "very sad. It will always be sad to me."

"The necklace with the dove," she said, her eyes now locked on the page.

Shane didn't quite get where Grace was going. He put his arm on her shoulder. "Right," he said. "The necklace."

"Bundy had taunted my mom with a reference to that necklace."

"You can barely make out the dove," he said.

"In fact," she said, now looking into her husband's eyes, "you can't."

Shane leaned closer and focused his sleepy eyes. "I guess you're right. But I don't think I'm following you."

"My mom was fixated on that letter from the minister. The dove letter."

"I know," he said, trying to be patient at a very, very late hour.

"My dad said that if Ted was trying to push her buttons from the grave he'd used the missing poster as a reference. You know some little detail to make her feel that he knew something. Or better yet, was holding something back."

"But if he didn't get the dove reference from the poster, where did he get it? The newspaper?"

Grace set down the ice-cream-store-colored album and led her husband back to the bedroom. "No. The newspapers never mentioned it. The necklace was something only the killer could have known. They were sure that Ted had kept it after Tricia's murder."

"As a trophy."

She nodded.

"But you're saying now that he didn't."

"I'm not sure what I'm saying. I'm just thinking out loud here. If Ted was taunting Mom and Dad with the dove comment it wasn't coming from him seeing it on the poster—that was always what the original case detectives told them."

"So if not from the poster, from someone else?"

"Maybe," she said, taking Shane's hand as they walked back to the bedroom.

"A real possibility was someone in prison. Someone he met. He wasn't in isolation until Florida, death row."

Grace slipped under the covers and kissed Shane.

"Maybe it was just a coincidence," she said letting her eyes close. "Maybe my mom and dad were wrong all these years."

Shane lay still, listening. He could feel her body going limp as she fell into much-needed slumber.

CHAPTER 30

Tavio Navarro started a new job—a complete yard remodel with a stone pool, a fountain, and a pergola that would frame the garden view of a large home in North Tacoma. He wasn't responsible for the pergola. Another contractor had been hired for that. In another time or place, Tavio would have been overjoyed with the prospect of such a prestigious job. He wasn't just a yard boy anymore. He, with his company, Green Ways, was seen as one of the better landscapers in the area, an up-and-comer who not only designed yards of distinction, but did so with a mind for easy maintenance. That was key. Less watering. Less pruning. More time for the home owners to enjoy the benefits of their gardens. A few of his workers chided him for designing them out of regular weed and water service, but he laughed it off.

That day, however, he wasn't laughing at all. Tavio had been a wreck ever since he found the dead, dismembered girl along the Puyallup River. He'd questioned Michael, but he seemed evasive and angry at the mention of anything related to what he said was the worst mistake of his life.

The girl on the news looked like Catalina and her eyes haunted Tavio. So had her mother's pleas for help on TV. He wondered if Catalina's mother had begged the same way when she heard her daughter was missing. He wondered how hard she'd cried when her body was found three days later.

Three days after he and his brother moved from Yakima.

Those had been the darkest of times. They had no money. No food. And they had the specter of the law chasing after them. When they picked cherries in Wenatchee or apples in Cashmere, they never did so without repeated glances over their shoulders.

But no one came calling. No one went looking for them. They just disappeared. They were given a chance to start over and make a new life—a new life with the ghost of Catalina always hovering near, whispering that she did not love Michael; whispering that one day he would face her and he would pay for what he'd done.

Tavio told his trio of workers to get busy.

"This section," he said, pointing to a weedy patch of lawn near the new water feature, "needs to be done today. *Vámonos!*"

The workers—two young men straight from Guatemala, and Michael—nodded and did as they were told.

Tavio watched his brother as he instructed the boys. His heart was heavy and he felt sick to his stomach.

"Going to the store," he said. "Be back in *un momento.*"

There were few pay phones in the area, but he knew of the one in the parking lot of the 7-Eleven. He parked his truck and went to the phone, depositing the coins that had warmed deep inside his pocket. He dialed 911 and told the dispatcher that it was not an emergency.

Though deep down, he felt that it was just that.

"Detective, uh," he said, "Alexander. The lady police officer on TV."

Grace Alexander was at her desk, a small cubicle that was more office worker than TV cop. She knew the irony of the world's view of police work. Everyone assumed that detectives drove nice cars, wore expensive clothes, and worked in an environment befitting stars. The truth was that while the Tacoma Police Department boasted a state-of-the-art facility—interview rooms with two-way mirrors, a forensic lab that rivaled what the state crime lab had—it was decidedly mundane. She had a collection of Mariner bobbleheads on one side of her cubicle desk and a picture of her and Shane when they'd summited Mt. Rainier that summer. It hadn't been that difficult of a trek, but it still came with some bragging rights.

"Next year, Everest," Shane had teased as the guide snapped the photograph.

"Next year, *Hawaii*," Grace had shot back.

She smiled at the memory as she picked up the phone.

"Alexander," she said.

"I want to know something," said a man with a Latino accent.

"How can I help you? Who is calling?"

"I don't want to say my name. But can I still ask a question?"

"This isn't the help desk at the library, sir."

There was a short pause. "Yes, I know. I want to know something about the girl I saw on TV. The girls you were talking about."

"Kelsey Caldwell? Lisa Lancaster?"

Another short pause, followed by, "I need to talk here. Go away."

"I'm not going away," she said.

"No. Not you. I want to know if she has DNA on her."

"Sir, we don't disclose that kind of information. Who are you and why are you asking?" The caller ID on her phone indicated a pay phone. *Damn!*

"Please look into a case in Yakima. Her name was Catalina Sanchez. Please check on her. Do the DNA. Please."

"Catalina Sanchez?" Grace repeated as the phone line went dead.

Paul Bateman, in the next cubicle, had heard part of the conversation and had quickly planted himself in front of Grace.

"That sounded like a crazy or a good tip."

"You don't get many like that. The guy basically told me to try for a DNA match on another case in Yakima."

"Yakima? Pretty far from here."

"Far, yes. But let's turn a few stones."

Grace typed C-A-T-A-L-I-N-A + S-A-N-C-H-E-Z into the database and pressed the SEARCH key.

Her eyes met Paul's as the screen flashed with a hit.

"Three years ago. Nineteen-year-old girl. Migrant worker. Unsolved."

"Suspects?" he asked.

"None."

"Interesting, but what's her connection to Tacoma's vics?"

Grace clicked through the report and a photo of Catalina Sanchez filled her screen.

"Jesus," Paul said, refraining from using the Spanish pronunciation, something that undoubtedly took a lot of willpower. Dead girls were nothing to make light of and he knew it.

Grace looked up. "She looks like she could be Kelsey's sister."

Paul nodded as he bent closer to get a better view. "Same eyes. Same hair. Same everything."

"Right, same everything," she said. "Except this one's unsolved. We're going to solve our homicides?"

"Case still active?"

Grace looked back at the photograph of the dead girl from Yakima. She and Kelsey *were* a lot alike, except for one vital detail. Kelsey's dad was not about to rest until someone led them to their daughter's killer. Catalina Sanchez had no such champion. It made a difference, and every member of the media and law enforcement knew it. There were the moms of victims who had made it their lives' missions not only to remember their daughters, but to make sure that every single person out there did, too. Beth Holloway never missed a moment to fan the flames of publicity surrounding the disappearance of her daughter Natalee while away on a school-sanctioned party trip to Aruba. Beth had gone so far as to even confront the chief suspect, a Dutch ne'er-do-well named Joran van der Sloot, while he awaited justice in a Peruvian prison. Same with Sharon Rocha, who had taken up the task of ensuring her pregnant daughter Laci Peterson's murderer was brought to justice. Scott Peterson, a fertilizer salesman who'd wanted to be free of the constrictions of a family, awaited execution on death row in California.

And yet there was no one, it seemed, to mourn Catalina. The biographical background on the Yakima victim was devoid of any helpful information. For her parents it merely stated, *migrants, address unknown*. Her last place of employment was Jonogold Orchards in Selah. And as if it needed to be noted, Catalina Sanchez's "illegal status" was listed by the report writer, the responding officer.

"Let's find out what happened to Catalina," she said, picking up the phone.

"You really are something," Paul said, with a tiny trace of sheepishness.

"How do you mean?"

"Nothing," he said.

"You started it, now go on."

"Something Lynnette once said."

"Pillow talk," Grace said. "Great. I love the idea of you and her cuddled up talking about me."

"Not so much about you. About the kind of person you are. The kind of cop."

She kept her eyes on him, barely blinking. In a way, it felt a little good to make him squirm. "What's that?"

"She said you were the kind who never left a stone unturned, a dog with a bone."

Grace exhaled. The comment was either a compliment or a derogatory remark. She just didn't know which.

"Thanks," she said. "I guess."

"Yeah. Anyway, what was it about the caller that makes you think it's worthwhile to follow it up now? We got hotter stuff to work, you know."

"Really? That's news to me. Anyway, there was a kind of pleading in his voice. He might not know who killed Kelsey, but my bet is that he knows exactly who killed Catalina Sanchez." She looked down at the photo on her computer screen. "She deserves justice, too."

Paul thought of saying something about Lynnette once telling him that she thought Grace was not only a by-the-booker, but a little self-righteous. He held his tongue. Even though Grace's statement hadn't needed to be said, there was no getting around it.

She was absolutely right.

A report from the Washington State Patrol crime lab landed in Grace Alexander's overstuffed email in-box. It brought with it the kind of news that no homicide investigator ever wanted to read. Her heart sank with each word. The DNA sample taken from Catalina Sanchez's rape and murder had been lost among scores of other pending evidence in what had been the state's criminal justice Armageddon the previous year. A small fire had broken out in the lab and the sprinkler system had done what it was supposed to do . . . gone off. And off. And off. It had ended up drenching and destroying evidence from almost every county in the state. Particularly hard-hit were counties with lesser means: counties that wholly relied on the state crime lab.

While the memorandum from the lab in Olympia indicated that, in fact, there had been a sample taken, it had been destroyed. Even the supporting documentation had been destroyed when a couple of employees had had the bright idea of using hair dryers to mitigate the loss of the original documents. Unbelievably, the electric dryers manned by none-too-bright, but well-meaning, workers had sparked a second fire.

Catalina's case was among many relegated to complete and tragic limbo.

As Grace scrolled through the electronic file she noticed that only one item had survived—a partial witness statement indicating someone had seen a couple of young men carrying something to the river's edge the night of Catalina's disappearance. The witness, a Hispanic man named Tomas Martinez, had provided no address. He'd indicated he was following the harvest and would be in Central Oregon the next week. He had no phone, but he promised that he would contact the police again when he could.

But, it appeared, he never had.

Grace wondered if this Tomas Martinez had been the man who'd called her with the tip.

She printed out a photograph of Catalina and added her to the others pinned under the fluorescent tube that ran under the bookshelf of her cubicle.

Kelsey, Lisa, Catalina, Emma.

The similarities could not be denied. Each of the pretty girls was dark eyed. All had long dark hair, parted in the middle. She ran her finger along the row of photos thinking to herself that they had so much more in common than their mere physical resemblance and their youth. Each had died in a violent manner. Each had been violated in the worst possible way. Each girl was a victim who cried out for justice.

I hear you, she thought. *I hear all of you.*

Grace hated the crime pundits who immediately jumped on the "serial killer among us" bandwagon whenever even the hint of similarity became apparent. It was too much. Serial killers were exceedingly rare. While endless books were churned out about Gacy, Bundy, Ramirez, and the other big-league killers, among serial-killer aficionados there seemed to be the hope that a new one would emerge. The idea of it disgusted Grace Alexander. Serial killers were the ultimate evil. While she faced the victims with an unblinking eye, she wanted to tell each of them that she hoped they were not killed by the same man. The sum of three individual killers was far less a man whose sole predatory focus was to kill a stranger.

It just was.

It rained all night and the wind knocked over the neighbor's old-school galvanized aluminum garbage can, but that wasn't what kept Grace awake. It was the rotating series of the faces of the dead girls that clicked through her mind. They morphed into one another like an old MTV video—back in the day when the cable channel actually played music videos. The girls were so, so young. So pretty. So much like the sister she both loved and hated. It was so strange, the rotation of faces and how Tricia had been one of them.

She woke up her husband.

"Honey," she said.

His sleepy eyes stayed shut.

She turned on the light and nudged him once more.

"Are you asleep?"

Shane pulled one eye open and looked at his wife.

"I was," he said, trying to hold his sarcasm. It wasn't easy to do. He looked over at the bedside clock. It was after three.

"Sorry," she said, rolling closer.

"I know it's the case," he said, "but what about it?" Again, he tried to keep his feelings in check. It wasn't that he didn't care about Grace's work or what troubled her. It was that it had become more than fifty-fifty in their relationship. More like eighty-twenty. It had become increasingly difficult for Shane to share about his work, his colleagues in the field office, whatever was bothering him.

"I keep thinking of my sister," she said, her voice nighttime soft.

"What about her?" he asked, a little surprised to hear that Tricia was the source of Grace's insomnia.

"If sounds silly, I know."

"What does?"

"That I keep thinking of the similarities in the case and how no matter what outcome there will be sisters like me. Mothers like my mom. You know, people who will carry the tragedy in some way for the rest of their lives."

"It doesn't have to be that way. You'll solve the cases," he said.

"They didn't," she said.

"They aren't *you*. Besides, the killer isn't Ted. Get some sleep."

"I know." She turned away from him, and looked out at the black water of Puget Sound.

CHAPTER 31

Grace felt a slow leaking of air coming from her lungs as she looked at the report from the Washington state crime lab in Olympia. It was both interesting and disappointing. In reality, the report indicated little more than what she'd surmised already—at least about the bones themselves. The bones were female. Young. The report didn't say exactly how long the victim had been dead, but indicated the skeletal remains were likely less than fifty years old. What she needed and wanted to know more than anything, wasn't there, of course. The lab didn't have the capability to determine whose bones they'd recovered from the shoreline near where Samantha Maxwell's body had been recovered. DNA extracted from bones was possible, but not an easy endeavor. Even a single hair follicle would have been a better bet.

Maybe the FBI can do better, she thought.

The report itself was brief, only three pages. It was the last page that held her interest came near the end of the document:

Significant traces of arsenic and lead were
recorded with the bone sample. The soil samples
collected from the immediate vicinity do not
carry those metals; however, locations near the
former site of the ASARCO smelter do.

The ASARCO smelter had been a Tacoma land-
mark, though not an especially lauded one, since the
turn of the previous century. In its day, the 562-foot
smokestack spewed the foul by-products of copper
smelting into the air, giving the city its "Aroma of
Tacoma" nickname. The smelter dumped lead and other
chemicals into the atmosphere, sending a toxic cloud
over much of the immediate vicinity. Prevailing winds
sent the plume points farther. Arsenic, a heavy metal
by-product of the copper smelting process, was collected by the company for use in insecticides. At least
some of it was. Over time, tons of arsenic sprinkled
over the water, shoreline, forests, and the front yards of
homeowners closest to the smelter. In the early 1980s,
the United States Environmental Protection Agency
named the former smelter a Superfund site—one of the
most toxic in the country.

As Grace dialed the number for the crime lab, she
remembered how she and her mother gathered with
friends on Verde Avenue and watched in awe as the
massive smokestack was reduced to rubble in 1993.
The town of Ruston, just below the bluff along Commencement Bay, had been freed from a dark shadow
cast by the monolith.

"Detective Alexander," she said.

The lab supervisor, a nice woman named Bea Carter,
answered.

"You're fast. Got the report, I take it?"

"Yes," Grace said.

"I figured you'd have a question or two."

"You know me well."

"I know your case. And I really wanted to find out who those bones belonged to. I was hoping right along with you."

"Will you send them to the FBI?"

"Already on their way," Bea said. "No telling when they'll get to them. They don't exactly pounce on everything, especially something this old."

"I know. Thanks. One thing I was wondering about on the report. The arsenic. Are you saying that the victim was killed by arsenic poisoning, or were the bones contaminated by the soil?"

"No. No. Not poisoning. The arsenic had leached into the bones, but had settled in after death. This was not a poisoning death at all. My feeling, based on what the techs found and sent along for our lab, is that the victim was buried elsewhere. Shallow grave, too."

That detail puzzled her. "Why shallow?"

"Most lead and arsenic from the smelter—and that's where this came from, I'm almost sure of it—only penetrated the top eight to twelve inches of the soil. I'm thinking that whoever killed our Jane Doe barely buried her."

"And then moved her later?"

"That's what it looks like. None of the soils around the point of discovery have anything like those parts per million found in the femur."

"Just the femur?"

"I think so. Hang on. Let me look. I'll put you on hold. Sorry for the Muzak."

A moment later, Bea came back on the line.

"Just the femur. The other bones were mostly clear."

"What do you think that means?"

"Good question. I've thought about it a lot. We all talked about it at lunch today. I think the body was buried with the arms folded up and over the victim's chest. On her back. In repose. Not with the arms at the side. I don't know, rain, or water, or some way it leached around the body, settling on the legs—and I'd say the back and the back of the skull if we could find anything else."

"And then moved later?"

"Right. Dug up. Moved. Long after death."

"Why do you say that?" Grace asked.

"Because of the way the heavy metals leached into only the lower part of the femur. Somebody dug up that body—and remember it wasn't very deep—and moved it."

"Why would someone do that?"

Bea paused before answering. "Maybe they were afraid someone would find it."

CHAPTER 32

Mimi Navarro, smelling a little like the paint she'd used on the baby's room, nuzzled her husband and whispered in Tavio's ear as he faced the wall and tried to calm his heartbeat with a prayer of forgiveness for what he'd done. On any other occasion, Tavio would see his wife's movement as an invitation to make love. He wasn't interested in that. Not at all. Not when he felt so sick to his stomach for making the call to the police. It felt like a betrayal and there was no getting around that.

"Tavio, you didn't leave your name?" she asked.

"No, Mimi. No."

"You didn't use your cell phone?"

"No, no, I did not."

She slid closer and wrapped her leg over his. "The police cannot find you."

Tavio felt the baby kick, but he didn't remark on it. He had been so torn up over the whole thing. The suspicions were eating him alive. If Michael had been doing what Tavio thought he might be, then his brother was a monster and had to be stopped. And yet, there was the possibility that he was innocent. Tavio had hoped for that. Whenever that hope tried to stir, he thought more about the night Catalina died.

They were driving back to pack their belongings. They didn't have much beyond a few changes of clothes and a couple of family photographs, a Bible, and a small pistol that traveled with them from orchard to orchard. *Just in case.* As Tavio drove in the blush of the morning light, he felt his face grow hot. His tears sizzled against his burning skin. He didn't cry out. He rolled down the window to let the air dry his face while his brother started singing along on the radio.

"You cannot be singing now! Catalina is dead!"

"I'm sorry," Michael said, switching on a sad and confused demeanor that was alarming in its swift change. "I didn't mean to."

Tavio had felt funny from the minute he'd seen his brother and the scratches on his face. How was it that he was scratched? The only reason could be that Catalina had tried to stop him. He had noticed something else that was strange, too. Michael said that Catalina had fallen on a rock when they were making love.

"Rough sex, yes, that's what it is called," Michael had said, altering his story for the second time.

Catalina's injury was not on the back of her head. It was on the front. It was there not because she'd fallen while they were making love. It was there because Michael had likely slammed a rock into her face.

"You told me you didn't mean to do this," he said.

Michael tried to shake it off. "I guess I didn't. I can't remember."

"Remember? You just killed a girl. What do you mean, you can't remember?"

"Quit yelling at me, Tavio. I was so mad at her. I don't really remember what happened when."

"I want to ask you this, and I want a real, a true, answer."

Michael lit a cigarette and tossed the match into the roadway.

"Go ask. You can ask what you want. I know what you're going to ask. But, yes, go ahead, Tavio."

"Did you kill her on purpose? Did you?"

Michael exhaled. "No."

"I can tell when you are lying."

The reality was Tavio couldn't tell when Michael told a lie. No one could. Michael had a kind of strange skill when it came to lying. He'd always found a way to be less than truthful whenever it benefited him to do so.

"I will answer. But I don't think it is fair that you keep asking me."

"I just helped you push Catalina Sanchez into the river!"

"That's right, *you* did. And that makes you just as responsible. An accomplice."

Tavio could barely believe what he was hearing. "Are you serious? Are you threatening me now?"

"Just the truth, Tavio. You seem to always want the truth."

Tavio knew then that his brother was not like other men. His brother did not seem to feel guilty. Not when he got extra money by mistake. Not when he cut in line to get the best row in the orchard. Not ever. Michael Navarro was not like Tavio at all. They were brothers.

They had the same mother and father. In their veins the same blood flowed. Yet they were not the same.

Not at all.

Two years after Catalina had been murdered, Mimi was putting away laundry. It was a chore she despised, but because of her part-time schedule of work and classes, she took it on. She did most of the cooking, too. Sometimes she wondered out loud if America really was a place of equality. She did almost everything her sisters back in Mexico did—plus school *and* a job. Mimi almost never went inside her brother-in-law's bedroom, but there was no getting around it that particular day. She had three stacks of laundry and only two hands. She pushed his door open with her hip and proceeded to his dresser. She set down the folded and sorted laundry and opened the top drawer. She wasn't snooping at all. It wasn't Mimi's style to pry, but she couldn't help but notice a bottle of lubricant nestled atop some photographs of girls.

Naked girls. Not of the ilk that would pose for *Playboy*, but the kind of images that would grace some pervert-visited website on the Internet. Indeed, the photographs were laser printed, not from the glossy pages of a skin mag.

Nasty, Mimi thought as she tried to set aside the unfortunately very obvious and graphic scenario of what Michael was doing with the lubricant and the photos.

Disgusting!

Before she shut the door—vowing never to go in his room again—she noticed something about the photographs. All were of dark-haired women. Women with long, dark hair. Mimi had never seen Catalina Sanchez, but she'd once met her sister. The girls that Michael were fixated on all had what she was sure were Catalina's build and features. Tavio had told her the story after their wedding when they were talking about the worst things they'd ever done—the things they could never undo. Mimi was sorry that she'd once made out with a boy—not all the way, but closer than she should have.

Tavio's ultimate transgression was decidedly worse.

"I helped my brother hide a body," he had said. "He killed a girl accidentally."

At first, Mimi had thought it was a joke. She figured he was saying something to make her feel better. That he was conjuring up something completely absurd. Because he loved her so, so much.

"I'm not kidding."

She studied his eyes.

"You're not?"

Tavio shook his head, his eyes grew wet, but he did not cry. Later, he would wonder if he'd lost part of his humanity because the mention of what he and his brother had done no longer produced the same emotion. Shame had replaced horror by then.

"Oh my God," Mimi said. "You are not kidding."

Tavio tried to explain, but it was a difficult thing to manage. "I will regret it forever. It was an accident. At least I think so."

Later, he'd tell Mimi that once their baby was born, his brother would have to leave.

"I don't trust him," he said. "I don't trust him to be good."

Every now and then, Mimi would try to test Michael to see if he was just an immature young man or something sinister. He seemed to like girls. She and Tavio had gone out on several double dates with Michael.

One time she asked Michael if he dreamed of getting married.

"I guess so," he said. "I don't know if I will find anyone like the girlfriend I once had."

Mimi held her tongue. She wanted to say, "You mean the one you killed?"

Yet she didn't. There was something about her brother-in-law that scared her. More than what he'd done in the past. It was a fear about something he might do to *her*. It would probably be easier to kill a second time.

It was late, well after midnight, when Michael Navarro returned from wherever he'd been all night. He'd been evasive about what he was doing over the past few months, but neither Tavio nor Mimi pressed the issue. There was no real need for it. After all, they'd made a deal. Michael had said that when their baby was born he'd find a new place to live. He'd volunteered and the agreement had been amicable. Michael needed a place away from his brother, to start over, to begin his own life. It was true that he and Tavio would continue working together at the landscaping company, but there would be no more long drives to and from work locations. It was, Tavio agreed, the right thing to do.

"Best for you. Best for me," he said.

Tavio was up watching a DIY show about landscaping—always good for a chuckle—when Michael came home that particular night. His younger brother literally kicked off his shoes and threw down his jacket.

Though he was sometimes hard to read, this time there was no room for doubt. Michael seemed agitated about something.

"You pissed about having to move?" Tavio asked.

"No. Pissed about other stuff."

Tavio studied his brother. His facial muscles were taut and he stood with his feet planted firmly. It was almost as if he was daring Tavio to take him on, to push him.

"Like what?" he asked, weighing his words and watching for the reaction. "Other stuff?"

"You wouldn't understand," Michael said.

"I might," he said. "But how would I know if you don't tell me?"

"You have everything, Tavio. I have nothing."

Tavio motioned for his brother to sit, but Michael refused. "I worked hard," Tavio said. "You work hard."

Michael shook his head. "It isn't about that. I don't care about that," he said, looking at the big-screen TV. "I am stuck. I'm trying not to be. I'm trying to do like what they talk about on the radio. Move on. I want to move on."

Tavio didn't ask from where or what. He had an idea, a hope.

"Talk to me, Michael."

"I won't. I can't. Sometimes I feel like there is a beast inside of me, eating me, clawing at me from inside my stomach."

Tavio glanced at the TV, the sound of a commercial loudly filling the room. He pushed the MUTE button and turned to talk to his brother, only to find that he was alone.

Michael was gone.

* * *

The next morning, the *Tacoma News Tribune* ran another article on the dead and missing girls and women. Since there had been no real news, the reporter went for the easy way to advance the story by highlighting other Northwest cases that had held the attention of the region in years past.

GIRLS MISSING: Remembering Other Cases That Rocked Our Region

The article, which included a timeline and bonus online features, highlighted the Ted cases from the 1970s and made mention that the lead detective in today's case had a personal connection to the crimes.

Detective Alexander's family has always maintained that Tricia O'Hare was a victim of Bundy's. She disappeared just before the string of murders, but her remains were never found. She's been listed as a victim by a number of authorities, including the FBI.

Tavio and Mimi Navarro sat in his landscaper's pickup truck across the street from the Tacoma Police Department on Pine Street. They'd never been to a police department before—they'd never had a reason to. Both also knew there was a risk at coming there—a risk that by sharing their concerns with those who carry a badge they could destroy their family. Mimi, who had the most to lose, had been the most insistent of the pair.

"If another girl dies," she said, "then it is blood on our hands. I cannot live with that."

"But what about . . ."

Mimi didn't blink. She was completely sure. "I would rather be sent back to Mexico than live knowing I could have stopped Michael from hurting another girl."

It was more than *hurting*, of course. The Navarros were heartsick about the possibility that Michael was a killer.

"Remember, we are here with the hope that he didn't kill that girl," Tavio said, reiterating a kind of fantastic wish that seemed like the longest shot imaginable. Everything had pointed to Michael.

Grace Alexander met them in the lobby among the historic uniforms and other relics that played out the history of the Tacoma Police like a mini law enforcement museum. The Navarros followed her to a second-floor interview room and she offered them coffee or water, but they declined.

"I know this is difficult," the Tacoma Police detective said. "And I know your circumstances concern you, but do not worry. I'm not concerned with that. I'm not looking at causing you any harm, I just want to understand why you think your brother killed the girls found by the river."

"I am not a police officer," Mimi said, stating the obvious. "But I do watch *CSI* and *Investigation Discovery* all the time."

Grace smiled. "Yes, many people do."

Tavio spoke up. "I don't watch them. But I do fear, I mean, *know* that he killed that girl in Yakima. I am sorry that I never said anything before. I am very, very sorry.

I think I just believed him enough to stop me from telling anyone. And when they found the girl, what more could I do anyway? She was dead. There was no bringing her back. He's my brother and I will always love him right or wrong. At the time, I didn't want to think that he really killed her. . . ."

Grace leaned forward. "But you know he did, right?"

Tavio nodded. "Yes. Are you going to arrest him for that?"

"No," she said. "That's not the case I'm working, but the police in Yakima will be taking another look and we will see some kind of an outcome concerning their investigation later. I'm more interested in learning more about your brother and how it is that you think he's involved in the murders here."

"Yes, but what will happen with Yakima?" Mimi asked.

"I talked with the police there," Grace said. "Other than your statement, it looks like there is not much evidence."

"What about his DNA?" Mimi said, a little proud that she could bring up a technical term. Although she was taking classes, she didn't have much opportunity to talk about things like that. Tavio was a good man, but he was not complicated.

"Unfortunately, the samples from Catalina's body," Grace said, "were compromised." She didn't tell them that the samples had vanished from the crime lab.

As Mimi listened to the detective, she reached into her purse and pulled out the photographs of the young women she'd found in her brother-in-law's bureau drawer.

"Makes me sick, this stuff," she said.

Grace looked down at the images. None of the girls looked familiar. No Kelsey, no Emma, no Lisa. It was a collection of porn, disturbing, certainly. Evidence, possibly.

"Look," Mimi said, "All of the girls look the same. Just like the missing girls in the newspaper. He must be collecting these for some perverted reason, Detective."

Grace turned the photos over. She didn't say that the girls were a match, because they weren't. Not really. Yes, they had dark hair and dark eyes, but they were Hispanic.

None of the missing or dead girls were.

CHAPTER 33

Palmer Morton was good looking in the way that men with money can afford to be. He wore the best clothes—clothing that he purchased on trips to New York because he insisted that Seattle or, even more so, Tacoma, had no sartorial finesse. He didn't admit to it, but he dyed his hair—or rather had a stylist come to his house and do it. No Grecian Formula for his locks. Palmer was a small man, but like actor Tom Cruise, he carried himself in such a way that most people didn't realize that he was under five-foot-eight. Lifts in his custom Italian shoes didn't hurt the perception, either.

Yet right then as he stood in his son's room over-stuffed with the accoutrements of a father with a guilty conscience—a plasma screen that nearly covered one wall, and a computer workstation that would have made computer geeks Apple-green with envy.

"You little shit," Palmer said, jabbing his fingers into Alex's shoulder as the teenager sat up on his bed.

"Hey! That hurts!" Alex yelped.

"You ungrateful little shit. You made Calla cry!"

Alex shot his dad a lightning-fast cold look—so fast

that he hoped his dad hadn't seen it. "That's what you're mad at? You made Mom cry when she caught you screwing Calla at the beach house."

Palmer jabbed at his son again, but Alex pulled back in time. This brought an even darker red hue to the older man's face. His eyes were now bulging and the veins on his neck pulsed in time with his anger in a staccato fashion.

"Alex, that's done," he said, seething. "You mention that one more time and you're going to go to a state school. Don't ever make Calla cry again. Don't ever threaten her again. Got that?"

Alex got up and not so skillfully hid a package of cigarettes from his father's prying eyes. "Can we forget about her?" he asked, looking up. "I'm in trouble, Dad."

Palmer shed his jacket. He was hot and angry. He knew he'd already blown up, but there was always the threat of an aftershock of anger.

"You are always in trouble," Palmer said. "You seem to make a sport of trying to find ways to piss me off and make me wish I pushed harder for an abortion when I had the chance."

Alex had heard that particularly hurtful regret before. His father claimed that his mother tricked him into marriage by getting pregnant. His dad had never wanted him.

"The cops came today," he said, refusing to look into his father's eyes.

As Alex predicted, Palmer exploded again. "Jesus! What did you do? Shoplift at Frye's again? What an idiot!"

Alex pulled back and let his eyes look into his father's only for a half-second. "No. No. I haven't done that in a long time."

Doesn't he know the difference between shoplifting and real trouble?

"Good, because the next time you do I'm not going to bail you out by paying off the manager. He's using me like a damn ATM. So what is it now?"

"The cops came today about Emma. She's missing."

"Is that the chick you were doing?" Palmer asked, a smirk now spreading over his face.

Alex glared at his father. "I didn't *do* her, and yes, it was the girl I really liked."

Palmer shook his head in utter disgust. "Liked? God! You're nineteen, grow a pair and use 'em. Use 'em a lot. Forget *liking* any girl. There's time for that later."

Alex hated his father so much just then. More than he ever did. He knew that his dad had no real attachments to anyone. Not even Calla. Certainly not to *him*. Alex knew that there were things about him that were genetically linked to his father—his eyes, his build. Thankfully *not his height.* By his sixteenth birthday, Alex had been a good five inches taller than his dad— an achievement that made Palmer Morton bitter. As Alex watched his father, he often worried that his near sociopathic personality had transferred to him. His dad was an ass. He probably had some of that in him, too. When he'd told a friend about what he thought, she'd told him that he "absolutely" wasn't like his dad at all.

"The fact that you recognize what kind of person he is and that you don't want to be like him is proof enough that you're not headed down that path."

It was Emma Rose who had said those words. And when she had, he'd fallen for her. Hard. It was as if for the first time ever he'd found someone who wanted to believe that he had some good inside him. He wasn't just the rich kid with the blowhard dad. He wasn't a petty thief who shoplifted iPods and other stuff he didn't need.

Palmer pressed on with the quasi interrogation of his son. "Why did the police come to talk to you about her?"

"She's missing. I told you that."

"Look, I can't remember every detail of your social life, as puny as it is. But why did they come to *you* about Emma?"

"You know, because we went out a few times. That's all. They were just looking for information."

"What's the big deal then?" Palmer asked.

Alex searched for the right words. Some things his dad could never understand. "I don't know."

Palmer unbuttoned his shirt collar. His anger still percolated, but it had subsided a little. "Alex, I can't fix this if I don't know what kind of problem we're facing here."

"Dad, I'm not sure. We had a big fight. Emma actually dumped me. I said some stuff about wanting to get her back. I didn't want her to break up with me. Now, you know, she's gone and it looks like, well, bad. Real bad."

Palmer sighed. "What a pussy you are. Jesus! I never thought I'd have a dickless wonder for a son. But I'll fix it. I always do."

CHAPTER 34

In the manner articles highlighting a mysterious crime always do, the latest GIRLS MISSING article in the *News Tribune* prompted a series of calls to Grace Alexander. One tip after another that, in the interest of justice, had to be followed up in some way. Most went nowhere. Most had no real connection to the case. The call from an elderly woman was one of those. She spoke with the throaty deep voice of a smoker with a slight wheeze, suggesting that her lungs were ravaged by emphysema.

"You better find who killed those three girls," she said.

"The department is doing its best," Grace said.

"Your best wasn't good enough. You never caught the SOB who killed my Susie."

Grace instantly recalled the name, and the voice. Susie Sherman's photo was on the wall of unsolved cases, like her sister. It was Susie's mother, Anna, on the line.

"I'm sorry, Mrs. Sherman," she said.

"I'm sure you are. I'd be sorry, too."

Anna Sherman and Grace Alexander shared a bond.

There was no doubt about it. Years after Susie's disappearance in 1972, her body had been discovered in the woods off a remote stretch of Highway 401 under the shadow of Mt. Rainier. Anna's voice still held the unmistakable sharp pain that came with each utterance.

Like my mother.

Like my father, too.

Grace knew that tragedy either bound family members tightly together or tore them completely apart. She'd seen her own parents' marriage disintegrate over the years. Within the heavy walls of Anna Sherman's throaty voice Grace could still hear echoes of her own mother's grief. It was, she knew, a grief that never went away. While it was clear that Mrs. Sherman couldn't exactly shed any light on the cases that were consuming every moment, there was no way she would ever refuse the invitation the still-grieving offered.

"Come and see me. I think I know something about serial killers who prey on young women," Anna said.

"Are you a psychologist?" Grace asked, wishing a second later that she hadn't.

"I'm a mother," she said.

Grace felt embarrassed. "I'm sorry. Of course. I didn't mean . . ."

"That's all right. I corresponded with Ted Bundy."

"You did?"

In that moment, Grace wondered who *hadn't* corresponded with the serial killer. Authors, her mother, and now, Anna Sherman. It seemed Ted Bundy might have been in need of a social secretary.

"Don't be so surprised," Anna said. "If you thought someone killed your daughter you would have done the same thing. I thought I could get him to tell me something, you know, before he fried in the electric chair."

"Did he tell you anything about what happened to your daughter?" Grace asked.

A beat of silence.

"No. Not really, but he told me enough that made me feel that the world was a safer place for everyone when they finally put him out of his miserable existence. I don't mind telling you I had a glass of champagne the night he cooked on the electric chair."

"I understand," Grace said, though she never admitted to anyone that she didn't believe in the death penalty. Her job had been about tragedy and death and there was no need to add to it by taking another's life. *Even Theodore Robert Bundy's.*

"Anyway," Anna said, again with a wheeze, "I think Ted might be able to help you better understand what might have happened to the missing girls."

The words were perplexing. *Ted is dead.*

"Sorry?" she asked.

"Come and read the letters. I have a stack of them. Better than some hifalutin profiler on the *Today* show. I know all about you. I think you're smart. Besides, I make pretty good banana bread and I'll have some out of the oven by the time you get here."

Anna Sherman was in the Island Home retirement center not far from the Target off Union in Tacoma. Grace knew the location; she had visited there with her seventh-grade choir to sing Christmas carols to the elderly residents. As she went inside to find Anna, the wafting smell of old people filled her nose. It was as if the scent of the people who had been there two decades prior still lingered like summertime lavender and, she thought, a little bleach. That wasn't the case, of course. Places like the Island Home always smelled that way. Anna lived in the assisted-living section of the community. She had been moved from the "live alone" to "needs a little more help" series of buildings cheerfully painted in red, blue, and yellow—a color combination that Anna thought must have been a painter's mistake.

"If they were going for something patriotic, they blew it big time. I mean, really, yellow? Who pairs yellow with blue and red?" she'd asked when her daughter and son-in-law moved her there four years ago.

Grace found a place to park under a big fir tree. A yard keeper ran a leaf blower over the sidewalk and a couple of young people went toward their car, the woman crying. It was, Grace imagined, a typical morning in a place that always needed to look pretty for someone's final days.

Anna was in Rosedale Bungalow, room fourteen. A nurse's aide named Brigitte let Grace inside. In a wheelchair by the window, a small gray-haired woman with driftwood-gnarled hands and hunched shoulders brightened. At her side was a blue plastic file box. Anna was an impossibly tiny woman. She sat ramrod straight watching a dog chase a cat across the parking lot. It wasn't a pretty view, but it held her interest.

She turned to the detective and smiled.

"You look like you did when you were a little girl, Grace. Just as pretty as a picture."

"I thought you wouldn't remember me," Grace said,

bending down to give the old woman a gentle, but heartfelt hug.

"I'm as old as the hills," she said, pointing to her temple, "but I've still got everything right upstairs. Knock on wood." She looked around and smiled at the obvious fact that there was no real wood in her room. "All vinyl and plastic. Ugh. I don't know why they think everything has to be completely hose-able around here."

Grace smiled. "You look lovely, Mrs. Sherman."

"Anna," said the elderly woman with glossy white hair and bright-red fingernail polish—a trademark look she'd held on to all of her adult life. "You're not a child anymore."

"Fine, Anna, then." She took a seat across from Anna's wheelchair. A nurse's aide looked in and nodded.

"How is your mom getting along without your father?" Anna asked, inching the wheelchair a little closer.

"About the same," Grace said. "She has her good days and bad days."

"I was sorry to read about your father's passing. He was a kind, decent man."

"Thank you, Anna."

"You're not here about Susie, are you?"

Grace shook her head. "No."

"The three girls I've been reading about."

Grace nodded sadly. "Right," she said, not even a little surprised that Anna Sherman read the paper. Of the members of her parents' group, she was unquestionably the best informed. In another time and place, Anna Sherman could have been a female version of John Walsh. Whenever a new missing girl was reported, Anna already had in hand whatever public information she could glean. She had friends at the police department who routinely copied public information files for her—through whatever channels she was able to create on the sly.

"I know it sounds far-fetched, but when I read about Emma Rose—that's her name, right?"

Grace smiled inwardly; Anna Sherman hadn't changed one bit.

"Right," she said. "Emma Rose."

Anna looked away at the dog in the parking lot. She wasn't distracted by the animal. She was thinking, pulling together the threads of what she wanted to say.

"When I read about the circumstances of her vanishing, I thought it seemed a lot like what happened to Susie. That Lancaster girl reminded me of your sister's disappearance."

Grace, of course, had thought the same thing. Emma and Susie had been taken after closing at their respective jobs. Emma, Starbucks. Susie, a produce stand and gift shop on the west side of Tacoma. Lisa Lancaster and Tricia O'Hare were both college students last seen in a Pacific Lutheran University parking lot. All four girls had never given the authorities any reason to suspect that they'd run off willingly. If any had a secret boyfriend or lover, it would have been news to their families. *Big news.*

And all four girls had one thing in common—their physical appearance. Susie, Lisa, Kelsey, Tricia . . . all were brunettes of a similar body type and build. They were lovely girls; two lost forever. One was still missing—waiting patiently for someone to find her dead or alive.

"I'm thinking that you came here for help of some kind, Grace," the elderly woman said.

"Yes," Grace said, hesitating a little. It was the reason she'd come. Anna Sherman could read people better than anyone. "This is hard to ask, but I've been thinking about Ted Bundy and . . ." Her voice trailed off and the look of recognition came to Anna's face. Her dusty blue eyes were instantly full of emotion. Even all those years after everything happened, the name still brought back a flood of memories. None of them good.

Anna locked her eyes on Grace. She didn't say anything. She just looked.

"I was thinking about the similarities of the cases . . . and, you know, the letters to and from Ted."

"Tell me about the letters," Grace said.

"You're interested, then?"

She nodded and looked at the blue plastic box. "Yes, that's why I'm here."

By the looks of them, the letters had been typed on a manual typewriter. Some letters, most notably the E and R, seemed to stick and were rendered slightly above the baseline of the words in which they were used. It was double spaced and signed: *peace, Ted.*

Dear Mrs. Sherman:

I want to call you Anna, but I don't know if you want me to do that. I look forward to each of your letters and though I wish I had some information to ease your mind, I know I don't. Every time I write to you without the response that you are looking for, I think you will stop writing to me. I would hate for our friendship, however tenuous, to end because I will not make up a story about your daughter just to give you peace of mind. I guess everyone wants peace of mind. Even me.

Especially me.

So that we can continue our correspondence, I will offer you something. Not an admission of course—because that's not the truth—but I will offer you my most sincere, my most heartfelt, most genuine condolences for your loss. Your daughter was a beautiful girl and undoubtedly loved by many. Whoever killed her is a complete monster.

But I am not that monster. I'm a guy who made some mistakes and now I am paying the price for it. I'm not saying that my mistakes weren't big ones, but the measure of my supposed crimes is far less than those who want to kill me would have.

I am sorry about Susie. I have seen her photograph many, many times over the years. She's always put up with the string of girls from Oregon to Washington. I admit that she looks like whatever the world seems to think I'm responsible for, but I never would have killed her.

He scratched out the last few words and wrote with pen: *never would have killed anyone.*

The correction was very telling. Anna knew it when she read it the first time. It was a slipup. Ted had edited himself. A sociopath of the highest order, yet devious enough to know the denial of killing a particular girl was not a strong enough protestation on its own. A normal person—one who didn't suckle on the bloodlust of a murder spree—would dismiss the entirety of the question.

Ted was good at reading people. He was always good at second-guessing what someone would think or do. That was how he'd been able to pick the victims who would help him with his sailboat, change a tire, carry some books as if he were on his way to some political science class.

Ted Bundy, the up-and-comer. Ted, the young Republican. Ted, the manipulator. But more than anything, Ted the predator.

Grace's eyes met Anna's, and she went on to the next letter.

Dear Mrs. Sherman:

Tell me more about you. I want to know what kind of home Susie was raised in? Did she have a lot of friends? Was she as pretty as her picture? Did she seem to have a bright future? Do you think you will ever stop hurting because she is gone?

Sometimes when I was a kid I thought that the world was a big ugly place. I had no real idea how ugly it was, how petty people could be. I tried my best to fit in wherever I could. Sometimes I thought that people were just jealous of me. Don't get me wrong. I'm not an egomaniac. I'm good looking. That's one thing I got from my dad, I guess. People used to say that

*I looked like Johnnie Bundy. What a joke that
was. He wasn't even my dad. I was nothing like
him. He was a goody-goody, all right. My mom . . .
my mom. Hard to even talk about her. I know she
did the best that she could for me, given the
times. Yet, she was the one who spread her legs
and nine months later out popped me!
Sometimes I wonder if she was easy and didn't
know who my dad was or if it was just that she
was naïve about sex. I don't like slamming my
mom. She stood by me through all of my
troubles and that's better than the rest of the
Bundy clan.*

   *I bet your family never stopped praying for
Susie. Did you decide if you can send me her
picture? I'd like to see what she looked like in a
decent photograph. The ones I saw in the paper
were always her high school senior photograph.
Those always look cheesy. I know mine did. Mrs.
Sherman, it would mean a lot to me if I could see
her photo. Will you please, please send me one?
You mentioned that you vacationed with Susie
the summer before she died. . . . Was it on the
beach on the Oregon Coast? Maybe you have a
photograph from that trip you could send me?
Did she wear a bikini?*

Grace felt her stomach turn somersaults. It was beyond belief that Ted Bundy would seek a swimsuit
photograph of a girl he'd probably killed. She could
only imagine that he'd wanted to relive whatever he'd
done to Susie Sherman. It was disgusting, vile, reprehensible.

"You didn't send him a photo, did you?" she asked

Anna shook her head and motioned for Grace to pour her some water from a plastic pitcher on a tray next to her bed. It was the first time that Grace noticed the oxygen tank—at the ready, but not in use.

"Of course not. I thought of sending a picture of some minor TV actress or even another family member and saying it was Susie. Someone who looked like her. I wondered what he would do if he knew that I didn't trust him."

"But you *didn't* trust him, did you?"

Anna sipped her water and set down the glass. "Of course not. But I didn't want to lose him. I didn't want him to go away. You know how you cops on TV sometimes try to keep someone talking on the phone so you can get more info?"

Grace nodded. "Yes, to trace them?"

Anna took another sip of her water. "Right. Well, I know with a letter you can't trace anything, but I thought that the more I could get him to write, the more he'd tell me. Maybe among his garden of lies, I'd be able to weed out a little bit of truth. Maybe I'd be able to get him to admit that he'd killed my Susie."

Grace understood completely. In so many ways, Anna was like her own mother. She wondered just how many others were out there wondering about their daughters and if Ted had been their killer.

A nurse came in with a small loaf of banana bread.

"We'll each have a piece," Anna said. "They make it from my recipe. Susie loved the cinnamon butter."

Grace smiled. It was a sad smile, but it was all she could manage. While the nurse set down the banana bread, she read another letter.

Dear Mrs. Sherman,

You are well, I hope. They want to kill me, as
you probably have heard. All I want is peace.
Did you know that I've been corresponding with
other friends of yours? I know that you are a
game-player. That's all right. While I prefer peo-
ple be direct, I'm sure that there are others who
are less inclined to be honest. I'm not saying
that you're a liar, Anna Sherman, I just know
that you can't be trusted.

peace, Ted

Grace put down the short letter, a note really, and fastened her eyes on Mrs. Sherman's.

"Was he talking about my mother?" she asked, a little unsure. "She was playing him, too."

Anna finished a bite of banana bread and brushed a crumb from her chin.

"Honestly, I don't know. The way I always looked at it, Ted probably got more mail than Santa Claus back then. Everyone—reporters, victims' families, groupies, what have you—wrote to him."

"If he wasn't referring to my mother, what other 'friends of yours' was he getting at? If you know?"

Anna shook her head. "Not sure. It could have been Peggy Howell."

Grace put the letter back into the envelope, the look of recognition washing over her face. "Peggy?"

"Yes," Anna said. "*Her*. I know your family has a history with the girl. I guess I did, too. She befriended me over Susie's death, and, of course, you know your sister's connection to Peggy."

*   *   *

Emma Rose hadn't given up all hope. Not completely. As dire as things had been, there was still plenty for which she could be grateful. Yes, she'd been tied up and her skin was colored by bruises that had passed from blue and black to a ghastly yellow hue. But he, the creeper, hadn't tied her up for a while. As she lay on the smelly mattress in the dank subterranean space, the so-called apartment, Emma had taken to keeping her eyes tightly shut. Truth be told, what was there to really see? The only time she bothered to open her eyes was when he came down the stairs. When the door opened and the stabbing light cascaded against the walls, Emma would run her eyes over every surface. Was there a door? A boarded-up window? Was there a way out of there?

She'd never seen any.

As she lay there, something else crossed the young woman's mind. At first, she wasn't sure if it had been a dream, a hallucination. Emma felt something. *Air.* Air ran over her cheek. It was cold, not the hot breath of the creeper who'd held her. Cool. She licked her palm and pressed her hand outward; turning it slightly like it was a metal detector or radar device.

There.

Emma felt the unambiguous movement of air. *Air!* It brushed against her in a slight, but steady stream. *Air!* Emma felt her pulse quicken and she instinctively turned to listen for her captor. Was he coming? Was she dreaming? No. All quiet. Next, she slid her feet to meet the floor and she stepped slowly and quietly closer to the moving air. She moistened her palm a second time, no longer reviled by the filth of her own skin.

She ran her hands, cut and sore, over the cement and cinderblock wall. She held her breath.

And there it was, air was pouring in through a crack at about knee height. She stuck a finger into the jagged fissure.

Could this be a way out?

Had God answered her prayers?

Or was this just a cruel joke made by a man who'd kept her like a zoo animal?

She heard his footsteps and she hurried back to the mattress. If it was the promise of a way out, she wasn't going to squander it by lamely standing next to it. She wouldn't tip off the man. She'd kill him first.

He opened the door.

"Stay down," he said. "Or I'll beat you until you can't stand without being bound to a two-by-four."

He set down the tray and shut the door. The lock dropped back into place. Her mind on the fissure in the wall, Emma Rose still needed to eat and drink. She started on the sandwich and washed it down with a different drink, a citrus-flavored soda.

Her legs started to wobble and she went back to the mattress.

CHAPTER 35

Grace Alexander studied the man across from her. They didn't get many like him in an interview room at the Tacoma Police Department. Paul Bateman looked at her and nodded. Palmer Morton, dressed in a European cut suit with shoes that probably cost a week's wages—a detective's wages, that is—was a smug little prick. He was puffed up and trying to appear as if he was a gracious sort of person.

It wasn't a good fit for his personality.

"Glad we could have a little talk," he said.

"Frankly, we're surprised to see you," Paul said. "You know, without an attorney."

Palmer smiled and shrugged a little, his perfectly fitting suit flowing effortlessly with each muscle movement. "If you ask me, attorneys and accountants have ruined the world."

The remark was meant to be a kind of "everyman" statement. But he was far from everyman status.

"Real estate developers haven't been so great, either," Paul said, with a slight laugh. It was meant to be a little dig, but Palmer didn't bite. He was there for a reason and taking the obvious bait was a fool's mistake. He prided himself on being a smooth negotiator and that's just what he was there to do. He considered Alex a piece of crap, but the boy was *his* piece of crap. If his kid went down, he'd go down along with him.

"It's nice of you to stop by. But really, we'd like to interview Alex," Grace said. "Maybe you can call him and have him come down."

"He's a kid," Palmer said.

"He's nineteen. He's an adult."

Palmer ignored the detective's remark and didn't say anything. It was strategic, a way to get the detectives to reveal more about their motives in talking to Alex in the first place.

"We're surprised that you wanted to see us," she said.

Palmer Morton folded his hands on top of the table. "I was on my way to a meeting and I thought I'd stop by. A little out of the blue, I guess. Hope I didn't interfere with any of your investigation into the disappearance of the girl."

"That girl is Emma Rose," Paul said.

A look of obvious recognition over his face, Palmer nodded. "Yes, Emma. Nice girl. Some problems, but nice."

Grace could have guessed it. Palmer Morton was there with a gas can. He was going to douse Emma Rose's character and drop a lit match. It made her even more suspicious of Alex and what kind of role he might have played in her disappearance.

"What kind of problems?" Grace asked, not giving away her irritation.

"I don't know how to say this, because I want to be PC," he said, looking first at Grace then at Paul.

"We're trying to find her, so tell us what you know," Grace said.

"I hate talking about anyone like this, but she was like a lot of girls. She wasn't interested in my son at all. She was just using him."

"Using him how?" she asked.

Palmer shrugged a shoulder. "Using him, you know . . ." His voice trailed off. "Look, my son's not the brightest bulb in the box and he sure as hell didn't inherit much of anything from me. Looks like his mother's side, that's for sure."

"I'm sure your family tree is fascinating, Mr. Morton," Grace said, her tone a little less polite than she'd intended. "But what, exactly, are you getting at?"

Palmer stared hard at Grace. "She was a little bit of a whore, a gold digger. She just cozied up to my son because of his big, fat trust fund."

"I see," she said, barely believing she'd heard him correctly, but knowing full well that she had.

He didn't like her tone and bristled right away. "Don't look at me like that, Ms. Alexander."

"Detective," she said, coolly correcting him. "How do you know this?"

"I know it because I saw it. Look, I don't want to embarrass my boy. He's already embarrassed. But Emma hit on me."

"Hit on you?" Grace asked, suppressing the desire to roll her eyes at her partner. The man across from them really was the biggest jerk in Tacoma. *Bar none.*

Palmer Morton fiddled with the money clip in his pants pocket. It was a platinum affair that had an angel on one side and the devil on the other. "Look, it happens a lot," he said in his best imitation of being somewhat sheepish. "I get it. Girls are looking for their daddies. Roll in some serious money and a manse like mine and it happens. All the time. Truth be told, I'm kind of sick of it."

Grace didn't need to make a mental note. With that remark there was no doubt that she and Paul would be joking about that ridiculous line for years to come. *So sick of being hit on!* And really, who in the world but an egomaniac uses the term "manse"?

"I imagine it happens a lot," she said, convincingly deadpan. "Considering who you are."

Palmer brightened a little. "Then you get it, right?"

She nodded. "Oh yes. Big-time."

The interview with Palmer Morton over, Grace hurried to her desk to get her purse and coat.

"Where you headed in such a rush?" Paul asked when he caught up with her by the stairs.

"Got an interview," she said.

"I'll get my coat."

"No. This is personal," she said, heading down the stairs.

And it was. Very.

Across town, Anna Sherman looked at the box of Ted stuff she'd kept all those years and noticed that inside a copy of *The Only Living Witness*, she'd hidden that horrible letter that Ted had sent her. Not one that he'd written, but one that he'd *sent* her. On purpose? Or a mistake?

She'd forgotten about it completely. She'd forgotten

about many things and it scared her. She could no longer recall Susie's laugh. That hurt so, so much.

She reread the letter. With each word, she felt a pang of worry, anxiety.

> *Dear Ted,*
>
>   *Sometimes I just want to call you Teddy! You are my huggable Teddy Bear! Don't be embarrassed. I know that you don't mind a pet name. I saw a new photograph of you on the news this morning. I think it was an older photograph. Maybe taken last year? You are wearing a turtleneck and it fits you like a glove. I thought that jail made guys pudgy. But not you. You are just as handsome and fit as ever. I am looking forward to seeing you. I have been over at Tricia's mom's house just to keep in touch with the O'Hares. You know, keep your enemies close. I tried to tell Tricia's mom that she would be surprised when the real truth comes out, but she says that I'm a fool to think that you are innocent of anything. She's the fool. She thinks that I care more about doing interviews with the newspaper than trying to prove who killed her daughter. Tricia is dead. She is over. What is the point on trying to assign blame now? No point if you ask me. Let Tricia rest in peace and leave me/us alone.*
>
>   *Now back to you. I heard an old song on the radio today and it made me think of you. I don't know if you will think that this song is silly, but I kind of think of it as our song. It is called "Love Will Keep Us Together." The group is a husband*

and wife group called The Captain and Tennille.
I almost didn't want to tell you about this, but I
really do think it fits us. No matter what
happens, Ted, love will keep us together.
    I promise to write tomorrow. I'll keep the
letters coming. I haven't heard from you in a
week or so. I hope you get this.
                        Love, Peggy

Peggy. Peggy Howell. Just as Anna finished reading, a nurse came in to check on her. It was medicine time. She put her hand up to her chest.

"Saved the best for last," the nurse said, like she always did. "The pink one."

Anna didn't respond. Usually she laughed and said something about how the blue pills were her favorite. She sat motionless, clutching the letter.

"Anna, are you all right?"

The old woman shook her head.

"Do you need the doctor?"

"No, I'm fine."

"I need you to do something for me," she said, pushing the letter into the nurse's hand.

The nurse, a younger woman with a normally sunny disposition, took the letter, her eyes falling on the paper.

"You can read it," Anna said. "But it won't make sense to you. I need you to fax this letter over to Detective Alexander at the Tacoma Police Department. Her card's over there on the table."

PART THREE
SON RISING

"Murder is not about lust and it's
not about violence.
It's about possession."
—TED BUNDY

CHAPTER 36

Phillip Marciano was in his mid-seventies and he looked it. Maybe even older. His hair was combed over his pink pate in three parallel striations and his skin was white parchment. He looked slightly frail and he moved slowly. Very slowly. He and Jackie, his wife of almost fifty years, lived in a condo in Gig Harbor. It was a two-bedroom home, but the second, smaller bedroom had been converted to a library, befitting the world literature professor that he had been at the university. Or, would always be. He and Jackie had lived in Gig Harbor since his retirement, fifteen years ago.

Grace Alexander had called ahead, something she didn't always do when working a case. She didn't want to give a potential witness a head start in either running or in conjuring some kind of cover story. This case—her sister's—didn't really call for either.

At least that's what Grace hoped.

When the detective appeared in their doorway, he introduced her to Jackie.

"This is Grace, Jackie," he said, letting her inside. "She's one of my students. She's working on a novel."

Jackie, a beautiful woman with cobalt eyes, and an orange scarf around her slender neck, smiled warmly.

"I wish Phil would finish *his* book," she said with a little laugh. "Maybe you can inspire him."

Grace nodded, going along with the lie as the old man led her from his wife to the library.

He shut the door and his smile faded.

"Look," he said, "I understand how this is part of your family history. I recognize that you want answers, but this is my life now. We can't always go back and fix things. I answered everything I could years ago. I truly don't know how I can help you."

He'd tried to shut her down, but Grace was undeterred.

"First, I'm grateful that you are seeing me now," she said.

"What choice do I have? If I didn't, you'll blow this all out of proportion."

"I'm not here to cause you any harm."

"Just being here causes me harm."

"May I sit?" she asked.

He nodded and motioned to a settee. Grace looked around the room. The walls were floor-to-ceiling books, many, judging by their covers, rare. This was not a library for show, but one that showcased the best novels ever written, amassed by a collector who could quote from many of them. On some of the shelves were family photos—Jackie, Phillip on vacation at the Grand Canyon and the Caymans, and other family members.

"Sorry, of course. No matter what you think of me, I still have manners."

Grace looked up. Mrs. Marciano had entered the room with two cups of tea and a plate of biscotti.

"Darjeeling," she said. "Just like Phil always served in his one-on-one sessions back in the day. Cookies are homemade."

"Thanks, honey," he said. "We're going to get started."

His tone was dismissive, but Jackie didn't appear to mind. *She's probably used to it*, Grace thought.

Grace took a cup from the table where Jackie had carefully placed it.

"She doesn't know, does she?" she asked.

Phillip swallowed some tea, pondering it. "I honestly don't know," he said, softly. "I hope not. I have done everything I can to keep it quiet, to keep her out of it."

"She suspected, though," Grace said. "I read it in the interview report."

"Yes. She made some complaints. She was fighting to keep me, not to hurt me. I was the fool here. Not her."

He stopped talking, pondering once more.

"How was my sister . . . was it my sister?"

Silence.

"Professor?"

He shook his head. "Sorry. What were you saying?"

"Are you all right?"

Again, a slight pause. A beat of silence. "I have pancreatic cancer," he said. "I don't know how much more time I have, how much I should say."

"I'm sorry," she said, which she was. She'd had an uncle who'd died of the same devastating disease. He'd go fast. "Do you know what happened to my sister?"

"I think I'm too tired to talk," he said. "Maybe we should do this another time."

Grace set down her tea and stood, inches from the

professor, who now seemed smaller, frailer than he had when she arrived. She couldn't allow herself to feel sorry for him. If he knew anything at all, he was a bastard for keeping it to himself for so many years. He was small, cruel man.

"You owe me and my mother an explanation," Grace said. "Were you having an affair with Tricia?"

Finally, a look in his eye—a snap of recognition came to his face.

"No, no, I wasn't, but . . . she knew about it, Detective. She saw me with her. She told me that what I was doing was wrong, which I already knew."

"When did she confront you?" she asked.

"A week before she disappeared. It didn't have anything to do with her disappearance. I wasn't having an affair with her. I agreed with her that it was wrong. I broke it off."

"How can you be sure it didn't? Professor, how can you be sure?"

The professor looked up, his eyes full of tears.

"Because I've lived every day since then telling myself that very thing. That it didn't matter. That it couldn't matter."

"Who was the student?"

Phillip kept his eyes cast downward. "Margaret Howell."

The name was like a bullet to Grace's chest.

"Peggy?" she asked. "You were involved with Peggy?"

The professor shook his head and finally looked up. "I was, like I've admitted to you a moment ago, a fool. I don't like the word *involved*. It seems too personal. Too committed. I was stupid. We both were."

He's still justifying it, she thought. "The reports I

read indicated that the affair was only a rumor, that you were exonerated by the school."

Phillip looked over in the direction of his wife as she moved down the hall toward the living room.

"She forgave me," he said, overcome by emotion, but fighting to hold it together. "She told them that she'd lied. She gave me a second chance."

That's all that Grace wanted, too. A second chance.

"What did my sister do about it? Peggy was her best friend."

The professor nodded. "The last time we had coffee, we talked about it. Your sister had urged Peggy to stop seeing me and she promised she would. For the most part, it was over. It really was."

In the second-floor generic-as-can-be interview room, four people gathered to discuss Emma Rose. Only one knew something. *Maybe two.* Alex Morton looked worse than the proverbial deer in the headlights. The teen's tough-guy attitude had evaporated. He trembled a little underneath the thin graphic T-shirt of some band Grace had never heard of, and his breath seemed a little short. He moved his hands from his lap to the table, as though he couldn't seem to get comfortable. Not even a little bit. And in what was not a shocker to the detectives, in the seat next to Alex Morton was a lawyer, not his father. Nor was it surprising that the lawyer was one of the best in Tacoma.

Kiernan Weber was about sixty, a kind of genteel fellow who had served as a superior court judge in Tacoma before retiring to private practice. He came with the best reputation.

The best that money could buy.

A lot of money.

Palmer Morton's money.

"I understand that you have some questions for my client," he said in his characteristic deep baritone, a voice that routinely sent shivers down even the toughest defendant's spine. Prosecutors and defense attorneys, too. "I hope we can answer them to your satisfaction today," he said.

Grace had testified in Judge Weber's courtroom a few times. This was the first time she'd seen him off the bench. She respected him, like most in the department. Yet, she wondered if money was so important that a man like Weber, with a pension as big as the moon, really needed to scoop up more of the green stuff.

"Judge, as you know, we've met your client."

"And your client's father," Paul added, never missing a chance to turn the blade for a reaction.

Judge Weber nodded, refusing to play. "That's right," he said. "I understand all of that. And as far as I know, both have been cooperative."

"Reasonably so," Grace said, wanting to add something about how they had probably lied to her, but she let it go. Goodwill to the man next to the teenager trumped a sarcastic remark.

"That's good to know," he said. "I've always been on the side of cooperation."

"We have some new information and we're hoping that you can shed some light on it."

"That's why we're here. Tell me, detectives, is my client a target of your investigation? There was certainly some drama in getting us all here this morning."

"We're trying to find a missing girl, Judge. We need

help. We have reason to believe your client wasn't completely candid when we talked with him at his residence," she said, holding back the word *mansion* because it seemed so ludicrous to use that kind of loaded word. The kid was a kid. Whatever money he had came from inside his dad's wallet.

Paul spoke up. "We also think that your client's father wasn't so truthful, either."

Judge Weber's face betrayed no emotion. He just listened and took it all in. It was hard for Grace to think of anything other than testifying in the judge's courtroom. Hiring him to defend his son was a brilliant move on the part of Palmer Morton.

But maybe not enough so to save Alex.

"You've come across something new. Not sure if it's evidence of anything, but something you wanted to talk about this morning."

"Right," Paul said.

"We want to show you something," Grace said, sliding the DVD of the surveillance video from mall security into the player. Showing the image of Emma Rose talking to someone with the Mortons' BMW 3 in the background was powerful. Powerful enough to maybe jar Alex into actually saying something of value. Grace and Paul had discussed the idea before the rich kid and the judge showed up. Neither saw it as tipping any hand to a potential killer, because there was no body, no clue, no nothing about the whereabouts of Emma Rose. Playing the clip of the parking lot was all they had. If he was charged later, Alex Morton would get to see the video through discovery. There'd be plenty of time for him to come up with an excuse, of course.

Alex sat stiffly in the chair. He was still by then, apparently, giving up the notion of getting comfortable in a place that could never be so.

"Do you mind if we ask your client a few questions?"

"I do mind, and I've advised Alex that it might be in his best interest to answer some. But he wants you to know that he liked the girl."

"Are you talking about Emma Rose?" she asked.

The judge nodded while Alex just sat there, doing as he had undoubtedly been coached.

"Yes, of course. Emma Rose."

"Fine," she said. "May I direct a question to Alex?"

The judge looked at Alex and the young man nodded.

"Before doing so," Judge Weber said, "is Alex a target of your investigation?"

Grace shook her head emphatically. "No."

"Is he a suspect?"

"No," she said, again decisively.

"Is he a person of interest?"

There was a slight hesitation, but Grace answered. "We're just trying to find a missing girl. Alex might be able to help. Our focus, our sole focus, is on finding Emma."

"All right," the judge said. "What do you want to know?"

"How long did you date?" she asked the teen.

Judge Weber indicated for Alex to answer.

"A little while," Alex said. "Not much. It wasn't that serious."

"But you liked her, right?"

Again, a little nod from the judge.

"Yes, I liked her."

"Did you break up with her or did she break up with you?" Grace asked.

Before Alex Morton could answer, Paul leaned forward.

"She dumped you, right?" he asked.

Alex's throat tightened and tried to remain calm. "I guess so. I guess she dumped me. So what? It wasn't going to go anywhere."

"You didn't like being dumped, did you?" Paul asked.

Judge Weber shook his head. "Look, we're not in a courtroom and by the line of your questions, I'm thinking that you've gathered us here for more than a little mere fact finding." He turned to Grace. "I thought you had a video clip you wanted to show us? Isn't that why we're here?"

"Yes," she said, her eyes fastened on Alex. "Getting to it."

"You said that my client isn't on the clip, correct?" he asked, his voice deeper and more forceful than ever.

She nodded. "Correct."

Judge Weber appeared to size up the detectives before speaking. "You want us to look at the tape to see if there is anything Alex can tell you to be helpful. That's all, correct?"

"Yes," Paul said, a little irritated with the way the former judge was trying to control things like he was still in the black robe.

"Fine then. Then let's roll the tape so we can get out of here. I have a Rotary meeting at noon."

Grace reached over and pressed the PLAY button. While the DVD played, she kept her eyes on Alex. She knew that even a junior sociopath like she presumed he was would betray his feelings. Provided he had any. She'd done some background work on the boy—abandoned by his mother, being raised by an insufferable blowhard father—and she almost felt sorry for him. But if he had anything to do with Emma Rose's disappearance, any sympathy she had would be gone. Right then everything was about trying to find the missing girl, hoping that she would be alive.

Hoping that she wasn't the victim of a serial killer.

The screen showed the mostly empty parking lot. A few carts. A few cars. Then a figure of a young woman appeared. She was small, lithe. She started from the direction of the Starbucks and moved across the screen toward the transit stop.

"That's Emma," he said. "Quality sucks, but that's her. She practically skips when she's in a hurry."

Alex kept his eyes riveted to the plasma. Grace kept her eyes on Alex.

Emma turned around and started talking to someone in the direction of the Starbucks. The angle was so poor it was hard to tell if she was angry, laughing, or what. Her shoulders moved rapidly and one hand flew up in the air. But it was hard to say if it was a gesture of recognition or one meant to rebuff someone.

Like the potential stalker former boyfriend across the table from her.

"Do you know who she's talking to?" she asked Alex directly.

"How would I know?" he said.

Paul had been itching to move the needle. All this making nice, all this respect for the rich judge with the rich client, was turning his stomach.

"You weren't there that night?" he asked.

Before Alex had the chance to answer, Judge Weber put his fingers to his lips and the teen clammed up.

The judge didn't say anything, but it was clear to both detectives that he saw what they hadn't noticed at first, second, and fifteenth view of the tape—the car.

"This interview is over," he said, his eyes meeting Grace's with a cold, decisive stare.

"Do you drive your dad's car?" Paul asked.

Judge Weber stood up, pulling his client to his feet and pushing him toward the door. "Don't answer, Alex. We're done now." Before exiting the interview room he turned to Grace.

"I always thought you were one of the good ones," he said. "Guess there really aren't any more of those around here, are there?"

"Glad to know you're able to double dip. Must be nice to get a pension and have a job at the same time," Paul said.

The judge smiled. It was a cold smile, the kind meant to punish or humiliate rather than charm.

"Yeah, it is. And yes, I make a lot of money. Good-bye, Detectives Alexander and Bateman. Rotary at noon. I enjoy being a part of my community. You know, because I can afford to."

Paul turned to Grace.

"Jesus, I don't know who's more of a prick—the judge, the kid, or his dad."

"Did you have to piss him off?" Grace asked.

Paul glowered. "Did you have to be so respectful?"

"Don't go there," Grace said, frustrated by the whole situation. "I'm not the one with a thick Internal Affairs file."

"Low blow. But so what? Did you see the look on the judge's face when he saw the car?"

"Oh yeah. Let's name him."

"Suspect?"

"Person of interest. Let's rattle the Mortons' gilded cage a little and see what falls out."

CHAPTER 37

Jeremy Howell was six when his mother, Peggy, told him who his father was. Peggy would later say she held off for years because her son was too young to completely understand. It wasn't that she thought the boy was dumb. Far from it. After all, how could he be anything but brilliant? Indeed, there was no arguing that Jeremy was smarter than the average second grader at Geiger Elementary—the same school his father attended when growing up in Tacoma. Jeremy had been reading at the fourth-grade level and could recite all fifty states and their capital cities—something that Peggy was sure was nothing short of genius.

Peggy, her son, Jeremy, and daughter, Cecilia, were living in her late mother's house on Ruby Street back then. She told people she was a widow whenever they asked about Jeremy's father. Most assumed the boy's dad had been killed in a car accident or maybe in combat in the Army or Air Force. With a pair of military bases nearby, it was easy to allow people to think whatever they needed to believe.

Peggy could never tell anyone that he'd died in the electric chair.

Jeremy was watching a Superman cartoon when Peggy decided the time was right. She went over to the set and turned off the sound.

"Hey, Mommy, I was watching that," the boy said.

"I know. But what I have to tell you is more important than a cartoon."

He looked at her, studying her face for some kind of hint about what could be more important than what he was doing at the moment of her unwanted interruption. He didn't like it when his mother talked to him like that, as if she knew what was best for him. He knew best all by himself. He looked back at the silent TV as Superman went after Lex Luthor.

"Jeremy," she said, taking a seat on the sofa—the sole piece of furniture in the front room. "Your daddy was a very important, famous man."

This seemed to interest Jeremy and he turned his attention away from the silent TV to his mother.

"Who?" he asked.

Peggy wanted this particular disclosure to go perfectly. She'd planned it over the past several nights as she lay in her bed staring at the ceiling and conjuring the words that would not scare, but make him understand the importance of what she was imparting.

"I will tell you," she began. "But I want you to know something first." She waited for him to acknowledge the meaning of her caveat, and the six-year-old nodded slightly.

"What, Mommy?" he asked, using the "mommy" word because he knew that she liked it when he did so.

Peggy looked serious. "This is very important. Remember when I told you that sometimes people hate other people for no reason."

"Like you hated your mom?"

Peggy shook her head. "I had reason. No, I mean, like sometimes people get the wrong idea about someone and they just decide that hating is better than understanding."

"Okay," he said.

"Your daddy was accused of doing bad, bad things. He did not do them. He was not a bad man, but a lot of people thought he was."

"What did they think he did that was so bad? Was he in jail?"

Peggy nodded. "Yes, he was in jail. They said that he did terrible things."

"But what terrible things?"

Peggy swallowed, this was the hard part. He'd been raised in a world that condemned evil. Horror and shock were the routine responses to murder. Repulsion, too. "They said he killed someone."

Jeremy's eyes widened as he took in that bit of information. "Who did they say he killed?"

"Some girls. Some girls."

Jeremy pushed his mother to be as direct as she could.

"Did he kill them?" he asked.

Peggy shook her head with exaggerated vehemence and patted him gently on one knee. The boy recoiled a little; his mother's touch was a rarity and he didn't always like it when she tried to show any affection. Affection seemed foreign and uncomfortable.

"No, son," she finally said, "he did not. He absolutely did not. He never should have been in prison. Not for one minute."

"Is he in prison now?"

Peggy looked at the TV. She hadn't thought things completely through. She thought that she could explain what happened to Jeremy's father after he was a little older. It was the stupid school's fault having to shove a stupid "family tree" assignment at her. It seemed so unfair. *What about those slutty moms who can't figure out which guy is their child's father? How were they going to wriggle out of the school assignment?*

"No," she said, her eyes now welling with tears. "Your daddy died in prison. He never got to get out and be with us. He wanted to. He really did. He loved you and he loved me. No matter what anyone says about him, remember that. Remember what I'm telling you."

Jeremy nodded. "What is my daddy's name?"

"Theodore," she said.

Jeremy shrugged a little, searching for a connection. "Like one of the Chipmunks?"

Tears were streamed down Peggy's face. The emotion was genuine. "Yes, like one of the Chipmunks. But everyone who knew him called him Ted."

Jeremy thought a moment and reached for the remote control. He didn't ask his dad's last name. The name Theodore was bad enough.

Despite her tears, Peggy felt relieved. She patted Jeremy once more and went to the kitchen cabinet, where she kept a bottle of inexpensive vodka hidden behind a box of Rice Chex. A drink was in order. Her son would get the full disclosure later. She had to ease him into the truth with lies. In due time, he'd find out just how special he was. There would be no shame at all. Just the kind of pride that comes from knowing that greatness courses through a family bloodline.

CHAPTER 38

Grace wanted to believe that her husband, her mother, her partner, would understand her obsession with her sister's murder. And yet, she didn't really understand it completely herself. Lisa's and Kelsey's murders and Emma's disappearance were fresh, new. They called for her to help them claim justice, but it was her sister's case that propelled her forward. She hadn't slept for two days. She'd been living on coffee and junk food. While Paul was working the missing girls case file, she excused herself.

"I don't feel so good today," she said.

"Bug's going around."

When he said that, she thought of Ted's VW bug. Every word now seemed tied to the serial killer.

"I'm going to head out, okay?"

Paul nodded. "Sure. Got things covered."

Ted didn't cover his victims, she thought. He left them out in the open.

She logged on to the DMV database and retrieved a name and address for Daphne Middleton.

She'd pay Ted's old girlfriend a visit. Daphne was the girl that many in the media pontificated had been the catalyst for his murders.

Daphne's cross to bear was bigger than Mt. Rainier.

CHAPTER 39

There were a lot of things Jeremy Howell would like to forget. For a time, he really tried. He thought that if he took prescription drugs from his mother's stash in the kitchen cupboard (behind the iodine and bandages— no matter how many times he'd hurt himself, she'd never seemed to be able to find those first-aid supplies). He'd once read that electroshock therapy had been used to literally jolt the memories from those haunted by things they could not escape. One time in the basement, he cut the cord off of an old desk lamp, thinking that he could attach the loose wires to his temple and some-how get relief. He didn't go that far. He was too afraid that if there was anything good inside him, that, too, would be obliterated. In time, Jeremy came to under-stand that there were things that were etched so deeply in his memory that he could not erase them no matter how hard he tried.

He was only twelve the first time.

It was autumn and the chill of the tail end of Octo-ber came at him like a thousand tiny pins stabbing his body. His mother had always insisted that it was healthier for her son to sleep with the windows open, but Jeremy, who always felt cold, didn't agree. No matter how many times he told her, she insisted she knew best. She was like that. *Always right.* Always the first one to say that she was the expert and that he was her student. Over time he acquiesced. One night when the temperature outside had dipped below freezing, Jeremy got up, shivering, and went to secure the window, open as usual. He shut it as quietly as he could and he dropped the shades to the windowsill and returned to his bed. He wore no clothes, a habit that Peggy had forced on him when he wet the bed in first grade. It had only been one time, but Peggy raged at him as if he'd been the greatest disappointment that any mother on the planet could have.

He was weak.

He was a failure.

"Only a big baby wets the bed. I won't be cleaning up after you again. Strip. Take off your wet PJs. You're never going to do this to me again," she had said in her harsh, gravelly voice. She never soothed. She just didn't have it in her.

Jeremy, as always, did as he was told. He'd learned long before that morning to fear his mother when she yelled at him. To disobey her was to be sent to the basement, to the bunker-like space that she'd created for him. She called it the "Time Out" room. Whenever he was been sent there to reflect on how much of a disappointment he was to her, he felt his hate for her swell. Hate and fear. With his mother, those emotions went hand in hand.

But that night, when he was twelve, Peggy Howell crossed the line—albeit a squiggly line, because she was never exactly consistent with her edicts. Her rules and admonishments fluctuated like the Northwest weather. All of her warnings, rules, and edicts raced around Jeremy's head as he slipped between the sheets and the heavy dark wool army surplus blanket.

What happened next, he never told anyone. He didn't want anyone to make a big deal out of it. He had plenty of reasons to want to destroy his mother, but what she did that night was not one of them.

It was late and he was asleep, curled up on the edge of the bed, lying on his side. The mattress moved a little and Jeremy opened his eyes. Someone was with him. He could feel the presence of another person. His heartbeat amplified. He noticed a beam of light under the covers, piercing the darkness.

It was his mother. She was under the blanket with a flashlight.

What was she doing?

He inched away. She didn't touch him. She was looking at his naked body. It was wrong. Sick. Creepy. And though it was all of those things, Jeremy didn't say a word. It was as if he were wrapped in flypaper, unable to move, to speak.

He thought she was going to touch him, *there*. But she didn't. Not that time. She simply turned off the flashlight, put her feet on the floor, and left the bedroom. A sliver of light flashed from the hallway.

Although not yet a teenager, Jeremy had no doubts whatsoever something was very, very wrong with his mother.

He just didn't know what it was.

* * *

The next time Peggy Howell cozied up to her son, he was fifteen. Again, it was very late at night. It was spring and the smell of lilacs blooming outside wafted from the open window. After that night, Jeremy would never to be able to smell that sweet, heady fragrance without gagging. This time, Peggy dropped her robe before climbing into his bed. She pushed her naked body next to the teenager, close, but again, not touching.

"Ted, tell me you love me," she said, her breath caressing his exposed ear.

What?

Her voice smelled of alcohol and cigarettes, a mix of odors that Jeremy knew only too well. Every night before bedtime, she begged him, *ordered* him to give her, a kiss on her dry and wrinkled lips.

The lilacs wafted more, weighing him down. Pinning him so he couldn't move.

"Tell me, baby. Whisper in my ear," she said. "Love will keep us together."

At first, that night when there was no doubt that he was old enough to know better, he pretended not to hear. She wasn't really touching him, so he thought that it wasn't abuse. Not in the way that men abuse children. He told himself that it was not sexual. That his mother was lonely. Sad. Depressed.

"I'm not Ted," he said, finally. In his head, he was screaming it at her, but in reality his voice was but a whisper. "Mom, please go away."

Silence. Just the sound of the breeze blowing through the blinds.

"Go, Mom," he repeated, his voice full of fear, but still low.

The bed moved. She inched closer. "You are my Teddy," she said, ignoring the fear in his voice.

Jeremy inched farther away. "No, I'm Jeremy," he said.

She let out a laugh. If his voice was soft, hers was loud. She didn't care who heard her. She never cared about what anyone else thought. Occasionally, he'd admired her for that. There was a fierceness about his mother that made her different from the other moms.

"You are what I say you are," she said. Her tone was flat. It was as if she was feeding on his anxiety, sucking in every drop of his fear. As he lay there, he couldn't help but wonder if his mother got off on the fear that she induced wherever she could.

Threatening a clerk she felt had slighted her at the grocery store: "You'll be eating cat food once I get finished with you. No job. No place to live. Just Little Friskies."

"I'll make a wallet out of your scrotum and I'll give it to the Goodwill," she'd once screamed at the paperboy when a copy of the *News Tribune* arrived wet on their doorstep. "Don't think I won't. Only a fool would underestimate me and what I will do when I'm pushed. Got that, you little prick? I want my paper dry next time."

There was no next time. Despite declining subscription rolls, the paper's circulation director dropped the Howells from home delivery. It wasn't just the boy's complaint. Jeremy watched his mother as she tried to wriggle out of a problem of her own making when the police came by. She was good. Very good. Somehow, Peggy Howell managed to convince them that the kid was overreacting.

"He was smoking pot on my front steps two weeks ago. You should be arresting *him*. The little creep scares the crap out of me. Other neighbors have complained."

"What neighbors?" the officer asked.

"Look, I'm not a gossipmonger. I'm a truth teller. I'm not going to give you names of anyone. If they don't have the balls to tell you when they're being messed with, then too bad for them."

"I see," the officer said, though Jeremy, who was listening from the hallway, doubted anyone could see what his mother said. She was tough. She didn't suffer any fools. But she didn't always make sense.

Jeremy was always on edge and Peggy liked it that way.

One time she read him the riot act after he'd set the table with the forks and knives transposed in the place setting.

"Who's to say I won't poison you tonight, you little piece of garbage? Maybe you shouldn't eat. I don't think I would."

"Sorry, Mom," he said.

"Sorry is an excuse for the weak and stupid. You are neither. At least you shouldn't be. I'm not. Your father certainly wasn't," she said. "Stay put."

She picked up his plate of macaroni and cheese and disappeared into the kitchen.

A moment later she returned, a satisfied look on her face.

"You love me, don't you?" she asked, setting the plate down.

"Yeah. What did you do with my food?"

"You have to trust me," she said. "You have to eat it. Whatever happens will be a surprise."

"Did you put something on my macaroni and cheese?"

She balled up her fist. "What did I tell you about questioning me?"

He looked at his plate, his eyes scanning the pasta for something, he wasn't sure just what.

"That I never, ever should do that. Question you."

"Eat your dinner, Jeremy."

She put a forkful of food in her mouth and grinned. "So delicious. Potato chips on top, just the way you love it."

He looked at his plate.

"We have nothing if not trust," she said. It was her game. It was always her game. Later, he would read about people like his mother, those who enjoyed inflicting pain and fear on others.

"I'm scared," he said.

"Then you are a little bitch and if you don't eat that special macaroni and cheese, I'll make you wear my dirty panties to school again. And, this time, I'll call the school and tell the principal that you are stealing my clothes and that I want them to examine you in the nurse's office."

Jeremy's eyes welled up with tears, but he willed himself to stop the deluge. He put the macaroni in his mouth and swallowed.

"Sometimes, Jeremy, I wonder what will become of you. You're nothing like your father. In fact, you're nothing at all."

* * *

After the time Peggy came into his room and made her "love me like Ted" come-on, Jeremy stopped thinking of her as his mother. A mother wouldn't do that. He vowed never again would he let her come into his room like some kind of pervert freak. He didn't care if loneliness was her motivator. That was *her* problem.

Before he climbed into bed at night, Jeremy arranged a trio of empty Dr. Pepper bottles in front of his closed bedroom door. It was the only thing he could think to do. When Peggy swung the door open—drunk or high as she frequently seemed to be—the bottles fell and clattered on the hardwood floor. It was both an alarm and a deterrent. No more "midnight specials" with her son. No, no. No more of the cuddling that she desperately wanted. No more of her pretending that her son was her precious Teddy.

One Saturday afternoon Jeremy went outside with a handsaw and cut down the lilac bush. At the time, his mom was engrossed in a true crime book about mothers who kill their children. She had fanned the book at him as he exited the back door. Everything she did was an implied threat, a promise to be kept. He bundled up the limbs and put them in the trash. Before closing the lid to the garbage can, Jeremy threw up all over the branches. He studied his vomit like it was some kind of a work of art. Masticated particles of a ham sandwich stuck to the cut twigs and heart-shaped leaves of the remains of the lilac bush.

It was the prettiest thing he'd seen in a long, long time.

CHAPTER 40

Peggy Howell took a deep drag on her cigarette and watched her son as he toweled off after showering. She'd removed the bathroom door by then, telling Jeremy that any need for privacy was merely a desire to deceive her. She was not having any of that. Steam curled against the ceiling and he pulled the shower curtain closed. He'd long thought that his mother's control of him was beyond what others could imagine. He didn't know for sure, though. Jeremy had no close friends. In his entire life he'd never had a single friend come over to hang out in his room. He stopped asking his mother if he could. After a while there was no reason to ask anymore.

All he had was her.

"You have to man up if you are going to fulfill your destiny," she said, the smoke coming from her lips like a dragon. Her eyes stayed on his naked body. "You have your father's lean physique."

Jeremy tied the towel around his waist. "You talk like a freak, Mom."

"When your father was your age, he was already

taking chances. You just come home from school and watch TV."

"I don't have any friends, Mom. I don't want any friends," he said, a lie he learned to tell.

She nodded. "Friends can only hurt you, they are deceivers and users."

"I know," he said.

Another lie.

"By the time your father was your age, he'd been arrested for burglary, auto theft. Dumb, yes, but he was learning from his mistakes. You have to make mistakes in order to get better. Don't you understand that?"

"I guess so," Jeremy said, moving past her toward his bedroom. "But I'm afraid."

She sat down on the edge of the bed. He dropped his towel and started to dress. He hated her just then.

"Good," she said. "That's good. Feed on that. Feed on the fear you have, and gather it up for those around you. Fear, you idiot, is absolute power. Use it. Sometimes I give my head a shake and wonder to myself if you are stupid or just weak."

He nodded. He wasn't sure how to even answer her half the time. If answering made any difference at all?

"Jeremy, after you're dressed," Peggy said, "I want you to massage my feet."

As the water swirled down the sink, through the strands of hair that collected in a fuzzy, matted circular shape, Peggy Howell thought of the man that she loved above all others. Her life was running through the drain. She'd loved Ted with everything she had. She knew that he didn't see her as he saw the others. *The girls before her. The girls before everything happened.*

She traced his history long before crime writers sought to weave a marketable tale of his life story. After high school graduation in 1965, Ted went to a succession of universities. First, he enrolled in the University of Puget Sound, but after only a year he felt it too small, too local. He wanted out of Tacoma, away from his past. He told acquaintances—as by his own admission he had few, if any, real friends—that he wanted more, that he *deserved* more. In 1966, Ted made good on his grandiose vision for himself and transferred from UPS to the University of Washington in Seattle, ostensibly to study Chinese.

Peggy found that part of Ted's history so utterly appealing. *Chinese?* It was such a difficult language. Who but the most brilliant would even think to take on such a demanding course of study? Only Ted. *Ted.* So ahead of his time, her Ted.

The girls who were Peggy's rivals were not on anyone's list of Bundy victims, at least not in the true sense. Ted never spoke of the girls; only one time did he reference them in a letter to Peggy written four months before his execution.

My Peggy,
    Daphne and Liz were never anything to me. At least not to the degree that some of my detractors and the leeches who make money off my name will have the masses believe. I was young, a college student. I wasn't in love. I didn't get dumped by either of those girls. Stephanie, in

*particular, has slung some mud in my direction,
but I'm not a game player. I won't even give her
the dignity of a reply. When she's talking about
someone who is immature and directionless,
she's talking about herself. Whatever you have
read about the influence these women had on my
life is so totally overstated as to border on the
absurd. I'm laughing to myself right now as I
write this. Peg, you have been everything to me.
You have stood by me. That's love. That's what
keeps me going. In you, my legacy will continue.
You are a great gift.*

                              peace, Ted

In 1973, Ted was accepted into the law schools of the
University of Puget Sound and the University of Utah.
It wasn't his grades that got him there, but the letters of
recommendation from Republican Party leaders in
Washington, the foremost of which was Governor Dan
Evans. Ted earned Evans's accolades by way of his
support during the governor's reelection campaign. His
support was either clever or devious depending on
whether one wore a donkey or an elephant on his or her
lapel.

Ted, masquerading as a college student, followed
Evans's democratic opponent throughout the campaign
of 1972, recording speeches from the inside and passing them along to the state Republican offices. He was
ingratiating. Smart. Always there when he needed be.
There were times when staffers would find themselves
next to him, as if he were some kind of phantom who
came and went on footsteps that made no sound.

* * *

Peggy Howell never felt more disappointed than when Jeremy failed his LSATs, precluding him from following his father's path to law school. Her blood simmered whenever she recalled the day she'd beaten him to the mailbox and found the rejection letter, in its starchy crisp envelope. It was a knife in the back, a betrayal that only served to make her seethe with disappointment and rage.

Though years had passed, every now and then it all resurfaced and she'd pull a bloody tipped arrow from her quiver and aim it at him.

"You're nothing but a telemarketer! A goddamn annoyance to everyone who has the misfortune of picking up the phone when you call with some piece of crap that you want them to buy! Sometimes I go to bed at night and thank God that your father never had to see the man you've become. It makes me sick. Your dad was a lawyer! You're supposed to do better than your father, not worse!"

Jeremy knew enough about his father and he also knew that to challenge his mother was a mistake he would never make more than once. He could have stopped her right there and told her the truth.

Ted Bundy never got his JD! He had too many distractions in the form of pretty young brunettes, Mom! Pretty ones! Not like you, Mom!

And yet he held his tongue, tight like it was ensnared in a woodworker's vise. To challenge her was too, too dangerous.

* * *

"You are the prettiest by far," he said.

His words came at Emma like poisoned darts. He'd barely said anything up to that point, and now, when he did she wished he hadn't. She knew that horror movies were often considered more frightening because of what they didn't show. The unknown was always scarier than something visible in the light of day. Once the shark in the old movie *Jaws* was actually shown on screen, his menace palled. It didn't matter that he was snacking on an old sea captain or half-naked swimmer. It was scarier when his presence was hidden under the inky confines of the sea.

Emma's captor no longer wanted to be as anonymous as he had been from the minute that he took her. And the choice of his words in that first real utterance made his intentions all too clear.

Emma broke it all down.

"The prettiest" indicated that there was a component in his aberrant behavior that encompassed her physical beauty. He was attracted to her. That part was easy enough to decipher. He'd given her a brush and mirror. He wanted her to look a specific way.

"By far" was also telling and perhaps the most frightening thing she'd ever heard directed at her in her life. It seemed clear to Emma right then in the dim light of the room that she had not been the first. There had been other girls.

In the apartment?

And if so, where were they now?

"Thank you," she said to the man on the other side of the room. She did so because of her mother's advice for dealing with a school bully one time.

"Kill him with kindness," her mom had said. "I

know it seems lame, but I know for a fact that it works every time."

"You're welcome, Emma Rose," the man said.

She stiffened at the use of her full name. He'd never really called her by name, at least that she could be certain about. She searched the darkness, trying to see him. To see what it was that he wanted.

"Why don't you come out of the darkness and talk to me?" she asked, still a little frightened about what the perv might look like. Old, nasty, wrinkly, fat, and smelly. She knew *Beauty and the Beast* from the ice show that her mom took her to in Tacoma.

She also knew the *Silence of the Lambs*.

Both scenarios ratcheted up the fear and disgust that swelled inside her whenever she felt the air move in the apartment.

"Later," he said.

"When is later? It isn't like I have a lot to do here but read these stupid magazines."

"When I'm ready. When you are ready. I promise. You are the prettiest by far."

Emma saw the shadow move and she moved toward it. But it was too late. The door shut and the dead bolt fell like a thunderclap.

CHAPTER 41

Among the data collected from Emma Rose's laptop were the usual musings of a teenage girl. She had a blog—with only one entry. She had a Facebook account with a respectable two hundred friends, most of whom she actually knew. She had a Twitter account, but used it only for following various affinity groups.

Grace looked at the report provided by the forensic computer specialist, Darian Hecla, a brainy twenty-five-year-old who many thought should be writing code instead of cracking it. There was a little truth to that, but circumstances had sent him to law enforcement, a job he actually liked. His personnel file had been sealed so that even the nosiest records clerk couldn't get his or her prying eyes on it, but Darian was working there as a part of a plea agreement. When he was twenty, he'd hacked into the office of the governor and read things that would have been extremely embarrassing for her. The secret plea deal was the best solution for everyone.

Darian went through Emma's laptop, leaving no one or zero unturned.

Hunched over the printout, Grace used a yellow

highlighter to mark what she thought might bring the investigation closer to a resolution. To her way of thinking, the only resolution would be bringing Emma home.

Alive.

"Anything interesting?" Paul asked as he looked over her shoulder.

Grace looked up. "I think so," she said taking the yellow marker and rubbing its tip through a passage in the report. "Read this."

Laptop owner had three primary interests,
at least two of which intersected. She routinely
re-tweeted Tweets posted by @SafeSound and
@Envi_Live. Both are local environmental
action organizations based in the Pacific
Northwest. Both promote clean Puget Sound
water.

"We all like clean water, Grace," Paul said, lifting his eyes from the report.

Grace made a face. "Read on, please." She tapped her fingertip to the next paragraph, one she'd also highlighted.

Laptop owner's last three emails were to Alex
Morton. Verbatim:
"Alex, I'm really upset. Why don't we try to
work something out?"
"You have to care. This is more important than
money. You have to tell."
"If you don't do something about it. I will."

Paul finished reading. Grace turned in her chair to meet his gaze head-on.

"Something's not right here," he said. "What's she talking about?"

"I don't know, but we need to talk to Alex."

Grace Alexander and Paul Bateman parked around the corner from the Morton mansion—or "manse": the detectives had suddenly taken a perverse liking to referring to it this way.

When Morton's BMW 3 passed by in a black smear even in the residential neighborhood, they circled back to the house and knocked on the door.

"Shouldn't the kid be in school?" Paul asked as they waited.

"Kids like Alex don't think they need to learn anything more," Grace said. "They have it all handed to them."

"As much as I hate his prick of a dad, at least he worked hard for all this."

She nodded.

The door knob twisted, and Alex Morton stood there.

"I figured you'd be back. Dad said you'd try to do an end run on me. On him."

"You saw us through the video cam, didn't you?" Grace asked.

Alex indicated he had.

"You opened the door."

"Yeah. I did. I don't think you need to be here, but I figured if I told you the truth you'd get off of our backs and go find Emma. She's cool. I liked her."

"You liked her so much you killed her?" Paul said.

"You got that all wrong."

Grace looked at Paul. They were inside the house. The kid was talking. She tried to telegraph to her partner to ease up.

"We're here to listen, Alex," she said.

"Come on," he said, nodding in the direction of the stairs to the basement. "Let's talk downstairs. I have something to show you. I'm really, really sorry. I am. I know you think I'm a big piece of crap, and I guess I deserve that. I really am sorry."

Grace was all ears.

"Sorry for what, Alex? Tell us, what happened?"

Alex Morton told the detectives that he had seen Emma Rose at school the previous year, but they'd never spoken. He'd run into her at a few parties. Despite all his bravado, the kid hadn't had enough gumption to ask her out. She was too pretty. She didn't seem to care about his money or who his father was. Emma seemed more interested in saving the planet or ensuring that those in third world countries had safe drinking water.

"She had interests, plans. I guess that impressed me. I never really thought about anything other than the next video game that came out or how I might squeeze my parents for some extra dough so I could buy something. Dumb things. I just wanted stuff. Emma didn't give a crap about stuff. She just wanted to do right."

"You said you wanted to show us something," Grace said as they stood in the cool air of his basement crash pad. A big-screen TV was on mute, playing some kind of hair band music video from the eighties.

"In here," he said, leading them past a double door, to a smaller room. "My dad keeps an office down here. That's where Emma saw it."

"Saw what?"

Alex led them over to the computer. "My dad changed the password. So I can't get it to work now, but when Emma was over his password was Trump1234."

Paul suppressed the urge to roll his eyes. Palmer Morton was an egomaniac. He had better hair than Donald Trump, but there was no way he was going to best the New York real estate developer when it came to financial success.

"What did she see?" Grace asked.

"It was an email. My dad had left his email screen up. I normally don't care about his crap, but Emma sat down and started reading. She blew up at me. I had to get her to calm down. She told me that she was going to the police, the papers."

"Alex, what did she see?" Grace asked.

"When was this?" Paul asked.

"It was a week before she disappeared."

"Right, okay. But what was it?"

"It was about the cleanup going on at The Pointe. My dad had paid some contractors to get rid of the last bit of contaminated dirt. The contractor screwed up. They hired out a sub. Some cheap labor so they could rake in the dough. The subcontractor took the last tailings from the cleanup and dumped them into Puget Sound."

"Do you know where?" Grace asked.

Alex shook his head. "Not sure. Somewhere around Point Defiance, I think."

"What did Emma do?" Paul asked.

"She told me that my dad wouldn't go to jail if he didn't know about it. She thought that he was making a big mistake by keeping it quiet."

"Did you tell your dad about this?"

He nodded. "Yeah. I did. I told him, and he and Emma talked about it. She said she'd keep her mouth shut if he did the right thing. You know, if he had it cleaned up right away."

"What was his reaction?"

"At first he was really mad at her, at *me*. Then he calmed down. He said he'd take care of it. He'd cleaned up a Superfund site. He could clean up this mess, too."

The detectives talked to Alex a while longer, pinning down the information to make sure that had everything right. As they started up the stairs, Paul remarked about the double doors.

"Looks like that's bolted up better than Fort Knox," he said.

"Wine cellar. Dad has some mega expensive wines in there. And if you're thinking he doesn't trust me, you'd be right. Dad doesn't trust anyone."

Grace asked the million-dollar question. "Do you think he had anything to do with Emma's disappearance?"

Alex got real quiet. "I don't think so. He saw her that night. But he told me that after they talked in the parking lot she left for the bus. She was alive."

Grace waited until the car was moving before she spoke.

"Maybe we've got this all wrong," she said. "Maybe

Emma's not a victim of the same killer as Kelsey and Lisa."

Paul didn't disagree. "I don't like Morton for the serial killer type."

"Right," she said, putting the car in gear and heading up the street. "He's almost too rotten to be a serial killer." It was a half joke, but there was a little truth to it. Serial killers, in general, spiral out of control. They are unable to hold down jobs, unable to maintain relationships. They are killing machines and unable to focus on much more than that. The idea of the serial killer as the benign neighbor next door was more an invention of Hollywood. Most were frazzled and preoccupied.

Palmer Morton was focused like a laser beam on his business. He didn't have time to run around killing young girls.

He might have, however, had time to kill just one.

"What if he'd met her at Starbucks after work? Maybe she threatened to tell and he abducted her right then? Killed her to shut her up. A scandal over The Pointe would destroy plans for his development," Paul said.

Grace looked down at her phone and read a text. "It could shut him down for years," she said.

Paul nodded and looked out the window.

"Forever," he said.

They passed a sign for Morton's condo project as they drove back to the police department.

GET THE POINTE. KILLER VIEWS.

"That's pretty ironic," Paul said tapping on the glass.

Grace's mind was reeling. And it wasn't about The Pointe or the interview they'd just conducted. It was from the text message she'd just received. She was going to see Ted Bundy's old girlfriend.

"No kidding," she said to Paul.

"Have you been down there?"

"No," she said.

"Some big plans they have."

The Pointe at Ruston Way was an enormous complex with condominiums, townhouses, and apartments flanking edges of the sparkling blue waters of Commencement Bay. No one could argue that real estate developer Palmer Morton's vision had been realized in a beautiful way. No expense had been spared to design and build what the website and brochures promised was "World Class in the City of Destiny," a nod to Tacoma's motto and its reputation as being somewhat less than world class. The penthouse condos went for well over one million dollars and the cheapest rents on the apartments made living there only in the reach of BMW-driving professionals. No one without a two-hundred-thousand-dollar-a-year salary need apply.

The bulk of The Pointe at Ruston Way was built on the cleaned-up land that surrounded the former ASARCO smelter. Getting it built had been a battle—the EPA, the old-timers who didn't want any change (even though the previous landholder had poisoned the air, soil, and water, hardly something to champion), and a considerable consortium of homegrown environmental groups who wanted the land cleaned up and returned to its pristine state.

Palmer Morton had been in it for the long haul. He dug in and fought all warring factions and prevailed. He had money. He had balls of steel. He just wouldn't lose.

CHAPTER 42

Grace stopped for gas at a mini-mart just off the freeway in Redmond. She scanned the area by the cashier and grabbed a package of barbecue potato chips, regretting it the instant she pushed it across the dingy counter. The clerk told her that she could get a bigger bag for "just forty-nine cents more."

Grace smiled. "I really should save the two dollars and skip the chips altogether, but I'm hungry."

"We have some good Polish dogs," said the clerk, a large woman who apparently never got off her chair. She indicated a hotdog machine that turned two sad, shrunken hotdogs on hot rollers.

Grace shook her head and smiled politely. She was an expert at hiding her feelings. Her stomach was rumbling and the chips, bad choice as they were, were all she had time for. "Vegan," she lied, not even sure why. It just seemed better than saying "your hotdogs look like they've been there since Bush was in office," which is what she was really thinking. The pit of her stomach was sour, but it had nothing to do with hunger pangs. It was all Ted. Ted Bundy was like an insidious virus. Once more she was moving through her life chasing a man who already had been killed by the executioner.

She paid and went back to her car, checking the address she'd printed out on Google maps before leaving Tacoma.

212 Marymoor Lane

Everything he touched became infected with evil. People who studied Ted—law enforcement and serial killer groupies alike—considered Daphne Middleton to be victim zero. Daphne had been Ted's girlfriend, his confidante, the one he trusted above all others.

It wasn't hard for Grace to find her. Daphne had changed her name, but not her Social Security number. She'd moved around the Pacific Northwest and back to her home town of Des Moines, Iowa, before returning to Redmond, Washington, and the condo at 21 Marymoor Lane.

Grace didn't call ahead, but she kept her badge in her palm when she knocked on the door.

The door opened a crack and a slender woman with short gray hair answered.

"Daphne?" Grace asked.

A split second of fear came over the woman, but she quickly dismissed it. "There's no one here by that name." Her eyes, nestled in crinkled folds of over-tanned skin, flickered in that way that lets a person with genuine sensitivity see that a lie is being told.

Grace knew that she was trying to force something open that Daphne Middleton wanted sealed forever. Her past. Her history. Ted. Yet she persisted, because persistence when it came to Bundy was in her DNA.

"Daphne, my name is Grace Alexander. I'm with the Tacoma Police Department," she said, proffering her badge.

Daphne shrugged; her shoulders were tent poles holding up the loose cotton blouse that she wore untucked over a pair of faded blue jeans.

"I guess that's supposed to impress me," she finally said. "And, if I were Daphne, I'd probably be inclined to be so. But, as I said, my name is Jennifer."

She hadn't said her name was Jennifer.

"Daphne, please," Grace said, her tone more businesslike than pleading. "I'm here to talk to you about my sister. I'm here to talk to you about Ted."

Daphne/Jennifer looked around, past Grace. She scanned the parking lot.

Looking for a TV crew maybe?

"Why are you doing this to me?"

If there was a moment in which Grace knew that her obsession didn't trump the rights of others to just be left alone, that was it. She knew that while she meant Daphne Middleton no harm whatsoever, there was no way that her appearance on her doorstep could be anything but harmful. She was there to get something. She wasn't there to give Daphne anything—not new information, not closure, not comfort. She was a leech, a parasite.

And yet she persisted.

"I'm not," Grace said. "I'm doing this to help my sister." Even those words rang a little hollow. It was true that she'd been counseled her entire life that she was doing this for her sister's memory, that the truth that had eluded her family was something that was owed to

Sissy. It was no longer about that. Not really. It was really about what she had to prove.

Daphne moved the door open a bit more, letting the light fall on her face. "Come in," she said, her tone more resigned than welcoming. "But please, don't make me have to move again. Don't tell anyone you've found me. You have no idea what it's like living in the shadow of that man."

Grace didn't say what was going through her mind just then: *Yes, I do.*

The condo was spotless and modern. A pair of black Barcelona chairs flanked a gas fireplace. A glass coffee table with a Nambé bowl as its centerpiece was placed in front of a bright red leather sofa, also Italian, like the Barcelona chairs. Daphne Middleton had excellent taste and a flair for the dramatic.

"Coffee's brewing," she said. "Follow me."

Daphne led Grace to the kitchen, where an automatic coffeemaker beeped, indicating that it had just finished brewing. She poured a cup for herself and one for the detective. They sat at the kitchen table and talked. First Grace told her about Tricia and her mother, and how their lives had been wrapped up in the drama of a serial killer. It was part therapy, part fact finding.

"I think your mother wrote to me back in the late 1980s," Daphne said.

Grace nodded. "I'm sure she did. My mother wrote to anyone with a connection to him, from his grade school teachers on up to a cellmate he had in Florida."

"I see. I'm in excellent company, then," Daphne said without a bit of irony.

Grace liked Daphne. Despite all of it, she could still find something in the darkness that made one smile.

Daphne looked up. "Sugar? Milk?"

Grace shook her head. In the middle of the conversation they were having there was room for the mundane. It was odd and comforting at the same time.

"Black's fine," she said.

She examined the woman in early sixties across from her. She wore a pair of gold hoops and a necklace fashioned of stars linked together. Her brows were dark and they moved as she spoke. She was beautiful and expressive and she'd been through a lot.

Daphne was the only Ted victim who had chosen to be with him, then rejected him.

"I know what you're thinking. I know what everyone thinks. If I didn't kick him to the curb, those girls would still be alive. Your sister would still be alive. All of them. Live with that for a little while and come back here and tell me how that feels."

"No one blames you," Grace said.

Daphne laughed, but it was forced and as fake as the fur trim on the coat that hung on the hook in the kitchen.

"They do," she said. "You're a cop. You know better, but deep down you probably do, too. It's always been about when the killings happened. The date always comes back to me. Authors and TV people have speculated over the years that a broken heart might have been the trigger for his madness, or whatever it was."

"When you broke up with him," Grace said.

"That's been completely overstated, Detective."

"Grace, please."

Daphne nodded and swallowed her coffee. "Right, Grace. Just so you know—and no one seems to listen to me on this—the breakup with Ted was less dramatic.

He was immature. He needed growing up, you know, to find his own way. When we parted he didn't seem upset. He just vanished. Later, when I tried to reconnect—after he'd started law school and become a bigwig in the Republican Party, he acted like we'd never met. Some traumatic breakup."

Grace looked around the kitchen. Daphne had planted an herb garden in the window. The smell of mint and oregano perfumed the tidy space.

"All right, fair enough. But tell me, what was Ted really like?"

"Exactly why are you here? I mean, really. Missing girl in Tacoma? I read the papers."

Grace thought for a moment. The answer was more complicated than any one case. It was her sister's, the others, the life that her parents fashioned for her when she was growing up. She had a need to know people who knew Ted.

"Yes, the Tacoma case. But also," she said, "my sister's case. Tell me about him, please."

Daphne rummaged in a cupboard for a package of Lorna Doones.

"The only connection that exists from my time with Ted is our fondness for shortbread. His favorite. I stopped eating them for ten years, maybe longer. I started buying it again a few years ago. Funny how innocent things can sometimes feel evil for a time."

She put them on a plate and inched them over to Grace. She took one for herself and watched as Grace, her stomach still rumbling from the mini-mart snack, declined.

"Tell me about him," she asked. "I need to understand him from someone who knew him."

Daphne set down a cookie. "All right. There were two Teds. Maybe more. There was the Ted who could charm the socks off of anyone. He just could. He was quick. Funny. He had the kind of charisma that made people feel they were close to him even if they weren't."

"Like you?" Grace asked.

Daphne hesitated. "Yes, like me."

The look on her face spoke volumes. It was clear that even though none of it was her fault, even though she knew in her heart of hearts that Ted had been a monster before she ever met him, she felt that twinge that comes with responsibility—no matter how off-base.

"You say there were two Teds. What was the other? How did that other personality differ?"

Daphne indicated the coffeepot and Grace shook her head.

"The other was the Ted that killed your sister," she said. "The monster, the man without a conscience. The one who told me that he'd break my neck because I confronted him one time about stealing a TV. I knew he didn't buy it. I wasn't stupid. He was a thief. He stole other things, too; skis come to mind. I was pretty sure of it. After I saw that look in his eyes when I asked him where he got the goods, I knew I was never, ever going to push him again."

Grace was in full detective mode just then. "Was he violent?"

"That's the thing. Not violent in the way abusers are. Ted's rage was always under the surface, his anger poking through just enough so that you would take two steps backwards just to save yourself from the possibility."

"Please, go on. What else did you observe?"

Daphne picked at the necklace of stars that shifted and shimmered when she moved and thought for a second before answering. "You mean in the way he acted?"

"Either. Both."

"All right," Daphne said. "Weird stuff. Stuff that he shouldn't have or didn't have a real reason to have."

"Like what?

"You'll know the second I say it, but back then I didn't know what it meant. If it meant anything at all. I saw medical stuff around the house. Plaster of Paris, crutches. It was strange, but I didn't really say anything. Later, you know, after everything came out, I knew that those things were items he used to set his trap for those girls."

Weak Ted. Weak Ted was really strong, clever Ted.

"What else?"

"Oh and he had surgical gloves, too. Why did he need those?"

Both women knew the answer.

"I didn't ask him, you know," Daphne said, on a roll. "I just looked at the knives, the meat cleaver, the ropes and stuff he kept in his car and just accepted it. He even had a bag of women's clothes. I just accepted his excuse that he was gathering things up to give to St. Vincent's. I didn't even think about whose clothing it might have been. It wasn't mine. Oh, yes, he also had a wrench that he'd fashioned with a better handle for gripping. Today, of course, I probably would have looked for blood on it, but that was back then. Before *CSI*. Before serial killers, really." She stopped herself and considered the obvious, her audience. "Ted changed a lot of things, didn't he?"

There was undeniable truth in what she said. Ted had altered the way people looked at a man in need. In the Seattle Summer of Ted, he'd changed how safe a young woman felt walking in her own neighborhood. In the days before Ted, the only kind of footsteps that sent chills down a young woman's spine belonged to a man who looked scary—a bum, a hoodlum.

Not a handsome young man in a suit jacket and wingtips.

"Were you ever afraid of him?" Grace asked.

Daphne turned away, her eyes welling with tears, though none fell. It was as if that one real break in emotion could be stemmed.

"One night we were in bed," she began, her eyes still looking out the window. "You know, just saying that makes my stomach sick. Just the idea that I was in bed with a man who would rather have sex with a dead girl, a girl that he kills, makes me want to throw up. What was I to him? Just a placeholder? Nothing at all?"

Grace wanted the rest of the story. She'd talked to crime victims before. Hundreds of times. She knew that each word was like spitting out razor blades, but getting to the essence of truth wasn't ever an easy endeavor.

"What happened, Daphne? Tell me," she said.

Daphne nodded. "Right. We were in bed, as I said. It was late. I just woke up. It was like some kind of a strange feeling came over me and my eyes just opened. Ted was under the covers with a flashlight, Detective. He was under the covers looking at my body with a goddamn flashlight. And you know what I did about it? I mean, I was so mortified, do you know what I said to him?"

Grace shook her head.

"Nothing. I said nothing. I didn't know what to say. I pretended that I hadn't caught him, but the rest of the night I just laid there wondering why I stayed with someone like Ted. I thought maybe there was something more wrong with me than with him. There had to be, because what kind of a woman just looks the other way?"

There were millions of reasons, of course. She was in love. She was trapped in a relationship that she was unable to escape. She was like a lot of women back then, unsure of her own worth and whether her life was somehow diminished if she was a single woman. Grace offered none of those. Instead, she changed the subject, trying to give Daphne Middleton a break from her moment of realization that Ted had literally inhabited her nightmares, both awake and asleep.

"I know this is hard. And I am sorry. Really I am."

"Thank you."

"All right. Can I ask you about your hair?"

Daphne, now composed, nodded. It was as if she knew that one was coming. If she'd been the inspiration for the killings, why didn't she look like it? Her hair was cropped, not long.

"Even if I wasn't involved with Ted," she said, "I doubt very much that I'd be one of those women with the same hairstyle they had in high school. You know the type. You see them everywhere at the market. I cut my hair short after the Ted stuff hit the news, but I would have anyway."

"Was he fixated on your hair? Was that part of his obsession? You know, some people think that the hairstyle was so common back then that it couldn't really be crucial for why Ted stalked the girls that he did. My sister wore her hair long, parted in the middle, too. When I looked at her yearbook, about half the girls wore some variation of that style."

Daphne set down her mug and looked directly at Grace. Her eyebrows stopped moving and she spoke in hushed tones.

"I know. But I think so. I really do. I think that Ted was fixated on my hair. One time I told him that I was going to get a new haircut. Lots of girls were going shorter then. Girls on TV, girls in sports. Not everyone had to look like Jaclyn Smith."

Grace didn't get the Jaclyn Smith reference, but she'd look it up later online. She thought of the row after row of victims and their dark, long hair, parted in the middle. She knew from reading about Daphne that she'd had that look once, too.

She pressed Daphne for more. "Go on, what did he do?"

"He had a fit," she said. "An absolute freak-out fit. It was completely over the top. It was almost like a tantrum. I remember him saying that if I cut my hair he'd go crazy and he might do something drastic."

"Kill someone?" Grace asked.

"No. Don't be silly, Detective. I thought that he was going to get drunk or something. Get on his hands and knees and beg me not to do it. He actually looked like he was going to cry. Ted had pulled that kind of stunt before—you know, acting like he was crying when all he was doing was pretending to be so, so upset."

"So what did you do?"

"I didn't cut it, if that's what you're thinking," Daphne said. "No man was going to tell me how to dress or wear my hair. I made a decision a little bit later that Ted wasn't the man for me. He wasn't mature."

"You didn't think he was violent or that he would hurt you?"

Daphne shook her head. "I wish I could be as dramatic as some of those Bundy girls who got away from him—what are there now, about ten thousand who almost got murdered by Ted?"

It was a true statement, a kind of proof that Ted had morphed into Pacific Northwest folklore status like D. B. Cooper and Bigfoot.

"Probably," Grace said.

"I just dumped him. I told him that he needed to grow up. And that was that."

"How did he take that?"

"Not very well. He basically gave me the big FU. I honestly didn't care. He was immature and he was creepy."

There was at least one other question that never seemed to have the benefit of a decent answer. None that Grace could find. None that her mother could uncover. After Ted was released on bond in late 1975 and was awaiting his trial in Utah, he split his time between the house in Tacoma and Daphne Middleton's place in Seattle.

The question was short.

"Why?" Grace asked.

Daphne nodded slowly. "Why did I let him stay with me? Don't you think I've asked myself that a million times?"

"I'm sure you have, but why? Why did you? Did you think he was dangerous? Did you think that he would hurt you if you told him to get out of your life?"

Daphne fiddled with the stars around her neck again. "No, it wasn't that. I would like to lay blame on the concept of a battered woman and the fear that makes someone stay close to the enemy instead of retreating. But that wasn't it."

"Then why?"

"It sounds so foolish, but it's true. It was my own vanity, I guess. I think I thought that I picked him and it said something awful about me if I admitted to the world that I was going to bed with a killer."

"But you were," Grace said, coming very close to crossing the line. "And you did."

"Right. Right. But seriously, the whole time I was with him, I was pretending. That's what's so messed up about it. I was pretending that I supported him, when all I was doing—I swear to God—was telling myself that he couldn't have done what they were saying."

"But you saw all those things that bothered you— the plaster of Paris, for example."

"Yes, I know. And I talked to investigators—one right after another. They all told me what I just couldn't admit. I was kind of trapped. The truth about the whole thing was that if he got convicted, I felt only then I could drop him. Only after that could—please understand—could I be free."

Shane was waiting for Grace at the bottom of the staircase at Salmon Beach. She'd phoned that she'd be home at seven and it was nearly right on the dot when they met at the landing. Her interview with Daphne had made for a long and unsettling day.

"It's been a long time since I had a greeting this nice," Grace said, before reading the concerned expression on his face. "Something's wrong. Is it my mom?"

Shane held her. "No, baby. Not your mom. It's your sister."

Grace pushed him away a little. "What do you mean?"

"The bones," he said. "A friend at the bureau tipped me off. The bones were Tricia's."

Shane's mouth was still moving, but Grace couldn't hear anything more. Her mind zipped through images of her sister. The flash cards. Ted Bundy. Her bedroom. The dove necklace. Her mother's face. The last time she'd seen her father.

Tears came to her eyes and rained down her cheeks. Shane was still talking, holding her close.

"Are you, are *they*, sure?" she finally said.

"Yes. It wasn't the bones that did it. There were three strands of hair wrapped around the femur. Not intentionally, just there by luck. One had an intact follicle. That's how they did the match, Grace. She's found. You found her."

Grace nodded. "We have to tell Mom," she said.

Sissy O'Hare didn't shed a single tear. She simply sat there on the sofa next to her daughter and listened, her fingertips barely touching the strand of pearls she always wore. The big clock ticked. The room shrunk. But she just sat there. Calmly. Quietly. Shane excused himself and stepped into the kitchen to give mother and daughter a little time alone.

Finally Sissy spoke; her words came softly. "I've always known she was gone, Grace. I stopped looking for her twenty years ago. I knew in my heart that she loved me and she loved your father and she never would have left us. She had to be dead."

Grace knew that wasn't completely true. Her mom never changed their phone number. When she finally got a cell phone in the mid-nineties she made sure that the mobile carrier provided the same number—in case Tricia ever called. Her mother barely made a change to her sister's bedroom—and only did anything major when a leak in the window frame caused some water damage and the entire room had to be repainted. Sissy had chosen the same color, but it didn't look exactly the same.

"I know, Mom. I know."

Sissy stared into Grace's eyes. "Will you be able to tell anything else?"

Grace knew that had been coming, but still she clarified. "How she died? Is that what you mean?"

Sissy nodded. "Yes, and who killed her?"

Grace shook her head. "No. No, we won't. There's not enough there."

"That's all right. I already know. I've always known that Ted killed her. Ted killed all the pretty girls that year."

In the car on the way back home, Shane asked Grace if her mother would be all right.

"Maybe we should stay with her?"

"She'll be fine," Grace said. "She'll probably sleep better tonight now that she knows for sure Tricia is gone forever."

"Are you doing all right?"

She looked out the window at the Tacoma skyline as they drove toward home.

"I think so. I didn't know her. I'm just relieved for my mom. I wish my dad had lived long enough to know."

"Don't you think they've always known?" he asked.

"Probably. You know as well as I do that hope makes a joke out of logic."

"Do you still think Ted's the killer?" he asked.

"I'm not so sure."

And she wasn't. Not at all.

CHAPTER 43

Emma Rose wasn't sure exactly how many days she'd been in the so-called apartment. It likely wasn't more than a few, but with no daytime and nighttime indicators in that windowless, airless room, it was hard to really know. *Three? Or ten?* Emma plotted and schemed all the scenarios that would free her from her captor, but she didn't know if she had the strength to carry them out. The fact of the matter—and she knew it deep in her soul—was Emma was running out of time. With each passing hour or day or whatever measure of time there was in the real world, Emma was feeling weaker and weaker. While fear still coursed through her body, it did so at an increasingly sluggish pace. She knew that her captor was going to rape, torture, and kill her, but her body reacted slowly to the urgent messages that her brain was sending. *Get out! Kill him first! You only have one chance.* What was wrong with her? She'd taken self-defense classes in high school. She knew that every second she was alive there was still the hope that she could survive, no matter what he was planning.

When she thought about her weakening state, her grogginess, she wondered if she'd been drugged by those awful sandwiches. She told herself that she shouldn't eat any more, but when she left food on the plate, he screamed at her.

"You are no good to anyone dead! Eat!"

"Not hungry," Emma said.

"Liar! You do what *I* say. Not what *you* want to do."

Still holding on to her resolve never to cry again, Emma protested.

"But I can't," she said.

Though it seemed impossible, his tone grew harsher and his voice louder.

"Eat or I'll force it down your throat!" he railed.

Though she hoped that he couldn't see her obvious fear in the dim light, her hands were shaking as she picked up the paper plate. Sitting in the dank dungeon, Emma worked with birdlike bites on the sandwich that she was sure was taking away her will to fight.

She vowed to seize the moment, whenever it came.

Emma's chance came when he left the door open when he thought she was asleep or passed out. Like her body had been wrapped in lead and she couldn't move. She could barely lift her head toward the brightness. Was she dreaming? Hallucinating? A slice of light pierced the dank apartment and somehow, Emma was able to crawl on her hands and knees to the spot where she could get a better look at the world outside.

Where she could escape to freedom. Go home to her mother. Get out of there and never ever come back.

The teen dragged herself a few feet and looked upward at the dagger of light that came into the room. *What was out there?* The images blurred like the TV set that her grandmother had in her back bedroom, sparking the only thought of something happy since her abduction.

Her abduction. A flicker of a memory came from soft to sharper focus. She remembered how she and Oliver had closed Starbucks. Then another. A confrontation with Alex's dad. Palmer Morton promised to fix the contamination of the Sound. And finally, something else . . . a man with a sling on his arm asked for help in putting packages from shopping into his SUV . . . and then nothing.

Someone had hit her from behind. But it wasn't the creeper. He had been in front of her.

It was so bright outside the hellhole in which he held her captive. She was a grunion following the moonlight. She was a mule deer staring into the headlights of a rapidly approaching car with a driver unable to swerve. Emma could barely move her limbs, but she could see and her mind was processing it like the world's slowest computer.

An old rolltop desk like the kind she'd seen in a museum had been placed on the other side of the room. It was like Emma was looking through a tunnel and she saw nothing else but the desk and the photographs that hung in a crisp row above it. Black and whites. A series of them that at first all looked the same. Young women. All Caucasian. All with long dark hair, parted in the middle. They were old photographs, like the kind that came out of high school yearbooks before color printing was readily available. The girls were pretty. Who were they? Why displayed in a row like that? As her stomach undulated and her now bloody knees ached, she lowered her head and summoned the strength to try to press onward. She heard the TV going again and the sound of footsteps above.

Where was she?

Who had taken her?

Emma told herself that this moment might be her only chance. She had to get out of there. She inched closer to the door and looked upward. *A window*. It was one of those basement openings that was narrow and cut into the earth by the foundation. It was the source of the beautiful streaming light. The light that was her pathway to freedom, her way to Elizabeth Smart.

The eyes of the eight photographs appeared to look at her. The young women with the dark hair all seemed to speak to Emma, telling her to run as fast as she could. To get out of that horrible place before it was too late for her . . . as it had been too late for them.

Who are those girls?

A shadow fell and a fast-moving figure eclipsed the light from the window. Emma looked up, groggy and terrified, and she started to lunge toward the bright-ness.

"You like my collection, do you?" he said, shoving her so hard she fell backward, her head barely missing the bed frame. She looked up at him, trying with all she had to see his face, to see if there was something about him that she could recall. There was something in his voice. Something . . . what it was she wasn't sure.

He slammed the door shut with such force that the air in the room pummeled her as she tried to stand.

And then the terrible sound of the lock made her prisoner once more.

* * *

Peg Howell opened drawer after drawer. Her eyes popped in anger and her gnarled fingers poked like hooks through the contents of a junk drawer—which was most of the drawers in her decidedly unkempt kitchen. *Where are my goddamn cigarettes?* She pawed through sewing bobbins, rubber bands, golf balls, and a bunch of other useless stuff. *Where are they?* For a second she was slightly distracted by a copy of a book on tape that she'd once listened to relentlessly. It was a former FBI behavior psychologist's take on serial killers. She was fascinated by the book because it could not have been more wrong. The female author's pseudo analysis traced the origin of Bundy, Gacy, and Ramirez and their ritualized killings to some psychosexual trauma that occurred when they were young.

This is not to say that all serial killers are victims of sexual abuse any more than it would be fair to characterize each major serial killer as a bed wetter. . . .

That line always made Peg laugh out loud when she played the cassette tape in her car on the way to work. Ted was no bed wetter. She'd asked him directly during one of those phone conversations when he was in jail in Colorado.

"Baby," she said, "I've been reading a lot lately."

"Reading is good, Peggy. I'd like to read more, but the crap they have here in jail is an insult to my intelligence. Only a person dumber than a bag of hammers would want to put up with the likes of *Reader's Digest* and the same four Louis L'Amour adventure novels."

"Can I send you something?" she asked, letting go of what she'd wanted to share about her own reading.

"No," he said. "They'd probably just steal it. Bunch of thieves in here."

She winced at the irony. "Were you abused? You know sexually?"

"Whoa! Where did that come from?"

"My reading. Just some FBI perv thinks that a lot of people like you, you know, have been abused."

It was his turn to let it slide. The "people like you" comment was made without judgment.

"Wish I could be with you. I'd like to take you for a drive. Maybe up in the mountains."

"I'd love that, Ted. More than anything."

"Guard says that I have to go now. Guy's an asshole. A couple of the jailers aren't so bad. Gave me access to a typewriter. I'm thinking of writing to my congressman to see if I could get a little consideration. Maybe even the president. Bet he'd like a letter from Teddy Bundy."

"I'd like a letter, Ted," she said.

"Okay. Will do."

And then the call was over. Peg Howell didn't know it, but it was the last phone call for a very long time that she'd get from the guy she'd fallen in love with.

The first letter came four days later. It was stamped by a jailer that it had been opened and reviewed for content. Peg wondered what it was they were looking for in the letter. Ted was an eloquent, thoughtful writer. He wasn't going to put anything on paper that wasn't in keeping with his very important stature. He was also a lover, the gentlest she could imagine.

Dear Peg,
*   You probably have a little idea about how*
lonely I am. Because judging by your last letter,

you are too. I sit in my cell all day—except for one fifteen-minute stretch where they let me go out into the so-called yard for exercise. It is a total joke. The "yard" is about the size of a Ping-Pong table. I walk around it about a hundred times and then my time is up. I am glad that you are in my life. I think about you all day—and all night. If you were in the yard with me, I'd bet we'd figure out real fast what we could do in fifteen minutes. Are you blushing? I bet you are.

Hey, I'm about out of cigarette money. Can you send me some? Same as last time? The food here is crap too. I wish you could fix me one of those sausage and peppers dinners you were talking about in your last letter. Sounds good.

Tomorrow I have a psych evaluation with the county-appointed shrink. I'll ask him if I'm supposed to be a bed wetter!

Love, Ted

She answered back right away. In fact, Peg Howell never put off writing back to Ted. A man like him—refined, charming, handsome—was not the kind of man a woman should ever keep waiting. Peg always wrote in longhand and she sprinkled some Jontue on each of her love-laced missives. She was fascinated by him and so very much in love. There was no way that she could explain to anyone that she'd fallen for Ted Bundy, because no one could ever understand. Their love for each other was epic, beyond all reason. She knew it. He knew it. No one else in the world mattered.

Dear Ted,

*I was thinking that when you get out we
should move far, far away from Tacoma. It holds
nothing but bad memories for both of us. Maybe
we could go to Idaho or somewhere where no
one would know who you are. That sounds dumb
now that I've committed it to paper. I don't think
there is a person on this planet who hasn't heard
of you. I want them to know the Teddy that I
know—the smartest, most handsome man that
ever walked the earth. I mailed a check for $100
for your canteen. I wish that you'd quit smoking,
babe. It isn't good for you. You'll die of cancer or
something, and then where will I be? I'm letting
my hair grow out like you want me to. It is
getting longer and longer by the day. I'll be
ready to send you a photo in a couple of weeks.
Well, that's all for now. Have got a lot of things
to do.*

Love, Peggy

Peggy Howell hurried inside, the package held tightly
in her arms. She spun around the kitchen looking for a
knife to unzip the clear plastic tape that sealed the box
shut. The outside of the box was emblazoned with the
logo WIGS BY GABOR. Her heart pounding with antici-
pation, she pulled the two facing pieces open. Inside,
under a blanket of cellophane, was shiny swirl of hair;
a wig with a style name of SUSAN. There was no saying
who Susan was, but when Peggy saw the photo in the
back of the *National Enquirer* she was sure it was
styled after the actress Susan Dey, who played Laurie,

the eldest daughter, in the ABC TV series *The Partridge Family*.

She lifted it out as if it was a treasure beyond every expectation. Gently. Respectfully. She held it on her balled-up fist and shook it carefully, letting the genuine synthetic locks fall around her upright arm.

Peggy bent forward and placed the wig over her own hair. As she hurried down the hallway to the bathroom, her heart beat faster and faster. She flicked on the light switch and nodded in approval.

"Oh Ted," she said as her eyes ran over her face in the mirror, "you really like it? I grew it out just for you." She tilted her head and twirled a long strand. "Honestly, I don't know what I was thinking wearing my hair so short before. This is so, so much more attractive, don't you think?"

Peggy wasn't sure who she'd get to take her picture. She didn't have any real friends. There was always her mother. As much as she hated her, her mother could probably be put to use in some way. She owed her something.

That night in her dreams, Ted came to Peggy. He appeared out of the darkness next to her bed like some unbelievably handsome phantom. His eyes flashed a kind of wild sexiness that made her blush. It was as if he knew that he could do anything he wanted to her and she'd let him. She'd *beg* him. The window was open and Peggy reasoned that he'd come from somewhere outside. Ted was shirtless, in blue jeans and Nike running shoes. His brow, his tangle of brown hair, his chest were sticky with sweat.

"Ted?" she asked.

"Yes," he said, studying her with a grin stretched across his face.

She sat up in the bed. "Where were you?" she asked.

"I was out running," he said. She couldn't quite determine if his tone was dismissive or angry, as if she dared to question him. She hadn't meant it in an accusatory manner, just a question. And yet he seemed a little on edge, so she pushed harder.

"Where?" she asked, this time with more force. She wanted to know where she stood with Ted. Was she a lover? A confidante? Or just another groupie of a man who other girls swooned over? His dangerousness. His charm. His ability to weaken them at the knees. She was sure she was more than that, but she asked anyway.

Ted stood still by the open window as the air sucked right out of the room. "Nowhere, really," he said. "Just out. Trying to sort things out." When he looked away, a shard of light caught his cheek and Peggy noticed three parallel scratches ran from his temple to his jawline. Pinpricks of blood oozed from each scratch.

Panic and concern replaced Peggy's omnipresent neediness. She wanted to be strong, but she knew that she could barely manage that when it came to Ted Bundy.

"You're hurt, Ted. What happened?" She slid toward the edge of the bed, and beckoned for him to sit next to her. "Tell me, Ted." She patted the mattress.

He didn't even look at her before he started back toward the open window. She wondered a second if that was how he'd made his way into her bedroom.

"Not really hurt, Peg," Ted said over his naked shoulder. "Just a scratch from running. Hit a damn branch."

Peggy put her feet on the dust-bunny-littered wood plank floor and started to fumble in the darkness, clawing toward him, her handsome, elusive Ted.

"Let me help you," she said, pleading as though her life depended on it.

Silence echoed in the bedroom.

"Let me take care of you," she said. "Come to me. Don't make me beg, but if you do, I will. I want you. Whatever it takes."

Ted Bundy had a cold side. She knew it, though she'd never directly experienced it before. Not even in a dream. That changed when Ted came through her window. He actually glowered at her.

"Don't need help from some stupid bitch," he said, his voice a little soft, as if he was trying to mitigate the true meaning of his words. Yet there was no mistaking it. No matter how clever Ted was or wanted to be. It was still loud enough to hear.

Peggy's chest tightened and tensed. She wasn't sure of the meaning of Ted's words, if he was directing them specifically at her or, she hoped, someone else.

"Theodore, what in the world are you saying?"

He turned toward her, his eyes dark and cold. A puff of warm air came from his mouth. "Kidding, Peg. Love you. Love your hair, too." Then he winked.

She looked downward and touched her hair—the shimmery, silky Gabor wig. The Susan was fashioned of long dark tresses, parted in the center with the precision of a ruler. It was just what he loved.

He loved the way she looked.

When she turned to embrace and kiss him, Ted was gone. A breeze caused the curtain to flutter. Peggy got up and rushed toward the window, holding her wig in place.

"Theodore, come back! Don't go to her! You only love me!"

"I can't wait to show you what I bought, Mother," Peggy said the next morning when she'd summoned the courage to model her latest purchase. Behind her back, she gripped the Gabor wig.

Donna Howell looked excited. "Did you get me my favorite chocolates? Almond Roca, you know. Tacoma's finest and famous candy."

Peggy shook her head. "No, Mother, not Almond Roca. Next time, I promise. But this is even better."

"Nothing's better than chocolate," the older woman said, a cigarette dangling from her thin lips. "Except maybe sex, but it's been a while since I've had either."

"Close your eyes, please," Peggy said. "No fair peeking, either."

"Good God, Peggy, will you grow up and quit playing games?" Donna closed her eyes and expelled a lung-full of smoke, and it joined the cloud of yellow and white that circled over her like a swarm of wasps. She loved Almond Roca and the pretty pink tins that the candy came in.

"You can open them now," Peggy said.

Donna looked at her daughter. She immediately had a disgusted look on her face. "What in the world have you got on your head now?"

"Mother, it's a wig. Long hair is very, very in, and you know mine takes forever to grow out."

"You look like some kind of a slut with that kind of long hair. Cheap. Like a dime-store floozy."

Peggy felt her face grow warm, but she vowed that she wouldn't argue with her mother. She didn't have anyone else she could really turn to. She needed that favor.

"I'm not so sure about it, either."

"I must be going deaf," Donna said. "I thought I heard you agree with me."

Peggy didn't, but she hated fighting with her mother about everything. "I said I wasn't *sure*. I looked in the mirror and I don't think I like it as much as I had hoped I would. It's a Gabor wig, you know."

"The *Green Acres* actress?"

"Yes," Peggy said, swinging her hair slightly as if to make it all the more real looking.

"Makes sense in a way. Like one of those wigs on Miss Piggy."

"Mother!"

Donna shrugged and reached for her smokes. "You asked my opinion. You get what you ask for when it comes to me. No holds barred. That's the kind of mother I am and always will be. No matter how stupid you are, I'll never feel sorry for you. Your stupidity came from your father's side."

Peggy pulled a small Instamatic camera from her purse.

"Will you take my picture? I want to see what it looks like in a photograph. It'll help me decide."

"Waste of film," Donna said.

"Please, Mother. I'll go to the mall and get you those chocolates."

Donna thought a moment. "I don't know. I don't know why I have to do something in order to get a gift from you. Doesn't seem right. You always were an unbelievably selfish creature. Got that from your dad, too. Bad genes."

Peggy ignored the poisoned words. As awful as her mother was just then, there were times when she was far, far worse.

"Please," Peggy said. "I'll get you a two-pound tin."

Another drag on the cigarette followed by two streams of smoke out of her widening nostrils and then she held her hand out for the camera.

"You look wretched," Donna said. "But I want the candy."

Peggy handed her mother the small Kodak camera. She posed with her hand on her hip and her lips slightly parted. It was her attempt at a come-hither look. She wasn't sure if she'd be able to pull it off. There wasn't going to be any coaxing from her mother to make sure the shot was just right.

"Take another, Mother, please. I'm at the end of the roll."

Peggy had known her mother would only snap one or two, so she'd taken a bunch of filler photographs before coming over.

"Waste of film," she said.

"Only three left. I could take your picture."

"Like hell you will. Unlike you, I know I'm past my prime. I don't need any reminders of what I used to look like. Too bad you didn't get my good looks. And too bad you got your dad's bad hair. Whole family on his side has bad hair."

The camera went off two more times and Peggy's mother pushed it back at her.

"Now get out of here and get me my candy, you stupid little bitch."

"Yes, Mother," she said. "Fuck you, Mother."

Donna narrowed her brow. "What did you just say?"

"I said, 'thank you, Mother,' " Peggy said.

Donna paused a moment, scouring her daughter's face for the trace of a lie.

"That's what I thought you said," she said.

Peggy spun around and went for the door, promising to come back right away with the chocolates.

A half hour later, she stood at the one-hour photo place and waited for the images to roll off the conveyor belt.

A spectacled worker in a white lab coat with a name tag that said ANSON met her back at the counter.

"Only three shots," he said. "The rest of the roll must have been damaged. Other shots look blurry like they were taken of a carpeted floor or something."

He was very observant.

"I'm sure they are fine."

"No really. I can give you a free roll."

"No, I'll pay for those now."

"Honestly, no problem, ma'am."

"Give me those photos," she said, her voice carrying the distinct tenor of a person impatient and annoyed.

Peggy didn't even wait until she got in to the car. She'd gone to a lot of trouble—not to mention the purchase of some chocolates for the woman she hated more than anyone in the entire world. It was ironic that her mother had taken the photos. Her mother would call her every name in the book if she'd known how she'd fallen for Ted Bundy. She would never, ever understand.

Peggy took a deep breath as she stood in the parking lot and opened the envelope. The first one had her sexy look approximating something closer to indigestion. She blamed her mother for that. She was always putting her down. The second photo depicted her with her eyes half closed.

Her mother's fault, too!

Finally, photo number three. Her last chance. Peggy took in a deep breath. "Oh God," she said loud enough for a box boy nearby to hear her. He probably thought she was looking at some baby pictures. She didn't know why people always acted so animated about such photographs.

She smiled and put the envelope in her purse.

Ted will adore this. I am the girl of his dreams and I alone can save him.

When Peggy got home, she ignored her cat and hurried to the kitchen table. The post office was open for another hour. He'd have the photo before the weekend—before their weekly phone call. Being in love with Ted was a dream come true.

That stupid professor would never have left his wife.

CHAPTER 44

Peggy Howell put on a coat and stomped out the door. She was irritated by a lot of things and she needed to get out of the house. She cracked her window and smoked her last cigarette as she moved into downtown Tacoma traffic heading east toward River Road and the smoke shop where she bought her weekly carton. She turned up the music on the radio and listened to another Captain and Tennille song, "The Way You Touch Me." Like "Love Will Keep Us Together," it always made her think of Ted.

Peggy Howell's best friend, the one who understood her above all others, the one who knew that she was worth something, was Ted. He was always the man of her dreams—smart, sexy, charismatic. He could have chosen any other girl in the world.

She looked over at the turnoff where the dead girls had been found. The yellow tape that announced a criminal investigation had been removed. She slowed her car and pulled over. The field of grass and blackberries had been trampled by the investigators as they sought to assemble the flotsam and jetsam of a murderer's work. She unrolled the window and looked around, noticing the tire tracks, the footprints, even a LUNA bar wrapper that someone had left behind.

Chocolate chip, she mused. Ted's favorite cookies were chocolate chip, not shortbread or oatmeal.

Next, she remembered a conversation they'd shared a few weeks before his execution.

"I can't believe they are going to do this to you," she said.

"I'm not done yet."

"I know. I have faith."

"Babe, we all need faith. Faith and peace."

"I wish I could see you."

"They won't even let Carole," he said.

"Do you have to bring her up?"

"She's my wife," he said. "But she's nothing compared to you."

"I know. But it still hurts whenever I hear her name. I would have done the same thing if you called me as a witness. I would be Mrs. Theodore Robert Bundy. Not her. She's not even pretty, Ted."

"She's pretty enough. Not all of them were . . . or . . . are beautiful."

There was a pause in the line and Peggy's heart raced.

"You still there?"

"I'm here. Just another snap, crackle, and pop in the electrical wires here."

It was a joke, but Peggy didn't laugh. Ted's nearly literal gallows humor was lost on her. She couldn't imagine a world without him. He understood her so much better than anyone ever could. His letters were pure poetry. Better than Rod McKuen, she once said in a compliment that Ted ate up.

"Rod's good, thank you."

"You're better."

"No, no, you are the best. You always will be."

Another crackle in the line.

"Ted?"

"Yeah, baby," he said. "I'm here."

"You are the best," she repeated.

"There will always be others to follow in my footsteps, Peg. I'd like to brag and say that I'm the best, but I'm told over and over by the matchbook university shrinks that they know better. That I'm an aberration, a deviant."

"Deviant means different than the others," she said. "And different can be a very beautiful thing. I love you."

"I love you, too," he said. "Have to go now. Will be looking at your picture and thinking of you tonight."

Peggy sat in the car looking at the slow-moving Puyallup River wondering if there was anything more she could have done for Ted. That was the last time they'd spoken. A week later, she'd watched the live feeds from Florida showing the crowd gathering there to celebrate his execution. She wanted to be with his parents on the other side of Tacoma. She'd met Ted's mother a couple of times at the grocery store. She'd pretended not to know who Louise Bundy was. Peggy was a shopper looking for a ripe watermelon. Louise was a small woman with thick lenses and quiet, shy demeanor. She barely looked up when she told Peggy to sniff the stem end of the melon.

"That'll give you a good idea," she said. "Don't bother pressing it to see if it is soft. The skin is pretty thick and it really isn't a good indicator."

"You're very kind," Peggy said as Louise moved on down the aisle. She wanted to add that "your son is a great man, like a great misunderstood artist." But she held it inside. She wasn't sure if Ted's mother would really understand, if she really knew the son that she'd once pretended was a little brother was a man of importance. Peggy thought of running after her and thanking her again, just to get a glimpse into her eyes. Ted's eyes. But she didn't. She held back. Way back.

A few days after Ted's execution, Peggy met a man at a bar on Sixth Avenue in Tacoma. She never knew his name. Never asked. Three months later, Peggy was showing. She ran into Susie's mother, Anna Sherman, outside the Fred Meyer store on Nineteenth.

Mrs. Sherman's eyes landed on Peggy's swelling abdomen.

"Honey, I didn't know you were expecting."

Peggy beamed. "I'm due in the fall."

"I didn't know . . . you got married."

"Oh, I didn't. I don't need a husband to be a mother."

"I guess that's very modern of you," Anna said. "I was always glad I had a husband."

Peggy patted her stomach and pushed her cart toward her car. The miracle inside her was always to be *hers*, and *hers* alone. Her son was going to follow in his father's footsteps.

He was going to be the greatest of them all.

Donna Howell showed up at Tacoma General Hospital the morning after her grandson was born. She came without balloons or flowers. Instead, the former grocery checker brought with her a kind of palpable bitterness that permeated every puff of her smoky breath. Indeed, Donna Howell was one of those women who'd thought she'd done everything right with the raising of her children, but she'd been repeatedly disappointed by each and every one of them. Peggy was at the top of that list, or at the bottom. The middle, too. Donna Howell considered Peggy a heartbreakingly sorry excuse for a daughter. That is, if she'd deigned to waste a piece of her heart on her.

Which, not surprisingly to any of those who observed her, Donna Howell seldom did.

Some women are not cut out to be mothers. They don't have the lovey-dovey component in their personality that makes 2 AM feedings and projectile vomiting forgotten with the baby's innocent smile, first laugh, steps.

Donna was one of those women.

"You're never going to lose that weight, Peg," she said, bursting into the hospital room where her daughter had labored for seventeen hours, alone. She looked over at the new mother in the next bed and zipped the curtain shut without even so much as an acknowledgment of her presence.

"Hi, Mother," Peggy said, barely looking up from her bed adjacent to the window. She never called her Mom, or Mama, or anything so cozy or familiar. It was always Mother, more a biological term than anything familial.

"Did the baby's father show up?" Donna asked, her voice as cold and sharp as an ice pick.

Peggy looked out the window, searching the gray Tacoma horizon for something with eyes that brimmed with tears. *Anything.*

"Figured," Donna said, her reflection spreading over the window like an oil slick. "You are so stupid. Now, fat and stupid and with a bastard boy to boot. Your life just couldn't get any better, could it?"

Peggy turned to face her mother, holding her emotion as tightly as she could. "Nice to see you, too, Mother."

Donna unzipped her black-and-white nylon tracksuit jacket. "Well, where is he?"

"He's in the infant care unit, if you must know. There were complications."

"Life is full of complications, *Peg.* You're an expert at creating them."

Saying the shortened version of her name brought back years of bad, awful, humiliating memories. Donna used to introduce her daughter as *Piggy* or *Pig* to strangers, and then pretend that she'd said it correctly.

"Oh, you misheard me. I said Peggy, not Piggy!" And then she'd laugh. Except it was never funny. Not to the sad-eyed little girl who ate too much and knew she was a little overweight. Nor was it funny to the audience of her mother's pretend non-joke.

Peggy did what she'd always done to survive. She changed the subject.

"Aren't going to ask what's wrong with your grandson?" she asked.

Donna slithered across the room and perched on her daughter's bedside. "I *asked*. He's going to be fine."

Peggy brightened a little. *Mother asked.* She must care some. At least a little bit.

Donna looked around and smiled. *No flowers. Good. No cards. Even better.*

"What are you going to name him?" she asked.

Peggy's eyes met her mother's. "I was thinking of naming him after his father, Theodore."

A look of exaggerated puzzlement came over the older woman. "Theodore? That's a hifalutin name for a bastard." Donna stopped herself for a second, the wheels turning. "That must mean you know who the father is, which I suppose is a minor miracle for a slut."

Peggy's face reddened. Her mother always knew where to stick the knife.

"Get out of here," Peggy said.

Donna shrugged it off. She tugged at her tracksuit jacket as if it needed straightening.

"Aren't you the brash little bitch, telling me to get out when I came all the way here to see you and your baby, my bastard grandson?"

"Leave or I'll ask the nurse to call security, Mother. I don't need this. When you said you were coming, I don't know, I thought just maybe you'd finally be what I wanted you to be. For once."

"That's funny coming from you. I thought you'd be what I wanted you to be—a decent daughter."

"Decent? Now you're almost making me laugh. You've had more live-in boyfriends than anyone in a trailer park, Mother—that's right, more live-ins than anyone in a trailer park. That's saying a lot about you, Mother."

"You disgust me," Donna said. "You always have. Your father was no good and you carry his poisoned blood."

"He left you, remember that? He left you!"

"I was glad he left. He's dead to me. Just like you."

A nurse entered the room, but backed off a little before finally speaking. The atmosphere was tense, brittle.

"Is everything all right here?" she asked.

"We're fine," Peggy said, her eyes riveted to her mother's. "My mother was just leaving."

"Oh . . . did she want to hold her grandson?" she asked.

Donna looked at the nurse, a young woman with strawberry blond hair and freckles like a seabird's egg. "I don't want to hold him or see him. My daughter, you see, is an unmarried woman and the baby is a product of one of her many one-night stands."

"Good-bye, Mother," Peggy said in her calmest tone, refusing to take the bait.

"All right then," the nurse said, opening the door and motioning for Donna to exit.

Donna, her face tight with anger, did something remarkable just then: She said nothing more. No parting shot. No cruel remark to make Peggy feel lower than the bugs that crawl in the darkest depths of the forest floor. Not another word.

"Are you all right?" the nurse said as the door closed.

Peggy nodded. "I am. I'm fine. My mother and I have a complicated relationship."

"That's putting it mildly," the nurse said, surveying the physician's charts.

"I guess so," Peggy said. The door was open a crack for a little sympathy, but she didn't seek any more of it. Her mother was her worst enemy. Her mother was her tormenter. Her mother never once gave her a drop of human kindness. Yet she didn't hold that completely against her. Her mother was all she had.

"Have you named your baby?" she asked.

Peggy brightened a bit. Her baby. That was someone wonderful. He was only a few hours old, but already he was the best thing that had ever happened to her. "No. I was thinking of a name, but now I'm not so sure."

"What name are you thinking of now? There's no rush, of course. I mean, it is nice to have a name before you leave the hospital. It helps with the paperwork, you know."

"I had thought of Theodore," Peggy said slowly as she measured her words.

The nurse didn't say anything right away. The hesitation clearly bothered Peggy.

"You don't like it, either," Peggy said, pushing the button to lower her head in the motorized bed. The hydraulics rumbled.

"It isn't that," the nurse answered. "I dated a guy named Ted once and it wasn't the best experience of my life. Kind of a control freak who thought he was better than anyone else. But that's got nothing to do with your naming your little boy. Just a reaction. Sorry."

Peggy wondered if it was *her* Ted that the nurse was indicating. Her heart beat a little faster and the monitor at her bedside began to pulse more rapidly. Certainly there were plenty of Teds around Tacoma, but even so the idea of another girl being involved with *her* Ted was a painfully sore subject. She wanted to be the only one for him, the only one he ever needed. Indeed, the only one who ever really understood his deep, deep hurt.

"Was that here in town?" Peggy finally asked. Her voice was soft and a little shaky. The monitor's light quickened.

The nurse set down the chart, looked at the monitor, and shook her head. "Oh no, back in Detroit. Just kind of funny how names carry the weight of past experiences—good and bad."

Peggy turned toward the window again, looking out and thinking.

"My mother was dead set against Theodore, too."

The monitor slowed.

"None of my business, but she seems like a very negative woman. She probably wouldn't like any name you selected. I'm thinking out loud, of course. And I have no standing here. Just putting it out there. A lot of families pressure each other, you know. You'd be surprised at how many change their minds on the names they'd once thought were perfect."

Peggy nodded. "Understood. Thank you. When can I see my son? When can I see Jeremy?"

The nurse smiled. "I like *that* name," she said. "Let me ask the doctor if your son can come into your room."

"He's better?"

"He's just fine. We were just keeping an eye on him. Rough delivery, but I don't have to tell you that."

Peggy allowed a smile to return to the pretty blond nurse. *She* liked the name Jeremy. And as much as Peggy hated her mother, she didn't want to make her a greater enemy. Jeremy might need family someday. The boy didn't need his father's name to prove a damn thing. Being Ted's son was greater than a mere label.

* * *

Outside Peggy's room, the nurse met up with her supervisor, an African American woman of about fifty who had been working at Tacoma General for almost three decades.

"How's she doing?" the older woman asked.

"Better, no thanks to her mother," the younger nurse said.

The supervisor ran her glasses down the bridge of her nose. "Was that the jogger?" she asked.

The blonde looked on as a woman and her husband walked by dragging the IV unit along the gleaming floor way toward the nursery. "Sorry?"

"The woman in the black tracksuit?" the supervisor asked.

"Yeah. What a bitch she was. So mean to her." The blond nurse hesitated, thinking about the tail end of the encounter she'd witnessed with the mother and the conversation she'd had with Peggy about naming her son Theodore. "Weird thing about it was that her mother reamed her and Peggy, the patient, just took it. Barely reacted. But when we started talking about my boyfriend, Ted, her heart rate escalated big time."

For the first time, the older woman looked half-interested. "Your boyfriend? Didn't know you had one."

She shook her head. "That's just it. I don't. But Peggy's vitals shot up when I mentioned his name. It was like she was jealous or something when she had no cause to be. My Ted was a doofus I dumped back in Detroit. You know, before I came out here to this lovely job."

The charge nurse looked down at the paperwork assigned to Peggy Howell. She ignored the younger woman's dig about the job. As if Detroit was some prize, after all.

"Says the father's name is Theodore Bundy."

The younger woman nodded as she processed the information. "Name seems familiar," she said.

The supervisor pushed the paper back into the folder. "She probably made it up. She's not wearing a ring and she isn't married, anyway. I don't know why these young girls bother. A few years ago they did the right thing and gave them up for adoption. Better for the kid. I mean, most of the time."

"Her mother was so mean to her," the blonde said. "I mean really, really mean."

"Some mothers are," she said.

Before passwords and Internet sites, some men kept porn physically hidden away from their wives and girlfriends. Stashes were kept in private places where a man, and some women, could pleasure themselves without fear of discovery. Peggy had a stash like that. It wasn't porn, however. It was her bundle of Ted letters. Jeremy had seen her put them under the false bottom of a dresser in the guest room upstairs.

He read them one time, looking over his father's words with both reverence and disgust.

Dear Peggy,
I don't know the song you mentioned in the last letter, but I do like the message of it. I'm doing fine. I have been getting all of your letters, but don't have the time to answer them. Just not

enough time, I guess. The days are filled with all
kinds of legal wrangling between the prison
staff, the lawyers. Barbara Walters wants to
come and talk to me, and I told the warden to
tell her to take a hike. I don't want to be put up
on TV until I'm exonerated. If I go on TV now,
they'll just try to trip me up. A couple of authors
have tried to get ahold of me to write a book
about my experiences, and I might talk to them.
My story isn't what the world thinks it is. You
know the truth. You are the only one who knows
the real me. My mom thinks she knows me, but
she doesn't. Not really. Anyway, I was wondering
if you could send me a picture of Tricia. You've
told me so much about her that I'd like to see a
photo if you can manage one. I bet you're a
thousand times prettier than her, but I'd still like
to put a face to the name. Don't put her name on
the photograph, but yours. Bye for now.

peace, Ted

Dear Peggy,
I know you understand me. You understand
my place in history. I know that. I know you
understand that my cases are more intricate;
more involved than someone like that piddly-ass
Boston Strangler. Mine involved girls all over the
country. Look at the TV, for God's sake. I'm as
big as the Beatles and they were bigger than
Jesus Christ. I'm not a braggart. I just want
some recognition, some confirmation that I am
the best at something. I don't know for certain,

*but it might be fair to say that Michelangelo or
Leonardo were the world's greatest artists. Is it
that much of a stretch, Peggy, to acknowledge
that I too have held some great place in this
world? Everyone wants to talk to me. Figure me
out. They want to cut out my goddamn brain to
see what makes me tick. They ask me if I wet the
bed when I was a little kid. They asked me if
Johnnie gave me the belt. Do you think they'd
pick apart some other kind of genius? No. I'll
tell you what. They wouldn't. They wouldn't dare.
Sometimes, Peggy, greatness just has to be accepted, appreciated, and revered for what it is.*

By then Ted had jumped onto the genius bandwagon, and although what he was writing to her would have offended most of the world, Peggy didn't care. She loved him. She agreed with him. She understood above all others that something could be beautiful and very, very dark. If Ted Bundy was some kind of an evil genius, she was content being part of his life. She felt a charge, a thrill, at his words. She felt love.

If Ted had been consumed by murder "twenty-four hours a day," as the lead investigator in the Washington cases had said so pointedly as the hours ticked toward the electric chair, Peggy had found herself consumed by Ted. There was no water, no air. No food. No sleep. All that existed in her world was Ted and the hope that if the law did what it had set out to do that his legacy of greatness would live on in some very real, tangible way.

He was Leonardo. She was his Mona Lisa.

* * *

Grace Alexander looked at the fax sent by Anna Sherman's nurse.

"What's that?" Paul asked as he hovered over her, dirty coffee mug in hand.

"Nothing," she said.

"It doesn't look like nothing."

"Paul, this is personal."

"You've been doing something personal a lot lately."

She wanted to tell him, but it felt foolish. They were in the middle of a major investigation. She had Emma, Kelsey, and Lisa to think about. And while their cases were at the forefront, she had that need to find out who had killed her sister.

"I'm leaving for a meeting."

"Now?"

"Yes, now."

It was time to go see Peggy Howell. Peggy had lived with her mother in Ruston, in the heart of the smelter's toxic zone. The arsenic in Tricia's bones had come from the smelter.

She looked up Peggy's address. Of course, she'd moved. She had to move.

So did the bones.

A second later, Grace was out the door.

CHAPTER 45

In January 1989 the air in Tacoma was heavy with the stench of the Simpson paper mill, an acrid odor to which residents of Washington's toughest city, Grit City, had somehow become immune. The air had been especially chilly after temperatures dropped following a green Christmas. Ice pricked at the edges of lawns and vapors melted into frozen masses where the O'Hares' dryer duct fed moist air outside. And yet as cold as it had become outside, the scene on the TV set in the O'Hare family living room was beyond chilly. Sissy, Conner, and their little girl watched the spectacle coming from Florida.

Burn, Ted, burn!

Conner held Sissy's hand and leaned closer to her. He spoke in a whisper so that Grace couldn't hear.

"His time has run out," he said.

"He'll get another stay," Sissy said, her face knotted with worry.

"No, he's out of time. I'm telling you, he'll die tonight."

She shook her head. "Not so sure about that," she said. "He always manages to find a way to survive."

Conner looked at his daughter.

"The man who killed your sister is going to finally be punished."

Grace didn't say anything. She didn't know what she could say that would matter. She looked at the TV, but kept most of her attention on her parents. They carried such a strange mixture of fear, hate, and hope. They seemed both elated and miserable at the same.

"He didn't answer my last letter," Sissy said.

"He's been busy," Conner said, and a grim smile came over his face.

When Jeremy Howell looked into his mother's eyes it was with fear and respect, rather than love. Peggy had told her son over and over that he was special and that his specialness had to be fulfilled. If he was to be what he was born to be, to follow in his father's bloody footprints, then he had to do more than seize the moment. He had to create it. He had to be wily, crafty, smart. He had to be ruthless. When Jeremy looked into his mother's eyes it was with the kind of respect and fear that came with hate.

And yet he loved her. He knew her struggles. She'd told him repeatedly that loving Ted had been the hardest part of her hard-fought life.

"My own family disowned me," she said one time when they sat in the car parked in front of his grandmother's house. "And when they disowned me, they disowned you. I hate them. I know you don't know them and you never will, but, honey, trust me."

It was always about trust. Jeremy had never talked to his father, of course. By the time Peggy had told her son about his important father, Old Sparky had zapped Ted into oblivion.

"They killed him. No one would kill a lion for doing what he does naturally, exquisitely. No one thinks anything of a killer whale eating a seal, for God's sake. It is what they do. Your father was like that. You're like that."

"Like that?" he asked.

His mother's face tightened. "Don't be stupid. What don't you understand here?"

He thought a moment, wondering if he'd had the ability to say what he was really thinking.

"What if I don't want to be like that?" he finally asked.

She looked at him, with those cold eyes. She took a moment, too. Conversations between mother and son were always like that. Long gaps between utterances, rather than quick exchanges fueled by any real connection.

Her eyes narrowed once more and she shrugged. He was a bug. A gnat. His questions were annoyances. "You will struggle for the rest of your life. You will die being a nothing. Nothing is worse than a promise or birthright unfulfilled."

The words didn't track and Peggy Howell could see that.

"Being your mother isn't easy," she said. "What I did for you just doesn't seem to matter."

She turned away and looked out at the house that she grew up in.

"I hate my parents and you'll probably hate me, too."

"I could never hate you, Mom," he said, lying.

"I could hate you," she said.

"You couldn't."

"Don't mess with your birthright," she said. "If you do, you'll be alone forever."

"I don't want to be alone."

She lit a cigarette and cracked the window.

"Except for Ted, I've been alone my entire life," she said.

"What about my sister? My stepdad?"

"He's dead and your sister Cecilia might as well be." She pushed smoke out of her nostrils, reminding Jeremy of a dragon. "Are you going to let me down, too?"

"I guess not," he said, still unsure of what she wanted.

"When Ted was only a little older than you he killed a girl."

Jeremy felt his pulse quicken. "I don't want to kill anyone."

Peggy turned away. "Then you're nothing. You're dead to me. And you know what? I'll be kind of relieved. Nothing I loathe more than a loser. Especially a loser who's been handed greatness on a silver platter. Be nothing. Fine with me."

Jeremy remembered going to his bedroom after that encounter with his mother in the car, his sister playing in the room next door. He'd cried a little, but the tears were oddly forced. He went to Cecilia, who was playing with her Barbie, and he took his belt and slipped it around her neck. Cecilia started to scream and Peggy came in, yanked the belt from her daughter's neck, and slapped Jeremy as hard as she could.

"Dogs don't poop in their kennel," she said.

He touched his face where the stinging pain came. "Huh?"

Peggy's eyes bulged. "You heard me. Now get out of here!"

"But, Mom."

"Don't 'but' me, or I'll beat the crap out of you."

"I was doing what—"

Later that same night, Cecilia came into Jeremy's bedroom, her neck still pink from the belt that had he'd twined around it. Her saucer eyes absorbed her brother.

"Jeremy, why did you hurt me?" she asked. Her tone was plaintive, but she didn't cry.

"I don't know," he said, now barely looking at her.

She touched him, but he pulled back a little. "Please don't hurt me ever again," she said, looking at him as she tried to understand.

"I'm sorry," he said. His words came at her, hollow and empty.

"I love you," she said.

"I know."

In that moment even Jeremy Howell's kid sister could see that there was nothing to her brother's apology. He had meant to hurt her. He wanted to hurt her.

Years later after Cecilia married and found fewer and fewer excuses to come home she told her husband about the time her brother tried to choke her with a belt.

"I don't want that sick SOB around our kids," Kirk Morris said.

"I don't, either, but I don't blame him. Not really. I think that the stuff my mom was doing to him was making him that way."

"What was she doing to him?"

"Not *that*," she said emphatically. "She was always whispering in his ear. Telling him things."

"What was she saying?"

"Empowerment stuff. I watched her lean next to him and say, 'You're better than the rest. You are special.' "

"What's so creepy about that?"

"It wasn't in the words," she said. "It was in how she said things and how he reacted. It was like something secret, maybe forbidden, dark. I don't know."

"Now you're acting weird."

"Maybe I am. I was a kid. Maybe I just didn't get it. But on more than one occasion I remember my mother telling him that being the best was a lonely endeavor, one that few could understand. She said, 'Your work will only be known if you get caught.' "

"Get caught?"

"Something like that. I don't know for sure. It was a long time ago. Really, when I look back, my brother never really had a chance."

"I don't feel sorry for him and I don't want him around our kids."

"I do feel sorry for him, but I agree. I don't want him around the children, either."

Although the Morrises lived only across the Tacoma Narrows Bridge in Gig Harbor, they never saw much of Uncle Jeremy. Their mother said he was too busy. A recluse. He had a demanding job. She never told her children that their grandmother actually lived with their uncle. Oddly, they never asked about her. They assumed that she, along with their grandfather, was dead. After all, why wouldn't their grandma come to see them if she was alive?

* * *

The crack. *The way out.* The source of the air. Emma Rose woke up, her mind still zeroing in on what she needed to do above all other possibilities. Her head throbbed and she wanted to throw up. But more than that, she wanted out of the apartment. She wanted to go home. She pulled herself up from the mattress and found her way to back to the wall with the crack. At least, that's where she was certain it had been the day before. On her knees, she ran her hands over the wall, but she couldn't find the opening. Had she gone the wrong direction? The room was not that large. How was it that she couldn't find the source of the airflow? It was dark as always, but she'd found it before by feeling the air pass through the opening. How was it that she couldn't find it now?

God, help me. Where is it? Where did it go?

The Howells had moved to a nice middle-class neighborhood in Tacoma, on North Howard, not far away from where Ted had grown up. Donna Howell had taken her relocation money from the old neighborhood in Ruston and paid cash for the two-story house with the brick façade and bright green louvered shutters—a house that Peggy had insisted was the perfect location. After Donna died in 1994, the house was willed to Peggy, who was already living there with her adult son, Jeremy. While none of the neighbors liked Peggy, they did appreciate Jeremy's dedication to keeping the yard in perfect shape. He never missed a mowing and, better yet, kept it sprinkled in the summer.

"I haven't seen you in years. Since you were a child. But I know who you are," Peggy said, when she answered the door. "You look a lot like Tricia, not quite as pretty, but a lot like her."

"Hi, Peggy," Grace said, looking her over. Peggy wore jeans and a sweatshirt. Her skin was wrinkled and her hair was long, but very thin. It dawned on her that her sister would be showing signs of aging by then— had she not been murdered. "May I come in?"

Peggy nodded. "If you must. I'm surprised you've come by. Your mom pretty much disowned me. Shoved me to the side when all I wanted to do was help bring Tricia back home."

"That was a long time ago, Peggy."

"Yeah, well, it still hurts," Peggy said, searching for her cigarettes. "I worked my ass off putting up flyers, you know. I did everything I was asked to do and then some."

"I came here to talk about my sister."

"You want a cigarette or a beer or something? I have some thick-cut potato chips if you're hungry."

"I'm not hungry, Peggy. But I am here for something."

"For what?"

"The truth."

"What kind of truth?"

"The truth that only you know. The truth that the only living witness knows."

Peggy, still looking for her cigarettes, gave up. "You're talking in riddles. Can you get to the point? I have to take my son out for a haircut later."

"Jeremy?"

"Yes, Jeremy."

"Is his father home?"

"No. His father is dead. Now you're going to have to

leave. You're making me uncomfortable and I don't like feeling that way in my own home," Peggy said.

"I thought that this was your mother's house."

"She's dead. It's mine now."

"Right. She was bought out by The Pointe developers, is that right?"

Peggy nodded. "She was. And they really screwed her over. They were supposed to give us six months before they tore down the house so we could salvage those gorgeous old leaded windows by the fireplace. But no, they didn't. Really made my mom mad."

There were several ways to conduct interviews. One way was to build up to the key question, one little drop at a time, until there was a bucket of water to toss over the witness. The other tactic was to just go for the jugular.

Grace used the second technique.

"You killed my sister, Peggy. Didn't you?"

Peggy stepped backward. "Jesus! Where did that come from?"

Grace had Peggy where she wanted her.

"Tricia wanted you to stop messing around with the professor, didn't she? Did she say she was going to tell? Did you kill her because of that?"

Peggy looked flustered and angry.

Where were those damn cigarettes?

"I have no flipping idea what you're talking about."

"I think you do. I think you killed her and buried her at your mom's house on Ruby Street in Ruston."

"What are you talking about? Killed her? Buried her? You are really going to have to leave now. My son is at work and when he gets home he's going to rip you a new one for treating me like this."

"The bones found at the beach were full of lead and

arsenic. They came from your yard. You know what I'm talking about. I can see it in your eyes."

Emma Rose could hear yelling going on above her. It wasn't the TV. It was louder, continuous. Two women were yelling at each other. She heard footsteps. Someone other than *him* was there. This was her chance. Her only chance.

She took the *People* magazine with Selena Gomez on the cover and rolled it up into a megaphone.

"Help!" she screamed. "I'm down here!"

She stopped and listened for movement, but there wasn't any.

Next, she did what she had to do. It was her last chance. Her only hope. The stakes could not have been higher. If she failed, she would die.

She took the match she'd found up from the floor and ran it against the concrete, but nothing happened. Only a white line.

You have to light! she thought. *Light! Please!*

She tried it again. She could smell the scent of a burning match, but there was no flame.

God, why don't you love me? she asked.

She thought of Elizabeth Smart. She'd made it. She'd found freedom.

The match lit and she held it the edge of the *People* cover. She knew that Selena had been through a lot of things in her life, and she would forgive her.

It was a torch. She was the Statue of Liberty. Emma Rose knew that the smoke would need to find the nose of someone who would help her. Someone upstairs. Someone yelling. For good measure, she took off her

T-shirt and doused it with Sam's Club diet cola and held it over her mouth and nose. Next, she carried the blanket to the chair under the furnace vent and lit it on fire.

If she died of smoke inhalation or even if she'd burned alive, it would be better than dying at the hand of the sicko who held her in the apartment. She held the Sam's Club-diet-cola-soaked T-shirt and waited by the door. She didn't cry. She wasn't even that scared. She knew that whatever happened would be for the best.

Whatever happened, she would be free.

Grace stopped talking. She breathed in cautiously.

"I smell smoke," she said.

"I don't smell anything," Peggy said. She was angry. Her face contorted. "I want you to leave."

"We need the fire department." Grace reached for her phone and Peggy shoved her, knocking it out of her hand. It spun across the floor like a gyro.

"Are you crazy?" she asked, already knowing the answer.

"Get the hell out of my house."

"The smoke must be coming from the basement."

"No, it's not. I was cooking earlier. Get out of my house!"

Grace picked up the phone with one hand, and pulled out her police issue. She pointed the gun at Peggy.

"What's downstairs, Peggy?"

She punched in 911 with her thumb and put the phone on speaker.

"I'm at 2121 North Howard and there's a fire. This is Detective Grace Alexander with the Tacoma PD. I need backup, too. This is an emergency."

Grace didn't wait for the dispatcher response other than to hear that "help is on the way."

By then Peggy was gone.

With her gun drawn, Grace made her way first to the kitchen, where the back door had swung open. The door to the basement was locked. She kicked at it, but it didn't budge. She stepped back a couple of feet and fired in the lock. It took only one shot and the door was open. She turned on the light.

Smoke oozed from the slot in the steel door.

"I'm down here!" It was a scream, but it was soft, muffled. It was not Peggy's voice, but even if it had been, Grace would have gone down there to get her. She wanted her in prison for what she'd done. Dying in a fire was too good for her sister's supposed best friend.

Her murderer.

The basement lights were dimmed by the curtain of smoke and Grace called out to whoever it was who was trapped down there.

"I can't see very well. Tell me where you are."

Emma started banging against the door with her shoulder. She screamed out. "I'm here! I'm in here. In the apartment."

The apartment?

Grace crawled on her hands and knees and found the door. Her hands felt for the knob, but it, too, was locked.

"Back away," she said. "I'm going to fire my weapon to unlock the door."

A muffled cry came through the wall. "Hurry."

The gun fired and Grace pushed at the door. It wouldn't budge.

"I'm going to try again. Please stay away from the door. Do you hear me?"

There was no response.

"Please stay away. I'm going to fire."

Grace steadied herself in the smoke and shot once more. This time, the lock split and the door crashed open.

Inside, she found a teenage girl, unconscious and half naked.

Emma Rose was alive.

Paramedics carried Emma out on a stretcher into the yard, next to a maple that had already started to turn yellow. Flashing lights and sirens had turned what had been tranquil and beautiful into a nightmare of sorts. Several neighbors had gathered to gawk. One of them was a blond girl, young, pretty. She looked like an angel. When Emma looked up at her she smiled through the oxygen mask. She spoke, but no one could hear her.

"Thank you, Elizabeth Smart," Emma said.

Grace Alexander sat on the back of the fire truck taking in some oxygen and insisting she was just fine.

"I need to call my husband," she said. "We need to catch Peggy Howell. She's responsible."

The paramedic put his hand on her shoulder; it was a soft, reassuring touch. "Husband's on his way. Your partner Detective Bateman's over there."

Grace looked over as Paul made his way through the

chaos of the fire. A neighbor on the west side of the Howells' house had the stream from a garden hose aimed at the roof of his garage, but that was hardly necessary. The Howell blaze was small, contained to the basement.

"We found the body. We found Emma's kidnapper. Weird thing. Coroner says he's been dead five days. Not long after he snatched Emma. This sick SOB."

She got up. "What body?"

"Her son, I guess. Maybe a boyfriend. Two neighbors had differing ideas about the relationship."

"Jeremy's dead?"

"Yes, been dead a while."

"Did you find his mother?"

"Sit tight. You've been through a lot today. But, yeah, we got her. Blues picked her up by the Safeway trying to buy, isn't this ironic, a pack of smokes with a stolen credit card . . . Diana Rose's Visa card."

Grace felt so much relief, she felt her legs go weak. She sat back down. She wanted to call her mother, too. She wanted her to know that it was finally over. Peggy had been the killer. She'd betrayed them all.

"We found some weird shit inside the house," he said, stepping back a little as an aid car left. "Good thing you're sitting down."

"What?"

"You think your mother was a Bundy collector? This gal had her beat tenfold. Photographs, letters, books, it's like a murderbilia stage show gone wild in there. She even had cue cards for Ted."

Grace didn't understand. "Cue cards? What do you mean?"

Paul held one up in a plastic evidence bag. It was an

index card, much like the kind her mother had used when she made Bundy flash cards. These were slightly larger and the writing on them was a sloppy printing.

TED: YOU ARE THE PRETTIEST BY FAR.

"Weird huh? Like she was making up some kind of play or something."

"Not a play," Grace said. "More like a fantasy come true."

"Grace, we also found this," he said, holding up the silver necklace with the dove dangling in the flashing lights of the aid car. "It was with her stash of Ted stuff. Right on top. Just sitting there."

She reached for it and he let it fall into her palm.

Peggy had kept a souvenir. Just like the others.

EPILOGUE
BONES TO DUST

*"I'm the most coldhearted son of a bitch
you'll ever meet."*
—TED BUNDY

Peggy Howell gave several interviews after she pleaded guilty to the murders of Tricia O'Hare, Kelsey Caldwell, and Lisa Lancaster, and the abduction and attempted murder of Emma Rose. She didn't proclaim her innocence, like Ted had done at first. Instead, she rather appeared to bask in the glory of her crimes. She was not charged with her son's murder. As it turned out, Jeremy Howell had committed suicide. His mother told a reporter for the *News Tribune* that "Jeremy was a wuss. He was nothing like his father." She went on to say that she had that her biggest regret was not the murders, but the fact that "Jeremy couldn't man up. I had to tell him what to say, what to do, how to hold a knife. When we caught Kelsey—that's the first girl's name, I think—he couldn't even do what had to be done. I did. I showed him. Girl number two was no better. I gave him one last chance to be the man that he should be, but hell, he took the easy way out."

Jeremy Howell was cremated after the autopsy that determined he'd died of a single gunshot wound to the head. His ashes remain unclaimed.

Emma Rose was released from Tacoma General Hospital after three days of treatment for exhaustion, smoke inhalation, and dehydration. She told *People* in a telephone interview from her hospital bed: "Three amazing women saved my life—Selena Gomez, Elizabeth Smart, and Grace Alexander." She quit Starbucks and went off to college in California. Marine biology is her stated major.

Anna Sherman died on Christmas Day, never knowing for sure if her daughter, Susie, had been a victim of Ted Bundy or not. When the staff cleaned out her room at the assisted living center, they found a box of Ted memorabilia addressed to Grace Alexander with a small note written on the top: *You did it for Tricia, please do it for Susie, too.*

Tavio and **Mimi Navarro** welcomed their first baby, a girl, on January 14. They named her Catalina. Michael Navarro vanished. Police were able to track him to the Mexican border crossing in San Diego. After that, nothing.

Palmer Morton was arrested two months after the fire on Howard Street and charged with twenty-seven counts of fraud in a case that halted The Pointe development. He certainly had the resources to wriggle out of the charges by blaming the subcontractor. But it was a statement made by Emma Rose that clinched the case: "When I confronted him, he said that no one would believe me because I was a kid. He said that the subcontractor was stupid and he told them to find another dump location, one farther out of town. He knew what they were doing all along."

Sissy O'Hare could finally really breathe again. Knowing what happened, who was responsible, had been the greatest gift of her life. She had never imagined that her daughter had been killed because she wanted someone—Peggy—to do the right thing. It seemed like Tricia.

Grace Alexander took a leave of absence from the Tacoma Police Department. She used the time to work on a book, *My Sister's Keeper*—at husband Shane's urging. She never finished it. She found out she was pregnant. Her baby was due in the the summer. She still has dinner with her mother every Wednesday. She told Paul Bateman that "my mom and I have never been closer. We both feel free of something that took over our lives."

Tricia O'Hare is no longer considered a Bundy victim. The day after Peggy's arrest, someone updated the victim list on Wikipedia by removing her name. Her bones were returned to Sissy the following spring, and she and Grace buried her next to Conner.

ACKNOWLEDGMENTS

I wanted to take a moment to thank some of the people who have been so instrumental to the process of writing *Fear Collector*. I'm grateful to my amazing editor Michaela Hamilton for her deft editing and consultation as this book came together. And I'm equally indebted to Laurie Parkin, my publisher, for her wisdom, support, and patience. Lots of each!

My appreciation also goes to Susan Raihofer, my literary agent for almost twenty years, for being such a great partner in this writing life. Finally, I want to thank my readers and my family (including Tina Marie) for keeping the faith and sharing the adventure. I love you all.

Turn the page for more excitement with an original
short story by thriller master Gregg Olsen,

"The Bone Box"

Featuring forensic expert Birdy Waterman.
First time in print!

CHAPTER 1

There was an irony in the return address that never failed to elicit a sheepish wince from most anyone who received something postmarked there. Maybe even a sardonic smile. *A reaction.*

The town from which the letter had been mailed was Walla Walla, a southeast Washington city with the somewhat ironic nickname "a place so nice they named it twice." While Walla Walla might be nice—it had a burgeoning wine industry, vistas of ruggedly beautiful landforms, and a state champion youth basketball team—it was known mostly because it was home to the state's oldest and toughest penitentiary. The most notorious killers and rapists, violent offenders of any kind, were housed in a razor-wire-and-sharpshooter-rimmed complex that was all about doing time, paying for their crimes.

In her modest Beach Drive rental in Port Orchard, Washington, Kitsap County Forensic Pathologist Birdy Waterman kicked off her sensible shoes, turned the CD player to a Stan Getz track, and rummaged through her refrigerator—a cache of zombie food that indicated a life too busy with things other than cooking. Selecting a Coors Light, she looked out at the water of Puget

Sound and watched as something under its shimmery gray surface caught the attention of a flock of gulls. Birdy had seen the address on the envelope dozens of times, of course. But this was a first. It was a letter addressed to *her*, not one she'd put in the mail to the prison each November when Tommy Freeland's birthday came around. She instinctively wiped the rim of the beer bottle and took a gulp as Getz's sax glided through the chilly air of the drafty old beach cottage.

It was Friday. She had no plans but to eat, go to bed, maybe dream about one of the cases she'd been working—a three-year-old girl whose mother claimed she'd been abducted from the bedroom of their Chico, Washington, home. Tulip Lawson's remains had been discovered by clam diggers ten days after she'd been reported missing. Little Tulip's body was now stored in the chiller at the morgue, Birdy's grim domain.

The letter sent from the ditto-named town in the southeast corner of the state beckoned. Birdy slid into her new sofa, a Pottery Barn camelback that she'd ordered to fit the smaller space of the old house's living room. She'd never ordered furniture from a catalog before—now she was hooked. No more endless browsing. Just click and order.

She swallowed some more beer and reached for the letter. In a very real way, she'd long hoped to hear from Tommy one day. It was one of the reasons she sent those birthday cards, year after year. Her other reason was deeper—and one she never gave voice to. It was to assuage her guilt a little. It wasn't that she had done anything wrong. She had told the truth.

The truth. She'd learned then, at a very young age, that sometimes the consequences of telling the truth are too difficult to bear. Her testimony at her cousin's trial was one of the key points that had helped send Tommy Freeland to the land of inmates, wineries, and basketball hoops.

A place so nice they named it twice.

The letter was typed, which surprised Birdy. She hadn't known Tommy knew how to type. She really didn't know much about him at all. He had been a nineteen-year-old high school dropout when he was sent to prison.

As the sax soared and the gulls circled, Birdy read.

Birdy, I bet you are surprised to hear from me. Yeah, I got all of your birthday cards and the notes. At first I thought maybe you'd been required by someone to send them. I also thought that maybe you were being cruel and ironic. After a while, I figured you were just being you. I've had twenty years to think about what happened to Anna Jo and how it was that I ended up here. I would like to say I'm sorry for all of it, but I can't because I know I didn't do it. I couldn't have done it. I don't blame you for what you did. I don't really blame anyone. I've learned a lot about life here in prison and one of the biggest things is knowing that forgiveness is the only way through salvation. You might not be religious, but sometimes forgiveness is something different than God stuff. Anyway, I am not a liar. I am not a murderer. I guess you know that I've been up for parole and all they want me to do is admit to killing Anna Jo. I can't do it. I can't admit to something I didn't do. So,

I've never asked you this. I don't have any
money to ask anyone else. Will you help me?
Will you come down here?—I know we've never
really talked since before the trial. I want to talk
to you. I put your name on my visit list. All you
have to do is fill out this form and you can come.

He signed it: *Yours, Tommy*.

As Birdy looked down at the visitor's registration
form, two things struck her. One, her eyes were slightly
moist. She was no crier. She never had been. There was
something about continually seeing the worst that
human beings do to each other that forced a person to
wall up their emotions. *Protection mode*, she called it.
It wasn't that it didn't hurt to see a strangled child, a
mangled car crash teenager, or a woman beaten to
death by her boyfriend. All of those things hurt like
hell, but Birdy never cried about them. Not her job to
cry, she told herself. Her job was about making sure
that the prosecutors had all the evidence they needed to
stop the perpetrators from doing it again.

Birdy dried her eyes.

The next thing she knew was she was reaching for a
pen to fill out the form. It was as if Birdy's response
was completely automatic. There was no dissecting the
pros and cons of seeing him. No need to analyze his invitation. And, she knew, it was more than curiosity that
would take her there.

She simply had to see him.

The rental house on Beach Drive had been built in
1951 and it looked every bit of its vintage—asphalt

shingles, aluminum-frame windows, and a screen door that couldn't stop a sparrow. It was, in the kindest possible terms, cozy. It would take a coin toss to determine which of the two bedrooms was larger. The closets were miniscule. The kitchen had been built at the time when people gathered around a table in a little nook to discuss their days.

Birdy, at thirty-four, lived alone. She had no one to gather around the built-in nook. While others considered her too smart, too pretty, too *wonderful* to be single, being single was just fine with her.

She'd rented the bungalow with the idea that it was a temporary residence and she'd find something bigger, better, and more in keeping with her desires for privacy. She worked with a real estate agent to find a more permanent residence, but didn't find what she wanted. The gray and white house facing Sinclair Inlet and Bainbridge Island was home. She'd clipped a few ideas from home-decorating magazines in hopes the Seattle owner would eventually decide to sell the house to her. She'd be ready.

That night before she tucked in, Birdy went into the second bedroom. It was ceiling-high with boxes, books, and furniture that she still hadn't found a place for since her move from Seattle. She'd planned on setting it up as a guest room, but the need for guests seldom materialized.

Birdy flipped on the switch and scanned the overstuffed room for the box that held the odds and ends of cases that troubled her. Her father had made the box to hold the tools he used for carving toy figures he sold to tourists for extra money. The container was precious, but so were its contents. She looked inside at the file folders that filled a third of the box, the manila folders protruding like the spine of a dead animal.

Not all these cases had been failures insofar as the courts were concerned, but something about each of them troubled her. There was the young woman who drowned in a boating accident off Agate Pass—her best friend and husband reportedly had done all they could to save her. The case troubled Birdy not for the facts as presented at the inquest, but for what happened two years later. The best friend and the distraught husband got married, left town, and used insurance proceeds to buy a ranch in Arizona. There had been no evidence to suggest that the woman who drowned had been murdered—at least not at the time of the inquest. Drownings without bruising to show a struggle or wounds to show a major fight were frequently difficult cases for prosecutors. It was never about the drowning, but about what happened before and after.

Sometimes *after* was too late.

Another case that had found its way into the cardboard box involved a teenage girl who was the purported victim of a serial killer. Tara Hanson fit the victimology of the three women who had been killed by a sexual sadist rapist and murderer named Percy Bosworth. She had been the right physical type (slender, blond, short hair). And like the other two victims, Tara had been a bit of a party girl, had lived alone, and had been abducted from a mini-mart—as all of Bosworth's victims had been.

And yet Tara didn't quite fit in. She was like the jigsaw puzzle piece that is just close enough go in a particular spot, even when the imagery—the hot air balloon, the kitten with the ball of yarn, or whatever—doesn't mesh accurately. Victims one and two were employed by Kitsap mini-marts—Shellee Casper in Silverdale, LeeAnn Tomm at one in Olalla. While Tara's car was recovered from a convenience store in Navy Yard City, she didn't work there. Further, Tara lived in Kingston, far north of the location of her purported abduction. All the victims had been strangled and posed after they were dumped, but only Tara had been strangled manually. The others were killed with the application of two kinds of ligature—the first victim was strangled with a bungee cord and the second victim had been murdered with the tie from a hoodie. While the spread of the fingertip bruising left on Tara's throat was a close match for Bosworth's, it was troubling that Tara's case—as Birdy famously and regrettably told a *Kitsap Sun* reporter—"stood out like a sore thumb." The headline put up by a copy editor with a decidedly wicked streak took the comment further:

Pathologist Still Coming to Grips With Hanson Case

There were other cases in the box, too, more than twenty. The case that she'd first put into that sad little file was the one involving her cousin Tommy and the murder of Anna Jo Bonners on the Makah Indian Reservation, where Birdy had been raised. At first, the Tommy/Anna file had been there just because Birdy's own personal history was tied up with that particular crime. Later, as she added cases to the box, she'd wondered if it had been unsettling for another reason—a deeper one.

Though she never said it out loud, Birdy Waterman had a name for her little cardboard repository of the unsettling, the unfinished. She called it the Bone Box. Not to anyone else, just herself. That night, she pulled the Bone Box out from the would-be guest room and brought it to her bedside. She lifted the lid and looked down at the neat row of file folders, some thick, some thin. She knew that after doing so she wouldn't have a decent night's sleep. There were a lot of reasons why visiting those files was unnerving. But one above the others niggled at her subconscious. Guilt is like a dripping faucet that can never be tightened or turned off. Even when the guilt is undeserved. More so, rightly, when it is.

Birdy just wasn't sure where she fit in that spectrum.

There were only three clippings in the *Port Angeles Daily News* about Anna Jo's murder. The lack of media coverage was a sad but powerful indicator about how easily crime on the reservation was accepted, ignored by the press. It was as if Native Americans were only the subject of some kind of charity profile written in a patronizing manner. Or, Birdy thought, there were the articles that made her people seem as though they'd never been able to make lives for themselves and were mired in social problems like alcohol and drugs. Those were the stories that seemed to find their way onto the pages of the Seattle papers. A murder of one Makah by another, apparently, was not so newsworthy.

The first article announced the arrest.

Indian Arrested for
Murder of Girlfriend

It described the basic circumstances surrounding Anna Jo's murder and the discovery by a "family member" of Tommy soaked in blood.

A second clipping included a photograph of Anna Jo and another of Tommy. Hers was a pretty image taken in the eighth grade. His was a glowering mug shot taken at the county jail.

Makah Murder Case
On Trial Next Week

It was on the front page of the paper, a preview of the evidence, including the passage:

Freeland's 14-year-old maternal cousin is one of the chief witnesses for the prosecution. Because the Makah native girl is a minor, the *Daily News* is not naming her. She's expected to testify about seeing the accused flee the scene of the stabbing.

And then, the final clipping.

Freeland Convicted
Of Bonner's Murder

SENTENCED TO LIFE

The article was short, only four inches. After it ran, Tommy Freeland had been sent away to prison and expunged from most conversations around the reservation. His wasn't the worst crime committed, but as far as Birdy Waterman remembered, it was the one her family never talked about. Only a couple of times had her mother brought it up.

"I know you saw what you saw, Birdy, but you didn't need to tell anyone about it. Bad things need to stay in the family."

Lastly, Birdy studied the autopsy report with its voodoo-doll-like outlined drawing of a genderless dead figure, accompanying weights and measures, and the deadpan commentary about a young woman and her horrendous demise. The medical examiner, Stephanie Noritake, had been an idol of Birdy's. She was one of the first women Birdy had heard of doing the work of speaking for the dead. Birdy had stood in line for two hours to get a signed copy of the doctor's *Among the Stones and Bones: My Life in the Autopsy Suite*. She felt like she'd gushed too much when it came her turn to get an autograph, but she couldn't help it. Dr. Noritake was a forensic science rock star, a woman who mixed care and concern with authority and science. There was no denying that the two shared a bond. Dr. Noritake was one of the first Asian women to hold the position of medical examiner in a major American city when she served in San Jose in the late 1960s. After retirement she moved to the Pacific Northwest, where her family had lived before internment in World War II. Dr. Noritake consulted on cases in Clallam, Jefferson, and Kitsap Counties.

One of those was the Anna Jo Bonner case.

She'd testified at trial that the blood found on the victim matched what had been recovered from Tommy's T-shirt—putting him in the cabin—but her most interesting testimony had been about the stab wounds that killed the girl.

From the autopsy report:

> . . . there are twenty-seven wounds, indicating overkill. Twenty of the wounds were made after the victim was supine on the floor; nine of those hit the floorboards after piercing the victim's upper torso . . .

It was, as Dr. Noritake said in her report, and later at trial, "a classic rage killing."

And while there could be no doubt that whoever had wielded that knife had overdone it—severing the carotid artery had done the job just fine—as far as Birdy could recall there was no mention as to why Tommy would have wanted to kill his girlfriend. If it had been a rage killing, then what was he so angry about?

The next morning, she faced the mirror in the tiny mint-green and black-tiled bathroom. Birdy wasn't big on makeup, but a hurried glance indicated her sleepless night and the need for a little help. Her brown eyes were puffy, and her skin uneven. She applied a light swipe of powder. Tying back her shoulder-length black hair with a rubber band, she pronounced herself presentable.

It must have been intentional because it happened every time, but Birdy Waterman found herself dressing down for her trips back home to Neah Bay. She commanded a good salary as Kitsap County's forensic pathologist. She dressed beautifully every day for work. Weekends around Port Orchard, she always put on dressy slacks and a nice top. Jeans—and not even new ones at that—were reserved for visits home.

She put on a pair of Lee's from Walmart and a sweater. In Port Orchard, she was *Dr. Waterman*, and she wore her accomplishments proudly. At home, where they would certainly be noticed, she was merely Birdy. And she did everything she could to keep herself from giving the appearance that she'd made it.

And, yet, everyone on the reservation knew she had. There were very few secrets kept among the Makah.

Maybe just one.

CHAPTER 2

The front steps of the old mobile home were spongy. Each tread had soaked in rainwater on such a steady basis that the fact they were intact was some kind of minor miracle in a place that was decidedly short on them.

Birdy knocked on the door and waited, feeling the past come at her like it always did. *Her mother's house.* The home she and her siblings had grown up in. It was only fiberglass, aluminum, and carpet that hadn't been changed since the home was delivered to the reservation in 1969 as a part of a government-sponsored effort to help impoverished Native Americans get a step or two closer to something that had eluded them— hope.

The Makah people weren't so foolish to think that a mobile home was the equivalent of the American Dream.

Birdy's father, Mackie Waterman, had put it very succinctly the day the doublewide was rolled into position.

"If this is their idea of making things even, they're working with the wrong set of scales."

As she stood there on the wobbly stoop, the memory of her father brought a smile. He'd been gone for a couple of years, but in a very real way, he was always with her. While her mother could be cold, her father had doted on her. He'd called her every variation of her name—Baby Bird, Purty Birdy, and when she was didn't do as she was told, he jokingly called her Birdzilla. She used to wait on those very steps for him to come home from one of his extended fishing trips or from the lumber mill where he'd worked in the off-season.

Birdy let the memory pass as she knocked. She knew the door wasn't locked, but it seemed that her mom and her boyfriend of the moment required the courtesy of a warning. Neither owned a car, so a vehicle check wouldn't tell her if anyone was home. Birdy hadn't liked what she'd seen the last time she opened the door without knocking. No child ever wants to see her mother doing *that*.

Natalie Waterman twisted the knob and the chintzy aluminum door swung open a sliver. Birdy's mother stood quiet for a second. Dark eyes scanning. Silver-streaked black hair going every which way like a turn indicator on an old car.

"You keep coming," Natalie said. "Don't know just why, but you do."

The door opened the rest of the way, and Birdy, feeling like she had when she was ten years old, went inside the small living room. The TV was blaring, smoke curling along the dingy yellow ceiling, leggy houseplants clawing their way toward the saggy curtain-framed windows that looked out over a chicken pen and a woodpile.

Just like it always had.

Birdy hugged her mother, who remained stiff. "I come because I love you, Mom. Even when you don't make it easy. I still do."

A cigarette dangled from Natalie's nicotine-stained fingertips, and she braced herself as she allowed the physical contact with her oldest daughter.

"My, my, aren't you the giver," Natalie said, falling into the recliner pointed at the home shopping channel, where a bubbly actress was promoting Christmas candles and wreaths "guaranteed to freshen a room with holiday smells."

It was the type of item Birdy hoped her mother would buy. She'd offered to help get the trailer home in order, but Natalie always refused. Charity, she said, was for losers and that simply wasn't her at all.

Birdy pretended to ignore the sarcasm that seemed to pour from Natalie's cigarette-puckered lips. "You looking for your sister? She's not here. She's at home with her no-good husband and her litter of no-good brats."

Her mother—a charmer, she wasn't.

"No, Mom," Birdy said, softly. "I came to see you today."

Natalie's eyes stayed fixed on home shopping, but she answered her daughter.

"Look at me. I must have won the lotto," she said, without even trying to offer a smile. "If you want some coffee, I'm out. Might have some instant in the cupboard somewhere."

"I'm good," Birdy said, as she took a seat across from her mother in the familiar green La-Z-Boy recliner that had been artfully crisscrossed with black electrical tape and silver duct tape. It had been her father's favorite chair. She ran her fingers over the armrest.

"I'm going to Walla Walla to see Tommy," she said.

Natalie sucked the life out of her cigarette before answering.

"What for? Haven't you done enough to that boy?"

"He's not a boy," she said. "He's almost forty."

"Fine, but why are you going to see him?"

"Because he wrote and asked me to come. And besides, Mom, I have never felt right about him going to prison."

"A little late for you to say that now."

"I liked Tommy. I probably even loved him, even if he was my cousin."

"You are making me sick now, Birdy. Let it be. Go back to the dead people you seem to love so much. Leave the living alone."

It was cruel remark and it hurt. Natalie was a sharp-shooter when it came to piercing her daughter's insecurities. She always had been. Where most mothers sought to comfort a child, Natalie seemed to seek ways to hurt. Counselors and teachers, mentors and friends, each had tried to convince Birdy that her mother's cruelty was a sign of her own insecurities, but that did little to alleviate a girl's pain.

"I knew you'd be supportive, Mom," Birdy said, in a futile attempt at jabbing.

"Leave Tommy alone," Natalie said. "Let him be. Let sleeping dogs lie. You got that, Birdy? You're never satisfied with the way things are. You understand?"

Birdy's neck muscles pulsed. Her neck. It was like a barometer of her stress.

"I understand what you are saying, yes," she said. "But I don't agree with it. I don't know what Tommy will tell me when I see him, but I do know I want to hear it."

"All you need to know is that he's in prison because of you," Natalie said.

Birdy laid her palm against her neck. "I was fourteen, Mom."

"I had my first baby at fifteen. Fourteen isn't so young. Being young isn't an excuse for anything."

"It wasn't an excuse, but a fact. I did what I was supposed to do."

The room went silent as Natalie Waterman pressed the MUTE button. She wanted to make her point without the home shopping hostess's over-the-top spiel about a "Christmas kitten ceramic coming up next."

"You went against the family, Birdy," she said. "Twenty years is just a drop in the ocean. Families never forget a betrayer. You're a smart girl. You'd think with all your schooling you'd understand something as simple as that."

The sound went back up on the TV.

"I don't know," Birdy said, "I thought that you'd be glad about it. Happy maybe. Something positive about seeing him."

"You don't know me and I don't know you. On second thought," Natalie said, pulling herself up from the recliner. "I'm pretty sure I'm out of that instant coffee. You better run along home. Go back to your precious job and forget about all of us up here. You're too busy. Too important. I'm surprised you even remember where you came from."

Birdy stayed planted, thinking that if she stood her

ground her mother would calm down a little and take back what she just said.

Yet that wasn't about to happen.

It was a stalemate and not the first one. "Are you waiting for something?" Natalie asked.

Birdy's heart was racing and her stomach was in knots, but she didn't want her mother to know that she'd gotten to her—like she always did. She'd seen a gentle side of her mother in the past and she craved it again. Didn't every child?

"I'm waiting for you to be a mother," Birdy said, her voice soft as though it was too much to even ask. "That's what."

Natalie laughed. "You don't need a mother. And I don't need a daughter like you. Why don't you go on now? I'm watching *Judge Judy* next, back-to-back episodes. Do me a favor, Birdy."

Birdy wasn't a crier. If she had been, she would have dissolved into tears right then. But not now. Not in front of her. Not with her mother's seeming indifference, or outright hostility.

"What's that, Mom?"

Natalie turned the sound up on the remote.

"Don't mention Tommy again and don't go see him," she said. "Leave it be. Let the past fade away. Leave it."

Birdy Waterman slumped in her car in front of her mother's house. All visits home were bad, but on the scale of their relationship, this visit had been particularly disastrous. Natalie Waterman had come up empty-handed if she'd sought a reason to be happy. Few on the reservation would argue that she had many reasons to be happy. She was an alcoholic. Her husband had died in a fishing accident off the Pacific coast. Arthritis had taken its toll on her joints. Natalie was angry at the world and maybe rightly so. Knowing all of that didn't make the pain pass any easier.

Somewhere in the time line of her mother's downfall were the murder of Anna Jo and the subsequent conviction of her nephew Tommy for the most reprehensible of crimes.

Birdy pulled out of the muddy driveway and drove west toward the trail along the coast. The sky was clear and sunlight jabbed downward through the thick covering of spruce trees that contorted away from the ocean. She parked her car and started down the trail, each step taking her back twenty years to the day she'd seen the unimaginable.

CHAPTER 3

Summer weather along the Pacific is governed by a kind of strange roulette wheel, one that makes anyone with concrete plans on the all-but-certain losing end of things. Not until the moment one ventures outside to experience the world of nature is it apparent if it is sunny or rainy or a mix of both. Its unpredictability is the only sure thing.

Three days after her fourteenth birthday, Birdy Waterman dragged a wagon down the coast trail to gather kindling. This was something she did nearly every day in the summer, and most weekend days during the school year. In the rain. In the snow. In the most blustery of autumn days. It didn't matter. Birdy's family heated their little aluminum box of a house with a woodstove. Wood was free if one was skilled with a chainsaw. She wore two layers of clothing, a T-shirt and a sweatshirt that she'd undoubtedly peel off once she got down to the business at hand.

Birdy was small for her age, fearless when it came to the noisy saw, and just hungry enough to help her mother and father in any way that she could. Helping each other was not only the tribal way, but the way of the Watermans. Natalie made money doing what she considered bogus crafts for the tribal gift shop, and Mackie Waterman fished for salmon up and down Neah Bay and over to West Port. Tribal fishing rights didn't always guarantee a good income—no matter what the non-Native fishermen said. So there, on that summer day, Birdy did what she always did: forage for deadfall along the coast trail that wound its way from the hillside down to the rocky beach populated by sea stacks and smelly sea lions.

She was on the east fork of the trail when she first heard the noise. It came at her like a locomotive, pushing, huffing, and puffing. Each breath was a gasp for air. At first, it didn't seem human. Birdy idled her chainsaw, then shut it off. She turned in the direction of the noise.

"Hey!" a familiar voice came at her. "Birdy!"

She looked through the tunnel-like pathway and strained to see who it was.

"Birdy!" It came again.

Coming toward her was her cousin, Tommy Freeland. He was in the darkness coming toward her. The ground thumped under his frantic feet. She set down the saw. Then, like a strobe light, his face was suddenly illuminated. It wasn't the handsome face of a much loved relative, despite the familiar flinty black eyes and handsome broad nose.

The twenty-year-old's face was dripping in red.

"Tommy!" Birdy cried out, and moved closer. "Are you okay?"

"Birdy!" he called again, stopping and dropping his elbows to his knees. "Help me."

By then she was close enough to see that the coloring on his coffee skin wasn't just any red. It was the dark iron red of blood. Tommy's T-shirt had been splattered with what instinctively Birdy Waterman, only fourteen, knew was human blood.

"Are you hurt?" she said, almost upon him.

His eyes were wild with fear. "No, no," he said as he tried to catch his breath. "I don't think so. . . . I think I'm okay." He looked down at his bloody hands and wiped them on his blue jeans, also dark and wet with blood.

Birdy shook a little as fear undermined her normally calm demeanor. "What happened? Who's hurt?" she asked.

Tommy, breathing as hard as a marathon runner at the finish line, swallowed. He started to cry and his words tumbled over his trembling lips. "Anna Jo. Birdy, I'm pretty sure Anna Jo's dead."

Anna Jo was a beautiful young girl, the kind other girls of the reservation aspired to be. She had a job, her own car, and she was kind. No one thought anything but the best of Anna Jo Bonners.

Did he say dead? The question rolled around in her head, but she didn't say it out loud. Something held her back. Maybe it was because she didn't want confirmation of something so terrible. Birdy took a step backward and fell onto the black, damp earth. Tommy lunged at her and she screamed.

"Hey," he said. "I won't hurt you. I was trying to stop you from falling. Don't be afraid of me."

"What happened to Anna Jo? What did you do to her?"

Tommy blinked back the recognition of what his cousin was undoubtedly thinking just then.

"No. I never. I just found her. Honest. She was at Ponder's cabin. She was already dead. I promise. I never hurt anyone."

Birdy found her footing and got up from the damp, dark earth. Her heart was pounding so hard inside the bony frame of her heaving chest just then, she was certain that she'd have a heart attack. She didn't want to die and she didn't want to find out what had happened to Anna Jo. She was too scared. Instead, she turned and ran, leaving the wagon, the chain saw, and her bloody cousin on the trail.

Twenty years later, as she walked down that same trail, the scene played in her head. Birdy hadn't thought about what she'd felt that summer day and the role fear had played in what she testified to at trial. She was the witness who had put Tommy on that trail covered in blood. She was the one who had provided the time line that connected the victim to the killer. While it was true that Tommy Freeland had had blood all over his hands and chest, and it was true that he and Anna Jo had had a bitter fight a few days before she died, he'd denied any part of the brutal stabbing that had killed her.

One of the last things Birdy remembered Tommy saying before they hauled him away after sentencing was, "I loved her. Doesn't anyone remember that? I loved Anna Jo. I would never have killed her. I didn't do this."

Over the years, in case after case, Dr. Birdy Waterman would hear similar statements from the convicted, but never would they be so personal, so directed at her ears. Tommy had been family. When he went away to Walla Walla, his disappearance caused a rift between sisters, aunts, uncles, cousins. No one who lived on that part of the Makah reservation was ever the same. People didn't talk about it. Ever.

Birdy watched a squirrel as it zipped up the craggy bark of a towering Douglas fir. A hawk flew overhead. The wind found its way through the evergreen canopy. The land all around her was as it had been when she was a girl. The place, she knew, should feel like home. But it didn't. It never could. A place where one feels unwelcome can never feel like home. Thinking of Tommy, Anna Jo, the trial, her mother, she wondered if there would ever be a way to fix any of it.

She walked back to her car and drove over to her sister Summer's brand-new mobile home, but no one was there. Same at her brother Ricky's place—a small wood frame house that he'd built himself. She decided not to let it pass through her mind that they'd avoided her on purpose. She was their sister—their blood. They had to love her, too, didn't they?

It was dark when she returned to the bungalow on Beach Drive. Birdy had driven all the way through with only a single stop for gas in Port Angeles. It was after nine when she finally pulled up. Too dark, she thought, to feed the neighbor's cat as she'd promised to do while they were away in Hawaii downing rum-infused tropical drinks—a prospect that seemed more than appealing right then. Birdy made a mental note to get up extra early to feed Jinx before the Coopers got home and found out that their next-door neighbor was an untrustworthy cat sitter.

Knowing Pat and Donna Frickey, there could be no crime worse.

Birdy took a beer from the refrigerator and a package of chicken-flavored Top Ramen from the cupboard. She took a drink from the bottle and unwrapped the ramen with no intention of cooking the noodles. She ate it dry, like a big fat brick of crispiness—a habit she'd acquired growing up on the reservation and having to make do with a package of the Asian dried noodles for two out of three meals of the day.

The message light on her answering machine caught her eye. There were three messages. She pushed PLAY.

"*. . . Election Day is fast approaching and we want to make sure that the Citizens for a Lovely Port Orchard can count on your support for our transportation levy . . .*"

Birdy sighed and pushed DELETE. *The Lovely Port Orchard group would be better served by focusing on cleaning up the streets they already had than on building new ones*, she thought.

Then next message came from her mother, probably just after her visit.

"*I'm sorry, sweetie. You really caught me off guard about Tommy. I think you should just leave him be, but you never listen to me anyway. Love you.*"

The word "love" came out of her mother's mouth in a cough. The voice message was so like her mother that it brought a smile to Birdy's face. While Natalie Waterman hadn't invented passive-aggressive behavior, few would dispute that she had perfected it.

The last message sent a chill through Birdy's bones.

"*Dr. Waterman, if this is you, I want you to know that you've caused enough trouble for Tommy and his family. If you know what's good for you—and I bet you do—you'll stay away from him.*"

The voice was unfamiliar. Birdy played it again. It was hard to determine if the caller was male or female. It was breathy and soft, the kind of voice that required concentration in order to fully comprehend.

She scrolled back on the caller ID function of her machine. The call had come from a pay phone at the tribal center—which wasn't much of a surprise. After telegraph, tele-native was the fastest mode of communication known to man. Someone from the Makahs had heard from her mother that she was going to see Tommy, and not only that, they didn't want her to.

Not at all.

"If you know what's good for you . . ."

CHAPTER 4

Tommy was barely forty, but he looked closer to sixty. Maybe even older. If DOC Inmate 44435-099 had once been the most handsome boy on the reservation, years behind bars—more years than he'd lived free—had stolen that from him. It wasn't merely that his jet-black hair had receded or that his once-clear skin was now loose and somewhat sallow. His eyes nestled in dark hollows. It was also obvious from across the poorly lit visitation room that whatever charisma he'd had, whatever inner light had radiated through him, was gone. *Pfft. Out like a soggy match.*

Birdy Waterman almost had to steady herself when she saw Tommy. While she realized that two decades had come and gone, she hadn't expected Tommy to look so old. Certainly in her job, she'd been around prisons and jails all her adult life. Most inmates seemed to make the best of their time on the inside by pumping iron in the yard. There wasn't much else to do. They looked like health-club regulars. Tommy, by contrast, seemed alarmingly frail.

She walked toward him, quickly so as not to show any hesitation. He was, after all, family.

Tommy, in a dingy gray T-shirt and off-brand dunga-
rees that seemed a size too big for him, stood to greet
her. "You look almost the same," he said, a broad smile
of recognition coming over his face. It was disarming,
the way she remembered Tommy Freeland could be.
*Maybe a part of him is still there, somewhere hidden
under the hard veneer of prison life?*

Tommy nodded for her to sit, and Birdy slid into a
bolted-to-the-floor steel frame chair. "You, too. But
you're a liar," she added, trying to hide her obvious surprise.

Tommy eyed her, taking in everything. It was a fast
and unequivocal search, the kind of once-over that an
inmate might employ to figure out that instant of life or
death in the laundry room, in deciding who to trust.

"Well, you have filled out," he said. "Not in a bad
way. But, you know, you're no longer Birdy Legs."

Birdy's face reddened. No one had called her that in
eons, and it made her feel good. It was funny how the
mention of a once-hated nickname elicited fond memories. Back on the reservation it had been a nickname
meant to torment her. Time changes everything.

"Thanks," she said, changing the subject. "I'm glad
you asked me to come."

He frowned slightly. "You were never *not* invited,
Birdy. It hasn't been like you didn't know where I
was."

"That isn't fair," she said.

"Well, from my knothole, there isn't anything about
the last twenty years that has been particularly fair."

Birdy nodded. There was no arguing that.

"Do you want a pop or something? I brought quarters," she said offering up her Ziploc bag of quarters.

Tommy smiled. Actually, it was not really a smile, but a kind of grimace. "No. I'm good. I've learned to do without. You know, without friends, family. Pretty much without a life. A lot of people played a part in making that happen."

He left those words to dangle in the air of the visiting room.

"I didn't lie," Birdy said, her tone more defensive than she'd intended.

Tommy leaned back and crossed his arms. As he did, Birdy noticed a series of jagged scars, some faint, others far more recent. Her eyes hovered over the scars, but she didn't remark on them.

"No," he said, biting off his words. "You saw what you saw, but God, Birdy, you know *me*. You know I couldn't have hurt Anna Jo. It isn't in me to hurt anyone, least of all her."

"Why didn't you say so?" she asked, though she knew he had. At least to her. He had told her on that sodden trail just after it happened.

"You mean take the stand to testify? Like anyone would believe an unemployed drug user like me? That would have been pretty useless, don't you think?"

Birdy wanted to disagree with her long-lost cousin just then, but she knew he was probably right.

"Do you hear from your family?" she asked, regretting the question almost the instant it came from her lips. Birdy hadn't meant it to hurt him, she just wanted to know. Tommy's mother, her aunt, had pretty much iced her out of that side of the family—payback for her testimony.

He looked away at a little girl playing a card game with her father and Birdy answered for him.

"I'm sorry. I thought . . ." she said.

"Mom's been married twice now. Somewhere along the way she's been too busy for me," he said. "Not like I'm a kid anyway."

Birdy didn't say so, but she understood. "I think I'll get a Coke. Sure you don't want one?" She looked at Tommy and a guard one table away. The man with a faint moustache and eager-beaver eyes nodded that it was okay for her to get up and go to the vending machines. Tommy followed her across the room filled with wives and girlfriends mostly, a few kids. Some passed the time playing checkers. Others read books in tandem like they were in some library for criminals.

Birdy inserted three quarters and the change tumbled to the coin return.

"Damn," she said. "Must be out of soda."

"Just tricky," Tommy said. "I'm not allowed to touch the machine, but I'm told you have to drop the change in very slowly. One, then the next, then the last."

Birdy did as he suggested and was rewarded with a cold can of diet soda.

"I'll take one, too," he said.

She looked over at the guard watching them. He nodded that it was all right for her to hand him the pop. She dropped three more coins and retrieved another can.

As Birdy turned, Tommy leaned a little closer and whispered, "I don't want anyone to hear me. Please, Birdy. I need you to believe in me."

"Are you being mistreated?" she asked, her voice as quiet as possible.

"Please return to the table," the faintly mustachioed guard said.

Birdy felt a chill and it wasn't from the icy cold soda.

"You've been up for parole twice," she said. "Just tell them you're sorry."

"I didn't do it. And if you don't get me out of here, I'll probably die here. I don't want to die in this place."

"You've served your time," she repeated.

"Here's something that might not have occurred to you. Prison is more than bars and the guards. Prison is how people see you. I have some honor, Birdy. Help me get home as a free man, a man who didn't kill the girl. I never would have done that. Tell me you understand that."

"I do. That's why I'm here. I came because of your letter."

Tommy looked confused. "What letter?"

"The letter you sent me. The reason I'm here."

Tommy shook his head. "I'm glad you're here, but I didn't send a letter to you. I mean, I did write to you years ago, like I wrote to everyone. You know, asking forgiveness for what I've done. Part of the program."

"I never got that letter," she said. "The letter I'm talking about came last week."

Tommy touched his chest with his forefinger. "Not from me it didn't."

They sat back down and faced each other. She hadn't dreamt it. She'd read the letter. She'd come all that way. *But if Tommy didn't send it, then who did?*

Birdy knew that she'd carried Tommy's case in the Bone Box all those years for a reason. Deep down, she didn't believe he really could have killed Anna Jo Bonners.

At the same time she wondered just why it was that

he—or someone—called on her to help now. It would take only moments for that answer to come to her.

An alarm sounded and the visit was over. Just like that. There was an awkward quiet, like the conclusion of a first date when both parties know there will never be a second. Birdy wasn't certain what she could really do, or why she should do it. Tommy and the other inmates stayed at their tables as the visitors filed out. Outside the visitation room, the forensic pathologist from the other side of the mountains lined up with the friends and families of Washington state's most notorious.

It was obvious from their chatter that many knew each other. Regulars. The word fit. For the most part the people leaving their men and boys behind were so very average. There was nothing scary about any of them. Not a single one of them, save for a woman who never managed a smile, looked like they even knew a hardened criminal. They were the other side of a violent crime. They were on the side of the perpetrator, the convicted. Every one of them had come to show an inmate something they could get nowhere else—compassion and love.

Birdy, at the rear of the line, started for the corridor that would lead her out of the prison, out the door to lives where no one knew they'd spent four hours and a bag of quarters playing table games and talking about the dullest of things. *Like anyone. Like people at home.* That is, if home included a baby-faced rapist, an axe murderer who ironically worked in the prison kitchen as a meat cutter, and a seventy-year-old man who had strangled his wife of almost fifty years one Christmas morning with the very necktie she'd given him ("Bea knew I hated plaid," he joked whenever the subject came up).

For every inmate with a visitor that afternoon, Birdy knew, there were probably scores of others who never had that human contact with anyone from outside. Never had visits with anyone, except maybe the occasional convict groupie or an eager-beaver churchgoer who wanted to save someone's hardened soul from the system that only existed to make them pay for their sins in an earthly way.

And then there was Tommy.

As far as Birdy Waterman knew, until that afternoon when she came calling, he hadn't had a single visitor. Birdy wondered if someone could be the same person they always were if they had no contact with those who knew him. Wasn't part of who you were how others related to you, feeding your personality traits, shaping your character with their own? And yet Tommy still seemed like Tommy. A little subdued, certainly thin and haggard, but still Tommy nevertheless. During the visit he occasionally punctuated what he said with a short laugh—even if nothing was funny. When she heard the laugh, she was transported back to the Tommy he was before he became the Tommy who killed Anna Jo.

Birdy remembered how the two of them had spent one insufferably hot day picking huckleberries. They'd cursed how small the berries were and worried that they'd never get enough to fill that half-gallon container that her mother had insisted was required for a pie. It was a couple weeks before Anna Jo's murder. Now it seemed like days ago, not decades. She and Tommy had picked and picked and picked for hours.

When it looked like they'd never get enough berries, Tommy had the bright idea of buying some from a vendor.

"Your mom is too much of a stickler," he'd said. "So let's give her what she wants to make her happy."

The berries cost him his last dollar, but he didn't care.

Natalie Waterman *did* care. The berries they bought were not huckleberries, but blueberries.

"Sorry, Aunt Natalie," Tommy said. "I thought they looked a little large for hucks." He flashed his bright white smile, gave that little laugh, and shrugged in the way that just made it easy. Everything was easier with Tommy, back then.

As Birdy followed the queue and turned the corner toward the metal detectors and the glass-walled station where the guards monitored every blink of someone's eyelash, a finger jabbed at her shoulder. It startled her.

"I know why you're here," a man's voice said, as she spun around. "Maybe even more than you do."

It was the same guard—the one who'd watched her and her cousin as they visited.

"Excuse me?" she answered, looking him over. She read his ID badge: Ken Holloway. He was smaller there in the corridor than he was when he commanded a chair upfront overlooking the prisoners in his quadrant of the room. He had soft green eyes and a pockmarked face. Not handsome, not ugly. Despite the fact that he carried a gun, worked with the worst of humanity day in and day out, Sgt. Holloway seemed concerned.

"Your cousin isn't well," he said.

"What do you mean *well*?" she asked.

The guard stopped walking. Birdy stayed with him

as the other visitors shuffled toward the doorway. "It was all he could do to get out of his cell and get down to see you."

"What's wrong with him?" she asked.

"It's none of my business," Sgt. Holloway said. "But I like the guy. He's probably the most decent guy in the prison—that includes the guards and the superintendent's so-called staff. Them for sure."

He wasn't answering her question. She asked again, this time directly. "Is he sick?"

Holloway shook his head. "Worse than sick. He's dying. Leukemia. He'll be dead before Christmas. At least that's what the docs tell him. Anyway, you need to know that."

"Why are *you* telling me this? Why didn't he?"

He stared into her eyes, searching. "He's proud, Dr. Waterman."

The use of her name surprised her. "You know who I am?"

He nodded. "Hell yeah, he's bragged about you for years. I know all about you, your backstory, the crime that sent him here. I know stuff you don't even know."

"Like what, for instance?"

"Like Tom Freeland didn't kill that girl up in Neah Bay."

"I'm sure you've heard claims of innocence before around here," she said, looking at an inmate pushing a laundry cart down the hall.

"Yeah. More times than you probably think. But Tommy's different. He has honor. He's never ratted on anyone and no one has ratted on him. He's taught at least a hundred inmates how to read; sent money—and he don't have much—to a cellmate's family. He's not perfect, but he's as close to decent as I've seen in this hellhole," he said, his eyes lingering over another guard and an inmate in belly chains down the corridor. A mother who moments before had been calmly playing cards with her son was now convulsing in tears as she moved toward the exit.

"My boy is being raped by his cellie! Why don't you people stop it?"

It was hard not to look at the woman, but Birdy faced the sergeant. "He didn't tell me he was dying," she said.

"Of course not. He's not the type."

"What's that supposed to mean?"

"Tommy's not one to make someone do something they don't want to do. He could tell you he's got months, weeks to live and you'd get all in a tizzy and try to help him because of that—not because you thought he was innocent."

"What kind of medical care is he getting?" she asked. "Maybe I can help."

Sgt. Holloway shook off her offer. "No offense, but don't you deal with dead patients? No disrespect intended."

"None taken," she said. "And yes, I do, but I also know doctors who actually deal with patients who are living. I know several very good oncologists in Seattle."

"Look, I'm sure you do," he said. "If you think that because he's a con, he's not getting the benefit of a cancer doc, then you'd be wrong. The state legislature has made it sure these guys get the best care possible when it's serious. Mantra around here is that medical care for cons is gold-plated. No more lawsuits coming at us because someone croaked before their time."

"I see," she said. It made sense to her. The whole world seemed to spin on making sure no one got sued, or if they did, they couldn't lose.

"Do you?" he asked, a little pointedly.

"Can I talk to him again?"

"Too late for today. Next week though. You staying in town?

Birdy shook her head.

"I can give him your number and he can call you collect. Visiting hours are over until Tuesday."

"I don't have my purse," she said. "You don't happen to have a paper and pen?"

Holloway put his fingertips to his lips and smiled. "Don't tell the other guards, but yes I do." He pulled a scrap from his pocket and a stub of a pencil.

Birdy took it and wrote as he called out his number.

"Do me a favor," he said.

She stopped writing and looked up, her eyes locking on his. "What?"

"Don't let him down," he said. "The guy deserves better than that."

"He's in prison for killing a girl," she said.

"So the jury concluded. But do you think—even for a minute—that the man you sat with today killed someone? He's a decent human being," he said. "Better than most by far."

"He's helped a lot of people," she said, searching the guard's eyes.

"I know what you're getting at and you're right. I'm one of those. Your cousin has taught me more about being a compassionate person than anyone. I'm here as a guard because of him. Some are here to punish, but

I'm here to help. So I'm asking you—for him, please, help him."

"You sent the letter to me," she said. "Didn't you?"

He looked down at the gleaming floor. "It was the only thing I could think of doing. He wasn't going to ask you. But if you could have seen his face when he got word that you'd asked for a visit, you would know that I did the right thing. Man, he was so happy. And you know what else?"

Birdy shook her head. "No, what?"

"You're doing the right thing," he said.

"I still don't know what, exactly, I'm doing. I've looked over the evidence file. I didn't see anything that can help him."

Ken Holloway looked around. "It isn't for me to say," he said finally. "But I will anyway. Your cousin once let it slip at a meeting that relationships some-times aren't all they seem. He said, sometimes you trust the wrong people."

"What does that mean? What wrong people?"

"He said that the girl wasn't all that he thought she was."

Birdy stood in the silent corridor. Was he referring to her? How she didn't stand up for him? How could she? She had told the police what she'd seen even though her mother and father told her to keep quiet.

Or was he talking about Anna Jo? And if it had been Anna Jo, then there was only one place to go. Back home.

CHAPTER 5

"**I** know who you are and why you are here."

Anna Jo Bonners's mother stood on the front steps of her house and faced Birdy Waterman with ice-pellet eyes. Carmona Bonner was a woman who, as Birdy recalled, seldom smiled. She had the kind of humorless face that owed more to the fact that she'd lost one of her front teeth in a car accident than to what kind of person she really was. She simply never smiled. After Anna Jo's murder, few thought she had many reasons to anyway.

Birdy braced herself against the chill by wrapping her arms around her chest. "My cousin is dying and I'm just trying to tie up some loose ends," she said.

"My daughter is dead and there are no more loose ends," Carmona said.

Birdy persisted. "May I come inside? Chilly out here."

Mrs. Bonners stood her ground. "No," she said. "You should have put on an extra sweater. Always cold up here this time of year. Maybe you've forgotten, living in the big city."

The remark was almost laughable. No one who visited Port Orchard would have considered it a big town, much less a major city.

"Really is cold out here," Birdy said, letting her teeth chatter for effect and because the chilly ocean air was pummeling her. A curl of wood smoke coming from the chimney indicated that there was no need to suffer on that stoop.

Carmona Bonners sighed and reluctantly opened the door. "Come in," she said. "But you can only stay a minute and you have to stay on the linoleum. I just cleaned the carpets."

She shut the door and the two stood in the miniscule foyer. A photograph of a group of Makahs huddled next to a whale carcass dominated the space. It wasn't a particularly old image. Despite outcries from environmentalists and organizations like PETA, the Makahs had established their continuing right to hunt for whales off the coast of Washington. They had done so only once in modern times.

"Mrs. Bonners, I really only want to know one thing and I think you might be able to help me. Something has troubled me over the years."

The woman regarded her visitor warily. "I guess you were probably traumatized, too. Not as much as we were. But seeing Tommy Freeland right after he did what he did to our Anna Jo must have been bad. Like I said, not like us at all, but hard, I guess."

"Yes, it was," Birdy said. "I don't even like bringing it up. Just thinking about it all these years makes my heart break for you and your family."

"Thank you, but that's not why you're here. I heard it through the grapevine that you're trying to clear his name."

The grapevine on the reservation was more powerful than a satellite receiver. "It isn't so much that," Birdy said. "I don't know what happened, but one thing that troubles me is all the violence against Anna Jo. They called it a rage killing. I don't know what Tommy would have been so mad about."

"Trust me," Carmona said, "he was mad. Do you need me to spell out what he did to her?"

There was no use suggesting that Tommy wasn't the killer. The focus had to be on gathering information and understanding. Not promoting something she wasn't even sure about.

"I guess so," Birdy said. "What was it?"

Carmona glanced through the window as a pair of headlights slowly meandered by. "You better go now. Let's just let sleeping dogs lie," she said.

Birdy wasn't ready. She wanted, *needed* some answers. "Didn't he love Anna Jo?"

"He said he did," she said, her words emphasizing the word "he" in a strange way. Birdy asked the victim's mother what she meant.

"Look, I know you have respect for our people," Carmona said, her voice whistling a little through the gap in her front teeth. "I know you haven't completely forgotten where you came from, so let's just leave it at that. Let's let Anna Jo be. Let her live in our memories as she was—not as you'd have her."

Carmona opened the door and held it for Birdy to pass. Birdy put her hand on the doorjamb to buy a moment more of conversation.

"Anna Jo didn't love Tommy, did she?"

"Good-bye, Dr. Waterman. Let my daughter rest in peace."

CHAPTER 6

It had been a quiet day in the Kitsap County Morgue, which meant it had been a good day. No one who worked there ever cursed their jobs because there was "nothing to do." An empty chiller meant a day without carrying the hurt of someone else's loss. A child. A wife. Even a friend. Birdy was in the midst of finishing up a supply order that needed to be filled when she looked up from her desk to see a woman in an orange North Face jacket and black jeans. The color combination was definitely on the Halloween side of the fashion wheel, which might have been intentional. The holiday was only a week away.

"You don't remember me, Dr. Waterman," the woman said, her voice soft and nearly reverential. She was slightly built, with the facial features of a Makah—intense eyes slashed above with eyebrows that never needed any help from Maybelline, and, most strikingly, a pronounced nose.

Birdy looked her over, racking her brain. *Who is this?* There was something familiar about her, but Birdy couldn't come up with a name.

"I'm Iris," the woman said. "I used to be Iris Bonners. Married to Randall Rostov now."

Birdy nodded. "Of course, I remember you," she said, a little unconvincingly, as she worked hard to reel in some kind of memory. She did recall Randall Rostov; he was the son of the first Makah to run a whale-watching business catering to the tourists from Seattle. If Iris hadn't said her maiden name, she would never have guessed who she was.

Iris was Anna Jo Bonners's little sister. She had been three or four grades behind Birdy in school, a gap of enough measure to ensure that their paths seldom crossed. It didn't matter how small a school was. And the reservation school was small by any standards. Only eighty students graduated with Birdy—and only three of those went on to college.

"It's okay if you don't," Iris said, taking off her jacket to reveal a cascade of black hair that had been tucked inside. "I was a lot younger than you."

Birdy smiled, a recollection finally coming to her. "I do," she said. "I actually do. Weren't you a dancer? I remember hearing that you went off to study dance back east. New York?"

Iris nodded. "Yes, I was. Back then. Made it as far as Milwaukee. A far cry from New York, that's for sure. Now I work in the bar at the casino. In the bar. So much for my brilliant career. But look at you."

Birdy deflected the compliment, if that's what it had been. With some of the people on the reservation mad at her for getting a medical degree and not returning to work in the free clinic, it was hard to know if Iris really thought her career had been brilliant or a betrayal.

"Coffee?" Birdy asked. "I was about to pour myself a cup."

Iris shook her head and declined. "Too late in the day for me. And really, I don't have much time. The longer I wait to get to the point of it all, the greater the likelihood that I won't be able to get up the nerve to tell you what I think you need to know."

Birdy scooted back into her chair, her eyes riveted on Iris. "Okay. No coffee. Sit down. Talk to me, Iris." She motioned to Iris to take one of the chairs across her desk.

"I'll stand," Iris said. "And first of all, before I say anything, I want you to know that as sorry as I am about everything, I'm also scared. Really scared. I have two kids. This can't come back to me. Promise."

"Promise."

"I hope I can trust you, Birdy. I'm hoping that given your job and your education, you'll be able to keep a confidence."

"I will," she said.

For the next twenty minutes, refusing to sit, Iris Bonners Rostov talked about her sister, how much she loved her, how she was sure they'd have been close.

"Not like you and your sister," the younger woman said.

"That's right, my sister and I aren't close," Birdy said, swallowing the sentence in one bitter gulp.

Birdy wondered why Iris had needed to make the jab. People often needed to hurt someone as a way to take away their own pain. Putting the hurt on another person sometimes made them feel better, if only by comparison.

"Iris, you came a long way to tell me something you think might be important," Birdy said.

"I did," she said, "but really I'm scared."

"It's about Tommy, isn't it?"

She nodded, but stayed quiet.

Birdy pushed for an answer. "Iris, what?"

Iris took a breath. "I don't know that my sister really loved Tommy. I know it is wrong to talk bad about the dead, but it seems to me that Anna Jo has had a long enough time to adjust to what she did—wherever she is."

"I'm sure she's at peace," Birdy said.

Iris looked away. "Not after what she did, maybe not."

"What did she do?"

"She cheated on Tommy. She was seeing someone else. I think that's why Tommy killed her. He must have found out."

The disclosure came out of nowhere. Birdy had thought that Iris was going to say something against Tommy, another reason why no one should forgive him, or that he'd gotten what he deserved.

"I didn't know she had another boyfriend," Birdy said. "I've never heard that before."

Iris's eyes were back on Birdy's. "Well, she did," Iris said. "She had two guys on a string. Tommy and the other guy."

Birdy got up. The intensity of what Iris was saying made her feel silly sitting in her chair while Iris stood, coat on, ready to drop the bomb and run away.

"Do you know his name? Was it someone from home?"

Iris shrugged a little. "I never saw him. She never

said his name. Not to me. I don't think he lived on the reservation, because I'd never seen him or his car. Whenever he came to get her, she had to walk all the way down the lane to be picked up. I don't think she wanted our parents to meet him. Maybe he was black or something. I don't know. My dad was kind of a racist and that wouldn't go over real big with him."

Black?

"What makes you think he was black?"

Iris looked around the room. "Nothing really," she said. "I was a kid and I just tried to figure out why it was that my sister hid him from everyone in the family." Iris shifted in her chair. She was on a roll now and Birdy wasn't about to stop her. "I thought we'd meet him after she died, you know, he'd come over and pay his respects at the house. That never happened. We never saw him. Not even one time."

"So you think Tommy killed her because he was jealous of this other man?"

"That's the only thing that makes sense to me. I remember my mom telling me that the police caught Tommy red-handed. He must have killed her for something. Anna Jo was hurt pretty bad. He must have been mad."

Twenty-seven-stab-wounds mad to be exact.

"Did you ever see Tommy threaten her? Act jealous? Angry?"

"That's the hard part. I always got the impression that he loved her, was gentle with her. The other guy always made her cry. One time I remember going into her bedroom when she was on her bed crying. I asked her what was the matter and she said she was in big trouble. I asked her what kind, and she said, 'boyfriend trouble.' "

"What do you think she meant by that?"

"I don't know. That was the last time I saw her. The next day she was dead."

After Iris left, Birdy went home to the Bone Box.

CHAPTER 7

The next day Birdy Waterman got in her car to drive to the morgue. She hadn't slept well. She'd been unable to shut down her thoughts about Tommy. Yet duty called.

A car accident the night before had taken the lives of a middle-aged couple from Bremerton. They had left a party in Port Orchard and the women crashed their late-model Jeep just outside Gorst, a tiny town clinging to a hairpin turn of highway populated by a strip club and coffee stands with half-naked baristas. Investigators theorized that the driver had been drunk. Birdy Waterman would examine the bodies, take the blood, look at stomach contents, and send tissue to the lab to determine if alcohol had been a factor.

As she dressed for work, she kept thinking about Tommy. She'd called the prison to confirm his illness with the medical staff there—from one doctor to another. Just as Sgt. Holloway had, the doctor on call said how much everyone liked Tommy and how "it is a shame he never got out of here."

Instead of turning up Division Street and heading

toward the morgue, Birdy did something she'd never done in her entire life.

She called off work.

"Joe, you can handle the crash all right? I'm taking a personal day."

Birdy despised the "personal" day excuse, but it seemed more legitimate than lying and saying she was ill.

"You under the weather or something?" the assistant asked.

Birdy pressed the gas pedal and headed toward Highway 16 along Sinclair Inlet.

"Or something," she said, still refusing to out-and-out lie. "I should be in the office tomorrow." She hung up her phone and started toward the highway for the long drive to the Makah Reservation near Neah Bay. *Home.* The scene of the crime. In her mind it was now both places, linked like that forever.

Birdy had two things on her mind, one trivial and one overriding. She was grateful she drove a Prius— gutless as it was, she'd been racking up the miles and was grateful that she needed to fill up only twice in the past week. Forensic pathologists are on a budget, too. She was also thinking about the right starting point to find out what she could about Anna Jo Bonner's murder and what role her cousin had truly had in it. Blood doesn't lie.

Not usually.

It came to her that the person to see was none other than Clallam County Sheriff Jim Derby. Twenty years ago, Jim had been the lead detective, albeit a young and inexperienced one, on the Bonners murder case. Since that time, he'd made a name for himself. A very big name. For the past ten years he'd served as the sheriff, an elected position he won by a landslide. At the moment he was preparing to run for Congress. His campaign motto had already been trademarked on his website: CONGRESSMAN DERBY: WINNER TAKES ALL.

Jim Derby was a flinty-eyed man with angular features and Sharpie eyebrows that only added to the hard-liner-against-crime persona that he'd earned rather than manufactured over a decade of law enforcement. Property crimes and drug manufacturing had been his primary challenges in the county in the very northwest corner of Washington state. His thick wavy hair had receded a little, allowing his scalp to catch the light of the fluorescents, and his belly hung over his oversized belt buckle like a floating shelf. If he had any enemies in the community or in the sheriff's department, none were bold enough to speak out against him. Jim Derby didn't suffer any fools, which was one of the reasons state Republican Party leaders thought he'd be the no-nonsense candidate to defeat Democrat Casey Laughton, who'd held the office for four terms.

Derby's office was completely impersonal save for a portrait of Mrs. Derby and their son, and a row of bobble-head sports figurines that commanded the majority of a shelf next to the window. The joke in the sheriff's office was that when "the sheriff talks, you just nod."

Birdy had called ahead and Sheriff Derby had agreed to clear some time for her.

"I've followed your career," he'd said. "Glad to see you made something of yourself." The words tumbled out a little patronizingly, but Birdy took them at face value.

"Thanks," she'd said, almost adding *Glad you did, too.*

"Not sure what I can tell you. Things change, time marches on, memories fade."

"That's fine. To be honest," she'd said—a phrase she hated because it signaled that everything else must have been a lie—"I'm not sure what I'm looking for."

It was true. She wasn't. All she knew was that her cousin had compelled her to help him. She wondered if her own sense of guilt had driven her to. She'd never lied about what she'd seen, but her statement to the sheriff and at trial was crucial.

She'd read the statement before heading up to Clallam County.

I had been cutting wood for my family. It was around three p.m., but it could have been later. I don't know the exact time because I don't have a watch. I heard a noise of someone coming down the trail toward me. He was screaming. I didn't know who it was at first. I was scared. I turned off my chain saw. I stared to run and then I heard my name. It was my cousin Tommy calling to me. I went to him. He was bloody. He was crying. He was saying that "she's dead. It's my fault. She's dead." I asked him who and he didn't answer for a long time. Then he said it was Anna Jo Bonners. I started to cry and then I ran away. I was so afraid about what happened, I ran as fast as I could. I got home and my mom told me not to say anything. The next day the sheriff found

my chain saw and questioned me. I agree that
this is what happened and is true.

It was signed with a signature that was half printed
and half cursive, and dated. It was *her* signature, at
least as she'd used to write it. Yet something didn't
seem quite right. Birdy remembered how a kind lady
with short blond hair had sat in the small room while
then-detective Derby urged her to "get it all down" and
"don't worry about the mistakes because Patricia can
fix them later."

Patricia. The name played in her head, but she
couldn't come up with any more. Who was Patricia?

When she walked into Derby's office, she was instantly reminded of the days leading up to Tommy's
trial. It was strange. The sense of familiarity didn't
come from seeing him in person, or even hearing his
voice on the phone. It was the odor that lingered in the
air of the office. Birdy caught the distinct whiff of
witch hazel, a scent that always led her back to the days
she'd spent waiting to testify, being questioned, all of
what came with being an eyewitness. At fourteen it had
been almost too much to take in. All the adults telling
her what to do, pretending they weren't telling her
what to say. The smell reminded her of all of that. Jim
Derby used witch hazel as a skin bracer or aftershave.
Apparently some things hadn't changed so much after all.

A secretary led her inside the bobbleheaded office
and the pair exchanged a few remarks about the congressional race, the reservation, and the time that had
passed. She told him that she'd seen Tommy and she'd
promised to look into his case.

"Not officially, of course, but as a family member."

"A little late to dig into that one," he said. "It has been a long time."

"Not really," Birdy said. "Not if he's innocent."

Sheriff Derby motioned to his coffee cup and Birdy shook her head at the offer.

"We got him dead to rights as I quite vividly recall," he said, folding his big hands atop his pristine desk. "One of my first big investigations. Who says he's innocent?"

Birdy didn't like his tone. Not at all. She'd come there to learn more about the case from the lead investigator. She hadn't come with the intention of defending Tommy. It wasn't about that. It was about finding out the truth for someone who really needed it. At that moment, she wasn't sure if it was she or Tommy who needed the truth more.

"He does," she said. "Always has. That's kind of the point. He has always said he was innocent, but once he was convicted, he just kind of stopped. He disappeared. There was no appeal."

Jim gave a knowing sigh; it was exaggerated like everything he did. "Maybe once he was convicted, he knew we had him and there was no point to fighting it anymore. Didn't testify at trial, either, as I recall."

"No, he didn't," Birdy said. "But you interviewed him."

"It wasn't much of an interview."

"So I gathered," she said, pulling out a slim manila folder. "I have a reference for it. Somewhere . . ." She shuffled through the documents she'd brought from the Bone Box. She'd flagged one page with an incongruent rainbow Post-it note.

"What's all that?" he asked, as she rotated the file and set the page on his desk.

"Material I collected," she said, watching his every nuance and facial tic. Was there anything to be learned from his folded hands? His sigh? In the morgue the dead say nothing, but their stories were part of their bodies.

"You probably have cases that haunt you, too, don't you, Sheriff?"

He sighed again. *Impatient? Annoyed?*

"I can assure you, Freeland's isn't one of them," he said, "but yes."

Birdy finished sifting through the folder. "Here it is," she said, pointing her forefinger at a line in an old police interview report. She started to read:

". . . subject was polite, but evasive. Didn't admit guilt, but attempted to deflect responsibility during the recorded session."

She pushed the paper at him, but he didn't reach for it. His fingers still threaded his hands together. "Yes, for a killer, I guess he was polite. Is there a point here?"

"The report makes mention of a recording, and yet as far as I can tell the recording was never played at trial. I've looked everywhere for a reference to it, but none."

The sheriff shrugged. "Maybe there wasn't much on it worth playing. Not like he confessed or anything. Sure I can't get you anything? Pop?"

"I'm good. No thanks. Back to the report here—it is your report, right?"

He nodded, his smile still in place, but his eyes no longer generating any kind of genuine warmth. He wasn't irritated, maybe a little impatient. Birdy tried to avoid reading anything into his demeanor just then. She was after something very specific.

"Says right here." She tapped her fingertip on the page and glanced at him. "Says 'suspect deflected blame.' What does that mean? If you remember, that is. I know it has been a very long time."

"It has been, I'm sorry. I wish I could help you. I can see you have a lot of passion in your eyes for this matter. I understand the family connection, and the importance of family on the reservation."

Again, he said all the right words. *At least mostly.* He had the badge of a law enforcement officer, but no doubt politics had been Derby's true calling. The last word was meant as kind of zinger, Birdy was sure, though she didn't let on. Law enforcement who worked the reservation never did so because it was a plum assignment. It was a stepping-stone. The people who lived there were never seen as they should have been— as mothers, fathers, and children. Just as big, messy family units, a mass of souls coiled together tightly in troubles that never ceased.

"Do you know what became of the tape?" she asked.

"Evidence locker at the county. Always thought the kid would appeal, but knowing that he's guilty as sin, probably did us all a favor by accepting his sentence. In my mind, that's the same as owning up to the crime."

"He didn't own up to anything," she said.

"No answer is sometimes the same thing as saying that you're guilty."

"That isn't how our legal system works, Sheriff Derby."

His eyes stayed on her. The bobbleheads moved

slightly behind them, a Greek chorus of plastic and spring necks. "Look, I understand where you're coming from. I wish I could help you and your people. I wish there was something that I could tell you that would make the world a better place, a place where the sun always shines, where no kids are hungry, and your cousin wasn't a killer."

Annoyance had clearly given way to genuine irritation.

"It is nice to dream, isn't it, Sheriff?" she said, getting up and reaching for her coat. "Thanks for your time. Thanks for all you've done for my . . . my *people*." She paused and turned, a smile on her face.

"I have often thought of the nice woman, Patricia, who was so kind to me during the trial," she said as they passed by a records clerk outside his office.

A look of recognition came over the sheriff's face, but it was fleeting. "Yes, Patricia Stanford," he said. "Nice and smart. Retired from the department years ago."

"Do you happen to know where she is?" Birdy asked.

Jim Derby, witch hazel balm oozing from every oversized pore, looked upward and then shook his head. "Sorry, but I lost track of her. I think, yeah, I think she passed away."

As Birdy climbed into her bright red Prius, a finger tapped at the window.

It was the records clerk, who'd overheard Birdy's conversation with the sheriff.

"Hey, don't know why he said that. I can only guess. He never liked Pat much. Not that I could tell anyway.

As far as her being dead, that's a complete crock. I chatted with Pat-Stan last month at the Antiques Mall in Port Angeles. She runs the place."

"He must have made a mistake," Birdy said, purposely a little unconvincingly. She didn't like Jim Derby at all. She was glad she didn't live in his congressional district. She would probably doorbell for any other candidate no matter what their qualifications.

"It wouldn't be the first time," said the clerk, a middle-aged woman whose county-issue name badge identified her as Consuelo Maria Diego. "But I don't think so. He just hated Pat. She quit here because of him. I don't know what the beef was, but Sheriff said, 'Pat didn't have a leg to stand on.' He could be mean like that, you know."

CHAPTER 8

The Wicker Avenue Antiques Mall was a gritty warren of old, musty collectibles of debatable value. Customers entered the tight rows of vendor cubicles with their questionable arrays of Strawberry Shortcake lunchboxes, milk jugs from defunct Northwest dairies, or the occasional 1970s-era kitchen set and were immediately skeptical that they'd find anything there that they couldn't get from the closeout section of the local Goodwill. In fact, the Port Angeles Goodwill had a better record for delivering the occasional treasure.

Patricia Stanford had snowy white hair that she wore down to her waist. She also had one more distinguishing feature. Pat-Stan was missing her right leg, having lost it in a meth lab shootout the year after she'd made it to the detective's rank.

Didn't have a leg to stand on. . . . What a jerk!

"Patricia Stanford?" Birdy asked, approaching Pat as she fanned out the items in a jewelry case around a handwritten sign that said BAKELITE SOMEONE HAPPY.

Pat turned on her good leg. "That's me. Can I help you find something?"

"I've found what I'm looking for," Birdy said. "That would be you."

Pat appeared surprised. "Me?"

Birdy nodded and introduced herself, and the flicker of recognition—at least of her name—came over Pat-Stan in the most pleasant of ways. The woman, who leaned a little because she didn't like the way the prosthetic leg felt on the stub of her thigh, managed a warm smile.

"You're grown up," she said. "You look the same in the eyes, but, well, well, you have grown up."

Birdy returned the smile. "I remember how kind you were to me back then."

"And you've come here to tell me that?" she asked.

"Not exactly," Birdy said. "I came for help."

Pat-Stan narrowed her focus, ignoring a couple of women haggling over a stack of vintage hankies. "What kind of help?"

"I came here for my cousin Tommy."

Pat-Stan shifted her weight and winced. "I don't know what you mean."

"Of course not," Birdy said, explaining that Tommy was ill and she wanted to help clear his name before it was too late.

"Where's he living?" she asked.

Birdy paused a beat. She wondered why Pat-Stan asked that. "Walla Walla. He never got out of prison."

The shop manager looked genuinely surprised. "But that was more than twenty years ago. I thought he'd be out long ago," she said.

"He won't admit to something he didn't do. And that's the only way he could have been paroled."

"I wish I could help you," she said, stepping away to twist the small padlock on the jewelry case door.

Birdy touched her shoulder. "You can. You don't have to wish."

Patricia took a small step backward, both hips now resting against the cabinet. "I don't remember anything," she said. "I was a secretary studying to try to get the god-awful job that cost me my leg. The pension is good. But I'd rather have my leg."

It was a joke, an attempt to defuse the tension between them.

"Actually, I'm a little surprised that you're alive. I spent a half hour with Sheriff Derby and he told me that you were dead."

"Interesting. He probably wishes I were dead. The man's a complete ass. He was a terrible boss, he's estranged from his only kid, his wife only comes out to pose for campaign photos. Messed up. I hate him."

Some common ground, good.

"You're not one to hold back," Birdy said, trying to keep the disclosures coming. "But why would he wish you were dead? I don't get that."

Again, nervousness took over and Pat-Stan called to the women fighting over the hankies that she'd be right over. She looked back at her visitor.

"I really don't want to get into it," she said.

Birdy pushed harder. "Does it have anything to do with Tommy's case?"

Pat-Stan waited a long time. Uncomfortably long. It was one of those awkward pauses that usually invites an exit from an uncomfortable conversation.

"Probably," she said. "No. Yes. I mean, I don't know.

Jim was not just a jerk yesterday. His jerkdom has been a long time coming."

"What about Tommy?" Birdy asked.

Pat-Stan pretended to search her memory. "I can't say. Really. I don't exactly remember."

"Please," she said.

"I've said all I should. I really do wish you luck. Don't know how it can help Tommy. He's served more than his time, that's for sure. Can't give back all those years."

"Do you think they should be given back?" Birdy asked.

Again, a long pause. Pat-Stan clearly wanted to spill her guts right over that tacky display case, but she held back the best she could.

"I will say this and it's against my better judgment. I transcribed his tape and I can tell you this. . . . When I saw his statement at trial I noticed that it was slightly different. Some parts were omitted."

"I have his statement here," Birdy said, pulling out the file.

"I don't have my glasses and I wouldn't remember exactly. Just something kind of bugged me. I told Detective Derby about it, but he dismissed it as a clerical error. That really angered me because, well, *I* was the clerk."

"What was different?" Birdy asked.

Pat-Stan shrugged. "Don't remember. Check the tape."

"Video?"

"No, audio. We taped all the interviews. Policy."

This interested Birdy. The transcripts—no matter who did them—didn't sound completely like Tommy. "Where are the tapes?" she asked.

"I've got some. When I left, I was so mad that I took a bunch of old case files. Don't lecture me. You've never lost a leg and then had your boss tell you that it would be best if you sat at a desk for the rest of your life. I get off at five. House is a mess, but I do the best that I can. Come over."

She wrote down an address on Hawthorne Avenue and went down the narrow aisle. No one would have known that she'd lost a leg. Pat-Stan had practiced her gait. She might have lost a limb, but she had never lost her sense of pride. As Birdy Waterman saw it, despite its place in the "sin" category of the Bible, pride could be a very good thing. Pat-Stan was angry about the contents of the report.

Anger, Birdy knew, could be a good ally.

CHAPTER 9

With a little more than an hour to kill, Birdy found a coffee shop that made ginormous cinnamon rolls. Even though the time of day was so wrong for that kind of indulgence, the forensic pathologist with a sweet tooth ordered one.

"Heated with butter?" a pleasant young man behind the counter asked.

"If I'm going to die from sugar overload, might as well go all the way," Birdy said.

As she drank her coffee and ate the gooey roll at the table in the back of the café, she reread her own statement and compared it against what Tommy told the detectives.

I was smoking pot and drinking beer that
afternoon in the woods alone. I had talked to
Anna Jo Bonners about meeting me at the cabin
so we could mess around. Anna Jo didn't show
up so I hung out by myself. I heard a scream
coming from the cabin later and I went inside. I
found Anna Jo Bonners in a pool of blood. I was
scared that whoever had hurt her was still there

so I grabbed the knife. I ran out of the cabin and
hurried down the trail where my cousin Birdy
found me. I don't know why I picked up the
knife, but I threw it away before my cousin came
up to me. I did not kill her. I really liked Anna
Jo. I think I might have loved her even.

All of the evidence supported the contention that
Tommy was the killer. He'd had Anna Jo's blood on his
shirt and hands, his fingerprints had been recovered
from the knife, and Birdy's eyewitness testimony had
put him fleeing the scene of the grisly homicide in Ponder's cabin.

Yet he said he didn't do it.

Surprised that she'd devoured half the roll, Birdy
pushed the plate away just as a call came in with a 509
area code, eastern Washington.

"Waterman," she said.

"Dr. Waterman, I hope you don't mind the intrusion," a man's voice said. "This is Ken Holloway. I'm
the guard you talked to at the prison. You know, about
your cousin?"

"Of course. Is everything all right? I didn't leave my
ID behind, did I?"

"No. Not that. It's about Tommy. He's been admitted
to the infirmary. They might take him out of here to
Spokane. He's not doing so hot. After you left, he changed
his family contact info to your name. Not changed. Actually gave a family contact. The spot on his file had been
empty since he got here."

Birdy felt sick and it wasn't the cinnamon roll,
which was now expanding in her upset stomach.
"What can I do?"

"Nothing," he said. "He wanted me to give you a message. He wanted me to tell you that . . ." The man's voice grew soft. For a second, Birdy thought he might be crying.

"Are you all right, Sergeant?" she asked.

"Yeah," he said, his voice clipped in an obvious attempt to snap out of his grief. "He just wanted me to tell you that even if you don't believe in him all the way yet, he's grateful knowing that someone out there thinks he matters."

Birdy asked, "Will you let him know I got the message? Tell him that I'm doing my best. I don't want to give him false hope."

"Hope is never false," he said. "Hope is what keeps the innocent from killing themselves. Hope is what makes me think that justice will be done."

She hung up and looked at the time on her phone. Pat-Stan was waiting for her.

Patricia Stanford produced an old audiocassette from the box of things she'd taken when she'd hobbled out of the Clallam County Sheriff's department. It had been kept in an envelope with the date and Tommy's first name scrawled on it in pencil. On the top right-hand side, a red ink stamp read: EVIDENCE.

Pat-Stan offered her some coffee, but Birdy declined. She was sick to her stomach.

"If you have any Rolaids," she asked. "I'll take a couple."

"Alka-Seltzer all right?"

Birdy nodded. Pat-Stan went into her kitchen and returned shortly with a fizzing glass of water.

"Lemon lime," she said.

As Birdy drank it, she couldn't help but think of Pat-Stan's need to collect some things from her office, her own kind of a Bone Box, maybe. She wondered if there were hundreds, if not thousands, of law enforcement people who carried away the flotsam and jetsam of cases that niggled at them, too.

"Why Tommy's tape?" she finally asked.

Pat-Stan inserted it into the player. "I guess I took things that bugged me. Things that I wasn't really sure about."

Birdy didn't tell her about her own stash. Pat-Stan, in some ways, was a kindred spirit. Maybe law enforcement was full of people like them; those who were on the right side of the law, but weren't as convinced as the men and women who lined up in the jury box. More times than she could care to admit, Birdy and her colleagues turned over the best information they could find, in hope that the jury would sort out the puzzle pieces that didn't really fit. Their job had been to gather the evidence, the prosecutor's job was to put it all into a story, and the jury was called upon to make the final call.

"Were you there?" Birdy asked. "In the room when this was recorded?"

She shook her head. "No. Not at all. Didn't have the right badge back then. Derby treated me like an office girl and flunky. My scores on the detective's test were twenty points higher than his. He's now sheriff and I'm a human tripod selling *Partridge Family* lunchboxes."

Even though the woman had clearly been wronged by her boss, in a very real, and very uncomfortable way, Birdy was grateful for it. Pat-Stan's anger was proving to be more helpful than she'd hoped. Bitterness, sadly, was something that she could put to use.

Pat-Stan pushed the PLAY button. The tape crackled and popped, but Tommy's voice was unmistakable. It was young Tommy. Broken Tommy. Not the man old before his time rotting away in prison. Tommy Freeland spoke in a deliberate, halting manner.

"I was smoking pot and drinking beer that afternoon in the woods alone. I had talked to Anna Jo Bonners about meeting me at the cabin so we could mess around. Anna Jo didn't show up so I hung out by myself. I heard a scream coming from the cabin later and I went inside."

His words were so precise that Birdy wondered if he'd been reading his statement. But he couldn't have been because the statement was a transcription of the tape, not the other way around.

"I found Anna Jo Bonners in a pool of blood. I was scared that whoever had hurt her was still there so I grabbed the knife. He told me to put it down. So I—"

"Stop the tape, please," Birdy said, looking up from the transcript of her cousin's statement, her heart beat a little faster. The Alka-Seltzer roiled in her stomach.

Pat-Stan complied. She kept her facial expression flat, but her eyes were alert and sharply focused. There was awareness behind them, and, Birdy thought, a kind of appreciation for what she was hearing.

Maybe even a little relief.

"Did you hear what I heard?"

"Yes. I guess that's why you're here, isn't it?"

"He says that someone told him to put the knife down," she said.

"That's right. That's what he says."

"But at trial he said he was alone."

"He didn't. Maybe you don't remember, but Tommy Freeland never actually testified. His lawyer told him not to. The transcripts were used."

"But the transcriptions are wrong."

The former detective nodded. "I know. I was there. The only comfort I've had is that all the other evidence so clearly indicated that Tommy was the killer. It was only after his conviction that I played back the tapes."

"Not only that, but doesn't he sound peculiar?" Birdy said.

Pat-Stan watched her visitor closely. "How so?" she asked.

"Stilted, calm. Not like someone who'd just killed his girlfriend and was looking for a way out of it," Birdy said.

"Funny that you should say that," Pat-Stan said, her finger hovering over the recorder to advance the audiotape one more time. "I saw him the afternoon they brought him in. He was a complete wreck. He was barely able to breathe because he was crying so hard. Also, this isn't an interview tape at all. It seems like a compilation, bits and pieces strung together. Did you hear how the hissing in the background stopped at the end of the sentence?"

Birdy was still stunned by the disclosure that someone else had been at the crime scene. "Not really," she said. "I'll listen more carefully."

Pat-Stan nodded. "I want you to follow along with your transcription, okay? You are missing something."

"Missing something?"

"Listen carefully. There's a hiss on the tape just as he says it."

"All right."

The tape resumed.

"I ran out of the cabin and hurried down the trail where my cousin Birdy found me. I don't know why I picked up the knife, but I threw it away before Birdy came up to me."

"Stop, please."

The former detective pushed the button, her finger hovering to advance the tape once more.

"He said that he threw it away, before he saw me."

"That's what he said."

"But when I read the report, it indicated that the knife had been recovered from the cabin."

"I don't recall that, but all right. What does it matter where it was found?"

"It matters to me. Not so much where, but by who?"

"That's easy. Detective Derby found it."

CHAPTER 10

Jim Derby's house commanded the edge of a hill overlooking the Strait of Juan de Fuca, an always choppy passage that divides Washington from British Columbia. It was a big house with shingled siding and a river rock chimney. Atop its second story was a widow's walk framed by ornate ironwork. It was the kind of place that drive-bys admire and covet.

Pitched in the front yard was a campaign sign as big as a car: THE DERBY WINNER YOU WANT.

Birdy parked and walked up the long cobblestone path. She wondered how a sheriff could afford such a place. A congressman, yes. They had a zillion ways to earn a fortune through sweetheart deals made when their constituents were home dealing with the real-life problems of their respective districts.

She knocked and Jim Derby opened the door.

"What do you want?" he asked, clearly not happy to see her. "It's late."

"I think you know why I'm here, Sheriff." Her tone was flat, without emotion. Her eyes stared hard at him. He had to know why she was there. It wasn't a social call.

"It sounds like you're threatening me," he said.

Witch hazel scented the air.

"Are you going to invite me in or are we going to have this conversation out here where the neighbors might hear?" she asked, refusing to yield to fear.

Jim Derby looked warily over the hedge next door. A light beamed from the porch.

"Come in," he said.

"Who's there?" a woman's voice called as Birdy followed the sheriff into a living room that had been turned into campaign central. Mailers, bumper stickers, and yard signs blanketed the coffee table, the sofa, and a credenza that ran the length of a bay window that overlooked the Strait.

"No one, Lydia," he said calling into the hallway. "Just a staffer."

"All right then," she said.

He turned back to Birdy. "My wife doesn't need to hear this. I made a few phone calls after you left. I know what you're up to. I just don't know why. I'm guessing that someone from the other side is trying to smear me. I get it. That happens. Don't be used. Despite Tommy being a family member, you and I are on the same team."

"Are we? My team doesn't frame people for murders they didn't commit."

"You better back off, Ms. Waterman," he said.

"Doctor," she shot back.

He looked flustered, maybe for the first time ever. "Fine, Doctor, back off. No one framed anyone. Are you working for the Democrats or not? Is this about hurting my chances for reelection?"

"No," she said. "But it does give me a little bit of

comfort knowing that what you did to my cousin and Anna Jo will stop you from winning the derby, as you like to call it."

"Just wait a second. You don't know what you're talking about."

"I found out that Anna Jo was seeing someone. Someone she didn't want her parents to know about. It was you, wasn't it?"

Derby took a step backward, but said nothing.

Birdy pressed on. "It wasn't that Anna Jo was embarrassed about who she was seeing. It was the other person—you—who was embarrassed about seeing her, a Makah girl. She meant nothing to you. She was trash to you, wasn't she?"

"I want you to leave," he said. "I will call my deputies and have them pick you up for threatening an officer."

Birdy gripped her keys. She'd planned on jabbing them in his eyes if he got violent with her. Instead, he was cowering behind the shields of the men and women who worked for him. Probably like he'd always done. Like he did to Patricia Stanton. "Fine," she said. "People like you ruin the law for everyone who actually gives a damn. You killed her and you set up Tommy."

"Get out!" he said, his voice rising to flat-out anger.

Again, Birdy felt her keys.

"Wait," came the woman's voice from the other room.

Birdy spun around and faced Lydia H. Derby, the woman who graced every campaign poster; the woman her husband wore like an accessory. She was a slender woman with dark-dyed hair and a flawless, powdery white complexion. She wore brown velvet sweatpants that she somehow managed to make stylish. She was the ultimate dream wife for a man with higher aspirations.

"Lydia, this is handled. Dr. Waterman is leaving now."

Lydia's face stayed calm. *Botox? A controlled wariness that had been practiced over the years? Resignation that what she was going to do was something that had to be done? Birdy didn't know.*

"This is going to come out," Lydia said. "I suppose it should. Owning up to something will set you free. Isn't that the truth, Jim?"

His eyes pleaded with her. "Lydia, don't."

Birdy held up her hand without the keys to stop him from saying anything more. "Mrs. Derby, you overheard what we were saying, didn't you?"

"Every word," she said.

"I'm right, aren't I?"

She shook her head. "No, you're half right."

It didn't track. "Half?" Birdy asked.

"Jim did frame Tommy Freeland, but he didn't kill Anna Jo."

"Then who did?"

Lydia looked at her husband. By then Jim Derby had dissolved into a chair by the credenza.

"I did," she said.

Birdy thought she didn't hear quite right. "What? You?"

Lydia Derby glanced at her husband, his face buried in his hands. "A couple of days earlier I followed Anna Jo to that love nest Jim kept with her." Lydia said, stopping a beat as her husband jabbed a finger at her.

"Shut up, Lydia!" he said, snapping back into the moment.

"You'd like to shut me up," Lydia said before returning her attention to Birdy. "I don't know how special Anna Jo Bonners was. All I know is that she was ruining my marriage. I had a little boy to think about. You were about to ruin my life, Kenny's life. I only wanted to threaten her with the knife. But something just took over. She was sitting there, waiting for Tommy or something. I just grabbed a knife from the kitchen and started . . ."

Anna Jo Bonners was dressing. She was young, beautiful. She was unencumbered by children, with a slender body that had never carried a baby.

"I know who you are," Anna Jo said, barely glancing at Lydia.

"Leave him alone," she said.

"You mean like you do? I'm giving him what he wants and needs. I know about your type. Needy. Always thinking of yourself. No wonder he laughs about you when we're in bed." Anna Jo started for the door. "You know what's so funny? I don't give a crap about Jim. I'm looking for a good time. You might try it sometime, Mrs. Derby. Jim says you have no passion."

"Please," Lydia said. Her body was so tense, she thought if she breathed any harder her breastbone would shatter into a million little pieces.

"I do what I want to do," Anna Jo said. She was not really a malicious girl, but somehow the fact that Lydia was so upset made her feel good. Jim Derby's wife's tears only served to egg her on. Lydia's anguish gave her power.

"We made love in his car the other day," she said. "You ever try that?"

Lydia was shaking. "Stop it or I'll stop you."

Anna Jo just didn't seem to care. "That's a laugh. You couldn't satisfy your man—how do you think you'll find the courage to stop me? Go home, Mrs. Derby."

That was when Lydia saw the knife. It was like an antenna transmitting its presence from the open kitchen doorway. Without another second to think it through, she grabbed it from the cutting board, spun around, and plunged it into Anna Jo's midsection. The first cut brought a muffled scream, a kind of guttural spasm of noise that undulated over the cabin's cedar floorboards. The second brought eye contact, a look of horror and disbelief.

"What are you doing?" Anna Jo said, grabbing at Lydia and the knife as she sank to the floor. Blood splattered over her bra as she moved her hand over her breast to stop the bleeding.

"You're getting what you deserve!" Lydia said as she stared down at the girl fighting for her life.

"Stop! You're killing me!" Anna Jo said, as she tried to regain her footing. Halfway up, she slipped on her own pooling blood.

The scene was beyond frenetic. Lydia stood over Anna Jo, working the knife like a piston. Over and over. Twenty-seven times. Later, when she spoke of what she'd done, she was unsure if Anna Jo's last words were really as she remembered them or if they had melded into some twisted fantasy of what had happened in Ponder's cabin all those years ago.

"Finally, got some passion," Anna Jo said.

Or maybe she didn't say anything at all. She died after the second or third stab into her carotid artery.

Lydia looked up as her husband entered the cabin.

"Good God, what did you do, Lydia?" Jim Derby asked, his eyes terror-filled as he dropped down next to his lover.

"I fixed your mess. Now you clean it up," she said.

Jim reached for Anna Jo's blood-soaked neck for a pulse.

"Anna Jo?" came a voice outside the cabin.

It was Tommy.

Jim led his now silent, almost catatonic, wife toward the back door.

"I'll clean up your mess, Lydia. I guess I owe you."

In a beat, he'd returned, pretending to see Anna Jo's body for the first time. Tommy was crying and trying to give his girlfriend mouth to mouth. His whole body was shaking. He picked up the knife and looked at it like it was some kind of mysterious object.

"Get out of here, and get rid of the knife. I'll clean this up."

"Who did this?" Tommy said.

The detective hooked his hand under Tommy's armpit and lifted him to his feet.

"Just keep your mouth shut. I'll help you," Jim said. "Get rid of the knife and get out of here."

"My husband later told me how he rearranged the crime scene. How he'd wiped away my footprints. Blamed his own on an uncharacteristic lapse in detective protocol. He called Tommy's appearance at the cabin a gift," Lydia said, looking at Jim. "I believe you said he was the 'perfect patsy,' " she said.

* * *

With Birdy looking on in the expansive comfort of the Derbys' magnificent living room, Lydia was crying her heart out as she confessed to what she'd done. She was literally crumbling into pieces, but Jim "Mr. Family Man for All People" just sat there. He didn't even try to calm his wife. Birdy wondered what he was thinking about—his political career diving into oblivion? He certainly wasn't thinking about Lydia.

Or Tommy.

Or Anna Jo.

He got up went for a desk drawer and got his gun.

"I'll say I thought you were an intruder," he said, coming toward Birdy.

"No, you won't," she said. She held up her cell phone. "I've had this on speaker. Your old friend Pat-Stan—the one you said was dead—is listening and recording this entire conversation."

"You asshole, Jim Derby," came Pat-Stan's voice over the cell phone. "I've already called the police—and not your bunch of deputies. The state patrol is outside now. Let's see who has a leg to stand on in court."

Tommy Benjamin Freeland took his last breath a week after getting word in his Spokane hospital bed that his cousin Birdy had cleared his name. The medical staff said their patient was unable to respond verbally, but he nodded slightly and managed the briefest of smiles. They were sure he understood.

Birdy had wanted to go see him, but a homicide case involving a high school boy in Port Orchard kept her planted in the autopsy suite. She left work when she got word of Tommy's passing.

Birdy wasn't a crier, but she couldn't stop just then. She hurried to her car and drove down the steep hill toward the water. Her mind rolled back to the boy she'd known—the one who had taught her how to fish a creek at night with a flashlight and, in one of her more disgusting lessons, how to dress a deer with only a pocket knife and a whetstone.

She parked the Prius behind the old abandoned Beachcomber restaurant and looked out at the icy, rippling water of Sinclair Inlet. She knew that she'd done all she could. She had been so late to come to the realization that Tommy had needed her all those years. It made her sick and sad.

Tommy, we let you down. I let you down. . . .

A young bald eagle, its feathers still a root beer float of brown and white, swooped down to the water and grabbed the silvery sliver of a fish. Its wings pounded the air like the loudest heartbeat imaginable as the bird lifted a small salmon and carried it upward to the cloud-shrouded sun.

Birdy Waterman was a scientist, a doctor. But she was a Makah and that meant a millennium of tradition and lore had been woven into her soul. Her connection to the water, the air, and the creatures that inhabited the natural world was different from that of people who didn't depend directly on it for their very existence. She watched the eagle as it screeched skyward, its talons skewering the now motionless fish.

Birdy felt a whisper come to her ears. It was gentle, like a breath of a lover.

"I'm free," the wind said.

She cradled her eyes in the crook of her elbow and

then looked out the windshield as she watched the young eagle fly away.

Tommy was at rest. He, finally, was free. And so was Kenny Holloway. The prison guard from Walla Walla who'd set all the events in motion called her after his mother and stepfather's arrest for murder and conspiracy. He wasn't celebratory, just grateful for the outcome.

"You meet all kinds of people in prison," he said. "Some bad with no possibility of redemption. And then sometimes you meet someone like your cousin. If he'd given the slightest reason to continue the coverup, I would have done so. My mother did what she thought she had to do and that monster she's married to made it all happen. I wrote the letter to you, because I knew you'd be the one to help fix the big ugly mess."

"Why didn't you just come out and tell me?" she asked.

"Telling something to someone gets you nowhere. Your cousin had been saying all these years that he was innocent, yet no one listened. Someone like you had to find out what happened."

Kenny Holloway ended the call with a thank-you.

"You did more for me than just about anyone," he said. "Anyone but Tommy, that is."

Inside her house, the Bone Box was lighter than it had been. Tommy's case file would not be thrown away, but no longer did it feel right to keep it there. There were the cases of a little girl found drowned off the fishing pier in Manchester; the two teenage boys from Bainbridge Island who had supposedly killed themselves in a secret pact; and so many others. It surprised her how many there were. How many times she second-guessed the results of the cases in which things just didn't add up. All the cases were different. All deserved another look.

Birdy turned off the light and slid under the covers. Her mother was right about one thing. She was never satisfied. That night as she went to sleep she remembered how she and Tommy had picked huckleberries and foraged for firewood. She imagined his laugh.

She'd fish through that box again. If all else had failed, if someone had gotten away with murder, maybe she could put her intuition and forensic science to good use. For Tommy and the others whose voices were never heard—some living, some dead.